VIXENS

Books by Bertrice Small:

The Kadin
Love Wild and Fair
Adora
Unconquered
Beloved
Enchantress Mine
Blaze Wyndham
The Spitfire
A Moment in Time
To Love Again
Love, Remember Me
The Love Slave
Hellion
Betrayed
Deceived
The Innocent
A Memory of Love
The Dutchess Rosamund

"The O'Malley Saga"

Skye O'Malley
All the Sweet Tomorrows
A Love for All Time
This Heart of Mine
Lost Love Found
Wild Jasmine

"Skye's Legacy"

Darling Jasmine
Bedazzled
Beseiged
Intrigued
Just Beyond Tomorrow
Vixens

Anthologies

Captivated
Fascinated

BERTRICE SMALL

VIXENS

BRAVA

KENSINGTON PUBLISHING CORP.
http://www.kensingtonbooks.com

BRAVA BOOKS are published by

Kensington Publishing Corp.
119 West 40th Street
New York, NY 10018

All Kensington titles, imprints, and distributed lines are available at special quantity discounts for bulk purchases for sales promotions, premiums, fund-raising, educational, or institutional use.

Special book excerpts or customized printings can also be created to fit specific needs. For details, write or phone the office of the Kensington special sales manager: Kensington Publishing Corp., 119 West 40th Street, New York, NY 10018, attn: Special Sales Department; phone 1-800-221-2647.

BRAVA and the B logo are Reg. U.S. Pat. & TM Off.

ISBN-13: 978-1-57566-856-7
ISBN-10: 1-57566-856-4

First Kensington Trade Paperback Printing: February 2003
Second Printing: July 2012

10 9 8 7 6 5 4 3 2

Printed in the United States of America

For Kate Duffy,
With love from her most faithful author,
Bertrice Small

A NOTE FROM THE AUTHOR

August 2002

My dear readers,

Twenty-four years ago I began to write a novel entitled *Skye O'Malley*. It was what we call a single title. But you loved Skye so much that I wrote a sequel to her story, and suddenly I found myself writing a series, "The O'Malley Saga." This first series spawned the second, "Skye's Legacy." It's been a lot of fun.

But 130 years have passed between Skye's birth in Ireland, and the conclusion of *Vixens*. When Skye was born, Henry VIII was on the throne of England; followed by his daughter, the great Elizabeth; her cousin James I; his son Charles I; the Commonwealth; and now Charles II. We've passed through a great deal of history, haven't we? And Skye's descendants number between 400 and 500. I can no longer keep up with them. So it is with regret I conclude the epic of Skye, her kith and her kin.

Of my thirty-one titles, only twelve encompass Skye and her family. I plan on continuing my writing, and if I'm lucky, I may invent another heroine as fantastic as Skye, and when I do, I hope that you will enjoy her adventures every bit as much. God bless, and much good reading from your most faithful author,

Beatrice Small

Prologue

QUEEN'S MALVERN

Autumn 1667

"Did she, or did she not murder her husband, Mama?" Charles Stuart, the duke of Lundy, asked his mother.

Jasmine Leslie, the dowager duchess of Glenkirk and the marchioness of Westleigh, looked directly back at her son. "If you would know the answer to that question, Charlie, then you must ask her when she arrives" came the quiet reply.

"*I must know!*" the duke insisted. "You are, after all, introducing this girl into the bosom of our family, Mama."

"*This girl,* as you call her, is your niece, Charlie. She is Fortune's youngest child. *She is family!*"

"She is a stranger, Mama, for all she is Fortune's daughter," he said. "We know nothing about her."

"*I know,*" Jasmine responded sharply.

"Then why will you not tell her?" he pleaded.

"Because it is a terrible tragedy for Frances. It should have remained private, but unfortunately, Lord and Lady Tolliver, newly returned from the Virginias, have been swift to bruit this disgraceful scandal about the court. This calumny should have remained on the other side of the ocean! Frances comes to us to escape the backbiting, and the uninformed gossips whose lives are so barren they must tittle-tattle this misadventure. Your sister and her husband have acted with incredible discretion and perfect good manners considering all that has happened."

"But I don't know what has happened!" the duke almost shouted at his mother. He ran an impatient hand through his slightly graying auburn hair, which was cropped very short in order for his court wigs to fit properly. His amber eyes were lively but his look quite disturbed.

Jasmine sighed deeply; still she reached out to take her son's hand in hers. "I have always acted carefully, Charlie," she began.

"Except with my father," he murmured and received a sharp pinch on his arm for his words. "Ouch!" he exclaimed, but he grinned.

"Mistress Frances Devers would not come into this house, Charlie, indeed I should not receive her at all, had I any doubts as to her character. I do not. Remember, my dear, that your sister has corresponded with me for thirty-two years. I have not seen her, or Kieran since that sad day when they left for Maryland, but I know everything there is to know about them and about their family. Aine is a nun. Shane is his father's heir. He has a wife and three children of his own. Cullen and Rory have their own plantations, with wives and children. Maeve is happily married and expecting her second child. Jamie and Charlie are out on the frontier exploring. Kieran is not well. He has worked too hard these past years to make his plantation thrive. Fortune writes it has weakened his brave and noble heart. And now this tragedy that has beset the family has played havoc with all their lives. It was better that young Frances leave the Colonies and return to England."

"But this rumor of murder?" Charlie persisted.

"If you would know what has happened, Charlie, then you must ask your niece," his mother repeated. "No charges were ever made against her, nor was she even brought before the king's magistrate. Unless your morbid curiosity overcomes you, dear boy, then you must be satisfied with that answer no matter the evil rumors. They will swirl about her for a time when we introduce her into court, but eventually some other scandal will catch the court's interest and Frances's difficulties will be quickly forgotten." Jasmine arose from the tapestried-back chair where she had been sitting. "If Frances cannot be welcome in this house, Charlie, then I shall open my dower house at your brother Henry's. I am, after all, the dowager marchioness of Westleigh as well as the dowager duchess of Glenkirk."

"Oh, no, you don't," Charlie said, suddenly laughing. "Barbara and I do not intend to be left in charge of those two vixens you have raised and influenced. And Cadby is not big enough for all of you. Nay, you will remain here, dear Mama, where I may keep an eye on this family's current crop of wicked wenches."

"Then I shall go and prepare for my granddaughter's arrival," Jasmine said. "The outrider arrived less than an hour ago. She should be here shortly. I requested she travel without a servant of her own. I have chosen a sensible Queen's Malvern lass for her." She turned and walked away from the old family hall. "I shall be down when the coach arrives, Charlie," she told him.

The duke of Lundy turned to his beautiful wife, Barbara, who had been sitting silently during the entire exchange. "*Well?*" he demanded of her. "What say you, my lady wife?"

"I have never known your mother's judgment to be wrong, Charlie," the lady Barbara replied. "Whatever has happened to young Frances, she has been charged with no crime. These rumors of murder will frankly make her far more interesting to the gentlemen of the court than if she were just an ordinary young widowed colonial coming to court with the backing of her influential relations. Indeed, I fear it may take the light from Diana and my own, Cynara. I want those two wed before they get into any difficulties we cannot get them out of, Charlie!"

The duke chuckled. "They are just high spirited, my darling," he murmured.

"They are a pair of young devils, Charlie! We have all spoiled them dreadfully. Young Frances's difficulties, whatever they are, will pale in comparison with the mischief Diana and Cynara can get into. They go to court this winter, and we will find them husbands as soon as possible," the beautiful duchess of Lundy said firmly.

"If you say so, my darling," he answered her.

Barbara shook her head, laughing. "I do say so," she told him. Then she kissed him. "Thank goodness we only had one child, Charlie. I do not believe I should have survived with a second like Cynara." The duchess sighed deeply. "I love her, but she is every bit a Stuart. Arrogant and proud."

"You think me arrogant and prideful?" he asked her, surprised.

"Yes, but you have those qualities in the nicest way. Aye, you are proud to be a Stuart, and because of your Stuart grandparents, you have never known any stigma of being born on the wrong side of the blanket. But you can become cold and proud when anyone has the temerity to suggest that you are any less for your birth than you really are. After all, your grandfather was king of England and Scotland. Your father was the heir to that throne before his untimely death. The late king was your beloved uncle. The present king your favorite cousin, and he certainly favors you. You are the not-so-royal Stuart, Charlie, but you are Stuart nonetheless.

"Our daughter, however, thinks that being a Stuart places her above everyone else. She believes that being related to the king gives her advantages and privileges that she really does not have. Your mother and I have tried to convince her otherwise, but Cynara will have her own way. One day, however, she will learn otherwise, of course."

Charlie looked troubled by his wife's words, but then the sound of a carriage coming up the driveway reached his ears. "She is here," he said. "Come, Barbara, and let us meet Fortune's daughter, who may or may not have murdered her husband."

"If your mother says it is all right, my darling," the duchess of Lundy responded, "then I will trust that it is. Lord help us, my husband. We will now have three vixens on our hands to marry off."

Part One

ENGLAND, 1667-68

THE KING'S FANCY

Chapter

1

Frances Devers had spent the several weeks crossing the ocean in a fog of sorrow and pain. A short year ago she had been courted by the handsomest man in all the Colonies. And then at Christmas Parker Randolph had asked for her hand, and she had accepted. He was a Virginia Randolph, although not from the more important branch of the Randolphs who were involved in the politics of the Colony. His family were distant cousins, but still he was a Virginia Randolph, her sister Maeve said enviously, admiring the diamond-and-pearl ring her youngest sibling now wore. Maeve was married to the eldest son of a local tobacco farmer.

The preparations had begun for a June wedding. There had been parties and balls and even picnics once the spring came. There was a trousseau to be made. A modiste and a tailor had come all the way from Williamsburg with their staffs to do the work, helped, of course, by the plantation servants. There were virtually no slaves on her family's tobacco plantation. Neither Kieran nor Fortune Devers believed in slavery. While they bought blacks at the slave auctions, the Africans remained slaves only long enough to be civilized. Then they were freed legally, paid a wage, and given shelter and food. Whether they remained was their decision, but most did for the Devers were known to be good employers.

The wedding of Frances Devers and Parker Randolph had been

one of the most anticipated affairs of the year in the Colonies. The guests had come from as far as Massachusetts Bay and Barbados. The bride was the youngest child of a very wealthy and distinguished family. The groom was a Virginia Randolph. No expense had been spared to make this a gala event. The bride was beautiful. The groom set hearts a-flutter among the female guests. And then, the girl in the duke of Lundy's coach shuddered, putting from her mind the terrible images that refused to cease torturing her.

In the scandal and the chaos that had followed that terrible day, she had been comforted by her family, interrogated by the local king's justice, and prepared to be sent away from Maryland after her husband's funeral. She would go to England. To her grandmother, a woman she had never met. To a part of her family she didn't know. Six weeks after her wedding, she was put upon a ship. The ship belonged to her family's trading company, she was informed. She hadn't been aware her family owned ships. She was distantly related to the ship's captain, she was told. His wife would be her chaperon. Her longtime, and loved personal servant, a young black woman named Junie-Bee, would not accompany her. The break with Maryland was to be complete.

The day Frances boarded the *Cardiff Rose II*, her entire family accompanied her to the vessel. Her eldest sister, Aine, a nun with the Sisters of Saint Mary, had come for the wedding. She remained on in the tragic aftermath to comfort their mother. There as well were her eldest brother Shane and his wife, her brothers Cullen and Rory and their wives, her sister Maeve and her husband, and all her nieces and nephews. The youngest of her parents' sons Jamie and Charles, unmarried and adventurous, envied her. But they all cried, even her roughnecked brothers who had been closest in age to her. No one knew if Frances Devers would ever come home again.

Fortune Devers was pale. She wept copiously at having to part with her youngest child. She silently cursed the Virginia Randolphs for not knowing their son. Kieran Devers was drawn and, for the first time in his life, looked old. His heart had not been strong these past few years. This dreadful misfortune and the resulting consequence had taken a toll on his now-frail health.

"I am so sorry, Papa!" Frances sobbed on her father's shoulder a final time.

"Nay, lassie," he reassured her, stroking her dark hair. "You were right." He should have listened to his voice within, for he had sensed something off about young Parker Randolph. But he loved his child too much, and so he had pushed his doubts away, and let her follow her heart. Now they were all paying for his mistake. And they would lose her for it.

"These people you are sending me to . . ." she began.

"Your grandmother knows the truth of the matter, lassie," he said. "She will love you, and you will love her. Jasmine Leslie is a good and sensible woman. Listen to her, my wee Fancy," he continued, using the nickname she had had since childhood, "she will guide you well. Your mother's family are wonderful people." And he kissed the top of his daughter's head. "You have her eyes, you know. Hers are that marvelous turquoise, too."

"They are?" Frances sniffed.

"Aye, they are," he said, smiling for the first time in weeks. "She was a princess from a foreign land. She traveled to England for over six months aboard a great vessel, the first one to be called *Cardiff Rose*. You will travel only a few weeks, my dearest daughter. And while I am an Irishman born, England is a lovely land, too. You will be happy there."

"Not without you and Mama!" Frances cried. "Not without my family, Papa!"

"You have a very large family, my child," Fortune told her daughter. "Most of them you have never met. But I have spoken to you over the years of them all. You will live with your grandmother on my brother Charlie's estate. You will have two of your cousins for companions. They are young girls like yourself. Your uncle is related to the king himself! You will probably go to court, Fancy! And one day, knowing my mother, you will again find a man to love, and this time he will really love you."

"*Never!*" Fancy spat.

"Surely you do not still hold an affection for Parker Randolph?" her mother said nervously.

"No, I do not," the girl said stonily.

Fortune heaved an audible sigh of relief, and remembering it Fancy Devers almost laughed aloud. No. She held no passion for her departed husband. But she would never again allow any man to gain the slightest hold on her heart. Men could not be trusted, except, of course, for her father, and brothers.

Finally the ship was ready to sail. With much kissing and crying, Frances Devers bid her family and her childhood a final farewell. She then proceeded to weep her way across the Atlantic until England came into her view. The captain's wife, a motherly woman who had raised two daughters of her own, was wise enough to offer Frances her warm companionship but no advice unless solicited. She coaxed the grieving girl to eat and spoke warmly of Lady Jasmine.

When their vessel had finally anchored in the London Pool, there had been a smaller boat awaiting her, a barge. They lowered her in the boatswain's chair from the deck of the *Cardiff Rose II* to the deck of her waiting transport. The little cabin was elegant with its green velvet bench and fresh flowers in crystal holders on either side of the enclosure. There were pink roses, daisies, and delicate ferns. Her luggage finally stowed aboard the barge, and a second river transport, Fancy Devers began her journey upriver to Chiswick-on-Strand where she would stay the night at a place called Greenwood House.

It was midafternoon of an early September day, and the great bustling city through which the river Thames glided was a revelation to a girl who had never before in her entire life seen a real city. She didn't know which way to turn next, or if she should be afraid. The door to her enclosure was open to allow the river breeze to cool her. One of the rowers kept shouting out the places of interest as they passed.

"There be Whitehall, miss. King's not there right now. The gentry likes the country in the summertime. There be Westminster Palace. There be the Houses of Parliament for all the good the gentlemen politicians do us common folk. There be the Tower where traitors are kept and then gets their heads chopped off, miss." This last was said with great relish.

Finally the barge nosed its way into a stone landing quay and docked. Liveried servants hurried down the green lawn to the water's edge and helped Fancy out. Her luggage was already being unloaded. A young woman servant ran down from the house and curtsied before her. She had dancing gray-blue eyes, and her hair was ash brown beneath her cap.

"I be Bess Trueheart, mistress. Your grandmother has sent me to serve you. We are to depart for Queen's Malvern on the morrow. Please come into the house. You will want a bath, I am sure, and your dinner. And a bed that does not rock," she concluded with a smile. Then she curtsied again.

Fancy laughed. For the first time in weeks she actually laughed. "Thank you, Bess Trueheart," she replied, "and you are correct. I am hungry, tired, and dirty."

In Greenwood House she had been greeted by the servants, many older than younger, who welcomed her warmly. They remarked on how very much she resembled an ancestress, whose picture hung in the Great Hall overlooking the river. The housekeeper took her there, and Fancy was surprised by the portrait of the woman that was pointed out to her. She had dark hair, skin like cream, and her head was held at a proud tilt. She wore an elegant gown of scarlet velvet, embroidered with pearls and gold thread. They did resemble each other, but Fancy thought the woman far more beautiful than she was.

"Who is she?" she asked the housekeeper.

"Why, miss, that be your great-great-grandmother, Skye O'Malley. But you do not have her eyes. You have the duchess's, your grandmother's, eyes. I never in all my born days saw eyes that color except in her, and now you."

The next morning, Fancy and her new maidservant departed for Queen's Malvern, outside Worcester. It would be a trip of several long days. Her uncle, the duke, Bess told her, had arranged for the best of inns along the way. She was not to worry herself about anything at all. The weather was usually good in early autumn. The roads would be, if not dusty, dry so they should be home in no time at all.

Fancy sat back and took Bess's advice. She closed her eyes and thought about Maryland, and her family, and tried to push what had happened from her memory. But along with the thought of tobacco being harvested, the sweet smell of it drying in the barns, and the long skeins of geese soaring above the Chesapeake as the trees began to turn, came images of Parker Randolph.

They called him the handsomest man in the Colonies, and outwardly he surely had been. He was tall and lean of body, with wavy dark blond hair, and the bluest eyes she had ever seen. His smile had been quick. His laughter infectious. His manners and his charm legend. *And she had believed him when he said he loved her.* Fancy blinked back her tears.

But Parker hadn't loved her at all. His soul had been as black as his features were beautiful. And she had found out too late. Too late to prevent their marriage. Too late to prevent the scandal that surrounded his death. Her dreams of love, a life of happiness like her parents had shared, had been brutally crushed. But she had at least been fortunate to escape Parker before he caused her worse pain than the reality of what he was already had. If only they had learned of his true character, and that of his family, before she had become his wife.

But they hadn't known, hadn't even suspected. After all, as Maeve so succinctly pointed out, he was a Virginia Randolph. His more important Virginia relations had helped Kieran Devers quell the storm of controversy that had erupted over Parker Randolph's death. Faced with the true facts of the situation, and as horrified as the few others who knew what had really happened, they had used their considerable influence to extinguish the uproar as swiftly as possible. The truth was not pretty and had it been known, the scandal would have been impossible to contain.

So they had agreed with Devers that the sooner the widow departed the Colonies for England, the quicker this disgraceful situation would die down. With Frances Devers gone, the talk would fade away, probably by winter, everyone was quite certain. And so she had been exiled from everything and everyone she had loved. But Parker Randolph had taught her a valuable lesson. He had taught her that men could not be trusted. He had taught her that her father and her brothers were unique.

And when she had asked her parents why they had not told her these things before she wed, her mother had wept bitter tears. They had been so happy together, Fortune explained, that the difficulties they had faced in their youth in England and Ireland had been forgotten as the years passed. Aine, her eldest sister, had known the real story. So had Shane, Cullen and Rory, who had been named for deceased relatives and friends in Ireland. When pressed, Maeve recalled something about their father's wicked younger brother but little else. Neither Jamie, Charlie, nor she had known a great deal of their father's early history. And they weren't particularly interested.

They knew about their mother's family, who it seemed were wealthy and powerful people. Their grandmother was, in their minds, a colorful character who had outlived several husbands and had had a royal prince for a lover. She had known dukes and kings. Their mother said that her mother's own father had been the ruler of a great land thousands of miles across the earth. Fancy remembered that as children they had not quite believed their mother's tales. She was, it seemed, a great storyteller, touched with the gift of gab, her father would tease, for their mother had also been born in Ireland although she wasn't raised there.

But now, Fancy considered, those stories did not seem quite as outlandish as she and her siblings had believed. The comfortable luxury she had experienced so far was eye opening. She had never before known servants who had been with a family for generations. She had never experienced the fawning respect given to her and her equipage as they entered the assigned innyards and the inns. The lady wished a bath? *At once!* The lady preferred duck to capon? *Immediately!* It was all most revealing, and her curiosity was piqued. She found she was anxious to reach Queen's Malvern. And then suddenly they were there.

The elegant carriage that had been drawn all the way from London by six perfectly matched bays with cream-colored manes and tails moved smartly through the gates of the estate. Interested, Fancy pulled down the window and peered out. Located in a small valley in the Malvern Hills between the rivers Severn and Wye, the house and its lands had once been a royal property. Late in the reign of Elizabeth Tudor, the queen, in need of monies, had sold the estate to the de Marisco family. They had left it to their favorite granddaughter, and it was her son, the duke of Lundy, who now possessed it.

Constructed in the reign of Edward IV as a gift for his queen, the house of warm mellowed pink brick was built in the shape of an E. The brick outer walls were covered in shiny dark green ivy except for one wing that had been burned during the Commonwealth and reconstructed just five years ago following the king's restoration. The windows were tall and wide with leaded panes. The roofs were of dark slate with many chimneys. It looked a comfortable home to Fancy. Waiting before the house upon the carefully raked gravel drive was a small group of people. The most striking of the group was a woman in a garnet silk gown, the cream-colored lace of her chemise showing above the neckline, a lacy shawl draped about her shoulders. The lady had silvery hair with two ebony wings on either side of her head. Next to her stood a younger woman wearing a silk dress of ocean blue. Her hair, a dark blond, was fashioned with elegant curls. Next to her was a tall gentleman in a black velvet suit with snow-white lace cuffs, and a white shirt. His auburn hair was cropped short, and he had silver buckles on his shoes. With these three stood two young girls, quite similar in appearance. One wore a gown of deep green silk, and the other a gown of rich violet. Both had dark hair as did Fancy. *How alike we are,* Fancy considered. *We could be sisters. How odd. I wonder if Mama knew. They are more like me than my own siblings.*

"The old woman is your grandmother," Bess said. "The gentleman by her side is the duke, your uncle. The blond lady is his wife, Lady Barbara. The two lasses your cousins, Lady Cynara and Lady Diana."

"Are they sisters?" Fancy asked.

"Nay," Bess quickly said. "Lady Cynara is the duke and Lady Barbara's daughter. Lady Diana is the duke of Glenkirk's lass."

Fancy struggled to sort out the relationships as her mother had explained them to her. "She's a Leslie?"

"Aye!"

"Her father is my mother's brother," Fancy said aloud. "He is the eldest of my grandmother's Leslie children. My mother is the youngest child of her second marriage to the marquis of Westleigh."

"If you know that," Bess chuckled, "you know more than me, mistress." Then she said, "Lady Diana is the sweetest lass you'll ever meet with, but beware of Lady Cynara. She's proud beyond all bearing of her Stuart blood. She don't mean to be difficult, but she can be. Don't let her bully you, and I hope you'll forgive me for being so frank, but here you are, all the way from the Colonies, and not knowing a soul. My conscience wouldn't let me rest if I didn't give you the lay of the land, Mistress Frances. You seem as good a lass as your cousin, Lady Diana."

"I'm grateful to you, Bess," Fancy quid. "It is difficult being so very far from home, and a stranger."

The coach now drew to a stop. The door on the right side was opened by a liveried footman, and the steps pulled down so its occupants might dismount the vehicle. The duke of Lundy stepped forward, and offered his hand to Fancy.

"May I welcome you to England, and to Queen's Malvern, Niece," he said, helping her from the coach. "I am your uncle, Charles Stuart, your mother's younger brother." He bowed and drew her forward into the group of her relations.

"I am your grandmother." Jasmine Leslie greeted Fancy with a smile, and then she kissed the girl on both cheeks. "You look nothing like your mother, but you certainly do look like your cousins, and all of you resemble my grandmother. Blood will indeed tell. Welcome to England, and to Queen's Malvern, dear girl."

"And this is my wife, Lady Barbara," the duke continued.

Fancy curtsied politely.

"And your cousins, my daughter Cynara and my niece Diana Leslie," the duke concluded.

Fancy curtsied again, and her cousins returned the gesture, but all three girls were eyeing each other curiously.

Jasmine put an arm about Fancy. "Bess Trueheart has taken good care of you, Frances?"

"Oh, yes, ma'am!" Fancy replied. "She has been most helpful. I wanted to bring my own servant, Junie-Bee, but Mama said my break with Maryland must be complete."

They entered the house and settled themselves in the old hall that was Jasmine's favorite room at Queen's Malvern. The servants took her traveling cloak and came forth with trays carrying goblets of fine wine and delicate little sugar wafers, which they passed about. The family settled themselves about the fireplace. It was blazing merrily, taking the chill off the late afternoon.

As they sat making polite conversation, Cynara Stuart suddenly burst out, "We're going to court this winter, Cousin Frances!" Her bright blue eyes were sparkling with excitement.

"We have been to court before," Diana Leslie said softly.

"But only to be presented to the king," Cynara replied. "They say he is the best lover in all the world." She smiled archly.

"Cynara, mind your manners," Jasmine chided.

"Well, everyone says it, Grandmama," Cynara replied.

"We only visited a day at court," Diana explained to Fancy. "We met the queen, too. She is not particularly pretty, but she is very nice."

"They gave us sobriquets," Cynara continued. "*Everyone* who is *anyone* at the court has a sobriquet. They called Diana *Siren*. They say she is so beautiful that she could lure men to their destruction, but I don't think she ever would. Diana is far too sweet."

"And Cynara they have called *Sin*," Diana added with a mischievous grin. "I cannot imagine why. I wonder what they will call you, Cousin Frances."

"My family calls me Fancy. I could not pronounce my name when I was a very little girl. I called myself Fancy in an attempt to say Francey, which is what my brothers first called me. Soon everyone was calling me Fancy. When someone calls me Frances, I wonder what it is I have done wrong," Fancy finished with a little smile.

"Your mother's first house was called Fortune's Fancy," the duke of Lundy remarked.

"I never lived in that house," Fancy told them. "It was destroyed in a fierce storm six years after it was built. It was one of those storms that sometimes comes from the Caribbean in late summer. The house that replaced it is called Bayview. It was built on the same spot and oversees the Chesapeake." She sighed, and her lovely face grew sad. "I will miss it." Her voice trailed off.

"Of course you will," Jasmine said briskly. "It would not be natural if you didn't. I am an old woman. I have lived all but sixteen years of my life in England and Scotland, yet I still think of the palace where I grew up. It was set on the shores of a beautiful lake in a region called Kashmir. As I was the last, and the youngest of my father's children, and my mother was English-born, my father thought it better I live there where the climate was more temperate than farther south where his court was, and the air tropical. My first husband was a Kashmiri prince. He was very handsome with dark eyes," she told them, smiling.

"How many husbands have you had, Grandmama?" Fancy asked.

"Three," Jasmine answered her, quietly pleased that this new arrival had addressed her as *Grandmama*. "The first was Prince Jamal Khan. He was murdered by my half brother. That is why my father sent me to my own grandmother in England. I traveled many months to reach here. My second husband was the marquis of Westleigh, Rowan Lindley. He is your grandfather, Fancy. My third husband was Jemmie Leslie, the duke of Glenkirk. And your uncle Charlie's sire was Prince Henry Stuart, who had he lived would have followed his father, King James, onto the throne."

"How did my grandfather die?" Fancy asked, curious. "Mama says she never met him and always thought of Lord Leslie as her father."

"Your grandfather was killed by a religious bigot in Ireland. The bullet was meant for me, however, but Rowan died instead," Jasmine explained. "I was just enceinte with your mother, dear girl." She smiled. "You have a very large family here on this side of the ocean, Fancy Devers. In time you will undoubtedly meet many of them. My own grandmother had six living children. They have in their turn spawned many progeny, who have done the same. I believe my grandmother's descendants now number over four hundred souls in England, Scotland, Ireland, and the colonies."

"Gracious!" Fancy exclaimed. "I did not know that. All Mama said was that we had family here."

"Has your mother been happy?" Jasmine asked.

"I have never known Mama to be unhappy until recently," Fancy replied. "She and Papa can sometimes be most embarrassing, for they seem to love each other fiercely. I thought . . . I hoped I might find that kind of love one day, but . . ." She stopped, and said no more.

"Love," Cynara said grandly, "is but an illusion, Cousin."

"Indeed?" her grandmother noted dryly. "Considering your lack of expertise in such matters, Cynara, I am surprised you should believe such a thing."

"I have heard it said," Cynara began.

"I am relieved to learn your opinions are not based on personal experience," Jasmine answered sharply. "It is unwise, Cynara, to repeat such things, as it only makes you look foolish and ignorant. You are, after all, only fifteen."

"You were married when you were my age, Grandmama," Cynara said pertly. She tossed her dark head, and her curls bounced.

"It was a different time and a different place," Jasmine answered. "My father was not well, and he wanted me settled before he died. My foster mother was not particularly happy about my youthful marriage at all."

"Did your husband make love to you right away?" Cynara queried her grandmother, wickedly.

"Whether he did, or he didn't, is not a topic for discussion!" Jasmine turned to her daughter-in-law, whose face was flaming at this point. "*Really*, Barbara! Have you no control over this girl? What Fancy must think of her I can only imagine."

Fancy, however, was already fascinated with her cousin Cynara. Cynara was so very beautiful, and she seemed so sophisticated, even though she was a year younger than Frances Devers. Wisely, though, Fancy said, "Would you think me rude, Grandmama, if I asked to be shown to my room? My travels have been quite fatiguing."

"Of course not, dear child," Jasmine said quickly. She arose. "I shall take you. I have chosen your room myself. It is near to mine, and Diana is on the other side of you." She linked her arm in Fancy's and led her from the hall.

"What do you think?" the duke of Lundy asked his wife.

"She is lovely," Barbara Stuart replied. "Is it not interesting how alike she, Cynara, and Diana look? She is tired now, but in a few days we shall get to know her better, but Charlie, I think your mama's judgment will hold as it usually does in these matters."

The duke of Lundy nodded in agreement. "I suspect that you are correct, my dear," he responded.

"Does Grandmama think she killed her husband?" Cynara asked her parents boldly.

The duchess of Lundy closed her eyes in exasperation. Cynara was so damned reckless in her speech. *And her acts*, Barbara Stuart thought. What was going to become of her?

"There is no evidence that your cousin killed anyone, Cynara," her father said quietly. "I will appreciate you not repeating gossip, especially unproven gossip." He stared hard at his youngest daughter.

"Well then, why is it said of her that she did?" Cynara demanded.

"There was some terrible tragedy," the duke explained. "Even I do not know the truth of the matter. But you will keep in mind that if a crime had been committed, then your cousin would have been charged, and she was not. A bridegroom dying after his wedding is very unusual. It is precisely because there is little knowledge of what happened that people have decided to make up these stories, Cynara. I hope that you will never find yourself the subject of such gossip."

"Does Grandmama know?" Diana ventured softly.

"I believe she does," the duke replied.

"Poor Fancy," Diana said. "How difficult it must have been for her to lose her bridegroom in some dreadful manner. And then be sent away from all she knows and loves for her reputation's sake."

"You left Glenkirk when you were eleven," Cynara said, "and it hasn't affected you at all, Siren."

"But I was delighted to leave the Highlands, Cyn," Diana answered. "I far prefer the elegance and sophistication of England. And I shall one day make a good marriage here. It would have been difficult for me to do that at Glenkirk. Besides, my family comes south almost every summer to visit. And next year my sister, Mair, will join us. Fancy, however, has crossed an ocean to come to Grandmama. When will she ever see her brothers and sisters, or her parents again?"

The duke smiled warmly at his niece. Diana Leslie was always so thoughtful of others. He had never known such sweetness and often wondered where she had gotten it. And yet when called up to be strong, Diana was exactly that. She was unlike his youngest child, and yet the two, so different, were fast friends. They had been since that summer his mother had asked his brother to leave Diana with them. The duke of Lundy had always hoped Diana would be a good influence on his daughter, but it did not seem that way. Yet there was a bright side to the situation. Cynara had been unable to foist her naughty ways on her cousin. "You have a good heart, pet," he told Diana.

Cynara rolled her blue eyes, but then she grinned. "Let's go see what kind of clothing our cousin has brought with her from the Colonies. Her traveling gown wasn't half-bad at all. I would not have thought a little colonial so fashionable. And what jewelry does she possess, I wonder? Grandmama will give her some, certainly. She has so much," Cynara noted. "Don't you just love the ruby ring she gave me for my last birthday?" She flashed the gem before them as she did at least several times daily.

"Please allow your cousin to settle herself before you burst in on her, Cynara," her mother suggested. "There will be plenty of time to rifle through her possessions over the next few weeks before we go to court. Fancy will be tired, and want to rest."

"Oh, very well," Cynara said, then turned to Diana. "Let's go riding," she suggested. "We just need to change our gowns."

"Go for a walk in the gardens," her father said sternly, "and leave your grandmother alone with this new grandchild. She has missed my sister all these years and is thrilled to be able to have at least one of Fortune's children with her at long last."

"The gardens are lovely right now," the duchess responded, helpfully.

"There are new puppies in the kennels," Diana volunteered.

"*Ohh!*" Cynara exclaimed, excitedly. She loved dogs, and had been promised a new puppy from the next litter to be born. "Are they Bella's?" she inquired.

"Yes," Diana said with a smile.

"I get first pick!" Cynara responded.

"You know that I prefer cats to dogs," Diana reminded her cousin as the two girls hurried from the hall.

The duke of Lundy chuckled. "I do believe that with Diana's help we have saved Fancy from our daughter. At least for the time being," he amended with a grin.

"Fancy looks so sad," the duchess remarked. "Poor child! I hope she will come to love and trust us."

"Why is it," the duke wondered, "that Cynara did not get your kind heart?"

"She is like my father. Practical," the duchess said. "And like my mother. Determined to have her own way in all things."

"You rarely speak of your parents," he noted.

"No, I do not," the duchess replied. "My father is long dead, and my mother died just before my first husband, Squire Randall. She was always jealous of my father's love for me and would have allowed that brute of a second husband of hers to put me into service, even though I had not been raised to be a servant. Thank God for Madame Skye! Who knows what would have happened to me if it hadn't been for her."

"She was a remarkable woman," the duke of Lundy agreed. "I wonder what she would think of these three great-great-granddaughters of hers, all of whom resemble her most strongly. My mother grows more like her each day," he remarked.

His wife smiled. "Aye, Charlie, she does," she agreed. "She will brook no nonsense from any of our girls, and she will certainly get Fancy past her melancholy longing for Maryland."

"I believe she will," he said, wondering even as he spoke what was going on upstairs in his house right now.

Fancy had followed her grandmother obediently from the hall. She was tired, but the worst was over. She had crossed an ocean in surprising safety and traveled from London to meet her relations. And she had liked them all upon their first meeting. She knew far more of them, she realized, than they did of her. Her mother had never ceased to speak of her family in England and Scotland. It had always been very obvious to Fancy that her mother's siblings were most dear to her. Of course her memories were of young men and women, little boys, and an infant sister named Autumn. But now all of those siblings were well into their middle years, even the baby sister whom Fortune never knew.

Her grandmother stopped before a carved oak door and opened it, stepping through. Fancy trailed after her, and there was Bess Trueheart waiting with a smile. Fancy let her gaze sweep the chamber. It was large, the walls paneled in an old-fashioned manner, but there was a large fireplace, already blazing brightly on this late afternoon; and there was a big leaden-paned bow window with a seat in it. The room was decorated with velvet draperies at the windows, of rich turquoise blue with gold fringe and rope tiebacks. The furniture was sturdy oak, well polished and obviously comfortable. The floors were covered with a thick wool carpet of turquoise and cream.

"How lovely!" Fancy exclaimed, pleased, and she bent to sniff at a bowl of late roses on a table.

"It was my room when I first came to Queen's Malvern," Jasmine replied. "Of course it has been redecorated since that long-ago time," she concluded with a smile.

"Come into your bedchamber, mistress," Bess beckoned. "There be another fine fireplace here too, and a bed big enough for a large family, I'll vow." She ushered Fancy into the room.

It was, Fancy saw at once, every bit as lovely as the previous chamber, but she was surprised. "Two rooms? For my very own?" she wondered aloud. It was certainly not this way in Maryland where she and each of her siblings had had a bedchamber for themselves, and not one as spacious as this suite was.

"It is called an apartment," Jasmine explained. "It is the custom in great houses to have a dayroom and a bedchamber."

"Mama never told me that," Fancy admitted.

"What did she speak about when she spoke of England?" Jasmine asked her granddaughter.

"She spoke of her family mainly," Fancy answered.

Jasmine nodded. "I wonder if she missed us as much as we missed her. I still cannot believe that I let my precious child go so far from us. I thought perhaps she might come home to visit one day, but then the troubles began, and King Charles I was executed. The years of the so-called Commonwealth were difficult. I took my youngest daughter and went to France after my Jemmie was killed in the Stuart cause. I could not bear to remain at Glenkirk after that."

"Mama has been very happy, Grandmama," Fancy said. "I think only if she lost Papa would things change for her. She is, I believe, very much like you in many ways." Suddenly Fancy hugged Jasmine. "You have made me feel so welcome," she told the older woman. "Thank you!"

"Why, my dear child," Jasmine exclaimed, "you are my granddaughter, even if today is the first time I have laid eyes upon you. I have known you, your brothers, and your sisters through your mother's correspondence, but I will admit that I am right glad to finally have you here with us, even if it is tragedy that has brought you. We will wipe away those awful memories for you, my darling Fancy."

"What do you know?" Fancy asked her grandmother tremulously. Her voice had begun to quaver, and tears sprang to her eyes.

"Your mother has told me *everything*," Jasmine said. "No one else in the family is privy to that information, nor will they be unless you decide to share it with them one day. We will speak no more on it, my child." She enfolded Fancy into her embrace, and kissed her gently upon each of her cheeks. "This is England, and you are here to make a fresh start. The misfortunes of last June are behind you."

Fancy hugged her grandmother back. "Thank you, Grandmama," she said softly. "I am still coming to terms with what happened. I cannot believe I was so foolish as to fall in love with a man who did not deserve my love. He was so handsome, and so charming, and everyone envied me. He was, after all, a Virginia Randolph."

"I suppose," Jasmine remarked dryly, "that in the Colonies that means something, but here in England it does not, dear child. And more young women than not have fallen in love with the perfect man only to discover that the apple has a rather large worm. You are quite fortunate to have been freed of your worm so you might begin anew."

Fancy giggled. "Somehow thinking of Parker as a nasty worm helps me put everything in perspective."

"Men, dear child, are best kept in perspective and taken with a grain of salt," Jasmine advised. "Now, I shall leave you to get some rest. Bess will bring your supper here in your apartment so you may escape for tonight, at least, the questions your cousins Cynara and Diana are undoubtedly dying to ask you. I think you must be well rested before you are thrown into the company of those two vixens."

"I already like them," Fancy said. "We look so much alike but are all so very different, it would seem."

"You will become good friends, of that I am certain," Jasmine assured her granddaughter. "I shall come and visit you after dinner to make certain that you are comfortable. Bess Trueheart will take good care of you, I know."

"She already has, Grandmama," Fancy replied. "How clever of you to pick just the right serving woman for me before we even met."

"I told you, my child, I know you from your mother's letters," Jasmine reminded the girl. She smiled. "I shall return later." Then she left the bedchamber, and Fancy heard the door of the dayroom that opened into the hallway close.

Bess bustled in. "A nice hot bath, Mistress Fancy?"

"Oh, yes!" came the enthusiastic reply.

"Let me get your skirts and bodice off," Bess said, "and then I'll see to the bath while you take a wee nap."

Fancy nodded. It all sounded wonderful to her. She stood still while Bess unlaced her bodice, removed it, and then undid the tapes of her skirt. Fancy stepped out of the puddle of material, and

Bess next pulled the laces loose that held up her many petticoats. They fell to the floor with a slight hiss. Fancy stepped over them, now clad only in her lace-trimmed chemise.

"You get into bed, mistress," Bess instructed her, gathering up the pile of garments. "When your bath is ready, I'll wake you."

"Oh, I won't sleep," Fancy said.

"Well, just close your eyes then, and rest," Bess suggested. Then she hurried from the room with Fancy's clothing, closing the door behind her.

What kind of a tub would it be? Fancy wondered, closing her eyes. The tub she had bathed in at home was oak and comfortably large. Her mother had always believed in almost-daily bathing, although Fancy knew that other people thought her mother overfastidious. Her eyes closed. Everybody was so nice to her, she thought. The duke and his pretty wife. Her grandmother. Her cousin Diana. And Cynara. She had never met a girl like Cynara. She would wager that Cynara would not have been taken in by Parker Randolph. She wouldn't have been a simpering little fool, boasting silently in her pride over having caught the handsomest man in the colonies. Cynara would have seen right through Parker Randolph. No one else, even her parents, had. Yet somehow, even on their briefest acquaintance, Fancy believed that Cynara would have immediately known Parker Randolph for what he was.

Her thoughts slipped back to her wedding day. Her gown was so beautiful, and Mama had given her a strand of pearls for her very own. Parker had looked so distinguished as he awaited her at the altar of the plantation church. Like all of Fortune and Kieran's children, Fancy had been raised with knowledge of both her parents' faiths. She preferred the Anglican religion of her mother as did her sister, Maeve. Her elder brothers practiced the Roman Catholicism of their father. Her younger brothers claimed their explorations kept them from church, but Fancy knew that they were simply not church-going men. One day again they would be, she was certain, but not now.

The ceremony had been beautiful. The feasting afterward had been lavish. And then she had been escorted to the bridal chamber by her mother, Maeve, and her sisters-in-law to be prepared for her husband's arrival. When she had been undressed, put into her silk-and-lace nightshirt, and her matching cap with its silk ribbons, Aine had come in, and said a blessing over her. Then they had left her to await her husband. The tears began to slide down Fancy's pale face. *I must put this from me*, she thought silently to herself. *What has happened has happened. Nothing can change it. Parker did not love me. He is dead. And I must begin a new life here in England.* Lord, her eyes felt so heavy. Her thoughts became jumbled. Fancy Devers finally slept.

Chapter

2

She had had a lovely bath and a hot supper. Bess had tucked her back into her bed, and Fancy had slept the night through. She was awakened by a wet tongue licking at her face and the sound of giggling. Her turquoise eyes flew open to see a small black, tan and white spaniel on her bed, and her two cousins Diana and Cynara standing nearby. "Good morning," she said with a smile, and stroked the wiggling dog. "And who is this?"

"It's Beau," Cynara said. "He's Bella's mate and has just become the papa of three puppies. Grandmama says we may each have one. Do you like dogs? Diana prefers cats, but she's going to take one of Bella's pups anyhow. I get to choose first."

"Perhaps it would be more polite if we allowed Fancy to have the first choice since she has just arrived," Diana suggested.

"But I want a male, and there is only one of them," Cynara protested. She looked at Fancy. "Do you want the male?"

"You may have it," Fancy told her. "I prefer females. They are sweeter in nature and less apt to roam."

"Then you and Siren can argue over the other two," Cynara said, well satisfied. "Are you rested now? Come, and get up so we may show you all about Queen's Malvern. It used to be a royal property, you know, but the old queen needed gold, and our great-great-grandmother bought it from her. It's a wonderful house, but a wing was damaged during the wars that happened before we were born. My papa restored that wing. He built a beautiful dining room with a marble fireplace, crystal chandeliers, and the most beautiful paintings! Grandmama prefers the old hall, but I love the dining room. You will, too. Come on, Fancy! Get up!" She removed the dog from the bed and tugged at the coverlet.

Fancy laughed. She had always been the baby of the family, but she was a good year or more older than both these cousins. Still, it was lovely to feel young and carefree once more. Her parents had been right, she suddenly realized. This exile to England was just what she needed. "Call Bess," she said. She looked at the pair. Their gowns were very simple, and not at all as elegant as the ones they had worn yesterday when they greeted her. "Can we go riding later?" she asked them.

"Yes!" they chorused.

"Shall I dress like you?" she inquired. "Do you ride like that? Surely not," Fancy wondered aloud.

"Just throw on something to go exploring," Cynara said.

"We will change later when we ride," Diana added.

"You don't need Bess," Cynara said. "Certainly you know how to dress yourself, Cousin."

Fancy nodded. "But I don't know where my clothing is," she explained to them. "I'll need Bess at least to help me find my clothes."

"Of course!" Diana laughed. She pointed to an embroidered bell-rope by the bed. "Just pull it. She'll come."

Fancy complied with the instruction, yanking on the pull. "What a clever invention," she said. "I must write to Mama about it."

"But how do you call your servants in the Colonies?" Cynara asked, curious.

"Our servants are always there when we require them," Fancy told her. "They seem to know when they are needed, and if they do not, well, we just yell," she finished with a mischievous grin.

Both her cousins burst out laughing, and Cynara said, "Ohh, I can see we are all going to get on very nicely, Fancy Devers."

Bess arrived. She curtsied. "Yes, mistress? You'll want to get dressed,

I think." She smiled, and then continued, "Now you two shoo. You can wait in the dayroom for her, and don't eat her breakfast. She's going nowhere until she is fed."

Cynara and Diana departed, and then Bess showed Fancy the small room off her bedchamber that held all of her clothing, both garments that hung and those in cedar-lined chests.

"From the look of those two, you'll want something easy," Bess noted. She pulled out a natural-colored linen skirt and a white shirt, exclaiming as she did so, "Why this be a man's shirt, mistress!"

"I find it more modest to wear it over my chemise with a skirt," Fancy explained. "The style is that of a man, but you will see the shirt is made to fit me. And the laces are of silk ribbon."

Bess held the shirt up. "And it is smaller than a man's. You'll start a whole new fashion, mistress," she chuckled.

Fancy washed her face and hands in the basin of warm water that Bess had provided. Then she dressed in her linen skirt and white shirt. She fastened a black leather belt about her narrow waist and slipped her bare feet into a pair of soft black-leather slippers. Her long dark hair she braided into a single thick plait, affixing the end with a bright scarlet ribbon. Then she joined her cousins in her dayroom where Cynara was eyeing her breakfast with an almost predatory look.

"Have you eaten?" Fancy asked her.

Cynara nodded. "But I'm always hungry," she added. "There wasn't a great deal of food about when I was small. 'Twas before the king was restored. I can never seem to get filled up."

"Share my food with me then," Fancy offered. "I couldn't possibly eat all that Bess has brought me. Diana?" She looked at the youngest of her cousins.

"Perhaps a bit of apple and some cheese," Diana murmured.

The three girls made quick work of the tray that Bess had brought. It contained a newly baked cottage loaf, a large wedge of sharp cheddar cheese, a shallow dish with several hard-boiled eggs, and a bowl of apples. There was also a pot of hot fragrant tea. Fancy had grown up drinking this beverage and was not surprised to see it on her tray. When they had finished, Cynara led them on a tour of Queen's Malvern, for it was her father's house. Although it would one day belong to her eldest brother, Freddie, she would always consider it home.

When they reached their grandmother's apartment, they were met by two elderly, wizened little women. Cynara introduced them.

"This is Fortune's youngest daughter," she shouted to them, and they smiled, nodded, and bowed to Fancy. "She is called Fancy." Cynara turned to her cousin. "This is Rohana, and her sister, Tora-malli, who have been with Grandmama since her birth."

"My mother has spoken lovingly of you both to me," Fancy said.

"Our lady has read to us each letter your mother sent. We know you well, mistress, and are sorry for your troubles," Toramalli said quietly. "Rohana and I are at your service." She bowed again as did her twin sister.

Fancy reached out, and taking Toramalli's hands in hers, pressed them first to her forehead and then to her heart. "Thank you," she said.

"*Aiii*, you have been well taught," Toramalli said in an approving tone. Rohana smiled at Fancy, nodding in favorable agreement with her sibling. "And you do not shout at us as does the duke's high-flown daughter."

"But you never seem to hear me if I speak in a normal tone," Cynara protested volubly, stung by their words.

"We hear what we wish to hear," Rohana spoke up. "It is a privilege, my lady, of our advanced age," and then she chuckled at the surprised look on Cynara's beautiful face. "You think because you are Stuart everyone must pay attention, but it is not so."

"May we show Fancy Grandmama's rooms?" Diana said politely.

The sisters nodded in unison and ushered the trio inside.

"These rooms were our great-great-grandmother's once long ago," Diana said quietly. "The one we all are said to resemble."

"My father was born in these rooms," Cynara said importantly.

"Your father was born in the bed in which your cousin from the Colonies now sleeps," Toramalli said. "Queen's Malvern was not our princess's house at that time. It was her home. Lord Adam and Lady Skye ruled here then. You do not know everything, my lady."

"But didn't the king and the queen come to see my papa when he was born?" Cynara ventured.

"They did!" Toramalli confirmed. "King James and Queen Anne were visiting nearby, and they came to see your papa. They were well pleased by him. King James took him from your mother, and after he had held him for a time, Queen Anne took him, scolding her mate that he was not holding the infant properly. Prince Henry, his father, had arranged to have your father inherit Lord de Marisco's titles as he had no son. The old king said, however, he should be a duke not an earl. Aye! I remember it well. I told my lady that the boy was a true Mughal for the way he howled when he wanted his own way. And a not-quite-royal Stuart, your grandmama replied." Toramalli laughed with her memories. It was a high reedy sound.

"Rohana and Toramalli have lots of wonderful stories about Grandmama and Uncle Charlie and all the family," Diana said. "You must get them to tell you, for they know things even your mama did not."

"There won't be much time before we go to court," Cynara said.

"We aren't going to court until December," Diana replied. "It is just September. There is more than enough time."

"Fancy has to have a new wardrobe made," Cynara said.

"Why?" Fancy asked. "I have brought my entire trousseau with me from Maryland, and the Williamsburg tailors are most up-to-date."

Cynara shook her head. "Perhaps for Williamsburg, and perhaps here in the country, but not for court. We must be shown to our best advantage at court; after all, we are going husband hunting."

"*Not me!*" Fancy said emphatically. "I neither want nor need another husband, thank you."

"Cousin!" Cynara was shocked. "You are sixteen and next year will be seventeen. If you do not catch another husband soon, you will be way too old for any gentleman."

"I don't care," Fancy said bluntly. "Men cannot be trusted, Cyn. I have learned that from my own bitter experience. If you don't marry them, you can retain your freedom, and freedom is, I think, more valuable than any husband."

"Gracious!" Diana exclaimed, both shocked and fascinated by her cousin's declaration.

"A woman can have her freedom *and* a man, if she is clever," Cynara said with a wisdom that was beyond her years.

"*Hee hee hee!*" cackled Rohana. "Her Mughal blood shows, Sister."

"If you have come to see your grandmother's rooms," Toramalli said sharply, "then look about you, and be on your way."

The three girls walked slowly through the rooms, which were very familiar to Cynara and Diana. Toramalli showed them the boxes of jewelry that Jasmine possessed, a great and famous collection. Besides necklaces, rings, bracelets, chains, pins, and earbobs, there were also bags of loose stones. Cynara held out her hand and waggled it.

"See my ruby ring? Grandmama had it made for me on my last birthday. She let me choose the stone I would have, and I picked this one. I find the tear an interesting shape. It is a pigeon's-blood ruby. Its color is so rich. I do love it! Do you have anything like it?"

"I have little jewelry, but for the pearls my mother gave me for my wedding," Fancy answered. "I do not think I will ever wear them again for I like not the memories they evoke."

"Ohh," Cynara said, "may I have them?"

"Lady, you are much too bold!" Toramalli scolded. She turned to Fancy. "Remember that your mama gave you your pearls, child. Keep them, and do not associate any other memories with them but your dear mama," she advised.

"Those who do not ask, do not get," Cynara said sullenly.

"Such common greed does not become a young lady of your family," Toramalli said quietly. "Now, you have seen your grandmother's apartment. Go along and show Mistress Fancy the rest of this wonderful house."

"You would think at her age she would be content to sit by the fire," Cynara grumbled as they walked downstairs to the hall. "She really does get above herself."

"That isn't fair," Diana quickly said. "Toramalli and Rohana have been with Grandmother her whole life. They may be servants, but they are privileged servants. They are family actually more than servitors. And they miss their menfolk. Adali in particular."

"My mother told me about Adali," Fancy said.

"He is dead now," Diana said, "and Toramalli's husband, Fergus, and his cousin Red Hugh who always guarded Grandmama. All who have served our grandmother, but for Toramalli and Rohana, are gone."

"They should be gone, too," Cynara muttered. "Despite their vast ages, they are as sharp-eyed as they ever were."

"And sharp of ear too it would seem," Fancy teased her cousin.

"Come on, and I'll show you where everyone is buried," Cynara said cheerfully.

They followed her from the hall, and out through the gardens. Beyond on a hillside was the family burial ground. It was neatly kept, the green grass trimmed, the gravel paths nicely raked, and open borders filled with flowers. It wasn't at all a terrible place. There were even marble benches upon which to sit.

"Here is where they are buried," Cynara said, pointing.

"Who?" Fancy asked.

"Our great-great-grandmother, Skye O'Malley, and her sixth husband, our great-great-grandfather, Adam de Marisco, the earl of Lundy. She was wed with him longer than any of the others. They grew old together, but it is said she was still beautiful to look upon even on the day she died. She had a smile on her face when she breathed her last, Grandmama says," Diana explained.

"Grandmama adored her," Cynara added.

In the hall that night Jasmine said to her three granddaughters, "Tomorrow we shall enter the storerooms, my dears. It is time to begin preparing your wardrobe for court. And I shall choose from among my jewelry suitable pieces for each of you."

"You will spoil them, Mama," Charlie Stuart said to his mother, but the tone of his voice was affectionate.

"Of course, I shall spoil them," Jasmine said with a smile. "Grandchildren are for spoiling, Charlie, as you yourself know."

"I do not spoil Brie's children a great deal," he protested.

"Only because they are at Lynmouth, and you do not see them as much as you should," Jasmine teased him.

"Who is Brie?" Fancy whispered to Cynara.

"My older half sister, the countess of Lynmouth," came the soft reply. "She was Papa's eldest child by his first wife who was killed during the wars. I hardly know her myself for she lives in Devon and was grown by the time I came into the family."

"Oh." This was such a huge family, Fancy considered. She wished now she had listened a bit more carefully when her mother had spoken of them. And where was Devon? She would have to ask or be considered a complete lackwit.

In the morning the three girls came to their grandmother's apartments, and Jasmine took them to the storage rooms, where they were faced with an enormous choice of materials from which to choose. Many of the bolts of fabric had been brought to England with Jasmine at the beginning of the century. The walls of the room were lined with cedar, and there were no windows that would allow sunlight to fade the rich colors of the materials. Cynara was openly, and greedily enthusiastic.

"I have always wanted to visit this room," she admitted. Her bright blue eyes swept about, trying to take in all the bounty before her. Finally she closed them for a moment. It was all too much.

"I think," Jasmine said quietly, "you should each choose a single color and its tones around which we will build you each a new wardrobe. It will make you unique amid all the others who will be at court this winter. Fancy, I think for you a rich turquoise blue to set off your beautiful eyes. There are many shades in the turquoise family, and you shall wear them all, dear girl. With diamonds, pearls, and Persian turquoise for your jewels. You may be a bit bolder as you are the oldest, and a widow. But I see you in teal blue as well." She looked at Cynara. "And for you, my proud and greedy pet, shades of red. Scarlet, and claret, and burgundy and crimson with diamonds rubies and pearls. And for our sweet Diana, shades of rose, and green also, to match your eyes. You shall have my emeralds, diamonds, and pearls to wear. You are like a flower, and we shall present you as one."

"Should I not wear a less conspicuous color, Grandmama?" Fancy asked. "I am, after all, a widow."

"The less said about that unfortunate misalliance the better,"

Jasmine said sanguinely. "You do not mourn Parker Randolph. Why be a hypocrite about it, my dear girl? He was a monster!"

Seeing an opportunity, Cynara spoke up. "What did he do that made him such a monster?" she inquired innocently.

"I do not choose to discuss the matter, Cyn," Fancy told her cousin sharply. "Perhaps one day but not yet."

"Did I not warn you that you were not to discuss your cousin's tragedy?" Jasmine said sternly to Cynara.

"Well, you brought it up," Cynara replied pertly.

"Cyn!" Diana hissed at her cousin.

"Nay, Diana, she is right. I did bring it up, but I have the advantage of age and authority, Cynara. *You do not.* You will obey me in the future, or you shall not have my rubies to wear to court, and I know how badly you want them." Jasmine smiled wickedly at her granddaughter.

Cynara laughed in reply. "I would do *anything* for those rubies, Grandmama," she responded, "but you know that, of course."

"Then we understand each other, *eh,* my pet?"

"That is precisely the problem, Grandmama. You have always understood me far too well," Cynara complained with just a faint hint of irritation that she dared not to show.

Jasmine laughed now. "There are times when you remind me of me when I was your age," she said. "I, too, was very determined to have my own way; and my own grandmother was equally determined that I should not for my own sake, Cynara. Life does not always play fair, as I suspect you will eventually discover to your regret. You have been fortunate, so far, but your luck may not always hold."

"Yours did," Cynara said.

"Not always," Jasmine responded quietly. "Now, let us choose the materials that we will have fashioned into wonderful gowns for you all. Fancy, my child, here is a marvelous brocade the color of Persian turquoise. It will make you a fine gown for your first visit to court. You shall be much admired. I always found the gentlemen attentive when I wore a gown the same color as my eyes."

"I am not certain I want to be admired," Fancy said softly.

"Fancy says she doesn't want a husband," Diana explained.

"Of course she doesn't," Jasmine agreed. "At least not yet. But there will come a day when she meets the right gentleman and changes her mind. My first two husbands were murdered, and my princely lover died suddenly. I decided that I was bad fortune for the men who loved me, which is why Diana's grandfather, my beloved Jemmie, had to spend two years chasing me." She laughed with the memory. "But when he finally caught up with me. *Ahhhh!*" She smiled, and grew silent.

"*Ahhhh?*" Fancy could not resist her question.

"I learned that I was wrong," Jasmine replied with a chuckle. "And one day you will learn you are wrong too, but you are not ready yet. It would be strange if you were. For now, you will go to court and have a good time the way all young women of your age and class should at this time in their lives. Ohh, look! This teal blue silk is heavenly!"

And so it went for the rest of the day. When all the materials had been chosen and were neatly stacked in three piles, one for each girl, the storage chamber was yet full. Jasmine looked about her.

"It never seems to grow empty," she remarked, "but then each time one of our ships returns from India or China, they bring me fresh bolts of cloth to add to this collection. Still, some of what came with me all those years ago is here."

Several days later a tailor arrived from London with his staff, which would be supplemented by the two seamstresses who lived on the estate. In Jasmine's youth, a woman named Bonnie had made all their gowns. Now it was her granddaughters, in the employ of the duke of Lundy and his family, who sewed. Each girl was measured carefully. The tailor's cutter began to dissect the materials into varied and sundry shapes, which the seamstresses, under the direction of the tailor himself, began to pin together and then baste. The gowns were carefully fitted upon each of the young ladies, and at last the serious business of sewing began. As each gown was almost completed, a final fitting was required. And with each final fitting, the tailor warned his young clients not to gain an ounce of weight.

Finally, it was all done. The beautiful garments were hung in the cedar storage room until it was time to pack them. In addition the estate seamstresses had sewn petticoats of both silk and flannel; chemises with their wide balloon sleeves, the wrists and necklines edged with lace; corsets, lightly boned, for none of the trio really needed a corset, but it was the fashion. Besides, it helped display the breasts wonderfully, Cynara insisted. The corsets were of fine white silk brocade decorated with pink silk rosettes and laced with pink silk laces. Each girl had several sets of drawers edged in lace, which were called *les calecons* and came from France. There were nightgowns of fine silk, all trimmed lavishly in lace, and silk stockings, each pair decorated with a different design, as well as matching garters.

The shoemaker came, and the girls were fitted for new shoes, boots, and slippers. The dress shoes had jewel-studded heels, and ribbon bows, or bejeweled enameled buckles. There were pantofles, which were half-slippers made of soft leather or covered in silk or satin brocade. Each girl had a fine pair of leather buckskins, calf-high close-fitting hunting boots with a turnover top. Jasmine told her granddaughters that when she was a girl in India her royal foot was measured using a strand of pearls. The leftover pearls were given to her servant.

There were accessories to be chosen. Perfumed leather gloves of fine leather; shawls of sheer delicate silk or cashmere, imported by the O'Malley-Small trading company; fringed parasols; silk ribbons; painted fans; fans of ostrich feathers; silk flowers in every color to decorate their hair; and satin misers, which were small purses with a tiny slit in their center. Each purse was fitted with a small gold or silver ring so that valuables might be kept secure in one end or another. And of course, jewelry.

Jasmine was generous with her granddaughters, loaning them some of her finest pieces. There were necklaces, long strands of pearls both creamy pink and black. There were dangling earbobs, bejeweled broaches, and rings of all kinds. Jasmine advised her three granddaughters in their selection, and then saw that it was all carefully packed with their trunks in ivory boxes lined with velvet.

The autumn deepened with clear dry days and crisp nights. Fancy began to enjoy this new life she was living. Her cousins were wonderful companions, and the three girls had swiftly become fast friends. It seemed impossible, Fancy thought, to think she might have spent her entire life without ever meeting them. Her letters to her parents began to take on a happier tone. And then in mid-November, Jasmine announced that the family would be leaving for court in a few days' time.

"Your uncle has his own apartment at Whitehall," Jasmine told Fancy, "but it is barely big enough for him and for Barbara. You and your cousins will stay with me at Greenwood House."

"Where I stayed my first night in London?" Fancy asked.

"Yes," came the brief answer.

"Is it yours?" Fancy asked.

"It once was," and then Jasmine explained. "Greenwood House was my grandmother's London home. It was confiscated during the rule of the Commonwealth and given to a man known as Sir Simon Bates. Sir Simon, however, was not Sir Simon. He was a spy for King Charles. He was actually Gabriel Bainbridge, the duke of Garwood, my daughter Autumn's husband. And so Greenwood House remained in the family, although it is now hers, not mine. I probably would have given it to her one day. I stay there when I am in London as does my daughter India and her family. None of them will be coming to court for the Season though, and so Greenwood is ours," Jasmine concluded. "You will find it is advisable to have one's own place in London. So many people come to court, and there is not enough accommodation for them. The house next door to us is owned by your cousins, the earl and countess of Lynmouth. Sabrina is your Uncle Charlie's eldest child. She lived with her brothers in Scotland during the Commonwealth period while their father was with his cousin, the king. My son Patrick and his wife, Flanna, looked after them."

"Diana's parents," Fancy said quickly.

"That's right!" Jasmine laughed. "You will get them all straightened out eventually, dear girl."

"What is court like, Grandmama?" Fancy wondered.

"It is a whole world for those privileged to be a part of it." Jasmine explained. "It is where the rich, the powerful, the not-so-rich and not-so-powerful come to see, to be seen, and to climb the social ladder toward whatever goal they desire. It is where families make matches between their children, and the society of the elite flourishes. It is, quite frankly, unlike any place on earth."

"It sounds exciting, and dangerous, and perhaps even a bit boring all at once," Fancy noted.

"Clever girl!" her grandmother approved. "It is all of those things and more, Fancy. If I may be blunt, you are still a true innocent where human nature is concerned despite your unfortunate experience with Parker Randolph. At court you will meet all sorts of people. Some will be exactly what they seem to be. Many will not. Do not be afraid to come to me, or to your uncle, or to your aunt, Lady Barbara, to ask for our counsel or advice. I do not want you hurt again as you were in Maryland."

"I won't be, Grandmama," Fancy assured Jasmine. "I know that I lack experience in human nature, but I shall trust no one except you, Uncle Charlie and Lady Barbara. I have come to love Cyn and Siren, but for all their talk, they know even less than I do. I will be careful, and I will come to you for your wisdom."

"You put both my heart and my mind at ease," Jasmine replied.

Finally the day came when they were to depart for London. There would be several coaches in their train. Three would carry the baggage, and two would be for the travelers. There would be their riding horses as well, for it was not expected that the three young ladies coop themselves up in their transport. There was also a fourth large carriage for the personal servants who were going with them. Rohana and Toramalli would be left behind as they were simply too fragile to travel with their mistresses any longer. In their place Jasmine was served by a French woman who had been in her daughter Autumn's service. Orane had found life in the north dull. Realizing her unhappiness, Autumn had asked her mother to take the woman into her service. Orane was willing, and the move suited everyone. Orane was clever enough to be respectful to her mistress's two longtime retainers, and hence by deferring to them, or pretending to defer to them, she had fit in quite nicely.

Jasmine bid her twin servitors farewell. "You will both be here when I return in early summer," she instructed them.

"We will be here," Toramalli said. Rohana bobbed her head in agreement but added, "But not for much longer, my princess. We are both very, very old now, and all those we dearly love are gone but for you."

Jasmine nodded with her complete understanding. "Wait until I return," she said softly, and then she kissed them both on their soft wizened cheeks. "Stay by the fire in the hall," she instructed them. "And keep warm at night. Wear flannel petticoats to bed as well."

"The cats sleep with us," Toramalli cackled. "They keep us quite warm, my princess. Go now. The family awaits you to depart."

The great train belonging to the duke of Lundy and his kin departed Queen's Malvern on a cold, gray late November morning. It traveled for over a week before reaching its destination at Chiswick-on-Strind, which was located on the nearer edge of the city of London than it had been in earlier days. The leaves were all gone from the trees in Greenwood's park when the carriages drew up to the door on an early December afternoon. It was already getting dark.

"Barbara and I shall go on to Whitehall," the duke told his mother. "I will come tomorrow and tell you what is happening. I think the lasses should rest a few days in order to look their very best when they are first seen."

"Give His Majesty my fond regards," Jasmine said.

"He has a *tendre* for you, Mama," the duke said with a grin. "What's this sorcery you seem able to work on the Stuarts, royal and not-so-royal?" Charlie teased her.

"I think it is you and your cousin who charm most," Jasmine replied, "but you surely know how to flatter an old woman. Go along now, Charlie. We shall see you tomorrow."

The duke's coach turned in the driveway and made its way back down the wide gravel road through Greenwood's gates, and thence on to the king's favorite palace of Whitehall. This palace had once been the London seat of the archbishop of York. It began as an ordinary two-story house, that under the auspices of Henry VIII's personally chosen archbishop, Thomas Wolsey, had been developed into a marvelous palace, augmented in width and breadth and height. Beautified, embellished, and ornamented by Wolsey, it became an object of the king's desire. When Wolsey failed Henry in the matter of his divorce from Katherine of Aragon, he gave this palace to his master in hopes of appeasing him. Henry rechristened the palace Whitehall and enjoyed it mightily while Wolsey fell from grace and died.

Henry enlarged his new acquisition, which had sat upon a piece of land between the River Thames and a road that led to Charing Cross and then on to Westminster Cathedral itself. The enlargement required more land, which Henry purchased, but he was unable to close off the public street that traversed between his palace and his new acreage. Hence Whitehall became an assortment of courts, apartments, galleries, and halls. It was a jumble of architectural miscellany on the outside but magnificent within. It meandered and sauntered through a maze of chambers and suites, most of which were seen only by the huge assortment of servants necessary to run the place.

Still it had all the comforts and conveniences that anyone, let alone a king, could desire. There were wonderful gardens and a broad walk along the riverside for strolling. There was a ballhouse where the ladies played featherball against the gentlemen. There was a cockpit for the beautifully bred cocks owned by the king and the nobility. A great deal of serious wagering went on at the cockfights. There were tennis courts, for Charles like his ancestors, enjoyed the sport greatly. There was a tiltyard for those gentlemen still so inclined, although most of the court preferred dancing, dicing, and card playing to the vigorous exercise engendered in the tiltyard.

Whitehall had three gates. The Whitehall Gate kept the public from straying onto the king's grounds. The King Gate and the Holbein Gate offered the court access to the royal park. They were at opposite ends of the palace. The King Gate opened directly from the park onto the streets. The Holbein Gate was near the royal Banqueting Hall. The king's late father had always planned to rebuild Whitehall to give it more uniformity, but Charles II had not the means to do so. Still the interior was magnificent, and that was what most people remembered when they spoke of Whitehall. Its hideous and unsightly exterior faded when one recalled the wonderful tapestries, molding, carved stonework, fine furniture, and magnificent paintings by the best artists of the current generation and generations past.

The duke of Lundy's coach drew up within the Great Court. Liveried servants ran forward to open the vehicle's door and to begin unloading the luggage. Well schooled, they recognized the king's cousin and bowed. A majordomo directed the footmen to the duke's apartments, all the while welcoming him back.

"Shall I make your arrival known to His Majesty?" he asked.

"Yes," Charlie replied. Then offering an arm to his wife, he moved off into the palace and toward their own apartments. By the time they reached them, Charlie found one of the king's young pages awaiting.

The boy bowed smartly. "His Majesty," he began in a high piping voice, "desires your presence, my lord duke."

"When?" Charlie asked, smiling down at the child who could not have been more than seven.

"Immediately, my lord," came the reply.

The duke sighed and, handing his cloak to his valet, kissed his wife. "Do not wait up for me," he said in resigned tones.

"I will not," she told him with a small smile.

Charlie followed the page from his own quarters through the winding corridors of the palace to the king's royal apartments. He was led into the king's privy chamber where Charles Stuart was waiting for him. The king grinned, waving a hand at his page.

"Thank you, lad, now close the door behind you," and when the child had obeyed, the king said, "Welcome back, Charlie!"

"Why are there so few outside in your chambers?" Charlie asked. Then he said, understanding completely for he knew his cousin well, "Ahh, you have the headache, my lord, eh?"

The king chuckled. "What most people do not realize, Cousin, is that it is hard work being a king. I am expected to be available to all at all times. Sometimes I grow weary of it."

The duke nodded, pouring them each a goblet of fine red wine from a carafe on the sideboard and handing the king one.

"Sit down," the king said, and together the two Charles Stuarts settled themselves into high-backed velvet chairs before the king's fireplace. "Every now and then I must develop the headache if I am to get some time alone."

"I know," Charlie said, "and I should have realized when I saw your outer chamber virtually empty. How they all hate it when you send them away. You are the sun and the moon around which the many constellations and stars of this court circulate. They do not like it when you are not available to them."

"Take supper with me, just the two of us, and tell me all your news," the king said, reaching out to the bellpull.

"I've brought my mother and her three granddaughters to court," Charlie began. "We have come husband hunting," he grinned.

"The glorious Jasmine is here? Wonderful!" the king said. "She is the most incredible old woman I have ever had the pleasure of meeting. And the lasses? Your daughter and the niece who has lived with you these past few years, of course. But who is the third girl?"

"My sister Fortune's youngest, from the Colonies," Charlie replied, waiting to see what the king would say, but at that moment the door opened, and the page appeared.

"Yes, Your Majesty?" he queried his master.

"Supper for two, Georgie," the king ordered. "And I am not to be disturbed except for the meal, laddie. Bar all comers!"

"Yes, Your Majesty!" the boy replied, and shut the door once more.

"The girl who killed her husband?" the king asked his cousin.

"Your Majesty, I do not know what the truth of the matter is," the duke of Lundy said.

"But your mama knows, I am quite certain," the king chuckled. "She would not allow anyone of bad character in her house no matter their blood tie to her. She hasn't told you?"

Charlie shook his head. "And I asked," he admitted, "but she says the tragedy of what happened is only for Fancy to tell."

"*Fancy?*" the king looked interested.

"Her Christian name is Frances, but as a child she could not pronounce it. She called herself *Fancy,* and it seemed to stick," the duke explained to the king.

"What is she like?"

"She resembles both Cynara and Diana. They all favor my mother's grandmother. There are slight differences," Charlie said. "Cynara has her mother's bright blue eyes. Diana has the Leslie green eyes. Fancy's eyes are the same turquoise shade as my mother's."

"Ahhh," said the king.

"And there are other small things. My daughter and Diana have my mother's fetching little birthmark. Mama calls it the Mughal Mole. Diana's mimics my mother's, being placed between her left nostril and her upper lip. Cynara's is on the right side in an otherwise identical place, but Fancy does not sport the Mughal Mole," the duke explained. "Other than that it is difficult to tell them apart."

"They will be a delightful addition to the court," the king decided. "I remember last year when you brought the girls to meet the queen and me, they caused quite a stir. I believe that they were even given sobriquets at that time."

"Diana is *Siren* and my daughter they called *Sin,* although I am not certain I am comfortable with such appellations," the duke smiled. "I shall make it quite clear to all who show interest in my daughter, or my nieces, that they are not to be trifled with and if you, Cousin, could lend your considerable voice to mine, I believe we may keep them safe from lechers and fortune hunters."

The king nodded his head in agreement. "How old are they now, Charlie?" he inquired.

"Cynara and Diana are fifteen, and Fancy is sixteen, although she will turn seventeen in the very early spring," the duke answered.

"Such wonderful ages!" the king enthused. "Women grow boring much past twenty, although I can tolerate some as old as twenty-five."

"How is my lady Castlemaine?" Charlie teased his royal cousin.

"As temperamental, and as demanding as ever," the king said gloomily. "Her greatest fault, however, is that age has caused her to develop an interest in politics. She attempts to advise me, and more often than not disagrees with my policies. I do not like it, Charlie. My former passion for the Castlemaine has burned out. I have made her duchess of Cleveland and provided my offspring by her with titles of their own and financial support. Still she attempts to behave as if it were five years ago. I would be finished with her, but she will not go away," the king admitted. "I am ashamed now that I forced her upon the queen when Catherine and I were first wed."

Charlie said nothing to that observation by his cousin, for he had told him frankly at the time that embarrassing the charming Portuguese princess he wed was neither wise nor kind.

"There is someone else now," the king said, a twinkle in his eye.

"I would certainly not expect that Your Majesty had embraced celibacy at this point in his life," Charlie noted dryly. "Will you tell me who the lady is, or am I to guess?"

"You have not been with the court, Cousin, and so you could not possibly imagine who my eye has fallen upon. She is an actress, and her name is Nell Gwyn. Never have I known such a darling girl!"

"Then I congratulate you, Cousin, on this delightful lady," the duke said.

"The Castlemaine is furious," the king chuckled. "As long as I flaunted no new woman publicly, she might continue to pretend she still held my heart in her greedy grasp. Now she cannot, and her influence will, I believe, eventually wane. She calls Nellie a little guttersnipe. Nellie calls her the termagant. When they meet in public it is most amusing. But Nellie is very respectful of the queen. She is really a good lass, Charlie. You will like her."

"If the Castlemaine does not like her," Charlie said frankly, "then I am certain that I will."

"She has a wonderful and irreverent sense of humor," the king said. "She calls Castlemaine *the highborn whore*, and herself, *the lowborn whore*." The king laughed aloud.

At that moment there was a knock upon the privy chamber door, and it was opened by the page to allow the servants in with the supper. They quickly set it up upon a table between the two men and exited, the page closing the door behind them. Not a word had been spoken. The cousins served themselves from platters, bowls, and dishes containing icy-cold raw oysters; prawns that had been steamed in white wine; lamb chops; a large turkey stuffed with bread, sage, and apples; artichokes dripping with sweet butter; tiny whole white potatoes; and bread and cheese. Charlie refilled their goblets as they ate. A dish of apples baked with sugar and cinnamon, and standing in a shallow bowl of thick golden cream, had been left upon the sideboard for them. Both men ate with good appetites.

"Tell me more about Fancy Devers," the king said as they ate. "The gossip as bruited about by Lord and Lady Tolliver is most salacious."

"Considering that the Tollivers were not at the wedding, nor are they acquainted with either the Randolphs or the Devers, I would certainly discount whatever they had to say. They were never privy to the situation. Remember, Cousin, my niece was never charged with any crime, nor brought before Your Majesty's magistrate in the Colonies. Whatever happened was a tragedy that both families chose to keep silent upon."

"Is she sad?" the king pressed further for information.

"Less now than when she first came," Charlie said. "She is just a young girl like her cousins, but that she has known some calumny. She says she will not wed again, but I think that will change when she finds a gentleman to love who loves her. Her late husband was obviously quite sought after. Fancy has admitted that he was called the most handsome man in the Colonies. I wonder that my brother-in-law allowed her to make such a marriage, but that like all fathers of daughters he loved and spoiled her," Charlie concluded.

"I never thought the day should come when you come to court chaperoning three young girls," the king concluded. "I remember you as a very gallant young man, courting your fair Bess."

"That was long ago," Charlie said, his face growing sad for a brief moment. Then he said, "Barbara and I share a birthday, which is how we first became friends. This September eighteenth saw us both well past fifty," Charlie admitted to his cousin. "Your Majesty's memory is a good one that you remember my courting days."

The king chuckled. "Pass me that bowl of apples," he instructed and, receiving the dish in question, helped himself to two of the baked fruits, ladling the heavy cream from the dish onto his plate.

"Simple things are often best," Charlie noted, and then he helped himself to the baked apples as well.

"Are your lasses here at Whitehall?" the king wondered as he spooned his dessert into his mouth.

"No, at Greenwood House with Mama. Autumn and Gabriel never come to London, but while Greenwood is theirs, everyone in the family who comes to town uses it."

"How is Autumn?" the king inquired.

"Countrified and maternal," Charlie chuckled. "She has five youngsters by Gabriel now. Her eldest French daughter, Mademoiselle d'Oleron, is on her estate at Chermont. Madeline is her father's child. She loves France far more than England. As for King Louis's Margot, she is still with Autumn, but Louis has said the summer she turns twelve he wants her back in France at his court. She, too, is more French than English. She is already spending half of her year at Chermont with her sister. It is hard for Autumn to let them go, but Maddy is fourteen now, and will soon have to choose a husband. There is talk of the young heir from Archambault. If that comes to pass, then the two estates could be joined," Charlie explained.

The king nodded. He understood such things. This was how the rich remained rich. This was how power was amassed. "Autumn was a delightful mistress, if only for a brief time. What manners she had! What style! She knew her place and when to gracefully withdraw. I always admired her for it."

"Your Majesty knows she deliberately set out to seduce him?" Charlie said. It was long past, but he had always felt uncomfortable with the situation that his beautiful youngest sister had created.

"Ahh, Cousin," the king laughed. "I am not certain even today just who it was who seduced whom."

"She wanted a title and a house," Charlie said. "I could never get over how blunt she was with me about her ends."

"And I rewarded her with what she wanted," the king chuckled.

"What if Gabriel hadn't asked for her?" Charlie asked his cousin.

"But he did," the king said with a smile. "I would have kept my word under any circumstances, Charlie. I do have a great weakness where amenable ladies are concerned, as all seem to know."

"And the ladies of my family do seem to hold a fascination for the royal Stuarts," Charlie remarked with a grin.

"They do," the king admitted.

Suddenly outside the privy chamber door a commotion arose. The door flew open to reveal the king's boy page attempting to bar entry the duchess of Cleveland.

"'Oddsfish, Georgie," the king drawled, annoyed, "what is this?"

"I heard that you were ill," Barbara Villiers, Lady Castlemaine, said as she pushed past the page. "You do not look ill to me."

Charlie arose, and bowed to the duchess of Cleveland. "Barbara," he said, "I had heard you had withdrawn from court and thought it marvelous that you should finally be showing wisdom at your age."

"I should not speak of age, my lord duke," Lady Castlemaine snapped back at him. "You can hardly claim acquaintance with youth any longer."

"I did not send for you, Barbara," the king said.

"*What?*" she screeched at him. "Am I a servant to be sent for then, my lord? There was a day . . . ."

"Long past, my dear lady," Charlie defended his cousin as he had always done when he could. He stood, and offered her his arm. "May I escort you somewhere, madame?"

"*You bastard!*" she hissed at him.

"Why, madam, everyone knows that of me. It is no secret. You but state the obvious," Charlie mocked her. He had always disliked this aggressive woman and was not unhappy to see her replaced in his royal cousin's affections.

And then suddenly the door to the king's bedchamber opened. In the portal stood the most adorable creature that the duke of Lundy had ever seen. She had a heart-shaped face, full lips, and dimples in her cheeks. Her tousled chestnut curls were short. Her bright eyes, hazel. Her face gamine, and her slender body shapely in all the places a woman should be shapely. *"Are we to be a threesome then, darling?"* she innocently inquired of the king, her eyes wide. She was wearing an outrageously sheer black silk nightdress lavishly adorned with lace.

The little page stared open-mouthed. And then the duchess of Cleveland began to spew a stream of invectives, which she hurled at the king. Even Charlie was surprised by the colorful and extraordinary abuse. He strode across the king's privy chamber, and grasping the furious woman by the arm, he dragged her out, through the royal apartments, and into the hall beyond. *"Madame, be silent!"* he thundered.

"How dare you!" the lady Castlemaine screamed and slapped him with a hard hand.

The duke of Lundy quickly slapped her back, much to her great surprise. Then he said to one of the royal guard, "His Majesty wishes this woman escorted from the palace immediately. She is not to be allowed admittance again this night." Charlie then turned and walked away.

"You will regret this, my lord!" came the cry after him.

The not-so-royal Stuart whirled about, his amber eyes blazing. "Nay, madame, 'tis you who will regret this scene. Have you no shame? Your time is over. Withdraw gracefully before you find yourself a figure of public scorn. There is nothing more embarrassing than an openly discarded royal mistress. Where is your pride? Or have you lost it all at long last? I somehow cannot believe that, so perhaps it is just that you are stupid as so many have claimed over the years."

Lady Castlemaine's visage drained of its color for a brief moment, and then she grew almost purple. Her lips moved, but no sound issued forth. She raised her fist at him, but then it fell to her side. Finally she turned and stormed away, followed by one of the king's men-at-arms hurrying to do the royal bidding, and put her out of the palace.

Charlie rubbed his face. The bitch had a rough hand, he decided ruefully. But then he grinned. He loved his country life at Queen's Malvern, but, God's blood!, it was good to be back at court again!

Chapter

3

The king sprawled on his carved upholstered throne, looking out over the reception hall at the entering guests. Both his breeches and coat were violet velvet. His cream-colored silk stockings were embroidered in gold sprays of flowers, and his garters were large cloth-of-gold rosettes with diamond centers. He had matching rosettes on his shoes. Next to him sat his queen, Catherine of Braganza, a Portuguese lady of sweet disposition, but no great beauty to Charles Stuart's eye. Still, she was a pleasant companion when he chose her company, her only fault being her inability to give him a legitimate heir. And the fault was obviously hers, for he had sired any number of bastards on ladies highborn and low. Poor Catherine, however, could not seem to conceive. Once or twice there had been a small ray of hope, but it had come to naught. His wife was barren. He might have divorced her and remarried. All Europe knew he had just cause, but Catherine of Braganza suited Charles Stuart with her gentle and docile personality. Another wife might not have been as thoughtful of his amoral habits as Catherine. Besides he had an heir in his brother, James, the duke of York, who already had two legitimate heirs.

The king's attention was suddenly attracted by a flash of brilliant turquoise blue. He focused his gaze. There was his cousin Charlie just now entering the room with his family. He escorted a lady on each arm: his elegant mother, the dowager duchess of Glenkirk, and his equally graceful wife, Barbara. They were followed by a trio of young girls. It was among these three the king had spotted the bright color. He recognized the girl in the scarlet gown as Charlie's daughter. The girl in the dusky rose as the Glenkirk lass. Therefore, the young woman in the turquoise velvet and silver lace had to be the gossiped-about Mistress Frances Devers.

"I see the duke of Lundy," the queen murmured to him. "I recognize all but one of his party. Do you know who the lady in blue is my lord?"

"It is his niece from the Colonies, Mistress Devers," the king murmured back. *What a beauty*, he thought. She was very much like her two cousins, and yet different.

"The *murderess?*" The queen was shocked. "The duke presumes upon your good nature my lord."

"Nay, my dear, I have already spoken to Charlie regarding Mistress Devers. While the details regarding this young woman's tragedy remain hidden from all but those involved, no charges were ever brought against her. You can be certain, however, that the dowager Jasmine would not have accepted this girl into her care had there been anything dishonest about her. Do you notice how she resembles her cousins? They certainly present a most charming picture, do they not?"

"But Lady Tolliver said . . ." the queen began, only growing quiet again when her husband raised his hand to silence her.

"Charlie assures me that the Tollivers were not guests at the wedding of Mistress Devers, nor were they personally known to either family. They have simply repeated the gossip that they heard while visiting their daughter in Williamsburg. I have already sent someone to speak with them about it, and I have given them a choice. Either they quell their rumormongering tongues, or they leave court. I should have sent them away myself, but that would only give rise to greater rumor." The king patted his wife's hand. "You will, of course, make your own decision, my dear, after you have met Mistress

Devers. And I hope that you will share your thoughts with me on the topic. You know how much I value your good judgment in such matters."

The queen colored, and the pink in her pale cheeks actually made her look very pretty briefly. "She doesn't really look very dangerous from a distance, Charles," the queen said softly.

The king laughed. "No," he agreed, "she doesn't." *But she does have the most kissable mouth*, he thought, his dark eyes narrowing speculatively. Were they related? No. Her mother had been a Lindley. Her father the son of some minor Irish lordling. Yet she was his cousin's niece. *But a widow and no virgin.* Her beauty attracted him, but he had reached an age where he wanted more than beauty in a lover.

"My lord, they come this way," the queen interrupted his musings.

The not-so-royal Stuart had seen the contemplative look in his royal cousin's eye. He recognized it from his long acquaintance with his relation. The look would not have been for his daughter, or for sweet Diana. *God's blood*, he swore silently. Then he pushed the suspicions from his thoughts. Of course, the king would be curious about Fancy given the scandal surrounding her. It was only curiosity. The king already had a delightful new mistress. Reaching the foot of the throne, the duke of Lundy bowed low saying as he did, "My liege." He then took the queen's dainty hand in his, and kissed it. "My lady."

The king stood up with a welcoming smile. "Cousin!" he exclaimed as if he were seeing Charlie for the first time in many months. "We welcome you back to court." The king was very elegant tonight in his suit of violet velvet. The buttons on his long coat, which ran from his neckline to his thighs, were diamonds set in delicate gold frames. The lace at his throat, and cascading from his cuffs, was gold. His dark curls were lavish and fell about his broad shoulders. Even as he stepped down from his dais, he was an extremely tall man. He took Jasmine's hand in his and kissed it. "Ahh, madame," he said in smoky tones. "If I were but ten years older." His look was smoldering.

Jasmine laughed heartily. "And I sixty years younger, Your Majesty," she told him, "but you do still have the power to charm this ancient heart of mine, for I have always had a weakness for the Royal Stuarts, as this ducal son of mine will give evidence."

The king chuckled. "You have not lost your edge, madame," he told her admiringly. Then he turned to the duchess of Lundy. "My favorite Barbara," he said, kissing her hand with a smile.

"Majesty, surely there is another lady who may lay claim to that title," the duchess of Lundy quickly protested.

"No longer," the king answered her casually so that those standing nearby were certain to hear. "Dark green favors you, madame," the king noted. He next addressed Cynara, "Welcome back to court, my lovely young cousin. And to you also, sweet Siren," he said to Diana. "But here is a lady I have not met amongst you." The black eyes turned themselves upon Fancy.

"My niece, Mistress Frances Devers, from the Colonies, Sire," Charlie said, making the introduction. "But she is called Fancy by those who know and love her. I do not know if Your Majesty ever met my sister Fortune. Fancy is her youngest child."

The king took Fancy's hand in both of his. "My dear Fancy," he began. "May I welcome you home to England?" He then kissed the delicate hand in his, but he did not let it go. "Come, my dear, and let me introduce you to the queen."

For a moment Fancy wasn't certain she was breathing. Cynara had said the king had charm, and he surely did. Remembering her manners she curtsied, saying breathlessly, "Your Majesty is so kind, and I thank you." Then as he brought her before the queen and made the introduction Fancy again curtsied low. "I am honored to be brought before Your Majesty," she said. "I never thought to meet my queen." She smiled shyly.

Why the poor child, the queen thought. *She is even farther from all she loves than I am.* She held out a beringed hand to Fancy, who immediately took the hand up, and kissed it. "We are pleased to welcome you to England and to our court, Mistress Devers," the queen said graciously, then she continued daringly, "We hope the sadness of the past few months may be wiped away by the good company of your family and of this merry court. You will be welcome in my chambers, Mistress Devers."

Fancy was stunned. She wasn't quite certain what the queen had meant, but she was intelligent enough to realize she had the royal approval. "Thank you, Your Majesty," she said. "Your kindness is almost more than I can bear." Tears shone in her eyes.

"And you have my favor as well," the king murmured low, kissing her hand a final time before releasing it.

Across the room Barbara Villiers, Lady Castlemaine, watched, her look sour. "He already plans her seduction," she hissed to the gentleman at her side.

"My dear cousin," the duke of Buckingham answered her, "you could not expect to keep his affections forever. You have had him longer than any so far. You have gained riches and position for all your children. What more can you want? You will never be queen, Barbara. Even you must realize that by now."

"He has taken to slumming lately," Barbara Villiers muttered. "First, that guttersnipe of an actress, and now this cow-eyed little colonial."

George Villiers, duke of Buckingham, laughed at her pique. "Nell Gwyn is most amusing, Barbara," he said, "but as for Charlie's niece she is only newly arrived, and scandal surrounds her. The king is merely curious. Nothing more. But, *if* he were more than curious, it would not be your concern, dear cousin. *Not any longer.* You must accept the facts, Barbara. The king is finished with you."

"He seeks younger women to convince himself that he is yet young," the lady Castlemaine said. "And I am now twenty-six."

"It is true you are not in the first flush of your youth any longer," her cousin replied, "but you are still a fine figure of a woman, Barbara. You could possibly have yourself a rich husband if you wished."

"I do not need a husband," she snapped. "What the hell would I want a husband for, George? I had a royal lover, and any other lover I take will not only pale in comparison to the king, but will certainly be my social inferior as well. How can I be another man's mistress after having been the king's? The bastard has ruined me for anyone else! I hate him for it!"

"You do not have to be any man's mistress, Barbara. Take charge of your life. Take lovers, many and varied. Then no man can say you are his alone, and that he now possesses His Majesty's leavings."

"How dare you speak to me like that!" Her voice was now raised and sharp. Those standing near her and the duke turned.

"Hush, sweet cousin," he soothed her. "You do not want to attract the attention of the court gossips now, do you? God forbid that anyone should feel pity for you, Barbara."

"You can be such a brute, George," she said low, and her gaze went back across the room where the king was now staring after his cousin and the women with the duke of Lundy. "'Odsblood, George! Will you look at that little colonial's jewelry. I am certain that it all belongs to her grandmother. The old dowager has always had the most fantastic collection of jewels. I remember seeing her once when I was a very little child. She had rubies the size of robin's eggs. I wonder who will inherit all her wealth."

"Her family tends to keep their wealth to themselves," the duke of Buckingham said in answer to his cousin's questions.

"'Twill be several lucky young men who wed those girls," Lady Castlemaine remarked astutely, watching as the objects of her interest withdrew from the royal presence.

"Did you see the way he looked at you," Cynara whispered to Fancy. "When you curtsied his eyes plunged so deep into your neckline that I thought he would not be able to raise them up again."

"I will admit to having felt the heat of his glance," Fancy said. "He is not a handsome man, yet there is something about him that is most fascinating. His eyes mesmerize you when he looks at you, yet I sense a kindness in him as well," she noted.

"They say he is very good to his women," Cynara continued.

"And he is a great lover," Fancy teased her cousin, "although how a respectable little virgin would know such a fact is a mystery to me, Cyn." She mischievously tweaked one of Cynara's sable curls.

"There is always a certain amount of truth in gossip, and I love good gossip," Cynara said with a grin. "Besides he has several . . . bastards, sons and daughters. He has recognized them all, and provided for them as well. The women he has loved adore him, except perhaps for my lady Castlemaine, who is now discarded in favor of an actress."

"Gracious!" Fancy laughed. "Where do you learn all of this?"

Cynara chuckled. "I listen," she said simply. Then she sighed. "'Odsfish! Diana is already surrounded by gentlemen. Do you wonder they call her Siren? There is little difference between the three of us, and yet they flock to her like bees to honey. I do not understand it, Fancy. What is it she has that we do not?"

"Well," Fancy said thoughtfully, "you, I suspect, are noted for your pride and your sharp tongue. I am surrounded by scandal. I am an unknown quantity. Our sweet cousin on the other hand is noted for her engaging ways and dulcet disposition."

"But I am a Stuart!" Cynara protested.

"And therefore less approachable," Fancy responded.

"Then what good is having a beautiful wardrobe and Grandmama's wonderful jewels if no one will pay attention to me," Cynara wailed.

"They will pay attention to us both soon enough," Fancy said. "We are all beautiful and all rich. Qualities gentlemen find most desirable in marriageable women I have been told." Her tone was suddenly bitter. "Be careful in this courting game, Cyn," she advised her cousin. "Be careful, and do not believe anything a man tells you else you will end up as I have and be miserable." For the second time this evening, her eyes filled with tears. She brushed them impatiently away.

Cynara saw her cousin's tears, but she said nothing. "Come on," she decided. "Siren cannot have all the gentlemen to herself. Besides, she does not really know what to do with them. Let's share in her bounty."

Fancy laughed. "All right," she said, and together the two young women joined their cousin. The royal reception lasted until midnight. There was much gossiping, some dancing, and gambling. The Season was just beginning. The cousins had agreed that when all was ended they would meet their grandmother in the Great Courtyard where their carriage would be awaiting them. Having bid Charlie and his wife good night, Fancy made her way with Cynara and Diana through the palace to their agreed meeting place.

A gentleman approached them suddenly, and bowing said to Fancy, "I am William Chiffinch, Mistress Devers. The king invites you to supper."

Before Fancy might reply, Cynara spoke up. *"Oh, dear!"* she said. "You must tell His Majesty that my cousin is regretfully unable to join him tonight as we are meeting our grandmother, the dowager duchess of Glenkirk immediately."

"However," Fancy now put in, "I should be honored if His Majesty would ask me again, when I shall be more than pleased to accept his kind invitation." She curtsied to Mr. Chiffinch.

"Of course, madame," the king's confidential servant replied, and he bowed to the three young women before turning away, and walking back down the corridor.

"The king asked you to supper, and you turned him down?" Diana was astounded by her two cousins' boldness.

"Silly goose," Cynara laughed. "When the king asks a lady to supper, she is meant to be the last course. He has just seen Fancy for the first time tonight. His ardor is more likely to increase if it is denied. Many a young woman has been ruined by accepting the royal invitation and then boring the king so she is not asked back."

"I am surprised he would approach me at all," Fancy said.

"You are beautiful, and you are widowed," Cynara responded. "The king would not approach Diana or me, for we are innocents."

"The way you advise our cousin, I sometimes wonder," Diana said. "How is it that you are so knowledgeable of men and their ways?"

Cynara shook her head. "I don't know if I am that clever, Siren, but when dealing with gentlemen, it seems to me that common sense should apply. When you can obtain something you desire easily, you lose your appetite for it. And men, I have noted, are mostly boys at heart. Boys crave excitement. Where is the excitement in an easily won prize?" She turned to Fancy. "You surprise me speaking up so quickly and telling Mr. Chiffinch that you would accept the king's invitation on another occasion. Would you really?"

"Yes," Fancy said quietly.

"I thought you were through with men," Cynara said.

"I said I didn't want a husband," Fancy replied. "I think I might prefer being a king's mistress to being any man's wife. A mistress, it seems to me, maintains her freedom as long as she is true to her lover. And if I would be a mistress, I would prefer to be a king's mistress than a common man's. The king seems a kind man."

"My lady Castlemaine might disagree with you there," Cynara said with a chuckle. "The king is through with her, and she is most put out about it all."

"I do not know her whole story," Fancy said, "but I do know she has enriched herself and her children in the king's bed. If she had any sense, she would retire gracefully and retain the king's friendship rather than make an enemy of him with her tempers."

"But Fancy," Diana said, her look concerned, "are we not better than my lady Castlemaine? Would you not prefer the comfort of a wife's place to the uncertainty of a mistress's position?"

"A wife and a mistress maintain the same position. *On their backs*," Cynara said laughing.

"Cyn!" Diana blushed.

"Do not fret, sweet cousin," Fancy said. "There is no guarantee that the king, having been refused, will ask me to supper again."

They had reached their carriage where Jasmine sat waiting for them. Liveried footmen helped them into the vehicle and the doors shut. The coach lumbered off out of the Great Court and through the Whitehall Gate onto the street.

"The king asked Fancy to supper!" Cynara burst out.

"Did he?" Jasmine said. *I must be getting old*, she considered. *I did not see that coming at all*. "And you refused him, of course."

"For now," Fancy replied.

"I had thought you would remarry one day," Jasmine said to her granddaughter. "There is little future in being a king's mistress."

"I find it a more preferable fate to being another man's wife,"

Fancy told her grandmother. "I find the king an attractive man, and he is said to be kind to the ladies who please him."

"Yes, he is that," Jasmine admitted, "and if you give him a child, he will acknowledge it. The Stuarts always accept their paternal obligations as I certainly well know. Your uncle has teased me about it, but it would seem he is correct when he says the Stuarts have a *tendre* for the women in this family. I was once Prince Henry's mistress, and your aunt Autumn, my youngest daughter, was for a brief time this king's mistress. You look nothing like her so whatever the allure is that we seem to possess, it is not in our similar features. Well, let us wait and see if you have whetted the king's appetite, or if your refusal has but put him off." She looked at her other two granddaughters. "You will say nothing of this to *anyone*," she instructed them both. "Diana, I know I may rely on you. But Cynara, my gossipy wench, if you should allow your tongue to wiggle-waggle, you could cause not just your cousin, but the entire family, great damage. Do you understand why, dear girl?"

"Yes, Grandmama, I do. I shall speak on this to no one," Cynara promised Jasmine. "Especially not Papa or Mama."

Jasmine's eyes met those of Cynara's. "Ahh, you do understand," she said, well pleased. Then she sat back, and closed her eyes. "I am far too old to be spending half the night up with you three wenches," she told them. "You have been properly introduced. I shall not always go with you after tonight. You have Charlie and Barbara there to chaperon you. I may, however, come to some of the masques. In King James's day the masques were marvelous, and I took part in many of them." She sat back and closed her eyes, not speaking again for the rest of their journey back to Greenwood House.

"Why does Grandmama not want Uncle Charlie and Aunt Barbara to know the king approached Fancy?" Diana asked when they were home again and seated in Fancy's dayroom with their shoes off.

"Because Papa would probably speak to the king invoking *family* obligations. Then the king would not approach Fancy again. He would forever be annoyed at Papa for having interfered with his desires and with Fancy for not having said yes to his first offer. If the king invites our cousin again, and she pleases him, her fortune here in England is made."

Diana sighed. "I'm glad the king did not approach me," she said. "All the young men who importune me but confuse me. If the king made advances toward me, I do not know what I would do."

Cynara laughed. "The day her parents left her here to be civilized from a Highland wench into a lady she said she could not wait to meet the king," Cynara explained to her other cousin.

"Well, I have met him," Diana said. "But I wouldn't want to be his mistress. I want a husband. I just can't make up my mind upon whom to concentrate."

"We are just come to court," Cynara said. "There is time to make those decisions. For now it is our duty to have fun."

"When shall we go back to court?" Fancy asked.

"Why tomorrow as soon as we are rested," Cynara said. "Perhaps we should get there in time to accompany the king on his afternoon walk along the riverside. Fancy, can your Bess bring our gowns for the evening? Then we will change our clothing in my father's apartments. I know he and Mama will not mind. It is such a convenience that he is housed at Whitehall," she noted.

"I'll bring the gowns, and I'll remain to help you all dress," Bess spoke up. "But now you must go to your own chambers, my ladies, and get some rest. You shouldn't have no purple circles beneath your beautiful eyes if you want to be the most beautiful young ladies at the king's royal court."

"You are so sensible!" Cynara said. "I wonder Bess that our grandmama did not give you to me instead of to Fancy."

"She didn't give me to you, my lady, because she knew I wouldn't put up with your nonsense like your good Hester does," Bess said pertly.

Fancy and Diana laughed, but Cynara looked very aggrieved.

"You are probably correct, though you are much too bold that you say so," Cynara snapped as she flounced from the room.

Diana kissed her cousin good night and, green eyes twinkling, followed after Cynara.

When they had gone, Bess escorted her mistress into her bedchamber saying, "Was you the belle of the court, mistress?" She began to unlace the turquoise velvet and the silver lace bodice.

"The king asked me to supper," Fancy said softly, "but it must remain a secret for now, Bess Trueheart. You cannot gossip to your friends about anything I confide in you."

"You have my word, mistress," Bess replied.

"I think I shall be uncomfortable confiding in my cousins should the king's invitation come again, and I accept it, which I will. Diana is a little shocked that I will go to supper with His Majesty."

"And Lady Cynara is full of self-importance, and all advice based on her *experience*," Bess noted with a small smile.

"Exactly!" Fancy responded. "Oh, Bess, I knew that you would understand! I am not a fine lady like my two cousins. I was not raised that way. You and I have more in common, though we be mistress and servant, than I have with my two cousins. I love them dearly, but I am not like them at all. You are a practical and prudent girl, as am I."

Bess nodded. "Aye, I am, and that is a truth, mistress. Your two cousins have the advantage of being known by society. Their lineage and their dowries are no secret. They'll find husbands quick enough when they wants 'em and decides to settle down. But you— well, to be frank, and meaning no offense, mistress—come from the Colonies, surrounded by scandalous tales. Most ain't yet discovered that your grandsire was the marquis of Lindley. That your pedigree is as good as that of your cousins. You need a little advantage with the court. If you decorates the king's bed and afterward retains his friendship, you will have that advantage," Bess concluded.

"Precisely!" Fancy said. "Ohh, I'm so glad that someone understands. And there is something else too, Bess. Cynara says the king's reputation as a lover is great. Is he a good lover, or do they say it of him because he is the king, I wonder? My . . . *husband*"—she shuddered visibly as she said the word—"was not a good lover. I might have been a virgin, but women know this instinctively about a man. I should like to have a good lover." Fancy loosened the tapes holding her velvet skirts up, and they fell to the carpeted floor.

"Well, mistress, from what I have heard," Bess began, "the king's reputation is the truth. His mother was a French lady, a princess, and she had some famous kings known to be great lovers in her family. And when the Stuarts come down from Scotland, they were also known to enjoy the company of the ladies. They have many cousins born on both sides of the blanket and recognized as family every one of them. Your uncle, the duke, is a fine example." Bess lowered her voice now, and leaned closer to Fancy. "Lady Cynara was born on the wrong side of the blanket, you know, but when her pa returned to England he wed with her mother and formally legitimized her in the courts. Now don't say I told you that. I mean it only as an example of the king's family, and how they approaches the folks about them. The Stuarts are good-hearted. The king has several sons and daughters by several ladies, not just my lady Castlemaine. He has acknowledged and provided for them all. His reputation as a lover is well deserved, I'm thinking."

"When he spoke to me tonight," Fancy said, "there was something about him. I felt I would not be able to resist him."

"It is lovely to fall in love," Bess admitted, "even if it is only for a brief time." Then suddenly she became her practical self once more. "Let's get you out of the rest of these garments, mistress, and ready for your bed. You want to look beautiful again tomorrow if you are to attract the king once more."

The next afternoon Fancy went back to Whitehall with her cousins. She was wearing a teal blue silk gown with an underskirt of teal brocade with silver threads that was looped up on either side so that it showed. Her sleeves were full, the top being teal, the lower half cream, and ending in soft lace cuffs. The puff sleeves were tied with narrow silver ribbons in two places. The top of her chemise, which came to her neck, was sheer lawn and edged with a pearl choker. She wore a tall-crowned hat trimmed with ostrich feathers.

The three cousins joined the king's party as they strolled along the walk bordering the Thames. At the very front of the troupe of walkers, they could see the king. He wore full breeches gathered into a band at the knee and decorated with red ribbons. His long black velvet coat was buttoned to the waist and his large black felt hat was decorated with white feathers and red ribbon trim. His red leather shoes were high-heeled with square toes and high tongues. They were decorated with large buckles of pearls and paste gems. He carried a long ebony cane topped with a carved ivory ball.

"'Odsblood," Cynara said softly, "he is so damned fashionable. I almost wish we were not related so closely."

"Cyn!" Diana's green eyes mirrored shock and disapproval.

"Don't be a ninny, Siren," Cynara said. "To be sought after by a king is an honor, but then I forgot," she teased her cousin, "the royal Stuarts bring misfortune to the Leslies of Glenkirk."

"Grandmama says it is true," Diana defended her family.

"But I'm not a Leslie of Glenkirk, and neither is Fancy," Cynara astutely reminded her cousin.

They suddenly realized as they walked that while they had begun at the back of the line, they were now in the front, and the king was just ahead of them. He turned his head slightly, smiled, and then beckoned them to join him in leading the court. Cynara moved quickly to the forefront with a flirtatious smile, half-dragging Diana and Fancy with her. Fancy wasn't quite certain how it happened, but the king was suddenly tucking her small hand through his velvet-clad arm.

He smiled down into her face. "Tell me about my colony of Maryland, Mistress Devers," he said to her. His black eyes were hypnotic.

Somehow she found her voice and, looking directly back at him, said, "It is a very beautiful land, Your Majesty. The Chesapeake is a series of deep blue bays coming up from the ocean. They are filled with all manner of sea life and game birds. The shores are forested in many places, but not so much now, my mother says, as when she first arrived. We call our estates *plantations*. My father grows tobacco, but not as much now as when he first came. He prefers raising horses. Slaves are needed for tobacco as it is very laborious work. My papa does not hold with slavery. He buys blacks, civilizes them, and trains them to serve us, or farm properly, and then he frees them. They usually remain with us and are paid for their work. He is thought odd by our neighbors, but I have seen the slavery system myself. It is inhuman in many cases. We also purchase the bonds of the English, the Scots, and the Irish who have been transported for crimes of one kind or another, or for debt. We have a lot of Irish at Bayview," she concluded. "My father is sentimental for the land of his birth."

"Bayview is the name of your plantation," the king said.

"Yes, Your Majesty," Fancy replied.

"And your father, if I recall the gossip, is Irish-born," the king remarked, "and a Catholic?"

"Yes, Your Majesty. That is why my parents left Your Majesty's Kingdom," Fancy replied.

"Prejudice is an evil thing," the king said. And then, "Did you know that you have the most extraordinary eyes, Mistress Devers?"

Fancy actually blushed. "I have my grandmother's eyes," she murmured softly.

"Your grandmother is an extraordinary woman," the king noted. "Was she really expecting you last evening?" His eyes twinkled at her.

"Ohh, yes, Your Majesty!" Fancy replied. "She was awaiting us in her coach in the Great Court so she might escort us home."

"Will she await you again tonight?" he wondered softly.

Fancy's heart hammered nervously, but she said, "No, Your Majesty, she will not. My grandmother says that she is too old to come to court every night, and now that we have been properly introduced she says it will not be necessary, although she will come sometimes."

"A most discreet lady, your grandmama," the king noted wryly. Then he said, "So if I were to send Mr. Chiffinch to escort you to supper you would come, Mistress Devers?"

"I should be honored to take supper with Your Majesty," Fancy said, and she smiled up at him, but it was not a flirtatious smile. Just a warm and friendly look.

The king took her small hand from his arm and kissed it. Their eyes locked. "I shall look forward to this evening," the king said. Then he released her hand.

"As I will, Your Majesty," Fancy answered him, and she curtsied before moving back to join her cousins who had now fallen behind into the midst of the troupe of courtiers. She felt strangely exhilarated. He was not the most handsome man she had ever met. Indeed, she was not certain he would qualify as handsome at all, but he did indeed have incredible charm, and again there had been that impression of kindness.

"*What happened?*" Cynara hissed.

"Later," Fancy responded.

"They are already gossiping that he singled you out," Cynara said. Her blue eyes were sparkling with curiosity.

Fancy remained silent, causing Diana to smile to herself. Diana fully approved of her older cousin's discretion. While she wasn't certain she favored Fancy's obvious course of action, she did appreciate her discretion. But if the king took her cousin to be one of his mistresses, there would be little prudence involved.

They napped in the apartments of the duke and duchess of Lundy. They ate a light meal that Bess had ordered from the palace kitchens. They bathed their faces and hands, and then prepared for the evening's entertainment. The Christmas season was almost upon them, and tonight the lord of Misrule was to be chosen by the court to rule over the coming holidays. Bess helped them all to dress. Diana wore a velvet gown of pale lavender. Cynara was in burgundy. Fancy in a blue-green. Bess did each of the girl's hair, fashioning the dark locks on the three heads into ringlets.

There was music and dancing in the king's banqueting hall. There was much laughter when Harry Summers, the earl of Summersfield, was chosen as the lord of Misrule. He was a tall, dark saturnine young man in his late twenties, whose sobriquet was Wickedness. Cynara eyed him almost greedily, remarking to her cousins that the earl was most outrageous handsome, no matter his reputation for mischief.

"He is not the sort of gentleman one marries," Diana said primly.

"I don't want to wed him, Siren," Cynara said. "I just want to know him better and perhaps play with him a bit."

"He looks as if he would eat you alive and not even leave the bones," Fancy observed. "I do not like men who are too handsome."

The evening wore on with Diana being surrounded as usual by a host of eligible, and not so eligible but hopeful, gentlemen while Cynara and Fancy found themselves once again on the perimeter of their cousin's circle of admirers. Finally Cynara had had enough.

"I am going to see if I can find the lord of Misrule himself, and get him to take notice of me," she said.

"Be careful," Fancy told her, and Cynara moved off into the crowd of courtier. Fancy, however, remained where she was. She didn't mind being ignored for it allowed her the opportunity to observe all that was going on about her. She watched the men attempting to gain Diana's favor with interest. Two stood out. They were identical twin brothers The duke and the marquis of Roxley. Tall with wavy auburn hair and blue eyes, they vied eagerly for Diana's attention.

"Mistress Devers?"

Fancy looked up into the face of the king's personal servant, William Chiffinch. "His Majesty has sent me to escort you to supper," Mr. Chiffinch said in quiet tones. "If you would please to follow me." He turned and moved away.

Fancy arose and followed him. She noticed that no one was paying the least bit of attention. Mr. Chiffinch was a man who could render himself invisible, and Fancy Devers was neither known yet by the court nor important enough to be noticed as she left the banqueting hall. She followed him through a maze of corridors, wondering if she would ever find her way out again. Finally Mr. Chiffinch stopped before a set of double oak doors. On either side of the doors stood a man-at-arms in the king's livery. Mr. Chiffinch opened the door and escorted Fancy inside.

"His Majesty will be with you shortly," he said, and then withdrew.

She looked about her, awestruck. She was in the most elegant room she had ever been in. The walls of the room were covered in red silk brocade and hung with huge magnificent pantings of landscapes and of romantic scenes. On one wall there was an enormous fireplace of red and black marble flanked on either side by carved pillars. The great andirons held large logs of applewood that burned with a sweet aroma. The furniture was golden oak, and the seats were upholstered in either dark tapestry or scarlet velvet brocade. Drapes of scarlet velvet brocade hung at the windows. A great crystal chandelier hung from the center of the ceiling. It was filled with beeswax tapers all burning brightly. There was a second door in the room as well as the one through which she had entered. Curious Fancy crossed the room and opening the portal peeped through.

It was a bedchamber with white and gold silk walls, a second fireplace that was also burning brightly, and the biggest bed that Fancy had ever seen in all of her life. Blushing, she quickly closed the door and, not certain what she should do, sat down to wait for the king. On the mantel an elegant clock ticked rhythmically. A gust of wind sent a rush of sparks up the chimney. The fire crackled sharply. Fancy stared across the room, her eyes unfocused. Was she doing the right thing? Was she really the kind of woman that a king would desire? For a moment her late husband's words on the wedding night slipped back into her conscience. *You are as cold as marble*, he had said to her. But had she been? Or had she just been afraid, and with good reason, considering what had followed. She shivered and again questioned herself as to why she was here.

The door to the apartment opened, and Charles Stuart, king of England, entered. Fancy jumped up, and curtsied low. It was too late to retreat now, she thought. And besides, weren't first thoughts always best? "Good evening, Your Majesty," she said breathlessly.

"My dear girl," the king greeted her with a warm smile. "May I say how lovely I thought you looked this evening. These shades of blue and green more than suit you." Reaching out he raised her up, and gazed into her eyes. "Amazing!" he said with another smile. "What beautiful eyes you have, Fancy Devers."

There was a knock upon the door, and it opened to allow a small line of servants into the apartment. They set up a table with linen, silver, crystal, and gold plates. The sideboard was filled with covered dishes, and then with the utmost gallantry the king seated Fancy at the table before the fireplace.

"I did promise you supper," he said with a twinkle in his black eyes.

"I never doubted it, Your Majesty," Fancy replied. "I have been told that Your Majesty is a man of his word."

The king laughed. "You have a quick wit," he said sounding very pleased. "I suspected that I was right about you, my dear."

"Right about what, Your Majesty?" she asked him.

"You are intelligent, sensitive, and amusing," he replied, smiling again as a servant placed a dish of raw oysters before him.

"Are you going to eat *all* of those?" Fancy heard herself asking aloud as a dish of prawns steamed in white wine was set before her.

His dark eyes met her turquoise ones. "*Every one*," he said with emphasis and began to swallow the mollusks.

Fancy nibbled at her prawns, suddenly nervous again. "It seems a great number of oysters to me," she noted.

"I am a man of vast appetites, madame," he told her. "Are your appetites large?"

"I do not know, Your Majesty, for my experience is slight," she responded. "But the ladies in my family do have a certain allure of sorts and seem to charm the gentlemen."

"If you have inherited from your grandmother not just her beautiful eyes, but the same allure that bewitched my uncle, then I suspect we may get on very well, Fancy. Do you understand me, my dear?"

"Your Majesty wishes to make me the last course in his meal this evening," Fancy replied with utmost seriousness.

Charles Stuart burst out laughing, and he laughed until he was weak and there were tears rolling down his face. When he finally regained control of himself, he asked her, "Are you always so bloody forthright, Fancy Devers?"

"I have always thought it best to be candid, Your Majesty," Fancy answered him. "I hope I have not displeased you by it."

"No, " he said, "you have not. More often than not I am spoken to with such delicacy of feeling and couching of phrases, that I often find it difficult to even understand some of the things that are being said."

A servant removed the dish of oyster shells from before the king, and another whisked away the remaining prawns. The gold plates that had been briefly removed from the table were now returned filled with a selection of foods. There was rare beef and sliced capon on Fancy's plate along with a serving of asparagus, obviously grown in the king's greenhouses, for it was December. The vegetable was covered with a delicate sauce. She lifted each stalk, holding it between her thumb and her forefinger, and ate it slowly with relish, her little tongue skillfully licking the sauce so that not a drop was wasted "These are so good," she told him. "What a delicious treat!"

He watched her, fascinated, particularly as he realized almost immediately that she had absolutely no idea how sensuous her dining on the asparagus was to him. He felt himself hardening briefly beneath the velvet of his breeches and considered if that pointed little pink tongue had any idea the uses to which it could be put. He knew in that moment that Fancy Devers was going to please him. He had never, since he returned to England, kept two mistresses publicly, but now that Barbara Castlemaine was almost gone, it was a distinct possibility. Even his cousin, the king of France hadn't done that yet.

"Aren't you going to eat?" she asked him.

"Yes!" he said, and turned his attention to his own plate, which had beef and ham and salmon, as well as asparagus, on it.

There was also a silver basket of delicate little breads on the table. There was sweet butter and several cheeses as well. The servants kept their goblets constantly filled, but Fancy was careful not to drink a great deal. She didn't know if she had a head for it, and besides she didn't want to miss what was to come by being drunk. When the little light supper was over, the servants carried away the table and its contents.

"Shall I call a maid to help you undress?" the king asked her when they were at last alone.

"I am sure Your Majesty has the skills necessary to help me," Fancy told him. Her heart was beginning to hammer a little nervously.

He escorted her into the bedchamber. The heavy gold-velvet draperies were drawn across the windows. The bed's satin coverlet was drawn back, the bedcurtains but half open. There was a bowl of red strawberries with a pot of clotted Devon cream, a carafe of wine, and two goblets on a table. The candles reflected within their crystal lamps upon the mantel, on the table, and by the bed. The king closed the door behind them.

Fancy started at the finality of the door's click.

He saw it and asked her, "Are you afraid?"

She shook her head. "Not of you," Fancy told him. "I simply worry my inexperience will displease you."

"You were married, I have been told," he replied.

She nodded. "For a few hours, Your Majesty."

"Are you a virgin?" he inquired.

"Nay, I had a wedding night," she told him, her voice suddenly tight with her tension.

"It was an unhappy experience?" he guessed.

"Yes."

"And yet you accepted my invitation knowing full well what I would demand of you. Why?" The king was distressed by her admission, and yet he still desired her very much.

"Cynara says you have a reputation of being the world's best lover," Fancy began.

The king could not help but smile at this.

"Women, even those lacking in experience, have an instinctive knowledge about lovemaking, Your Majesty. The man to whom I was married was the most handsome creature, with such charm that every woman who knew him loved him on some level," Fancy explained. "He was a terrible, no he was a brutal lover whose only need was to satisfy himself. He died for it, I fear, and widowed me before he could destroy me."

He had to ask. "Did you kill him?"

"No, and yet I was responsible for his death. I will leave you if that is what you desire, Your Majesty, but ask me no more now, I beg of you," Fancy said quietly.

"Let us return to the point when you knew he was an inferior lover, my dear," the king said as quietly. "If making love made you unhappy, then why are you here with me this evening?"

"Because of your reputation," Fancy said honestly. "The women of my family have always known the delights of passion. I would too, but I don't want to have to place myself in the keeping of another husband in order to discover what they know. And I can hardly question the amatory skills of a man before I wed him. Your Majesty, however, comes highly recommended as a lover. I should far rather have a lover than I would have another husband."

Charles Stuart digested this statement, amazed.

"Have I shocked you, Your Majesty?" she said. "I am so new to England and to the royal court that I hope I have not offended you with my bluntness."

He finally managed to find his voice again. "My dear," he told her, "I do not believe I have ever met a more candid lady than you. I can but hope that I am as skilled a lover for you as my reputation would have you and the rest of the world believe."

"From the moment I was introduced to Your Majesty," Fancy told him, "I had not a doubt."

He turned her about and began to unlace her bodice with adept fingers. "I think, my dear Fancy, that you will prove a most dangerous woman when you have grown up a bit more." Then he dropped a kiss upon the curve of her delicate neck. "Your scent is intoxicating. What is it?"

"It is night-blooming jasmine, Your Majesty," Fancy said. "My grandmother and her old maidservants distill it themselves. I love it."

"As do I," the king replied. The bodice unlaced, he turned her about again, and drew it off, laying it carefully upon a chair. "Now, my dear," he told her, "it is your turn. Will you remove my coat?"

Fancy's slender fingers painstakingly undid each of the carved gold buttons with their paste jewel centers that held the king's claret velvet coat closed. Stepping behind him she pulled it off, and set it upon a second chair.

The king turned about so that he was facing her. "Now, together," he said with a small smile, and he began to untie the ribbons that held her dainty lace-trimmed chemise closed. Fancy smiled back at him and loosened the ribbons holding his shirt closed. The garments removed, they were both naked to the waist. The king spun his companion around, and his hands as quickly cupped her two breasts. The twin beauties were perfectly round globes of firm, soft flesh. He closed his dark eyes briefly and allowed his other senses to take over.

His touch was so gentle, Fancy thought surprised. It was almost reverent, as if he were worshiping her. She had thought she might feel fear at first, but rather she was relaxed and leaned her head back against his shoulder. Eyes wide she watched as he caressed her bosom. His thumbs, like velvet, rubbed her nipples causing them to pucker sharply. His palms were warm and fondled her tenderly.

"*Beautiful,*" the king murmured in her ear. "Your breasts are the most beautiful I have ever seen, my dear. What perfect treasures you offer me. They are indeed fit for a king." He turned her around and, lifting her up, lowered her just enough so that he might kiss the spheres he was so obviously admiring. His lips were moist and hot, and she could not refrain from a quiver as excitement raced through her body.

He lowered her so that her feet were once again upon the floor. His hands cupped her heart-shaped face and he drew her so close that the tips of her nipples, just the tips, touched his broad and smooth chest. Then he began to kiss her—long, slow kisses with his big sensuous mouth. Again, and again, and yet again his lips took hers deeply. Her head spun with each kiss. At one point she wasn't even certain she was breathing. It was without a doubt the most delicious embrace she had ever in all of her young life experienced. Her late, and not lamented, husband had certainly never kissed her like this. Fancy sighed deeply.

He laughed softly, and her eyes flew open to find him smiling. "You like being kissed," he noted with understatement. Two of his fingers ran lightly over her lips teasingly.

She nodded kissing the fingers.

"What else do you like?" he asked her. "If we are to please each other, I would know."

Fancy shook her head. "I don't really know," she admitted.

"Then we must try to ascertain that information," the king told her seriously, but his dark eyes were filled with amusement.

"I suppose we must," Fancy agreed cheerfully.

"It will be difficult in all those petticoats," he noted.

"Then I must remove them, but should you not also remove a garment, Your Majesty?" She felt bold enough now to tease him.

"I am of the exact same opinion," he acknowledged. Sitting down upon the bed, the king removed first his shoes and then, standing up, his claret velvet breeches, even as Fancy struggled from her heavy skirts, and her several petticoats. "You are still wearing your shoes," he noted.

Fancy sat upon the edge of the bed and boldly held out first one foot to him and then the other. He drew the greenish-blue silk slippers with their turquoise and pearl buckles from her slim feet and set them aside. Then he knelt and taking a foot in his hand began to massage it between his palms. Her eyes widened with surprise.

"What delicious little feet you have," he noted, and he began to cradle her other foot, rubbing it with strong fingers. "And you wear silk *calecons*. How charming! But they must come off, my darling." His big hand slid up her legs, beneath her lace-trimmed drawers, drawing them down and off. Only her silk stockings with their green and blue vines and her silver garters remained to give the illusion of modesty. His hands smoothed over her bare thighs. His eyes admired the thick dark bush of tight curls between them.

"Turn about, Majesty," Fancy said softly.

The king stood, grinning. Seating himself again, he removed his stockings and garters. Then standing once more, he pulled off his silk drawers before kneeling before her once more. "Lie back," he said, and when she complied with his request, he began to undo her garters. Then he slowly rolled her stockings from her shapely legs. His hands slid over her calves and down her ankles.

Fancy was trembling with excitement. These last few minutes were the most thrilling she had ever known. If he did nothing more, she would have been satisfied, but then suddenly she realized that she wouldn't be at all. Even knowing what was to come, she welcomed it, for she had never imagined that a man could be so tender with a woman. He gently spread her milky thighs, and his dark head pushed between them. She drew a hard, sharp breath as he did so, and then a far more audible gasp of surprise as he parted her nether lips with strong fingers, and she felt the tip of his tongue touching her in a most incredibly intimate manner.

A man who had always been sensitive to women, the king raised his head a moment, asking her, "This has never been done to you?"

"No," she whispered, "but I do not think I want you to cease." She heard him chuckle as his head was once again lowered. At first there was just the sensation of his broad tongue stroking her. But then he seemed to find the most sensitive spot hidden within those folds of moist and sentient flesh. The movements of his tongue became more sensuous, and then as she responded with growing ardor, which was evidenced by her little cries, the tongue flicked relentlessly back and forth over that aching bud until she felt a distinct *snap* within her body and a wave of warmth, coupled with pure pleasure, swept over her.

The king's body was now covering hers. His manhood began to insinuate itself into the warmth and drenching wet of her love passage. He had meant to draw out his love play a bit longer, but her delightful enthusiasm had roused him more quickly than he had been roused in a very long time. She was as eager and as willing as he was. Then a look of complete surprise came over his face. He had just found his forward passage very much impeded. He drew back slightly and pushed gently ahead once more, but the previously easy path was most definitely blocked. *"You are a virgin!"* he gasped, and he struggled to maintain control over himself.

"No!" Fancy cried, "I cannot be!"

"We will not now debate the point," the king said through gritted teeth. "This will pain you, but only briefly, I swear." Then he thrust through her virgin shield in one quick motion, burying himself deeply within her love sheath with a groan.

It stung. There was a quick sensation of burning, and then it was gone. She felt him inside her, but the feeling was not at all unpleasant. He began to move on her now with slow, masterful strokes of his manhood.

"Oh!" Fancy exclaimed. "Oh! Oh! *Ohhhhhh!*" A wave of utter delight washed over her. She had never before known such a sensation. Stars began to explode behind her closed eyelids. His rhythm and acceleration increased. Her body was overfull with new feelings. She soared, and as she did she cried out, and then she wept uncontrollably. He kissed away the tears on her cheeks, all the while thrusting and pulling until with a great cry his big body stiffened, and she felt the rush of his juices as they poured forth, filling her. As he collapsed upon her, Fancy swooned with uncontrollable excitement.

When the king came to himself a moment later, he rolled off his beautiful lover and then gathered her into his arms. She lay softly against his broad, smooth chest. *She had been a virgin*, and yet she claimed that she was not. What had happened to make her believe that she wasn't a virgin? He knew in time she would tell him the secret of her husband's death, but this other he had to know now. She murmured low against him, and his arms instinctively tightened about her. There had been so many women in his life. Lucy Walter had given him his first son before he had been forced to flee England during the civil wars. And sweet Elizabeth Killigrew had given him a daughter two years later while he was on the run. And there had been Catherine Pegge's lad, born also in his exile. And then there was Barbara Villiers, his first real *maitress en titre*. Beautiful, sensual, greedy Barbara. She had given him five children, and attempted to foist a sixth on him, but he had known the sixth was not his and denied her. Her unfaithfulness was his escape. And recently Nellie Gwyn, saucy and greedy, but a good heart.

And now there was Fancy Devers. For he intended making her his mistress. She was not a woman to quickly bed and then discard. No. Fancy was a lover he would keep. She would be a nice balance with Nellie, and he knew she would be respectful of the queen. But first he needed to learn why this lovely girl had believed she wasn't a virgin.

Chapter

4

Fancy moaned slightly, then sighed deeply. The smell of sandal-wood touched her nostrils. Opening her eyes she discovered that she was cuddled in the king's embrace and lying upon his chest. She raised her head and met his glance. It was warm. "That was wonderful," she said to him. "Is it always that wonderful? Or is it just wonderful with Your Majesty?"

He grinned and then chuckled, flattered. "While I should like to tell you that it is only me," he said, "I am certain there are any number of gentlemen who please their ladies in a like fashion, my dear. But now we must talk."

"Oh?" She sounded distinctly disappointed. "I was rather hoping that we might do it again, Your Majesty," Fancy told him.

"Oh, we shall," he assured her, "but first I must know why you thought you were not a virgin, Fancy."

"But I couldn't have been," she replied. "My husband used my body on our wedding night." She shivered openly with the memory. "It was horrible! Not at all like Your Majesty's treatment of me."

"Sweetheart," the king said gently, "your maidenhead was quite intact, and I am a man who knows such things. Tell me what this man did to you, Fancy, and I will attempt to explain further. Did your mother not offer you the knowledge you would need for that momentous event in your life?"

"Mama said that she supposed that my sister Maeve and my friends had already told me what I needed to know, for all girls were inclined to chatter about such things. Then she told me to put myself into Parker's hands and all would be well. She said that a gentleman doesn't want his wife to be overly knowledgeable. That such a woman but frets a man since he wonders from where she has obtained her information."

"Had your sister spoken with you?" the king wondered aloud.

"Maeve was very impressed that I was to wed a Virginia Randolph. She said it was best I be pure as the driven snow else he be suspicious. So I asked nothing more. Oh, I knew that men kiss and fumble with your breasts, but other than that I had no knowledge."

"How did your husband make love to you?" the king questioned.

"He made me lie on my belly, and pushed my face into the pillows so none would hear my cries. He said he did not want to see my face when he did it. Then he pushed into me, and the pain was so terrible that I fainted dead away. So you see, Your Majesty, I couldn't have been a virgin."

The implication of her words slammed into the king's brain, and he closed his eyes for a short moment. The pervert had violated this exquisite girl in the most vicious and debauched way. *Were he not dead,* Charles Stuart, the king, thought, *I should kill him myself.* Then as his shock eased, he said to Fancy, "Sweetheart, you were yet a virgin for me because your husband used you in a corrupt fashion. No decent man would use a respectable woman in that fashion, particularly an innocent virgin. Someday you will tell me how he died, but even if you feel you are responsible for his death, he deserved to die, Fancy. Did you tell your parents what happened afterward?"

She shook her head. "There was such an uproar over Parker's death that I tried to put it from my mind," she admitted.

"Rightly so," he agreed, and then he bent and kissed her. "I shall never let any man harm you again, Fancy," he told her. "You have my royal word on that, my darling."

"And I do not have to speak of it again?" she said.

"Not until you are ready," he promised her.

She looked at him flirtatiously. "Can we do *it* again now, Your Majesty?" she queried him prettily.

He laughed. "So you like being fucked, my little colonial."

She looked a bit shocked by his use of the crude word, but then she answered, "Aye, I like being fucked by Your Majesty."

"What is it about you, Fancy," he wondered, caressing her face with a gentle hand, "that makes me want to keep you from all harm. You are hardly shy, or meek, and yet . . ." his voice trailed off.

Reaching up, she drew his head down to hers. "Kiss me," she said simply, and he did.

He made love to her a second time that night, and her passionate response to him set his senses reeling. He felt like a boy again. Afterward she fell asleep, but before she did he told her that these rooms were now hers.

"Are they not yours?" she said puzzled.

"I do not often take my mistresses to the royal apartments for I would not offend the queen," he told her, and she nodded her agreement.

"Am I to remain here?" she wondered.

"The rooms are yours if you choose to take up residence at Whitehall or they are yours in which you may entertain me and your friends. Shall I have a servant sent to you?" He arose from the bed and began to dress himself.

"I have a maid, Bess Trueheart," Fancy responded. "She will either still be in my uncle's apartments or will have returned to Greenwood House with my cousins."

"I will have her found and sent to you in the morning," the king said.

"But how will she find me? I have no idea where I am for Mr. Chiffinch led me down so many corridors and up so many flights of stairs, I am totally lost," Fancy said with a helpless smile.

The king laughed. "Whitehall is a hodgepodge, I will agree," he replied. "I will assign a page to serve you when you are here, my darling little colonial." He bent and ruffled her tousled raven's black curls. "Sleep well, my darling Fancy," he said softly. He kissed the top of her head. "We have but begun a lovely friendship." Then he departed the bedchamber, closing the door behind him.

The king quickly made his way back to his own apartments. He had to speak with his cousin about Fancy. *No!* He would not speak with Charlie. Not yet. He would send for the dowager duchess of Glenkirk. She must be informed of this turn of events. *Fancy had been a virgin!* He had certainly never expected it, and had they not been so far along in their amorous pursuits he might have been able to stop. But if the truth had been known, he didn't want to stop with her. The king knew that his sexual appetites were greater than most men, but it was just because they were that he had learned to control them. Considering the violence that had been visited upon Fancy Devers, he was glad that it had been he who had finally introduced her to the delights of passion. She could not have had a better teacher, he thought without bragging, for he knew that he was an excellent lover.

Page, his keeper of the privy closet, was awaiting him. He helped his master disrobe. The king quickly bathed and, clothed in a clean nightshirt, lay down for a few hours of rest. Soon enough he would be surrounded by the formalities and daily routine of his court. Time spent with his mistresses was private and precious to him. He fell asleep dreaming of turquoise eyes and perfect little breasts.

In the morning he told the keeper of his appointments to find a time in which he might speak with the dowager duchess of Glenkirk this very day. And when the time had been settled, a messenger was to be dispatched to the lady. The king's tone told the royal servant that he would not accept the excuse that his calendar was already full.

The keeper of the appointments bowed and said, "Yes, Your Majesty."

Jasmine, dowager duchess of Glenkirk, was sitting up in her bed drinking her morning tea when Orane bustled in holding a sealed packet. The maidservant handed it to Jasmine with a curtsy.

"This has just come from Whitehall," she said, "and the gossip is that Mistress Fancy did not come home last night with her two cousins. Oh la la, madame! The duke does not know whether to be angry, or not."

"I would advise he not be angry," Jasmine said with a smile. "A king is a king as we both well know, Orane." She broke the seal on the parchment packet and opening it, read the contents. When she had finished, she folded it back up again, and said, "I have an audience with His Majesty at four o'clock this afternoon, Orane. Bring me my jewel cases so I may decide what I will wear that His Majesty remember he is dealing with the Mughal's daughter and not just any old woman."

"Shall I send the duke to you?" Orane queried.

"Yes, I think that might be a good idea," Jasmine agreed.

Charlie came, and there was a frankly worried look upon his face. "You know?" he asked her.

"That Fancy spent the night at Whitehall? Yes. The king has requested my presence at four this afternoon," Jasmine said. "Does he usually speak with the families of those women he beds? You know him better than I do, Charlie."

"I can't answer that, Mama," the duke of Lundy said. "Barbara Villiers has always been a law unto herself, with the morals of a mink, and certainly no better than she ought to be. The others were all during his exile. He was on the run, and I doubt the proprieties, if there are such things in these cases, were observed. I don't know why he wants to see you, and frankly you will have to find out yourself, for I am not bold enough to ask him. I am hardly pleased that my cousin's very lustful eye has fallen on my niece, or any member of this family. What are we to say to Fancy's parents? You know what happens when the king beds any woman with regularity."

"We have babies," Jasmine said quietly.

"You loved my father!" Charlie protested. "It was different for you. Fancy is beautiful. A helpless young widow with no real knowledge of the king or the court."

"Fancy is a strong young woman with a mind of her own," Jasmine told her son. "If he decides to keep her for a time, if she gives him a child, Charlie, her chances of making a good marriage increase, or perhaps not. But you will not stop this. A child makes her fertile. There is always a suitor who is interested in a woman's fertility. And all of that salacious gossip that has circulated about her thanks to the Tollivers will be swept away with this new turn of events."

"The Mughal's court lost a valuable strategist in you, Mama," Charlie, the not-so-royal Stuart, complimented his mother.

"Fancy is a widow. It isn't as if she had anything to lose by the association," Jasmine said.

"You are the matriarch of the family, and the king respects such status," the duke answered his mother thoughtfully. "Do you think he wants your approval in the matter?"

Jasmine laughed. "When did your cousin ever ask for anyone's approval? He even defied the damned Scottish kirk! Now you know as much as I do, my son. Go away, and let me consider what I will wear to my audience with the king."

"A royal page came for Bess Trueheart last night," the duke said. "I suppose if anything had been amiss she would have come back to our apartments. I left Barbara sleeping. I had best return to tell her what little we know. Will you come and see us after your audience with His Majesty, Mama?"

"Yes, yes!" Jasmine said. "Now leave me, dear boy," and she waved him from her bedchamber.

The duke hurried from the house, down the lawns to the quay where his personal barge was waiting to return him to the palace. The Greenwood barge was just drawing on to the other side of the stone dockage. He almost blushed as his niece, accompanied by Bess Trueheart, alighted from the little vessel.

"Good morning, Uncle," Fancy said, and then she passed by him and moved up the lawns toward the house.

Bess Trueheart bobbed him a curtsy, and then she, too, was gone, hurrying after her mistress. Looking up, the duke saw his daughter and Diana in a window. He could almost hear their squeals of inquisitive excitement as Fancy walked toward the house. *'Oddsfish!* Was Fortune's daughter to be a bad influence on his and Patrick's girls? He would have to monitor the situation carefully, he thought, climbing into his own river transport.

Cynara and Diana were down the main staircase of the house before Fancy entered from the rivergate. They dashed down the hallway to meet her, shrieking with their excitement. "Tell us! Tell us!" they begged her in unison. And then they heard the stern voice of their grandmother who came up behind them, still clothed in her warm chamber robe.

"There is nothing to tell," Jasmine said. "Fancy, come with me. Cynara, Diana, calm yourselves with a walk in the garden. Orane has brought your cloaks and will walk with you."

"But, Grandmama," Cynara protested.

Jasmine took Fancy by the arm and walked her upstairs, away from the other two girls. She escorted Fancy to her own apartment, closing the door behind her as they entered. Then she turned and asked, "Did you lie with him?"

Fancy nodded. "It was wonderful, Grandmama!"

"Very well then, when you are ready to share your adventure with me, you will, I know," Jasmine replied.

"He has given me my own apartment at Whitehall," Fancy told her grandmother. "It is beautiful!"

"Will you not stay there?" Jasmine wanted to know.

"I am not certain I am comfortable doing so," Fancy admitted. "I think I must see what happens first."

"'Tis a wise decision," Jasmine said. "We will send a few of your things there should you need them, but Greenwood is your home, my darling girl. Have you eaten?"

Fancy shook her head. "I am too excited," she said, "so I decided to wait until I got back. Bess has gone to fetch me something."

"Then I will leave you. I approve your discretion and your prudence in this matter. I regret, however, that I cannot keep your cousins under control, and they will undoubtedly burst in here as soon as they have ascertained I have gone. Try not to overexcite them," Jasmine finished with a smile. She did not tell her granddaughter that she had been called to Whitehall that afternoon. Whatever the king wanted of her was between them alone. She kissed Fancy on both of her rosy cheeks and then left her. Out of the corner of her eye as she moved down the hallway to her own apartments, she saw the flash of Cynara's scarlet skirts. Jasmine smiled again.

Fancy was not surprised when moments after her grandmother had left her, the door was flung open. Both Cynara and Diana dashed into her dayroom.

"We have left Orane stumbling around the maze in the gardens," Diana said with a giggle.

"*What happened?*" Cynara demanded, quick to the point. "Did *he* make love to you? Was it wonderful? Are you to be his new mistress?"

"He made love to me. Yes, it was wonderful, and whether I go back is his decision to make, not mine," Fancy said. She wasn't certain yet if she should tell them about the apartment at Whitehall.

"There must be more," Cynara persisted.

"If there is," Fancy replied with a small smile, "I do not choose to share it. Making love, Cousin, is an intense and very personal matter. Besides, you are still a virgin, and I do not believe it is wise to share such details with an unfledged maiden."

"Oh, pooh!" Cynara snapped. "Women always compare details with one another. How else are we to learn what pleases a man if we do not learn from those who already know?"

"My mother has always said a gentleman does not want a bride who is overly knowledgeable else he wonder where she gained such knowledge," Fancy said. "Besides, this is the king and not just any gentleman. I should quickly lose his favor if I kissed and then told."

"I think Fancy is right," Diana spoke up.

"You would," Cynara muttered. "But I don't intend to marry for a very long time. I want to know what men are like. A great variety of men. It isn't like it was in our grandmother's youth, or even in her grandmother's youth, when women of intellect and wealth could have wonderful adventures, sharing their passion with any number of men!" Cynara said enthusiastically, and then she continued. "No. We are stuck in a deep wagon track of propriety and custom. Go to court. Flirt for a brief time, and then accept a marriage proposal from a *suitable* gentleman of good family, and equal or better wealth. *Marry.* Ruin your figure with babies. *Grow old!* It is all so damned

predictable! I don't want that kind of I life! *I want excitement!* If my
father wasn't the king's cousin, I should have attempted to seduce
His Majesty myself," she concluded. "How thrilling to be a king's
mistress!"

"Young women of our station and wealth are supposed to have
the kind of life you describe," Diana said. "That is why my mama
let me remain here with Grandmama. I should like to wed with a
duke or a marquis, an earl at worst. I look forward to my own home,
and the children who will cement my position in life. And I shall
have love even as all the women in our family have been loved. I do
not want the kind of adventures that Aunt India or Aunt Fortune
had; nor do I want to have to leave my homeland and my family behind over a matter of religion. I want a man who will love me above
all else and do whatever he must to have me for his wife! *That is what
I want!*"

"You both seek the same things," Fancy told them. "You just
have different methods for going about reaching your heart's desire."

"And you?" Cynara said astutely.

"I have been married. I don't choose to be again, but that does
not mean I don't want to be loved," Fancy answered her.

"You were married for less than a day," Cynara said scornfully.
"Whatever happened to you, you know that eventually Grandmama
will see that you are wed again. Besides after being a king's mistress,
anyone other than a husband would be considered a great come-
down socially."

"I was not raised socially," Fancy laughed. "And one night in the
king's bed hardly makes me his mistress."

"Nonsense," the practical Cynara said. "The Colonies have their
own form of society, I am certain. It is not like that of a royal court,
but do not tell me that you are all equals, for I know it is not, cannot
be, so. There are landowners, and merchants, and shopkeepers,
slaves, and bondservants, fishermen and simple farmers. Every civi-
lization has its social structure. We have learned that in our studies
with our tutors. Diana and I have been well educated. Grandmama

has seen to that. She says a woman must be able to speak intelligently with her husband after the passion, else he grows bored with her."

"What did you and the king speak of afterward?" Diana inquired innocently.

"There was not a great deal of conversation between us last night," Fancy admitted as Cynara rolled her eyes. Then she continued, "I will not kiss and tell, Cousins."

Bess arrived with a tray and set it down on the table. She sent a piercing look at Cynara and Diana that told them in no uncertain terms that they were to leave.

"We'll be back," Cynara promised.

"I am going to sleep after I eat," Fancy told them, and when they had gone, she giggled. "Did you see the look on their faces when I said that?" she asked Bess. "I suspect they think all we did the whole night long was make love."

"You didn't?" Bess was frankly curious, but Fancy knew by now that she could trust her servant.

"The king does not spend the night with his mistress. He always returns to his own apartments," Fancy explained. "He is most respectful of the queen."

"*Is he?*" Bess didn't think a man who fathered and recognized bastards at the rate the king did was particularly thoughtful of his poor barren spouse, but she kept those reflections to herself. "Eat your breakfast," she said to her mistress, "and then we will decide what you wish to leave in your apartments at Whitehall, mistress."

Fancy sat down and found her appetite was great this morning. She finished the tray of food Bess had brought her and then turned her attention to what she would send to the palace. It was at that point her grandmother's maid, Orane, arrived.

"Madame has sent me to advise you, mistress," Orane said. She then went through Fancy's wardrobe much to the outrage of Bess.

"Foreign cow!" Bess muttered.

Orane turned and laughed. "You can learn much from me," she told Bess. "And you had best pay attention, for your mistress is now in an especially high place. What would a country girl such as yourself know of those things? I, however, have served a lady who was mistress to not one but two kings."

"Who was that?" Fancy asked Orane.

"Your aunt Autumn," Orane said. "First, she was mistress to King Louis of France and bore him a fine daughter, Mademoiselle de la Bois. Then when she returned to England, she served King Charles in the same capacity. Her little son, by him, was born dead sadly."

"My aunt was the king's mistress?" Fancy was astounded.

"*Oui*, she was. And the king once attempted to seduce Lady Diana's mother, the duchess Flanna," Orane laughed.

Again Fancy was surprised. "Now I understand," she said slowly, "why it is said the women of this family are like honey to a bee where the royal Stuarts are concerned."

"*Mais oui*," Orane agreed. "You all have beauty, charm, and intellect, but there is also a *je ne sais quoi* about you that cannot quite be defined but is certainly enticing to the gentlemen." She stepped into the wardrobe chamber. "Now, let us see what you will need."

Orane chose two gowns that Fancy might wear during the day and two gowns she might wear in the evening. Then clucking, she hurried away to her mistress, telling Jasmine, "She has no robes de chambre to entice him, madame. Her night garments are plain. Simple. Tedious. They cannot possibly attract or seduce a man such as King Charles. You must remedy this lack at once if she is to keep his favor!"

"Can any of my robes de chambre be altered until we can have others made?" Jasmine asked.

"Madame!" Orane sighed.

"I know, I know," Jasmine said. "I am an old woman, but surely there is something among my things that can be made suitable, at least for tonight. Rohana! Look in my wardrobe."

"There is a new garment that could be recut," Toramalli spoke up. "Rohana, you know the one of which I speak."

Rohana nodded and went to fetch the required garment. She returned and spread it out for her mistress to approve. It was a garment of lavender silk, cut with a long skirt, and flowing sleeves lavishly trimmed with a waterfall of cream-colored lace.

"We can recut the round high neckline," Orane said, "and it will be perfect. We will also make a narrow belt to accentuate Mistress Fancy's dainty waistline. It will be suitable for tonight. Then we will have time to make others."

Jasmine nodded. "Can you two do it while I prepare myself for my appointment with His Majesty?" she asked her two elderly servants.

They nodded in unison and moved slowly off with the silk gown.

By the time Jasmine was ready to depart for Whitehall that afternoon, the gown was remade and packed with Fancy's other garments. Jasmine climbed into her large coach, Orane putting a fur robe over her mistress's knees. The dowager was magnificently garbed in a forest green and fur-trimmed velvet overskirt, which revealed an underskirt of green-and-gold-embroidered velvet brocade. The fur-trimmed scooped neckline was made modest by her high-necked pale gold chemise with its pearl-trimmed neckline. The puffed sleeves of the gown were trimmed lavishly with wide bands of thick brown beaver. Her matching cloak was lined and generously trimmed with the same fur. Beneath the hood of her outer garment was an elegant lace veil covering her silver head. Emeralds and diamonds dripped from her ears and spread themselves across the golden lawn of her chemise. Her brown leather gloves were lined in delicate gold silk.

The carriage departed Greenwood into the already dark winter streets and traveled through the city to Whitehall Palace. In the Great Courtyard, Jasmine alighted. A young page in the royal livery came quickly up to her.

"My lady Leslie?"

She nodded.

"Please to follow me, madame," the page said and hurried off. He led her into the palace, down several long corridors, finally stopping before a single door. He opened it, standing back, and gestured her into the chamber.

The king immediately came forward to greet her as the door closed behind her. "Madame, I thank you for coming," he said, leading her to a comfortable seat by the fire. "You must be cold. Did you come by the river?"

"Nay, the water is too chilly for a lady of my years, Your Majesty," she replied.

He sat down opposite her, and it was then she noticed a tray by his side. "Tea?" he asked her.

Jasmine was surprised. "Indeed, yes, Your Majesty," she told him and accepted the handless cup of the steaming brew that he offered her. "I did not think Your Majesty was a connoisseur of tea."

"I am not, but I know from Charlie that you are. I thought a bit of something warm after your trip would please you," the king replied. Then he raised a small tumbler of whiskey to her in salute.

Jasmine sipped at her tea, letting the heat from the aromatic beverage seep into her bones. Finally she put the cup back down and said bluntly, "You have favored my granddaughter, Fancy Devers, Your Majesty. I must assume that you have asked me here with regard to her future welfare. Is that not unusual for you, Charles Stuart? It is not your habit, I believe, to say, *'May I?'* "

The king laughed aloud. "Kings do not ask, madame, as you well know. But yes, I do want to speak to you about Fancy. I have given her rooms here at Whitehall. I will continue to favor her as long as it pleases both of us that I do so. But there is something that I must share with you, madame, for I suspect you did not know it."

Jasmine sat silent and waited for the king to speak further.

"Your granddaughter was a virgin when I took her last night," the king told the astonished dowager duchess of Glenkirk.

"It cannot be!" Jasmine finally burst out. "She was a bride. There was a wedding night."

"Madame, knowing my reputation, can you believe that I would be mistaken about a thing like this?" the king said.

"But when my daughter wrote to me she did not tell me this," Jasmine said slowly. "It cannot be possible that she did not know."

"When I realized the truth," the king continued, "it was too late for me to cease. You understand that? And afterward Fancy told me what had happened to her on that infamous wedding night. And her mother did not know, for there was so much ta-rah about the death of the bridegroom your granddaughter was both embarrassed and afraid to say anything more than she had already said," the king explained.

"Did she tell you *all* of it?" Jasmine asked him quietly.

"No. Only most briefly what he had done to her," the king admitted. "Madame, I know you have vowed to allow your granddaughter to tell her own tale, but I wonder if she will ever be able to do so. I would know the whole truth of this matter not just for curiosity's sake, but for Fancy's sake. I have never willingly brought pain to a lady who shared herself with me. I cannot force you to tell me, but if you could, I should be content to keep the lady's secrets."

"Give me some of that whiskey you are drinking," Jasmine said, holding out her little teacup. She sighed, her look troubled. "What else didn't she tell my daughter?" Jasmine asked. "And why did she believe herself not a virgin when she was yet one?"

"Your daughter assumed Fancy knew what was involved in the marriage bed," the king began. "She believed that Fancy had learned what she would from her older sister. She informed her that a girl of good family should not be very knowledgeable in such matters and told her to put herself in her husband's tender care."

"*God's blood,*" the dowager swore. "I know I did not teach my daughter, Fortune, to be so foolish or lackwitted. What on earth could have possessed her to send her youngest daughter to the marriage bed uninformed? This new generation has, I fear, no common sense at all. What happened to my granddaughter?"

"Her husband sodomized her madame. What happened afterward I do not know," the king said. "Fancy knew that a man enters a woman's body. She knew it should give her pain the first time. That is why she believed she was no longer a virgin."

Jasmine's beringed hand flew to her mouth, but it could not prevent the cry of anguish. Tears welled up in her turquoise eyes. For the moment, she was rendered speechless.

The king leaned forward and took her hand in his, rubbing and patting it in an attempt to comfort her. "I should kill him myself were he not already in hell, madame," he said. He pulled a silk handkerchief from his coat and gently wiped her cheeks free of the silent tears now rolling down them. "Will you tell me all of it?" he asked her again.

Jasmine nodded. "But swear to me that you will never reveal that I have," she said to the king.

"It will be *our* secret, madame," the king replied, and he kissed the elegant hand in his, smiling warmly into her eyes.

"No wonder the ladies adore you so, Charles Stuart," the dowager duchess of Glenkirk told the king. "Your uncle had the same charm. Now give me my whiskey, and I will tell you everything you need to know about the scandal surrounding my granddaughter."

He poured some of the smoky peat-flavored whiskey into her outstretched cup. She drank it down in one gulp, holding the cup out for more, which he immediately supplied.

"Did she really kill her husband?" he asked. "She told me she did not, but that she was responsible for his death."

"Her sense of responsibility is too deep," Jasmine began. Then she continued. "Parker Randolph appeared to be a perfect match for my granddaughter. He was the only son. His two sisters had been married off. The family owned several thousand acres of land in the Virginias. This boy was handsome, well mannered, and there was not even the faintest whisper of anything unsavory, or untoward about him. At twenty-five he was yet unmarried. When last year he set his sights on my granddaughter, it appeared that he had just been waiting for the right girl to come along. They had met at several parties. He asked my son-in-law's permission to pay court to Fancy. Under the circumstances, and especially as Fancy seemed to favor Parker, her father agreed. At Christmas last year they became engaged. The wedding was set for the month of June.

"My daughter and her husband spared no expense. The wedding was a lavish affair, marred only by the fact that the morning after it had taken place the bridegroom lay dead at his wife's hand."

"But both you and Fancy have declared her innocent!" the king said, confused.

"Parker Randolph had committed bigamy, Your Majesty," Jasmine explained. "There was on his father's plantation a young slavegirl who was every bit as fair as Parker and his sisters. His father had bought the girl when she was a child to grow up and to serve as a maid for his daughters. After these two young women were married, events that took place within a single year, they begged their father to give this faithful young slave her freedom. He did. The girl, however, asked to remain on the plantation as a paid servant to Mrs. Randolph, a frail lady who was happy to have her companionship.

"Parker Randolph fell in love with this girl, but she would not succumb to his blandishments. She told him he could only have her if he married her. He resisted for a time, but finally his lust overcame his judgment, if indeed he was blessed with any sense. He and the girl found a backcountry preacher who did not know either of them. They were married, legally and lawfully. The girl's name was, most fittingly, Delilah. Parker convinced her, however, that their marriage must remain a secret until the proper time.

"When he began to court my granddaughter, Delilah became angry, but Parker Randolph assured his naive and jealous wife that he was just doing it to make his family happy. When the marriage plans were announced, Parker explained to his wife that while he did indeed intend to wed my granddaughter, it was simply for her large dowry and for the great wealth she would eventually inherit. His family needed that wealth, and he had learned a secret about Fancy's family that would give him full control over them." Jasmine stopped here and sipped her cup of whiskey. She had suddenly realized how right it was that the king know the truth.

"What was the secret?" he asked her.

"Fancy had told him that her grandmother, her mother's mother, was a foreign princess from a land called India. The only thing Parker Randolph could remember about India from his few studies was that its people were dark skinned. He decided then and there that we were Negroid, which made Fancy a girl with African blood in her veins. He told his wife, Delilah, that he would threaten to expose this to all the Colonies if Fancy's family did not obey his every wish. Should this shameful knowledge, plus the fact that their daughter was really his concubine, and not his wife, become public, Parker reasoned, Fancy's family would be ruined in the Colonies. They would pay him whatever he desired, he told the gullible Delilah, to keep these secrets.

"Delilah protested that Fancy's children would be considered his heirs. Yet any children she gave him would be thought bastards. But Parker Randolph promised this woman that it would never happen. Fancy, he said, would never bear his children. Now I understand why he was able to promise his wife such a thing. But on the wedding night Delilah was unable to contain her jealousy. She secreted herself in the bridal chamber before the bride herself arrived. She watched as Fancy was undressed and prepared for the bridegroom. My daughter wrote to me that when Delilah saw her husband with Fancy, saw them make love, she was unable to contain herself. In a terrible rage she revealed herself to them.

"Parker Randolph was furious, especially when she told Fancy that she was not her bridegroom's real wife. Fancy was devastated. Of course he denied it and said that Delilah was mad and could prove nothing. My sweet granddaughter then cried that she believed him, and would stand by his side no matter what. It was then that Parker Randolph laughed and scorned both women as fools. He was indeed married to Delilah, he told Fancy. Then he went on to tell her exactly what he planned. She would be forced to pretend, while he reaped the benefits of her wealth. Delilah would be forced to watch, he said, as he enjoyed Fancy, and there was nothing she could do about it."

"But there was," the king said.

"Yes," Jasmine answered. "Delilah Randolph reached for the nearest thing at hand. It was a heavy silver candlestick. She hit her husband with it, once, twice, three times. That is when Fancy began to scream uncontrollably for help. It came quickly, but it was too late. Parker Randolph was dead, Your Majesty. The scandal of what this young man had done would have ruined the Randolphs. It would have ruined my grandchild had it become known that her virtue had been compromised.

"While her in-laws wanted to somehow blame her for the terrible tragedy, the more influential branch of the Virginia Randolphs would not permit it. They compelled their relations to face the truth. To soothe Parker's family, the portion of Fancy's dowry already paid was not reclaimed. Nor would my son-in-law allow the Randolphs to take out their wrath on Delilah. At first they claimed she could not have been wed to their son, but Delilah drew forth from her bosom the marriage lines the preacher had given her. Parker obviously never knew she possessed such proof. Kieran Devers sent Delilah north to Boston with enough money to start a dress shop. He told her if she ever showed her face in Maryland or the Virginias again he could not protect her."

"And Fancy came to England," the king said.

"She could hardly remain in the Colonies, Your Majesty," Jasmine said quietly. "The truth couldn't be told under the circumstances. There would have been no chance for my granddaughter. It was said that Parker Randolph had a fit and died on his wedding night. That in the midst of said fit he fell, accounting for the wound upon his head, much of which had been cleaned up before he was shown in his coffin," Jasmine explained.

"Why does Fancy consider herself responsible for his death?" the king inquired.

"She says if she had not married him, none of this tragedy would have happened. She realized too late that she was just in love with the idea of marrying the handsomest man in the colonies, she told her mother. As the youngest child in her family, she never did anything to distinguish herself until she caught Parker Randolph's eyes. Perhaps it is unreasonable for a sensible person to believe this, but she did at the time. I do not think so any longer. And that is the truth of the matter, Your Majesty, as my daughter related it to me in her correspondence last summer." Jasmine finished her whiskey and placed the small blue-and-white china cup on the table next to her.

"I will take good care of her," the king promised.

"I know you will," Jasmine replied. "The royal Stuarts have always been good to their women, and I should know, shouldn't I?"

"You would have made a magnificent queen," he replied.

"So it was said at the time, Your Majesty," she answered him, and then she stood up. "I shall go home now, my lord. Good night."

The king jumped to his feet and escorted her to the door. He kissed her hand, and said, "This will indeed remain *our* secret, madame. I would not like Fancy to believe that I had intruded, for I am sure she will eventually tell me in her own words what happened."

"I am certain too, Your Majesty," Jasmine responded. Then reaching up, she touched his saturnine cheek with her gloved hand. "You are nothing like your uncle," she told him. "He was all golden and blue eyed. You are very French."

"My mother said I was the ugliest infant she had ever seen," the king laughed. "She called me her black boy."

Jasmine laughed too. "But you have become a most distinguished gentleman, and more important, your heart is good, Charles Stuart."

"I think that as fine a compliment as I have ever received," the king responded. He bowed to her, and then Jasmine opened the door. Outside the little page jumped quickly to his feet to escort the dowager duchess of Glenkirk back to her carriage, even as the door to the king's privy chamber closed behind them.

Chapter

5

The afternoon was clear and cold along the Thames. A weak sun shone in an almost white sky, and there was the smell of snow in the air. The boatmen out on the river slowed as they passed the palace of Whitehall in order to catch a glimpse of the king and his court as they took their afternoon stroll. Wrapped in a peacock blue velvet cloak trimmed in rich marten, Fancy walked a step behind the king, whose silver-topped walking stick made a crunching sound in the gravel each time it touched the ground.

"Make way! Make way!" a shrill voice sounded behind her and Fancy found herself pushed aside by Lady Castlemaine. "This is not your place," Barbara Villiers said haughtily.

"Nor is it yours any longer, madame," Fancy quickly replied. "I am where I was asked to be. You are not."

Lady Castlemaine stopped in her tracks, as did Fancy, and the entire court behind them. "How dare you speak to *me* in that manner, mistress!" she snarled. Her tone was scathing, and older ladies than Fancy had been driven to tears by that icy timbre.

"You are rude, madame," Fancy replied. "Your position does not entitle you to be uncivil, and mannerless, although you believe it does."

Barbara Castlemaine shrieked at these words and raised her hand to slap Fancy. "How dare you address me at all," she screamed, "let alone attempt to reprimand me! I am Lady Castlemaine, and you but the child of an Irishman and the woman foolish enough to wed him, losing a great estate in the doing!"

Fancy caught the duchess's hand before it could deliver the blow. Her fingers wrapped strongly about her antagonist's wrist. She looked Barbara Castlemaine directly in the eye. "My mother, madame, preferred to keep her good name and took my father's most honorable name as her own in marriage, as opposed to the disgraceful behavior you have exhibited." Fancy loosed the wrist she held.

Now the king stopped, but he did not turn around. There was a small smile upon his lips, however.

Barbara Castlemaine gasped and grew red in the face as she attempted to say something, but before she might, another voice entered the fray as a third lady, garbed in a cherry red velvet cloak trimmed with gray rabbit's fur came forward to put herself between the two women.

"Well, my lords, and my ladies," the new arrival said, a most mischievous lilt to her voice, "here is a sight you will not likely ever see again. The king's highborn whore, his well-born whore, and his most assuredly lowborn whore all in one place at the same time." She laughed. The tension broken, the king and the court laughed with her.

The king turned about. *"Nellie!"* he scolded gently, but he was still laughing even as he admonished her.

"Will you allow that guttersnipe to speak to me like that?" Lady Castlemaine demanded in strident tones.

"Will you let that termagant speak to me like that?" Nellie Gwyn mocked her opponent. Then she looked at Fancy. "You are very beautiful," she said. "Can you share him peaceably with me, Mistress Devers?"

"I can," Fancy agreed. "Shall we walk together, Mistress Gwyn?" She offered her arm to the young actress.

The king chuckled, well pleased. He disliked scenes such as the one that Barbara Villiers had just instigated. He also appreciated the fact that his two new young and delightful mistresses had publicly agreed to get along. Life was so much easier when the ladies did not disagree over him, the king thought as he began to stroll once more along the riverbank. Then he stopped and turning, said to Lady Castlemaine, "Get you gone from my sight, madame. I would not see you again at court until after Twelfth Night. If then." Turning his back on the angry woman, he moved on again, calling to Fancy and Nell to walk with him.

Behind him the court moved past and around the Lady Castlemaine until she was left standing alone with only her small African page by her side. The boy waited nervously for instructions, bracing himself for the blow that was sure to come, for he could see his mistress's temper was high. But suddenly she seemed to shrivel and turning began a lonely retreat back to the palace, the page scampering in her wake.

Lady Castlemaine contemplated exposing Mistress Devers to the queen, but she quickly realized that Her Majesty probably already knew that the king was bedding not just that common little actress, but his cousin's beautiful niece as well. Except for a brief time early in his marriage, the king always treated the queen with the utmost affection and respect, both publicly and privately. After the initial shock of realizing her husband was a man of vast sexual appetites who would never deny himself, Queen Catherine had come to accept his peccadilloes. She even accepted the children the royal mistresses bore the king, and whom he proudly acknowledged.

Barbara Villiers was loath to accept that Charles Stuart was through with her. Defeat had never been easy for her. She would bide her time. He would eventually become bored with the guttersnipe and with his latest conquest, whom the court wits had now begun to call *the king's Fancy*. After all, Barbara Villiers reasoned, she and the king had been together for a very long time.

The king liked walking even on a cold day, and eventually many who began with him dropped away, returning to the comparative warmth of the palace. Fancy, however, born a country girl, was one of the few who could keep up with Charles Stuart.

"Come visit me later," she invited Mistress Gwyn, who finally decided to return to Whitehall.

"I will!" the young actress replied.

"You were kind to Nellie," the king noted as they walked.

"Why wouldn't I be?" Fancy wanted to know.

"She was born in a house here in London, little better than a brothel," he told her.

"You have accepted her," Fancy noted. "And she is amusing, isn't she? Besides, Your Majesty, I do not expect you will keep either of us around forever. Why would I quarrel with her over your favor? It is a well-known fact that Your Majesty's heart is almost as big as his—" She stopped, and her eyes twinkled when she looked up at him. "Besides, you are a king, and kings I have been told are permitted certain behaviors that we mere mortals are not."

"You always surprise me, Fancy," he replied. "Your lineage is quite excellent, and yet you do not behave quite like a lady of your background and blood should. Why is that?"

"I don't know," she answered him, "but perhaps my having been born in the Colonies has something to do with it, Your Majesty. Society here is so formal. Society in the Colonies, while proper, is not like it is here. We are more informal."

"It is odd to be king over a land you have never seen nor will ever see," Charles Stuart said. "Especially now that I know you."

"I think I am coming to like England better," Fancy told him.

They finally reversed their direction and began the return to the palace. The winter sun was already setting, and torches had been lit along the pathway. A wind had begun to blow off the water.

"It will snow soon," Fancy said.

"I will join you late tonight, my darling colonial," the king replied, kissing her lips softly before they entered the building.

"I shall await you," she responded, and then turned away as the king hurried off down one corridor, and she another. Fancy found her cousins waiting for her when she entered her apartments. They were seated, drinking chocolate and eating iced cakes. She laughed to see them like little girls on the floor before the fire, their pretty faces smeared with pink icing and their hot chocolate. "Are you quite comfortable, Cousins?" she asked them, handing her cloak to Bess and joining them.

"We need to change our gowns here tonight," Cynara said. "There is to be a wonderful masque directed by the lord of Misrule. It will take too long to have to go home, and so we brought our dresses here."

"Of course you may change here," Fancy told them, "but you cannot come back afterward for the king has told me he is coming tonight."

"We will go home directly," Cynara promised. "Whatever we leave behind can be collected tomorrow. You were quite wonderful this afternoon the way you stood up to my Lady Castlemaine. She is so rude!"

"It comes from all the privilege she has been accorded," Fancy said. "One must never allow such perquisites to be considered a prerogative. My mother always said that one meets the same people on the descent as one did when climbing to the top. My lady Castlemaine is quite overbearing. She is not the queen, nor does the king favor her thusly."

"They say he doesn't even sleep with her anymore," Diana said.

"I would not know if that is so," Fancy replied to her cousin. "It is not my business to query His Majesty over such things."

"Are you in love with him?" Cynara asked.

"No," Fancy answered honestly. "I am very fond of him, and he is very good to me. I enjoy the pleasure our bodies give to each other. I think we are friends. If you fall in love with a man, you find yourself at his mercy. I shall never allow that to happen to me again."

"Is his manhood unusually large as is rumored?" Cynara queried.

"*Cyn!*" Diana half-shrieked, blushing.

"Well, do not tell me you haven't heard the stories," Cynara rejoined. "We all have." She turned her gaze to Fancy. "Is it truth, or is it fiction, Cousin?"

"He seems a big man, but then he is big all over," Fancy said to her two cousins. "He is certainly larger than my husband was, but then I have little else to compare him with, Cynara."

"He's bigger than your average gentleman," said another voice, and Nell Gwyn sauntered into their midst. "In fact, he's right huge, and I've seen enough manly cocks in my day to make such an observation."

"Bess, get Mistress Gwyn a cup of chocolate," Fancy instructed her servant. "Will you have a cake, Nellie? My cousins have left us a few upon the plate."

"Thank ye, and I will," the young actress said with an impudent grin. She sat down before the fire with them. Her hazel eyes were bright with curiosity. "That was quick of you this afternoon," she noted. "I don't think anyone, not even the king hisself, has ever put the termagant in her place as you so neatly did. It did my heart good, and that's a truth." Reaching out she took one of the little cakes and popped it in her mouth, chewing it up, and swallowing it down.

"I am better born than she," Fancy noted, "and even if I weren't, I much dislike being spoken down to by a woman like that. She is an appalling opportunist."

"Are we much better?" Nellie asked.

"Aye," Fancy said. "At least we are honest in our desires. We do not pretend to be anything other than what we are, do we?"

Nell Gwyn nodded slowly. "Aye, and that's a truth," she agreed. "I was born in a tavern that was as much a brothel as a drinking house. Me mum told me if I was going to be a whore I should be a rich man's whore for the pay was better." She laughed. "I became an orange girl at the theater when I was ten, and I saw the fancy ladies and their gentlemen. I realized me mum was right so I became an actress."

"They say you sing and dance better than any," Diana murmured.

"You are the one they call Siren, aren't you? I have heard it said that even your rivals have no bad word to say about you. Have you yet decided which of those poor young gentlemen you will favor with your hand, my lady?"

Diana laughed. "I am not yet ready to choose a husband, Mistress Nell," she told the actress. "My cousins and I have just come to court, and I am having far too much fun."

Nellie nodded. "Enjoy it while you can, my lady." Her eye then turned itself upon Cynara. "You had best beware the game you think to play with Harry Summers. He devours little girls like you."

Cynara actually blushed, but then she said spiritedly, "I can take care of myself, Mistress Nell."

Nellie shook her head. "He's a right bad 'un, my lady. They do not call him *Wickedness* for naught." She sipped her chocolate. "Did the king give you these apartments, Fancy?"

"He did," Fancy admitted.

"I want a house," Nellie replied, "and I'll not settle for any less. Your family has a house here so it don't matter to you, I expect. And then, too, one day you will marry again and have another house. But poor lasses like me must struggle for our own. I expect that when I give the king a child, he'll give me my house."

"Do you think you'll have a child?" Cynara asked, fascinated.

"Of course! The king is as prolific as a rabbit when it comes to spawning bastards. All his women seem to be as fecund and fertile as a well-ploughed field except for our poor queen." Nell lowered her voice. "You know they say that the duke of York's father-in-law pushed for the Portuguese marriage knowing the bride was barren. His daughter is wed with the duke, and he wants his grandchildren to rule after our good king and his brother. They say when the king's mother learned that Prince James had married Anne Hyde she wept for days. Not that she could have done anything about it, and the bride ripening with a babe even before the marriage lines were spoken."

Fancy was absolutely fascinated with these tidbits of gossip Nell Gwyn was so content to share. Her two cousins had probably heard it all before, but new to England, Fancy had not. She had never met anyone like Nell Gwyn in all of her life, but she had immediately liked the young actress who was her own age. Nell might be a bit rough about the edges, but she was sensible and a great deal of fun. *I've made a friend,* Fancy thought and she was pleased with the knowledge.

Christmas came and went, and then Twelfth Night passed. The next event the court would celebrate with enthusiasm was the feast of Saint Valentine, patron of lovers.

"He ought to be patron of this court the way everyone carries on," Nellie Gwyn said publicly, causing the king to laugh aloud with the memory of it as he and Fancy lay abed.

"She has a wicked wit, our Nell," Charles Stuart, the king, remarked.

"I am not certain I find it flattering that you discuss other women while lying in my bed, caressing my breasts," Fancy murmured.

"Are you jealous?" he tensed her, kissing her round shoulder.

Fancy considered a moment, and then she said, "Aye, I believe I am, Your Majesty."

"Do you love me?" he asked her.

"Aye," she said slowly, "but not in the way you would think a woman loves a man," Fancy told him.

"How then?" he queried, curious.

"I love you in the same way you love me. I enjoy our passion. I treasure our friendship. I can never be more to you, Your Majesty, than friend. While many women I realize could not accept such a state of affairs, if I may be allowed the pun, I can."

"I am not certain if I am flattered or disappointed," he said, and he pulled her beneath him, kissing her mouth with a quick kiss.

"Would you have me be like my lady Castlemaine then?" Fancy said with utmost seriousness. "Unable, unwilling, to accept the inevitable and move on with her life? She shared Your Majesty's exile, but you have been more than good to her. She rewards your kindness poorly with her inability to give way."

"So when I say it is through between us, my little colonial, you will step aside gracefully?" he asked her.

"With regret, Your Majesty, but aye, I will not linger, or attempt to embarrass you, or make you feel guilty for being what you are. A most passionate and good gentleman," she finished.

The king laughed softly. "You have learned the ways of the court very quickly, my darling Fancy. I cannot help but wonder what you would have been like had you been raised in England. The women in your family have always been noted for their sagacity."

"And our loving natures," she murmured seductively, pulling his dark head back to hers and kissing him deeply.

He caressed her lovingly, for if the truth had been known, Charles Stuart, the king, had grown quite fond of Fancy Devers. She was intelligent and passionate, qualities he very much admired in women. He appreciated the fact that she accepted whatever he offered her with grace and was not in the least greedy as so many of his mistresses were wont to be. They had, as she had so cleverly pointed out, become friends. They would be friends forever, he realized, but for now they were lovers, and her response to his touch roused a fire in him.

Fancy sighed with total pleasure. This was what she had always thought passion would be like. The king's flat, broad tongue licked at her nipples and her round breasts. The tongue continued on down her torso; his lips nibbled at her sensitive flesh sending ripples of delight up and down her spine. Her limbs felt like warmed water, all liquid and relaxed. Her hands caressed him. Her nails lightly scored his broad back, and she sighed again as he entered her, filling her love sheath with his great length and thickness, moving on her until they were both crying aloud with their satisfaction. And afterward Fancy wept softly, her tears dampening his chest, and he caressed her until she was finally calm once more.

"This is what I have always dreamed passion would be like," she explained to him. "I am so glad to have known it with you."

"You will know it with a husband one day, my darling colonial," he told her. "I understand my worth as a lover, Fancy, but there are other men who know how to give and receive pleasure, too."

"I will not marry again," she told him.

"Aye, you will, one day, and I shall choose your husband for you, sweetheart, that I may be certain he is a gentleman who will value you every bit as much as I do," the king told her.

"You chose a husband for my lady Castlemaine and look how badly that turned out," Fancy told him pertly. "I want no reward, or pension when we are through, Your Majesty. Being your friend is more than enough for me. I never even considered when I was sent here to England that I would one day have your friendship."

He kissed her lips once again. "Sometimes I think you may be every bit as good as the lovely Siren," he told her.

"Oh no!" Fancy protested. "I am not at all like Diana, but neither am I like my lady Castlemaine. I need not prove to all the world that I was cherished by a king. What we have, Your Majesty, is ours alone." And she kissed him back tenderly.

"I do not think," the king told her, "that I ever met anyone like you, my little colonial."

"No," she agreed, "you probably haven't, Your Majesty." She was very happy. It would not last forever, she knew, but while it did she intended enjoying herself.

It was almost the feast of St. Valentine's when Nellie Gwyn came to her with a plan to stop the king, who had of late been visiting another actress named Moll Davis, as well as Nell and Fancy.

"Scolding him does no good at all," Nell lamented.

"He is the king, and kings do as they please," Fancy reminded her new friend.

"I know we can't keep him from dipping that big wick of his in every honey pot that catches his eye, Fancy, but I know Moll well. She is as coarse as gravel and given to airs. If she is not stopped, she will eventually make the king a laughingstock. So far he hasn't invited her to court, but she has been angling for an entry. She mustn't be permitted the company of Society or there will be no preventing a scandal. The king can see nothing else when he likes a pretty face and a pair of bouncy tits."

"But what can we do?" Fancy asked.

"The king is to visit Moll after the court festivities on St. Valentine's night," Nell said. "When he gets to her rooms, if indeed she does not send to him before, he will find Moll quite incapacitated," Nellie said with a wicked chuckle.

"Why?" Fancy demanded.

"Moll has a sweet tooth," Nell said. "A most greedy sweet tooth. She shall on St. Valentine's receive from a secret admirer a box of her favorite sweetmeats. There will be sugarplums and candied violets and the new chocolate treats that are becoming so popular. As I said, I know Moll well. She will believe the king has sent this marvelous box of treats, for the box will be silver gilt, lined in silver lace, and a pretty penny it cost me," Nell admitted.

"You're not poisoning her?" Nell asked nervously.

"Nay," Nell laughed. "The sweets have been made with a bit of purgative. By the time the king reaches her that night Moll will have consumed enough of the treats, all of them I suspect, and she will be on her chamber pot purging her bowels for several hours at least. The king will find her most distasteful, I believe. He has a kind heart, but no man can remain long with a woman who is either vomiting or crapping herself into a frenzy," Nell finished indelicately.

Fancy giggled, and her giggles turned into laughter. She laughed until the tears ran down her face. Finally she managed to say, "I think that is a terrible trick to play, Nellie Gwyn, but 'odsblood, 'tis funny. I do not think I should like to have you as an enemy. But how can I help you?"

"The king will return to the palace most disappointed," Nellie explained. "He will look for you, but he will not find you in your rooms. I do not have rooms at Whitehall, but he will not come to visit me for he will not want to leave the palace again. So he will go to his own lonely bed. *Where you and I will be awaiting him.*"

"Both of us?" Fancy had never heard of such a thing.

"Both of us. *And quite naked,*" Nell said.

"I never," Fancy began, and then her voice died away.

"Of course you never knew about such things, but I would wager if you asked your grandmama she will tell you of such behavior, and more, Fancy. Men like the king enjoy an occasional bit of variety with their passion. For some reason although I do not understand it, the sight of two women kissing and caressing each other rouses them greatly. Let us give the king this *gift* on St. Valentine's. Our naughty behavior in comparison with Moll Davis's disgusting behavior will put her from the king's thoughts very quickly thereafter."

"I don't know if I could . . ." Fancy said slowly, thoughtfully.

"Are we not friends?" Nell said, and then she turned Fancy's face to hers and quickly kissed her lips. "Was that so awful?"

"You are a wicked lass when you want your own way," Fancy noted, "but nay, that was not so terrible. And I have been naked before my sister Maeve and half-naked with Cyn and Siren. But will not our touching each other arouse us, Nell?"

"Of course it will," Nell admitted, "but it will also set the king aflame with his lust for us, and it is he who will satisfy our desires. By morning he will be a most content and happy monarch. We will be deeper in his favor while Moll Davis's star will flicker out."

"Is she really that undeserving, or are you just jealous?" Fancy asked astutely.

"I am jealous," Nell admitted honestly, "but she is also a dreadful trull, Fancy. She sold seats to her friends when the king planned to visit her so they might see she was in his favor. They hid behind the drapes in her dayroom and saw the king arrive. They listened outside the door after she led the king into her bedchamber. When he learned of it he laughed, but he was not pleased."

"You told him?"

"Of course I did. She boasted to all who would listen that she would replace me in the king's favor. One of her friends bragged to one of my friends about the incident, and my friend told me."

"She doesn't sound very nice," Fancy replied.

"Then you'll help me?" Nell asked.

Fancy nodded. "But I am still uncomfortable with the touching," she said. "I never imagined girls touching each other."

"A stroke here and another there," Nell said airily. "His royal imagination will fire up, and 'twill be him we're both touching not necessarily each other. And I'll show you some clever tricks to please a gentleman that I'll wager you've never thought about," Nell promised. "The king will not have suggested these things to you because he enjoys pleasuring a woman best of all, but it doesn't hurt a lass to be skilled in the amatory arts."

"Do you like these *things?*" Fancy asked Nell.

"I do!" Nell replied with a grin, "And one day you'll have a husband who will be delighted that you are so clever."

"I will not wed again," Fancy said firmly.

"Of course you will," Nell said. "You are a lady born and bred, Fancy Devers. Your family will not be content until you are safely married once again. The king will surely see to it himself."

"Like he did with Castlemaine? No, thank you!" Fancy told Nell Gwyn. "Would you want His Majesty to marry you off, Nellie?"

Nellie laughed, but it was an almost rueful laugh. "Girls like me don't marry, Fancy. I'm a king's mistress. I have no family or personal wealth to recommend me otherwise. I'll always be a king's mistress, and I had best save my monies while I am. The day will come when I won't be a king's mistress, and with no man to care for me I'll have to look out for myself and my children. Not that the king won't help, for he always accepts his own. The Stuarts are like that, but you would know better than I because of your grandmum. She is still talked about at court. Ain't she amazing!"

"Would you like to meet her?" Fancy asked.

"*Me?*" Nellie was astounded by such a suggestion.

"Yes, you!" Fancy laughed. "She is really quite wonderful, Nell, and not at all high-flown unless, of course, someone annoys her too greatly. Her own father was a king in India, you know. His title there was Grande Mughal. Grandmama has never forgotten that she is the Mughal's daughter. Nor has she ever taken a backseat to anyone."

"I should hope not!" Nell said. "They say your grandmama is a very great lady, Fancy. I saw her once, you know. One winter she came to the theater. I was nothing but a little orange girl then. She was with your Uncle Charlie."

"She is in London now," Fancy said. "The next time she plans coming to an entertainment, I will tell you, and you shall meet her. But *after* we play your trick on your rival. I am not certain that even Grandmama would approve of what we're going to do."

"But still you'll help me?" Nell cocked her curly head, her little gamin face questioning.

"We're friends, Nellie," Fancy said simply. Then she said, "And I have to admit to being curious about those *things* you mentioned."

"I'd show 'em to you anyhow!" Nell said loyally.

"And I'll help you because I have given you my word," Fancy answered back. "Besides, I have to admit to being curious about how the king will react to finding us both in his bed." Then she said, "I wouldn't want the queen to catch us, though. Neither of us is like Castlemaine for we respect the queen. It isn't her fault the king has appetites she cannot satisfy. Stuarts are like that."

"She caught me once," Nell said with a chuckle, "although she didn't know who it was. The king cried off from visiting her on the pretense of being indisposed. She, good woman that she is, came with all haste to see if she could comfort her husband. Mr. Chiffinch burst into the bedchamber, and I never seen anyone so pale, I can tell you. *The queen is coming!* he practically squeaked, and dragging me from the king's bed shoved me behind the window draperies. Thank heavens, it was a moonless night, I can tell you, else I would have been seen as naked as the day me mother birthed me by anyone outside those windows," Nell laughed.

"But how did the queen know that the king had been with someone?" Fancy inquired, curious and understanding now why the king rarely entertained his mistresses in his own bedchamber.

"After Mr. Chiffinch had stuck me behind the draperies," Nell continued her tale, "he saw my slippers by the bed. He only had time to reach for one, which he tucked in his pocket. He tried to shove the other beneath the bed, but he did not quite succeed. Then as the queen entered the king's bedchamber, he was forced to withdraw. The queen is so very sweet with the king," Nell noted almost sentimentally. "She asked him what was wrong, and he pled indisposition of the head and chest. She suggested he remain in a warm bed and drink hot, spiced mulled wine. He thanked her for her solicitude and to cement his illusion he sneezed twice. It was a mistake. The queen stepped forward to feel his forehead to see if he was fevered, and her foot hit my slipper. She bent and picked it up. I was barely breathing, but I peeped through the drapes to watch what was happening. She turned my slipper over in her hands several times, then set it back upon the carpet. *I had best leave you else the little fool now hiding catch herself a chill,* the queen said. Then she turned about and departed the king's chambers. When she had gone, the king laughed softly, calling me back to the warmth of his bed and telling me that his wife was a good soul with a tolerant manner. It was the only time I have ever felt guilty with him," Nell said.

"I should have been so frightened," Fancy said. "It is a wonder that you did not swoon dead away."

Nellie laughed. "It isn't the first time I've been caught in a gentleman's bed," she said. "I just ain't never been caught by the queen of England. But I don't believe she ever knew who it was."

Fancy couldn't help but laugh heartily at Nell's tale. "Let's just hope she doesn't catch the pair of us on St. Valentine's night. Discretion, my grandmama says, is paramount in such delicate situations as ours, Nellie. Besides, I'm not certain the king's window draperies could hide the both of us, and there will be a moon on that evening."

The king was in a merry mood on St. Valentine's. He had ordered that everyone at court must be dressed in either red or pink silver or white for the entire day. He danced several times with the queen. He danced with Fancy and Nell Gwyn. When, however, a ladies' choice was called, Lady Castlemaine was closest to the king and quickly claimed him for the dance. He was not pleased, but gentlemen that he was he danced with her until the music ceased. Then he turned abruptly away and moved quickly across the room. She could not follow him without it appearing that he had deliberately cut her. So she moved back into a crowd where her cousin, the duke of Buckingham, stood. George Villiers shook his head wearily at his relation, his meaning crystal clear.

The king departed a little after one o'clock in the morning. Fancy and Nell hurried to Fancy's apartments, and with Bess's aid quickly bathed and changed into their nightgowns. Then bidding Bess a good night they slipped from Fancy's room where Mr. Chiffinch, always amenable to a bribe, awaited them. Wordless he beckoned them to follow him. He led them through a door in the hallway into a hidden interior passage. There were no lights of any kind within the narrow corridor, but for Mr. Chiffinch's lantern casting a weak flame ahead of them. Then suddenly he stopped, and another door sprang open. To their great surprise the king's bedchamber lay before them. They stepped through into the beautiful room with its painted ceiling and huge bed. Mr. Chiffinch smiled silently at them and closing the door was gone. The room was very quiet. Only the steady ticking and tocking of the clock on the mantel and the crackle of the fire broke the stillness.

"What if he doesn't come?" Fancy whispered.

"He'll come," Nell predicted with a grin in equally soft tones. "I got a message earlier this evening that Mistress Moll had to cancel her performance tonight at the theater. She won't be well enough to be any man's lover tonight. *He'll* be here soon enough." Pulling off her pink silk nightgown, Nell climbed naked into the king's bed. "Come on!" she encouraged her companion.

Fancy swallowed hard, then drew off the cream-colored nightgown she had been wearing, and climbed into the other side of the bed.

"We'll keep the coverlet over us until we hear him coming," Nell said. "It's a damned cold night even here in this palace with a fire blazing." She leaned back against the feather pillows. "I'm going to have a bed just like this one day," she declared. "A good mattress, plump feather pillows, and lots of satin, and down! Do all the gentry sleep this way, Fancy?"

"I don't know any other way for a bed to be made up," Fancy admitted slowly. "From what you say, I expect there is."

"I've slept on the floor many a time with not even a blanket to cover my arse," Nell said. "I've got a mattress in my own rooms that's filled with a mixture of sweet straw and lamb's wool. It's better than the floor, or a plain straw ticking, but this is wonderful!"

"How are we going to know when the king comes home?" Fancy wondered aloud.

"Don't you worry none," Nell said. "Chiffinch will let us know. I paid him a goodly bribe and promised him more tomorrow if he does his job for us."

"I must help with that part," Fancy quickly replied.

"I won't say no to it," Nell answered her.

The two girls dozed for a brief time, and then they heard a voice saying quite clearly, "He's coming, ladies!" But they saw no one.

Nell threw back the coverlet over them. "Now don't get all excited," she whispered hurriedly. "What we do means naught, Fancy. It's just to get him cheered over his disappointment at Moll's. Put your hand on my breast now." Nell rolled onto her side and began to stroke Fancy's thigh.

Fancy blushed furiously, but she knew that her friend had no evil designs upon her. It was just to tease the king from the ill humor he would be in as he came through the door to his bedchamber. She began to fondle Nellie's pretty breasts, even as Nellie's fingers started to trail through the dark curls covering her Venus mount.

The doors to the chamber opened, and Charles Stuart, the king, stepped into the room. His black eyes widened at first with surprise and then lit with pleasure at the sensual tableau before him. His two current favorites were naked in his bed. He watched fascinated for several long minutes as they caressed each other, their delicate little hands like white doves, flitting from breast to buttocks, to thighs. Suddenly the two girls knelt facing each other. They kissed, the lips that kissed his so sweetly kissing each other every bit as nicely. The king groaned, a sound of distinct pleasure, and began to quickly tear off his clothing without the aid of his valet who was nowhere in sight.

"Let's help him," Fancy whispered to Nell, and the two young women arose from the bed to give aid to their master.

He kissed them each in turn, his arms enclosing each supple waist as they unlaced his shirt, unbuttoned his breeches. They pulled his shoes from his feet, rolled his stockings down his shapely calves. Nellie fell on her knees before the king, and taking his manhood between her ripe lips, she began to suckle upon it. As she did, the king turned to kiss Fancy, his hands strongly kneading her breasts as Nell's lips began to have the desired effect upon him. *"Enough!"* he finally growled, and Nell stood up. He led both women to the bed. "Which one first?" he wondered aloud.

"Both!" Nellie said with emphasis. "I'll wager Fancy ain't never seen it done. Let us broaden her education, Your Majesty."

He nodded and lay upon his back. "Come, my adorable little colonial, and mount me as you would your stallion. I've taught you to do that. You shall ride me to a finish, my darling."

Fancy did as he requested, sighing deeply with satisfaction as the king's large manhood slid into her love sheath. She leaned back enjoying the sensation of his length and his thickness as she began to ride him slowly at first, then faster and faster. Her turquoise eyes widened with great surprise, and her lush mouth made a small and startled *O* as Nell knelt over the king's head, and he began to lick at her hidden treasures. And all the while Fancy pleasured his manhood, and the king pleasured her; the royal tongue pleasured Nell, and the royal hands played with Fancy's breasts. Fascinated Fancy watched as Nell pulled her nether lips wide apart for the king, whose greedy mouth was now feasting upon her pink flesh. Fancy and Nell both began to moan as their *crisis d'amour* approached. As their soft screams of utter and complete satisfaction filled the air, the king's passion erupted, and he gave a loud shout of delight.

The trio fell helplessly into a heap, their limbs intertwining. Their breathing was rough and quick. Finally it began to subside, and Charles Stuart, the king, put a loving arm about his two mistresses. He had had a wretched evening after he departed Whitehall. He had looked forward to a romantic interlude with Mistress Moll Davis, an amusing, if vulgar, little actress. He had arrived at her rooms to discover that the lady was in extreme distress and could not leave her chamber pot. Even the outer room stunk of shit. Moll was alternately weeping and accusing someone of poisoning her. He had heard Nellie's name mentioned, followed by a rather unpleasant word. The king departed hastily, wondering what it was about Moll Davis that had attracted him in the first place.

He returned disappointed to Whitehall and decided to seek out his adorable little colonial, but she was not in her apartments. He was now beginning to find his mood turning into a hot temper. He had already stopped at Nellie's rooms in the city before his return to the palace, but she had not been there either. Were his two favorite mistresses cuckolding him? He would certainly learn the truth of the matter, and if they were he would punish them severely. And then he had entered his bedchamber to find the two women awaiting him and behaving in a very lustful, naughty manner. His anger had vanished.

"My darlings," Fancy heard him say, "what an absolutely delightful surprise you have given me."

"We have been planning it for some time, Your Majesty," Nell answered coyly to him. "It is our Valentine's gift to you, for what else might we find to please a king?"

"Nothing better than this interlude, Nellie," the king agreed.

"We had heard Your Majesty had left the palace," Fancy said wickedly. "We feared to be disappointed."

"But I was certain you would return soon," Nell added.

"*Were you?*" the king chuckled. While he would never ask her, he suspected that Nellie had been responsible for Mistress Moll's distress tonight. "Indeed, my dear, your name was spoken to me in most unhappy circumstances. It is, however, over now."

"Is it, Your Majesty?" Nell asked softly.

"Aye," he told her. "You two naughty wenches, however, will have to assuage my deep disappointment, and it will take, I fear, much of the night." He turned. "Fancy, my precious, fetch the basin and the cloths. You and Nellie will reverse position this time."

"I have never," Fancy began, and he knew immediately what she was about.

"I know," the king said, "and I have so longed to have you do it. Having seen Nell perform, you are not shy, are you?"

"A bit," Fancy admitted, "but Nell will instruct me."

They each bathed their private parts, refreshing them for the next tour of pleasure that was to come. Nell poured them each a goblet of rich wine to strengthen them for their new bout with Eros.

"Tell her what to do," the king said to Nell.

"Just don't bite him" was Nell's advice. "You can lick it, and suck on it like a sweet, as indeed it is the finest sweet known."

Fancy knelt. It was the first time she had ever come quite so near to the king's manhood. Even at rest, and relaxed it seemed rather large. She could see his pendulous royal jewels, lightly furred, behind the stalk of his manhood. Gingerly she wrapped her hand about it and squeezed. He murmured. The sound was not one of pain. Her tongue slowly slid from between her lips, and she began to lick at him. Then as she grew more daring, she slowly began to draw him into her mouth. She licked at him again. She drew upon him hard. The flesh within her mouth began to thicken and grow stiff. Soon she found she could not contain him. His manhood pressed hard against the back of her throat, causing her to gag slightly. She suckled instead upon the tip. His hand touched her head, and she heard his voice telling her to cease.

Now Fancy positioned herself as Nell had previously, and the king's skillful tongue probed and pleased her even as Nell rode their royal master to a delicious finish. Once again they lay in a tangled heap, replete with their satisfaction. This time the king had not loosed his love juices with Nell. Instead he covered Fancy's slim fair body with his own big one, entering her a second time, pumping her vigorously until she was half swooning and so filled with pleasure that she thought she would surely die from his attentions.

Charles Stuart, the king, performed with enthusiasm until the hour of the false dawn, and until his two favorites were admittedly exhausted with his lusty attentions.

Mr. Chiffinch was called to lead the two now-clothed ladies from the king's chamber. He waited while Nell Gwyn dressed with Bess's aid and then brought her to her carriage so she might return to her own rooms in the city. Fancy fell gratefully into her bed and did not awaken until midafternoon of the next day.

Chapter

6

The court moved to Greenwich to celebrate the month of May. Jasmine had taken a small house for herself and her granddaughters. Fancy had her own apartments at Greenwich as she had at Whitehall. With Mistress Nell remaining in London for a time Fancy was now the most visible, and favored of the king's women. Her position was made even stronger by the fact that the queen obviously liked her. This public knowledge pleased Charles Stuart, the king, as well.

When one of the queen's ladies asked her how she could be so cordial to her husband's latest inamorata, Queen Catherine replied, "Mistress Devers is well born, unlike some with whom the king consorts. She has beautiful manners and certainly knows her place, unlike some with whom the king consorts." This last a clear reference to Lady Castlemaine. "She is sweet-natured, and has always been most respectful to me when our paths have crossed. And, then, her family has a history with the Royal Stuarts, do they not? She is more of a good influence on the king than many others. This is a mistress I can truly tolerate."

"But what if she should have a child?" the queen's lady asked.

"Of course she will have a child," the queen answered. "They all have children." *But me.* The two words went unsaid, but all with the queen heard them as clearly as if she had voiced them aloud.

Another of the queen's women pinched the questioner for her foolish thoughtlessness. The queen was barren, and all knew it.

And Fancy was indeed with child. The St. Valentine's bacchanal of wine and unbridled lust that she had shared with Nellie and the king had had its result. She had only told her grandmother of her condition. Cyn and Siren would be unable to keep her secret. Now she must tell the king, which was why she had come to Greenwich with the rest of the court rather than returning home.

Unlike Lady Castlemaine who remained at court as long as possible so that everyone might be certain of her condition, Fancy planned to withdraw from court in early summer. She would return to Queen's Malvern to have her child, but whether she would come back to the court she had not yet decided. She did not approve of the way so many of these highborn English children were raised, rarely seeing their parents, and being brought up mostly by servants who could be abusive and were hardly a substitute for parental guidance, and love. Lady Castlemaine's children were a prime example of bad behavior. They knew they were the king's children, and bastards or no, they were arrogant and demanding.

"I do not want that kind of life for my child, Grandmama," Fancy told Jasmine one afternoon as they sat in the little garden of her grandmother's house "You raised your own children. My mother certainly did, as did your mother in Scotland. I don't want to leave my baby in order to follow the court. I already sense the king is growing less passionate. He has begun to favor Nellie more, but I am glad. Nellie needs him very much, and he enjoys her impudence and wicked tongue. She is really quite merciless to those who find her wrong side. You must meet her before I withdraw from court. I promised I would introduce you to her. She knows all the gossip, and the stories, and admires you greatly."

"Of all the friends for you to have made at court," Jasmine laughed. "You might have made some valuable connections among girls of good families for future use, but instead you became the boon companion of a common actress from London's slums."

"You disapprove?" Fancy was surprised.

"No, strangely I do not, for everything I have heard from your uncle about Mistress Gwyn is not unpleasing. I just wonder why," Jasmine said to her granddaughter.

"Why? Because Nellie was the only person at the court who accepted me, Grandmama. I came from the Colonies, a widow, who thanks to a pair of gossiping fools, was surrounded by scandal and innuendo everyone was more than willing to believe. Despite my family connections, mothers and guardians of girls my age shunned me. The king sought to seduce me the first day I arrived at court. Since I did not dissuade him from bedding me shortly thereafter, I was hardly considered respectable. I am unlike my lady Castlemaine, who has been with the court her entire life, who is cousin to the king's close friend, George Villiers, the duke of Buckingham, a lady for whom there is never enough power, wealth, attention. I have no great ambition for power. My only purpose was to please His Majesty because he was kind enough to show me that passion is neither cruel nor violent but a lovely thing. I have been approached on two or three occasions by people seeking my influence with the king, but I turned them away. His Majesty and I have, as our hot passion for each other has waned, become friends. I will not endanger that friendship, Grandmama.

"Consequently Nellie Gwyn was the only person with whom I had anything in common at court. She understands I will not stay; while I understand that her entire raison d'être is to remain the king's mistress. Being an actress, even a successful one, does not offer Nellie the security she desperately needs. I am a colonial, Grandmama. Our society is less formal than here in England. We are more accepting of people, not judging someone for their lack of family or of wealth. There are some now powerful people in the Colonies who came as bondsmen. They have worked hard and earned the respect of those who chose to come to the Colonies. I like Nellie for herself, as she likes me."

Jasmine nodded. She understood exactly what her granddaughter was saying to her. "Who knows of your condition?" she asked Fancy.

"Just you, Grandmama. I will tell the king before we leave

Greenwich to return to London. I have decided to depart the court in June for Queen's Malvern. The child is due in November, I believe."

"You know when it was conceived?" Jasmine inquired.

Fancy nodded. "St. Valentine' night," she told her grandmother.

"How romantic and what a lovely tale to tell your child one day," Jasmine said with a smile. "It pleases me that the king chose to spend that evening with you. He is not an ungenerous man, and you will probably receive a title, a small income, and perhaps even your own residence. We must make certain that it is near the family in Worcester, or Hereford. When you have spoken with the king about your condition, I will speak to him about the remunerations you are to receive."

"No, Grandmama!" Fancy cried. "You are no whoremistress to bargain for me. I am surprised that you would even suggest it."

"By openly becoming the king's mistress," Jasmine said, "you have in effect spoiled your chances of ever marrying an important man, my dear child. If you do not intend to follow the court, but bury yourself in the country, then you must be rewarded for your time of service, and for bearing the king's child."

"Can I not just live at Queen's Malvern with you?" Fancy asked.

"Queen's Malvern is your uncle's house. I live there most of the time as I prefer it, but it is not mine. Your uncle, however, would hardly dispossess me. I also have the dower house at Cadby, your uncle Henry's estate. Cadby would be too small for us, and as for Queen's Malvern, you would have to ask your uncle's permission to reside there permanently with your child," Jasmine explained. "The king should really give you a small estate where you may live and bring up his child properly. If you think you can negotiate such an advantage yourself then I shall not interfere, but if you cannot, then someone must. The Stuarts are generous but must be reminded."

"Nellie says the king will see me married off, Grandmama, but I do not want that," Jasmine told the older woman. "I see what happened when His Majesty married my lady Castlemaine off to poor Roger Palmer."

"If Barbara Villiers had cleaved to her husband only instead of flinging herself back into the king's bed, not that he didn't encourage it at that time, her marriage might have survived," Jasmine noted in sharp tones. "If the king could find a husband that the family approved of, it might just be the solution for you, my dear."

"Shouldn't I have to approve, too?" Fancy said dryly.

"Then you would consider it?" Jasmine asked.

Fancy sighed. "I should have to get to know any gentleman who sought my hand in marriage well this time, Grandmama. The last time I foolishly chose a man because he was handsome and so very sought after by other girls. Before, *if*, I speak marriage lines with anyone else, I must know him, and I must like him. I am not certain that I believe in love anymore, Grandmama; but if I find a man who is kind, and can laugh, and will treat my child as a good father should, then I will consider marrying again."

"You must also have control of your own monies," Jasmine added. "This has been the rule in our family forever. Our women manage their own funds. It ensures we do not become victims at the mercy of men."

"I did not know that," Fancy replied. "Mama never said it, and it was certainly not a condition of my marriage."

"It should have been, but then your mother adored and trusted your father completely. Fortunately he never betrayed that trust, but he might have. She was very lucky. You were not, and only that Parker Randolph showed his true colors immediately, you might have been caught in a terrible trap forever," Jasmine said.

"I don't expect I have a great deal of fortune any longer," Fancy said. "Papa had already paid the Randolphs half of my dowry portion. The other half was to be delivered the morning after the wedding. Under the circumstances it never was, but the first portion remained with them as part of the agreement between our families not to reveal the truth of what had happened."

"It was a foolish agreement," Jasmine responded. "By making such an agreement, they tarnished your reputation. You were the innocent party in the whole unfortunate disaster. The bargain your father made allowed the Randolphs to protect their name in the Virginias. It was not enough that you were not charged with a crime you did not commit. The gossips ensured that your reputation was damaged, and I am not certain that some of that gossip wasn't started by the Randolphs themselves in order to protect their own name."

"It is over and done with," Fancy soothed her grandmother, "and almost a year later. I am here with you in England, beloved of a king, and happy. I feel more at home here than I ever felt in Maryland, though at first I was very homesick."

Jasmine reached out, and took her granddaughter's two hands in hers. "Dear, dear child!" she said, and her eyes filled with tears.

"Now, Grandmama, do not weep," Fancy gently chided her, and she squeezed Jasmine's hands in hers.

"Tell the king soon," Jasmine advised. "If his interest is indeed waning, you want to make whatever arrangements you can while his feelings are yet tender toward you," she said, gaining control of her emotions and becoming more practical once again.

"The passion has gone," Fancy admitted, "but we shall always be friends. The king says there are few with whom he is at his ease, but I am counted among those few."

"Keep his friendship, my child. It will be your most valuable possession in the days to come," Jasmine told her granddaughter.

When Fancy returned to the Greenwich Palace later that day she found the king and some of the court out by the river, picnicking upon the lawns overlooking the river. To her delight Nellie had arrived from London in her absence. She joined them, waving to her two cousins. Diana was escorted by the duke and marquis of Roxley. Cynara, however, was seated near the earl of Summersfield and looking most arch. Fancy always worried when she saw Cyn with Harry Summers. She remembered Nellie's warning even if Cyn chose to ignore it.

"How is London?" she asked Nell as she sat down on the grass between her friend and the king.

"Warm for May and beginning to stink," Nell answered. "On His Majesty's advice I have retired from the stage for the interim. Perhaps next winter I shall return. *And perhaps not.* You are blooming. The country obviously agrees with you, Fancy," Nell noted.

Fancy looked directly at the king, and smiled. "It does, but if I bloom, dear Nellie, it is for other reasons as well."

"*Ahhh,*" Charles Stuart, the king, said and a pleased smile lit his usually saturnine features.

"I hope that Your Majesty is pleased with me," Fancy said softly, and she smiled back at him. "I shall ask his permission to withdraw from the court some time in June, for I am not a woman to make a spectacle of herself under these circumstances."

"When?" the king asked.

"November, I believe," Fancy said. "Around the fourteenth," she concluded with a mischievous smile.

"*Ohhh,*" Nell had finally caught the gist of the conversation, and her hazel eyes grew wide. "*Ohhh,*" she said a second time.

Both the king and Fancy laughed.

"It was a most memorable time," he said appreciatively.

"Not for Mistress Moll," Nell said wickedly.

"I have never asked you if you were involved in that naughty prank, Nellie, my angel," the king murmured.

"No, you ain't asked, and I'm grateful you didn't," Nellie said quickly. "Besides, you had a far better time that night than you could have ever anticipated, didn't you, Your Majesty?"

The king laughed again, and nodded. Then he turned to Fancy. "I am very pleased by your news, my darling little colonial. I assume that you will return to your uncle's house to wait out your confinement?"

"Yes, Your Majesty, but I cannot remain at Queen's Malvern forever, imposing upon my uncle's hospitality, can I?"

"No," the king agreed, "you cannot. I must think on it, and then we will discuss it, my darling."

"Thank you, Your Majesty," Fancy said with a smile.

"Who knows?" the king answered her.

"My grandmother, and now Your Majesty, and Nellie," Fancy told him. "I would prefer no public disclosure of my condition. Let them speculate after I have departed, if Your Majesty would permit me that small favor. I came into the court in a cloud of gossip, and I should prefer to leave quietly."

"But I may brag on you afterward, may I not?" the king teased her good-naturedly.

"Agreed!" Fancy said with a small smile. The pain of her marriage no longer hurt her, nor did the memory of that terrible night. It had been wiped away in the arms of England's king, who had showed her that passion was a wonderful thing to experience.

"I have a gift for you," the king told her, and he waved his hand toward a footman. The servant came with a small covered basket and handed it to his master, bowing as he did so. The king opened the basket, and there inside nestled a black-and-tan King Charles toy spaniel. He lifted it out as the puppy wiggled with delight at having been noticed. "He was born on your birthday," Charles Stuart, the king, said.

"When was your birthday?" Nell asked, surprised to have missed this important event.

"April First, All Fools' Day," Fancy replied. "I did not think Your Majesty knew it." Then understanding dawned in her eyes. "My uncle, via Grandmama," she noted with a chuckle. She took the puppy, and cuddled it against her cheek. "How precious, Your Majesty," she sold. "I thank you. I have a Prince Charles black, white, and tan at Queen's Malvern. She is a female and will make a lovely mate for this fellow when he is old enough."

"What will you call him?" Nell asked her friend.

"Why *King*, of course," Fancy said laughing. "Don't you think it an appropriate name?" She handed the puppy back to the attending footman. "Leave him with his mother until he is weaned," she said.

"Yes, madame," the footman said and withdrew.

"I thank Your Majesty for his gift," Fancy told the king.

"I would have rather had jewels," Nell murmured, but they heard her, and laughed. *"Or my own house."*

"I shall give you a house in the Pall Mall," the king promised, "but not until you give me what Fancy is giving me, Nellie." Then he arose from his place between them. "I see the queen coming," he told them, and he walked off to greet his wife.

Nell Gwyn smoothed her pale green skirts. "Will you come back, Fancy?" she asked her friend.

"I don't think so," Fancy replied, "but if I ever do, it will not be to the king's bed again. The passion is gone between us, though we remain friends, and always will, dear Nellie, even as I hope you and I will." She reached out and took her companion's hand. "I will miss you, Nell Gwyn," she told the young actress.

To her own surprise, tears sprang into Nell's eyes "I ain't never had a real friend," Nell admitted. "When you go, Fancy, I will be alone again. Most women, especially in our position, is so mean and jealous. We ain't never been jealous of each other, or our place in the king's life. I call Castlemaine *the termagant*, but I have always called you *the good lass*, and you are. Do you think your babe is going to be a lad or a lass?"

"I don't know, but I think I want a daughter," Fancy said.

"I wonder if they will marry you off," Nell considered aloud. "And if they do, who will it be?"

"I have told my grandmama that I cannot have another marriage like the last. I must know the man I wed well this time."

"You never really told me exactly what happened when you was wed," Nell said, openly and honestly curious.

"Then I shall tell you now, Nellie, knowing that you will keep it to yourself and not gossip my tale about the court," Fancy said.

"Does the king know?" Nell asked.

"Yes, I was finally able to tell him after the rather wild night we shared together," Fancy smiled. Then she proceeded to share the unfortunate story of her marriage to Parker Randolph.

Nell listened wide-eyed, and when Fancy had finished Nell asked, "What happened to his other wife, Delilah?"

"The Randolphs wanted to revoke her papers of manumission, and sell her south, but my father would not permit it. She was, he said, as white as any of them no matter her African ancestors. He gave her a generous purse and sent her north to the Massachusetts Bay Colony so she might begin a new life free of any taint of her own history, or of what had happened that night. She was, of course, well educated. She wrote my mother, who wrote it to me, that she had arrived safely, had opened a small shop, and was grateful for my family's kindness."

"You sound as if you forgive her," Nell noted.

"She did me no harm," Fancy replied. "It was Parker Randolph who was the villain of the piece, Nell. Now you know the truth of the story."

"And in a way 'tis far more colorful than what has been bruited about the court," Nell chuckled. "I'll keep your secrets, Fancy. I'll not even mention to the king that I know."

They celebrated the king's birthday at the end of May, and then the court returned to London briefly before the summer progressed. Fancy had told her uncle and his wife that she would be leaving the court, and asked their permission to make her home at Queen's Malvern at least until her child was born. Barbara, duchess of Lundy, put her arms about Fancy, and said, "You may remain at Queen's Malvern as long as you like, Fancy. I should not be unhappy to have a child in the house again. We are your family, and it is your home."

Fancy thanked them, but she was curious as to any arrangement that the king was making for her. She had heard the story about how her aunt Autumn had boldly requested a title and a house from the king. He had seen her married off to the duke of Garwood, thus giving her what she had required of him without it costing him a ha'penny. It was only good fortune that the duke had been wildly in love with Autumn and not cared about her past liaisons. Now Fancy considered what the king would do for her.

Jasmine, dowager duchess of Glenkirk, was equally concerned. When less than a week remained before Fancy's departure, she could bear it no longer and made arrangements to see the king at Whitehall. He welcomed her warmly, but the dowager came right to the point.

"What," she demanded of him as she settled herself in a chair and accepted a goblet of wine, "do you intend to do about my granddaughter, Your Majesty? We are to leave for Queen's Malvern in five days' time."

"I will, of course," the king said, "provide for my child, madame, and for Fancy as well; but frankly I am at a loss what to do otherwise for her. She says she will not wed again though I should prefer that my child have a father in the house to help raise it."

"Of course Fancy will wed again," Jasmine replied firmly. "She simply wishes to know the man chosen better than she knew Parker Randolph, and knowing her story, Your Majesty cannot blame her for proceeding with caution in any remarriage. I would like to see someone in the vicinity of Queen's Malvern, or Cadby, so I may be near this granddaughter."

"There is one possibility in that vicinity," the king said. "Christopher Trahern, the Marquis of Isham. They call him Kit. He is a widower."

Jasmine thought a moment. "Isham," she said, her still-facile mind seeking to identify the prospect. "Trahern. Trahern? Good heavens, of course! His wife died in a fire that partly destroyed his home. Now what is the name of his estate? Riverwood Priory! Yes, that is it! There was talk that the marriage was unhappy, and there was a child, I recall hearing," Jasmine noted. "There was some unsavory gossip too that he might have killed the wife, but nothing came of it. He is a recluse and rarely seen."

"He was one of my companions in exile," the king explained. "He was loyal, and I never knew him to be unkind to anyone. Indeed just the opposite. If anything, Kit Trahern is too good."

"He is Your Majesty's age?" she inquired.

"No, he is five years younger. I sheltered briefly at the priory when I was escaping the debacle of Worcester," the king explained. "He was just a boy of fourteen, but with his father's blessing he came with me," the king said, a smile of remembrance on his face. "After I had been restored to my throne, Kit returned home. His father was still living but died shortly thereafter. I think he waited to see his son a final time. I had heard he had married. There was no need for me to reward him for he had his title, and his estates were still intact. I told him if there was ever anything I might do for him he had but to ask. He never has. He's a proud fellow, madame."

"Would he do a favor for you now that so much time has passed since you last saw each other?" Jasmine wondered.

"I am the king, madame," came the dry reply.

She laughed and bowed from the waist. "Forgive me, Your Majesty," she said. "It has been a very long time since I have dealt directly with the monarch of England. If you believe that this man would be a good husband for my granddaughter, Fancy, then I beg you to communicate your wishes to the marquis of Isham. I only ask that you tell him that the final resolution must be Fancy's decision. You will not force her to the altar, but if she would wed again, it is he you would choose for her husband and to act the father to your child." She paused, and then added, "And you will tell Fancy of your decision?"

"I will. And you, madame, will encourage her to this marriage for her sake, and the sake of my child?" Charles Stuart, the king, said.

Jasmine arose and curtsied respectfully to the king. "Our business then is concluded, Your Majesty. If you should come our way again, I hope to see you. I do not believe I shall return to court. My granddaughters are able to conduct their own lives without my interference now that they have had a Season in Society."

"Your presence will be greatly missed, madame," he told her gallantly. "You will bid the queen farewell?"

Jasmine curtsied again. "I will, Your Majesty," she said, and then she backed from his presence.

That evening the king joined Fancy for the last time. "I have a possible husband for you," he said. "An old companion from my days in exile." He kissed her round creamy shoulder while untying her silk nightrobe. His hands moved to cup her breasts in his palms.

"I don't want a husband," she murmured, her head falling back against his shoulder. "Ohh, that is nice!" His thumbs were rubbing against her nipples, which had grown most sensitive, but his touch was, as always, exciting. She pressed her bottom against his groin in response.

"Now that I pay her little attention, Castlemaine takes lovers she thinks are a secret. I don't want you doing that, my sweet colonial," the king said. "You are a very sensual woman, and I cannot believe that you will be content to remain celibate for the rest of your life. You are a woman who is meant to have a mate, and more than one child."

"How can you speak to me of another man while you prepare to make love to me?" Fancy asked him. She could feel his love lance hard against her left buttock. "Does the thought of me in another man's arms excite you, Your Majesty?" she demanded of him wickedly.

"Oddsfish, madame! That is the first time I have ever seen your claws," the king drawled, amused. "To the bed with you!" He gave her bottom a spank. "You will beg my pardon for your pertness before all is through this night." And the king unfastened his fine dark silk robe, throwing it off to display his nakedness.

Fancy had pulled from his arms, and, turning about, she shrugged off her pale pink silk night robe. Her hands moved to cup her own breasts, teasing him with the sight even as she backed towards the bed. "Is your choice as manly and as well made as Your Majesty?" she asked him. "Will I be pleased with his skills, and will you think of me in his arms when you are alone in the night?" Her little pointed tongue swept swiftly over her lips, and they glistened.

"Ohhh, bitch!" he groaned, and, reaching for her, gave her a deep passionate kiss that left her weak with the familiar knowledge of what was to come. Pushing her down onto the bed he stared at her for a very long moment. She was so outrageously beautiful with her pale skin, and her dark hair, but most of all those wonderful turquoise eyes that had first caught his attention and engendered his lust from the moment he had seen her. And now she was ripening with his child.

Fancy held out her arms to him. "Come, Your Majesty," she purred softly at him. "Let us love for the last time." She smiled warmly at him, and reaching up drew him down.

"I can't wait," he said abashed. "You would think I was a raw lad, my dearest colonial."

"We have the whole night for our good-byes, Your Majesty," Fancy said sweetly, and she opened herself to him.

Mindful of her condition he was gentle, but their shared passion was as great this night as it had been the first night they had come together. It surprised them both, but they realized that the influence of parting and the small history they now shared were in part responsible for the heat they were generating. Finally sated after several delightful bouts with Eros, they slept for a time. Fancy awoke first, and knowing the king preferred to end the night in his own bed she awakened him.

"You must go soon," she told him.

"Then let me tell you of my wishes, my darling," he said to her, taking her hand in his.

She sighed. "I will listen," she promised him with a small smile.

"Christopher Trahern, who is called Kit by his friends, is the marquis of Isham, Fancy. He is five years my junior, and as a boy followed me into exile. He is loyal. He is kind. He is a widower who may have a child. I am not certain. His lands are near to your grandmother. Knowing your history I will not force you into any marriage, but it would please me if you wed with my old friend. You need not do it immediately. Get to know him, and let him know you. But for your sake, and the sake of *our* child, my darling, I beg you to consider such a match." The king put his hand upon her belly, which was just now beginning to show a faint rounding. "What do you think? Is it a son or a daughter that you will bear me, Fancy?"

She shook her head. "I don't know," she said. "I realize some women believe that they do know, but I do have no sense of this child quite yet, Your Majesty. One thing I do know, however. Lad or lass, it shall not have a Stuart first name. You already have Charles, Jameses, a Jemima, several Charlottes, and an Anne. I shall give my child its own name, Your Majesty. With your permission, of course," she smiled mischievously.

"Indeed, madame, you have it," he said. "I regret that the mothers of my offspring lack originality when it comes to naming their babies. You have our permission to name the child what you will, but it shall bear the Stuart surname as well. I promise you it will be the only one of my children to have that surname. Given your grandmother's history with my uncle, I think it appropriate."

Fancy felt tears spring into her eyes. She caught the king's hand up, and kissed it. "Thank you," she said.

He arose from the bed that they had shared and wrapped himself in his dressing gown once more. "You will promise me to consider the marquis of Isham, Fancy?"

"I will," she said.

He bent and kissed her lips a final time. "Farewell, Frances Devers," he said, with a smile, and he waved his hand to her as he moved quickly through the door.

"Farewell, Charles Stuart," she called after him, blowing a kiss as she used his name for the first and last time.

The door closed with a finality, and Fancy lay back in her bed to sleep. He had always been a vigorous lover, but now that she carried his child, their shared passion had, it seemed, been truly exhausting. *I am glad I am going home to Queen's Malvern*, she thought to herself. The king had not offered her a residence. Would he if she decided she didn't like this marquis of Isham? *I cannot upset myself*, Fancy considered. *It will all be fine, and after my child is born the king will reward me I am sure.*

In the morning Cyn and Siren came to eat breakfast with her and bid her good-bye. They would be traveling with the court for much of the summer and were very excited about it.

"What a pity you had to get with child," Cyn said thoughtlessly. "You will miss all the fun of a progress, but then they say the king has but to stare hard at a lady, and she gets a baby in her belly."

"It isn't quite that simple," Fancy laughed, and tearing off a piece of freshly baked loaf, she buttered it lavishly. Then spreading plum jam over the bread, she began to eat it. "And, Cyn, there is little fun in just staring. And how did you learn I was with child? I have not told you."

"Everyone knows," Cynara said dryly.

Diana laughed. "You have become so very sophisticated and not just a little wicked in your months at court, Cousin," she said.

"And you, darling Siren, are still surrounded by two eager, desperate young men. When are you going to choose one as a husband? Your parents will be at Queen's Malvern this summer, and they will want a report on your progress. What am I to tell them?" Fancy teased the youngest of the trio. "Here I am with a royal bastard on the way, and a prospective husband already picked for me, and what of you?"

"*What prospective husband?*" her two cousins demanded excitedly.

"Some fellow who is the marquis of Isham," Fancy said.

"*Kit Trahern?*" Cyn practically shrieked the name.

"Yes, I believe that is what the king called him. He was with the king in exile," Fancy said.

"We saw him once in Worcester," Cyn said. "There is a rumor that he killed his wife for being unfaithful," she added.

Now there was something the king hadn't mentioned. Did he even know? "What does he look like?" She was nonetheless curious. The king hadn't said she had to marry this man.

"He is gorgeous!" Diana burst out. "He's very tall and very lean. His hair is every bit as black as ours is. I thought his hands beautiful and strong looking."

"His face is all angles and planes," Cyn added. "His clothes, however, were not at the peak of fashion. Indeed they looked rather lived in and somewhat worn. But Siren is right. He was handsome."

"Then I already dislike him," Fancy said.

"Why?" Diana asked, puzzled.

"I have already had one handsome husband. Handsome men are dangerous and usually quite stuck on themselves. But for the king's sake, because I promised him, I shall meet this marquis. But I will not like him if he is as handsome as you claim."

"Don't you want your child to have a father?" Diana asked.

"The king is its father and will not deny it," Fancy replied.

"Nay," Cynara said. "A child needs a father in the house to love it and mentor it. I never knew my papa until I was eight years old, and he returned with the king from exile. For eight years I existed without him. I do not wish a fatherless childhood upon your child, Fancy. The king can acknowledge it as his blood, but he will never be there to kiss its tears away when it scrapes its knee, or praise it when it learns to write its name upon its slate for the very first time. If this marquis is suitable, and not unpleasant toward you, then damn it, marry him!"

"Gracious!" Diana said, green eyes surprised by her cousin's outburst. Cynara rarely mentioned her early years.

"You have never been married to a cruel and wicked man!" Fancy told her cousins. "A man whose soul was as black as night though he looked like a prince from some child's tale. A man who was the scion of a good family but who was as dishonorable as the devil's spawn himself. Every girl in the Colonies pined after Parker Randolph, for he was as beautiful as an angel. But he was evil. *Evil!* You think that because you have been at court these past months that you are worldly, and all grown up, but you are not, my dearest cousins. You are babes in the woods. If either of you choose a husband who is too handsome, I shall lock you away in one of Grandmama's old trunks until I manage to learn if your chosen husband is a good man or a bad man. I shall not have either of you suffer as I did!"

The two younger girls looked stunned, but then Cynara, who had always been the boldest of the two said, "What is the mystery that surrounds you, Fancy? Though the talk about you has, for the most part, died away because of the king, there are still some who whisper."

"They whisper foolishness," Fancy said quietly. "Not even your father knows my tale. Only Grandmama and the king. One day I may tell you some of it, but for now you must accept what I say and trust me. You are both yet too young and too innocent—yes, even you, Cyn—to know my story. A man, however, should not be judged by his appearance alone, no more than a woman should. What is on the surface is not necessarily indicative of what lies beneath the surface."

"But did you kill your husband?" Cynara demanded, refusing to be denied.

"Of course she didn't," Diana said. "Can you have known our cousin for all these months and yet believe she would commit such a heinous act? Fancy is no more capable of murder than you or I are."

Fancy reached out, and touched Diana's soft pink cheek. "Thank you," she said. Then she looked at Cynara. "No," she told her. "I did not kill Parker Randolph. I will say no more on the matter. You would be wise to leave it at that. But I wonder if you are wise, Cyn. I hear gossip that Harry Summers would seduce you and has wagered among his friends that he will succeed."

"I know that he thinks he can gamble on my succumbing to his charms," Cynara said, her cheeks pink. "He also believes he will escape my net unscathed, but he is wrong. I did not come to court to seek a husband, although my parents believe that is why I am here. I came to have fun, and I have had more than my share of it. But from the moment I laid eyes on the earl of Summersfield I knew that I wanted him for my husband. I shall have him! Harry thinks to remain a bachelor, but he will not succeed."

"You play a dangerous game," Fancy said. "Nell says he is a daring and wicked fellow."

"I am good at games," Cynara said. "I never lose, and I will not lose this match either, Fancy."

"Will either of you come home this summer?" Fancy asked them.

"In late July you may expect us," Diana said. "My parents will probably be at Queen's Malvern when you get there. It is a tradition with the Leslies of Glenkirk to have an English summer most years. This is the year my sister Mair is to come to Grandmama to begin her lessons in how to be a proper lady. Grandmama promised when she was old enough she could come. My father has been reluctant until now, but my mother has finally overridden him."

"I look forward to meeting them," Fancy said. "My mother always spoke of her younger brothers with such fondness. And many of your mother's clansmen came to us when they first arrived in the Colonies. My brothers are off with several of the Brodies in an area south of the Virginias. They say it is a beautiful area, filled with mountains and lakes, and much like the Highlands."

"My mother is yet a bit rough for all her years as the duchess of Glenkirk," Diana said. "But she loves my father with every ounce of her being, and she loves Glenkirk. You will probably get on quite well with her, for like you, her early years were more simple."

"Have you bade farewell to the king?" Cynara asked, curious.

"Yes," Fancy said, and no more.

"Was it wildly romantic? Did you cry? Did he?" Cynara persisted.

"It was very romantic, as was all my time with the king," Fancy said, "and neither of us wept, I fear to tell you. We are much too grown-up. We both knew my time was over. We have become such good friends. And I have the greatest gift of all from the king. My child." She placed her hands over her belly and smiled.

"Sometimes you disappoint me," Cynara said.

But Fancy just laughed, as did Diana.

On the day Fancy departed Whitehall, Nell came to see her friend and to bid her farewell. "Will I ever see you again?" she asked Fancy. "I hate to lose my only friend."

"You aren't losing me, Nellie; I'm just going home," Fancy told her. "I shall write you and tell you everything that is happening in my life. And you must write to me."

"I can't write," Nellie said proudly, "nor read, but I shall hire a secretary to do my correspondence with you so you won't be ashamed to show my letters about."

"I shall never be ashamed to admit to our friendship," Fancy told Nell Gwyn. "And if you come to Worcester, you will come and see me."

"Ain't likely to get there," Nell said gloomily.

"We'll find a way to meet again," Fancy promised, "but I will not come back to court, Nell. I've had my fun."

"What did he give you?" Nell asked boldly.

"A husband, if I want him," Fancy laughed. "A marquis."

"No title of your own? *No house?*" Nell looked glum.

"Perhaps if I don't like the marquis he will honor me after the child is born. I have his permission to name it what I will, and its surname will be Stuart. 'Twill be the only one of his children to bear that name. It is because of Grandmama and my Uncle Charlie."

"Well, that's something but not much. Can't put good wishes with the goldsmith," Nell said bluntly. "I'll talk to him. Castlemaine thinks now that you're going she can rise in his favor again, but I'll see she don't. She ain't good for him with her bad temper, and all her demands."

"Be careful, Nellie. She's a bad enemy to have," Fancy warned.

Nell Gwyn nodded. "The queen don't like her, but she don't mind me. I ain't considered much of a threat," she chuckled.

Fancy laughed. "Keep them underestimating you, Nell," she advised. Then the two women hugged warmly, and Nell cried a few tears.

When Nell had gone, Fancy looked around her apartments. They were empty. The baggage was on the cart. Picking up her cloak, she looked about a last time. Then humming beneath her breath, she departed.

Chapter
7

Kit Trahern, marquis of Isham, sat alone in his paneled library. A letter from the king lay in his lap. He ran an impatient hand through his night-dark hair, and his silver gray eyes were troubled. He had not heard from the king in several years, and now this. What had brought him to the forefront of the king's memory? He wasn't rich or powerful. Why had the king decided that he was the man for this distasteful assignment? The last thing he wanted in the world was another wife. Especially a wife carrying another man's child.

He had been through that previously, and before it all ended so badly, it had almost broken his heart until he realized he had never loved Martha at all. But he could not refuse the king. From the moment the king had sheltered at the priory, as he made his escape from the Commonwealth's murderous justice, Kit Trahern had known that he would serve this king unto death. The choice to leave his home as a boy and follow Charles Stuart, the king, had been his. He had never looked back. What followed had all been his choices. Now, for the first time, the king was asking a favor of him. *He could not refuse.*

He looked at the letter again, and one thing caught his eye. The girl was a granddaughter of the old dowager of Glenkirk and Westleigh. He vaguely recalled meeting her once, or twice, at some social function or other that he had attended with his late wife. An elegant lady with elegant manners. And still a great beauty despite her advanced age. Kit Trahern sighed deeply. Perhaps the girl wouldn't be too bad, but a colonial? He swore softly. The king had written that she was a widow. He wondered how her husband had died? Defending his good name from the wicked behavior of a lustful wife? What the hell was the matter with women today that they could not be satisfied to marry, and settle down as women in the past had always done?

He had not thought to marry again. He had fully planned for his title to die with him. He had no one in the world any longer. His own father had married late, and his mother had died at his birth. His father had not bothered to wed again, satisfied he had a healthy heir. And when his father had died, he had wed with the idea of begetting a son, but his choice had been driven by his lust. Martha Browne was a wealthy landowner's daughter, but there was not a drop of noble blood in her veins, which he discovered too late. He had seen her riding her white stallion at a breakneck speed across a meadow and thought the beast was running away with her. By the time he caught up, he realized his error. They had raced together until the horses almost dropped. And she had laughed through it all, her pale golden hair blowing unfettered in the breeze. He had immediately fallen in love, or so he believed, and he began to court her eagerly.

Her family, of course, was thrilled. They had never anticipated such a leap up the social ladder for any of their children. Their commercial wealth could but take them so far with the right marriages in this and succeeding generations. But for their daughter to have bagged a marquis was incredible. Kit asked her father for Martha's hand in marriage and was immediately accepted. The wedding had been magnificent. But then he had discovered his bride was not the virgin he believed her to be. An accident when she was riding, she swore to him; and because he had wanted to believe her, he had. Their passion had been intense at first. Then he noticed that his wife was spending a great deal of time out upon that big stallion of hers. While she might go out angry, she always returned happy.

Finally suspicious, he followed her one day, and his worst fears were confirmed. Martha had a lover.

The man was a big brawny stableman employed by her father. The marquis investigated discreetly. He learned his rival's father had been a passing Gypsy who had seduced a dairy maid, resulting in the son who had grown up to work in his father-in-law's stables. Martha had been wild and shameless as she fornicated in her lover's arms. Kit Trahern felt a sharp stab of jealousy for she had certainly never behaved thusly with him. He had withdrawn quietly from the lovers' stable rendezvous. When his wife returned home that day, Kit had coldly confronted her with his knowledge. Martha had laughed boldly in his face. Then she had screamed at him that she was now with child! There was naught he could do about it. *Whose child was it?* How could she know until it was born, she mocked him. It could be his, or it could be Wat's brat. Reminding her that they had not been together for the past two months as she had been refusing him with one excuse after another, he denied paternity. Martha laughed again. So the babe was her lover's, she said, and her lover's son would inherit the Trahern name and estates. There wasn't anything he could do about it. Unless, of course, he was willing to publicly admit to being a cuckold. And she laughed once more.

It surprised the marquis of Isham that the rage he felt against his wife took the form of an icy cold. He confined Martha to her apartment. He threatened his servants with death if any of them allowed her out. He sent Martha's personal servant back to her father. He replaced her with his old nurse, a woman he knew was completely trustworthy. After a few weeks had passed, his father-in-law came demanding and blustering. What exactly had happened to his daughter? Kit Trahern told him the unvarnished truth of the matter in his own words. Allowed to see her father, Martha, yet defiant, admitted her adultery to her parent, demanding he set her free.

Shocked, the gentleman departed determined to first whip and then dismiss and drive off the stableman who had caused all his family's difficulties. But even he knew there was nothing he might do to help his daughter. She was, he told his weeping wife, an unrepentant whore. She had made her bed and now must lie in it. Any infant she bore would be fostered out in a faraway place. Martha would be divorced by her noble mate and returned to her family, if they would have her. Squire Browne was not sure he wanted his daughter back.

The stableman, who with his master's daughter had helped to cause the shameful situation, came to the priory. His back had been lashed raw by his master, but he was as defiant as his lover. He stood beneath her window bellowing for her, but the windows were barred, and she could not reach him. Finally the man wandered off, never to be seen again in the vicinity. That same night a fire began in the imprisoned woman's wing of the house. While the marquis's old nursemaid escaped the flames which had begun in Martha's apartments, the marchioness of Isham died in the conflagration that followed, along with her unborn child. Fortunately only that one small section of the house had been destroyed. It was not rebuilt.

The local justice and the sheriff came to investigate. It was determined that Martha Trahern had started the fire in an effort to escape her husband, so she might go after her lover. The old nurse testified she had seen the mistress lighting her bed curtains with the candle, and when she had tried to stop her, Martha had pushed her from the room, barring the door behind her. Martha was buried in an unmarked grave in the woods.

And now, Kit thought gloomily, he was being told he must take another whore for a wife. What had he ever done to deserve such a fate? But the king did say that his child would not bear the Trahern name, nor would it be entitled to inherit Isham. Isham would belong to the son that this woman would one day give him. As if he would even consider lying with the wench. He was hardly interested in another man's leavings. Even royal leavings. But if the king wished him to marry the girl, he would do it. It was, after all, the only request that the king had ever really made of him. One could hardly refuse a royal solicitation. His mind finally settled on his duty, the marquis of Isham rode to Queen's Malvern to set the date for his marriage.

"I have not agreed to marry you, or anyone else," the beautiful young woman he was introduced to as Frances Devers told him bluntly.

"His Majesty wrote me . . ." he began, only to be interrupted.

"I do not know what His Majesty wrote you, my lord," Fancy said haughtily, "but I was told the choice was to be mine in the end. I do not know you. I am certainly not ready to make that choice yet. Your lordship is certain to notice that I am with child."

"Isn't that why the king wished you wed, madame?" the marquis demanded. She was so very beautiful, but she was obviously stupid.

To his discomfort, Fancy burst out laughing. "This child will bear the surname of Stuart and be formally recognized by its father, my lord. Everyone at court knows I am to give the king another wee bastard. His Majesty hopes that I will wed for the child's sake. He does not want this baby raised as his others have been. He desires that this child have as natural a life as any country-bred child. Therefore, he hopes I shall take you for my husband that there be both a mother and a father in his child's world. There is nothing more to it than that, but the choice is mine."

"I see," the marquis answered her stiffly.

"I believe my granddaughter thinks it would help if you both got to know each other," Jasmine said quietly. "I understand that your lordship's first marriage was an unhappy misalliance. My granddaughter, by coincidence, suffered a similar fate. This already gives you something in common, does it not?" She looked directly at Kit Trahern as she spoke. He was handsome, but not in a soft or dissolute way. There was a hard male look to him. *If I were only young again*, she thought, then smiled to herself.

"Perhaps, my lord," Fancy suggested, "you would like to stroll with me in the gardens. The gardens here at Queen's Malvern are said to be particularly beautiful." She looked up at him. He was very tall.

"Very well, madame," he agreed, offering her his arm. Together they exited the little salon where the family was gathered.

Charlie, the not-so-royal Stuart, looked at his younger brother Patrick, the duke of Glenkirk, and said, "Well, what do you think?"

"He's a wee bit stiff-necked," Patrick observed.

"Just as your own father was, I suspect, when King James said he was to marry me," Jasmine laughed.

"What do we know about him?" Patrick asked. "What happened to the first wife?"

"He married beneath him," Charlie replied. "A wealthy man's daughter. The lass was a born whore, and he caught her at it. She set his house ablaze and died in the fire. There is probably more, but that is what was gossiped about. I suppose we might ask him. I don't want to see Fancy unhappy."

"There is nae shame to haeing this king's bairns," Flanna, duchess of Glenkirk, noted. "Perhaps Fancy would prefer nae husband."

"She's better off with one," Charlie said. "She has no title or even a home of her own. I'm happy to have her here for as long as she likes, but I do not think she will be content for long."

"Wouldn't the king give her a title and a house?" Barbara, duchess of Lundy, asked. "He has never been mean with his mistresses, especially those for whom he still harbors a fondness. Fancy is certainly in his favor whether she is at court, or not. And the queen approved of her as well. Why force her to the altar?"

"You will force her to nothing, for she is more like me than any of my granddaughters," Jasmine noted. "But I agree with Charlie. She is better off with a husband. There is little adventure left in the world now, I fear. I want to know Fancy is settled and happy before I die. If not with this man, then another. And remember, my dears, the choice is hers first." She looked past them through the windows, and into the gardens where Fancy now walked with the marquis of Isham.

"You are very beautiful," Kit Trahern told Fancy. "I did not know if you would be."

"Does it matter?" she asked him, curious.

He shook his head. "No. The king has asked me to wed you, and fair or plain I will obey, for I am the king's loyal man," the marquis told her. "When is your child to be born?"

"In November," she answered. "You are very handsome, but not in the way I was led to believe."

"Does it matter?" he mocked her and then was surprised by her answer.

"Aye, it does. My first husband had the face of an angel, and the manners of a courtier, but he was black of soul and evil. What of your wife, my lord? For I am told you are a widower as I am a widow."

"Beautiful, and a born trollop who died at her own hand," he said candidly. "How did your husband die?"

"At the hand of his slave mistress," Fancy said, having decided with her grandmother that this was a simple answer, and easy for others to understand. "On our wedding night," she answered.

He was astounded, but his curiosity overcame him. "Before or after?" he asked her.

Fancy understood him completely. "I was a virgin for the king," she said quietly, "and as I am sure you are curious as to why I did not save myself for my next husband, I will tell you. I was told the king was the greatest lover in the world."

"And was he?" Kit Trahern's lips twitched with amusement.

"I don't know," Fancy said candidly. "I have naught to compare him with, my lord. I will tell you that the king knows how to offer pleasure to a woman. Women are known to enjoy their bedsport, too."

"You are very frank, madame," he noted. "I am curious as to how you would behave if wed again. Widow you may be, but it would appear you have little practice at being a wife."

"I have absolutely no practice at being a wife," Fancy said. "I was educated to be one, but I have never had the opportunity."

"Will you return to court after your child is born?" he inquired.

"No," she answered him. "I never thought to wed again, my lord Trahern. I was sent to England by my parents to escape the scandal of my husband's murder. I went to court with my cousins, who are a year younger than I am. I attracted the king's attention, and the rest you may learn easily, for our affair was hardly a secret. No woman the king beds can have a circumspect life while she is in the king's arms. But I have no desire to return to court and be the new Castlemaine, spawning one bastard after another and struggling to maintain my position. I like the king. We are friends now. We shall always remain so, I expect, especially as we are yoked by this child that I carry. But I have no desire to involve myself in the Society of the court. Nor do I wish to fob my child off on servants. I will raise my baby myself, here in the country, where I will teach my child proper values and good manners. My child shall not be an arrogant little beast like my lady Castlemaine's brats."

"You have strong opinions, madame," he said. "On first inspection, do you think I should qualify as a proper husband for you?"

"I do not know you well enough to make such a judgment," Fancy told him, "but on first inspection you do not seem a bad fellow. Tell me why you married your wife, my lord, and be honest with me."

"She was beautiful, and I lusted after her," he replied.

"So, like me, you were drawn to beauty and did not see the rot below the surface," Fancy noted. "We begin evenly this time, sir, for we must both admit to being fools. There is no great rush for us to wed, is there? Let us take the time until my child is born to learn more about each other. Then, if we decide that it is right for us, we will please the king and marry."

"You are a proud woman," the marquis said, but his tone was laced with his approval. "And a clever one."

"You are a proud man," she responded, "but I see no reason for us to spend the rest of our lives unhappy, even to please a man whom we both love and respect."

Kit Trahern nodded. Then he surprised her, reaching out to take both of her hands in his. Raising them to his lips he kissed them, saying, "We have made, I think, a good beginning, Frances Devers."

"I am called Fancy, my lord," she told him.

"The king's Fancy," he said softly, and he laughed.

Fancy laughed with him and seeing them from the salon window Jasmine was well pleased. *This is right*, she thought to herself, and she smiled.

The marquis of Isham remained at Queen's Malvern for several days. He had never had a family other than his father. He found himself a little surprised to be drawn firmly into the warmth of the dowager duchess's brood. Whether Fancy or he had decided to follow the king's instruction and wed, Jasmine Leslie and her family had already decided for them. Kit Trahern rather liked being part of the dowager's circle. She was a sensible old lady, and he began to see that Fancy was much like her grandmother.

They spent a great deal of time walking, but her family would not allow her to ride now, which irritated her muchly.

"My family raises horses," she told him. "I am used to riding all the time."

"But not with a baby in your belly, madame. A wee bit of caution cannot go amiss," he said in reply.

"They like you," she told him.

"I know, and I like them," he said.

"Your home, Riverwood Priory, what is it like?" she asked.

"The house is probably the same size and very much in the style of Queen's Malvern, but I have not as much land," he explained.

"What do you do with your land?" she questioned him.

He drew her down upon a marble garden bench so they might see each other when they spoke. For the first time he saw that she had eyes like her grandmother, yet she very much resembled a portrait of another lady in the old family hall. "I have cattle, some horses, and a few tenants."

"Is it profitable?" Fancy wondered. He had gray eyes.

He laughed. "We do not starve, and I have no debts," he said.

"Land," she said, "is meant to be husbanded and made profitable, my lord. You must invite me to your home so I may inspect it. My papa always said I had more of a head for business than any of my brothers."

"Then," he teased her gently, "you are considering me as a husband, madame?"

"It is far too soon for any decision to be made in that venue, my lord," she replied sharply. "I simply wish to see your home."

"You had best come sooner than later, for I do not imagine that traveling will be good for you in a few more weeks," he noted.

She nodded. "And, too, my cousins Cynara and Diana will be coming home from court shortly. I would be here when they come. Diana cannot make up her mind about a husband, and Cyn plays a dangerous game with an earl who has the sobriquet *Wickedness*. My uncle Patrick is going to be very annoyed at his daughter, for he wants a son-in-law so he may cease worrying about her."

"Are all families like this? Concerned with one another to such a degree?" he asked her.

"I do not know of other families, my lord, but I know that this family does care deeply for one another. Are you uncomfortable with it?"

"Nay, I think for the first time in my life that I am truly happy, Fancy," he told her in a burst of ingenuousness.

She smiled warmly at him. "You are not nearly as cold and haughty as you were a few days ago. I think I may learn to like you, my lord, but do not hold me to that promise quite yet."

"My name is Christopher, Fancy, but I am called Kit. It would please me if you would use my name," he said.

"Even though I am nowhere near to deciding our fates, Kit?" she said, and her turquoise blue eyes twinkled.

He nodded.

"Then Kit it is," she agreed. *"Ohhh!"* A look of surprise suddenly crossed her beautiful face.

"What is it?" he asked, his look concerned.

"My baby!" Fancy cried. "I think I have just felt my baby!" She arose from the bench. "Take me to Grandmama, Kit! I would tell her!"

"Do not run, Fancy," he begged her, suddenly realizing that he was concerned for her well-being. His hand on her arm gently restrained her as they hurried into the house.

"Grandmama!" Fancy cried, entering the old hall where Jasmine sat sewing. *"Grandmama!"*

The old woman looked up and, seeing the look upon her granddaughter's face, stood and hurried to meet Fancy. "What is it, my dear child?" she asked anxiously.

"The baby!" Fancy cried excitedly.

Jasmine paled, and Kit Trahern quickly moved from Fancy's side to take her arm. "Nay, madame, 'tis all right," he assured her.

The two duchesses came hurrying up to them.

"What is it?" Lady Barbara asked.

"I think I have felt the baby move," Fancy said, her eyes shining with her elation.

"A fluttering like there was a wee butterfly imprisoned in yer belly?" Flanna Leslie said.

Fancy nodded.

"Aye, then," the practical duchess of Glenkirk said. "Ye've felt the quickening, lassie. All is well." Having borne her husband a goodly number of children, Flanna Leslie was considered the expert in such matters. "Sit down now, lass, and calm yerself."

The marquis of Isham watched as the three older women settled Fancy, bringing her a pillow for her back, a stool for her feet, a cup of her grandmother's tea to soothe her nerves. The only women he had ever seen in his household before his marriage, and now that he was again alone, were servants. And his wife had never interacted with other women as these women now did with each other. It was a revelation. Was this what it would be like if he and Fancy were wed?

And Fancy. There was another surprise. She was nothing like he had imagined at all. He remembered Barbara Villiers in the days in which they all shared an exile from England. Beautiful and bold Barbara with her haughty airs and her extravagant demands. Barbara who had shamelessly flaunted her position as the young king's mistress. Barbara with her violent tempers when she was denied anything upon which she had set her heart's desire.

Oh, the king had had other little flings. The tragic Lucy Walter who had been involved with him even before he left England, and had given the king his first son and a daughter. Unable to accept her inevitable desertion by her royal lover after their second child was born, Lucy took to drink and other men. When her little daughter died, her downward spiral accelerated. The king took his son, placing him with his mother in Paris for his safety's sake. Lucy died alone and quickly forgotten. There had been two other passing fancies for the king. Elizabeth Killigrew, who gave him a daughter, and Catherine Pegge, who gave him a son, but it was Barbara Villiers that Kit Trahern thought of when he considered a royal mistress.

But Barbara's star had been eclipsed and was waning now. The king's royal eye had touched upon another woman, and Barbara was, if the gossip be true, going to go the way of other discarded royal mistresses who had shone brightly in history. Fancy spoke of an actress, a common girl, but an amusing one, with whom she had shared the king's favor. Now this girl was considered the king's favorite.

He looked across the hall at the women gathered about Fancy. A colonial, but certainly of good family. Her manners were charming. Her beauty undeniable. She was sensible and good-natured. Intelligent. Other than beauty, she was nothing at all like Barbara Villiers. Yet they had both fascinated the same powerful man. The king would have certainly never given Kit Trahern Barbara Villiers to husband. That task had fallen to the unfortunate Roger Palmer, now divorced from my lady Castlemaine. Why then had the king given him Fancy Devers?

She is a good woman, the king had written. *Her heart is bruised, but not broken. She is free to love.* Well, Fancy hadn't been in love with the king, for she had told him so. They had, however, been in delicious lust for a time, she explained. It had, she admitted, all been very new to her, for she had been raised to believe one fell in love, married, and there was an end to it. Yet it hadn't been that way for her at all. Nor had it been for him, and he certainly understood *being in lust* as Fancy had so quaintly put it.

That was how it had been for him with Martha, but he hadn't understood it at first. Martha had liked him well enough in the beginning for he was a new toy for her. Her family's excitement at such a large step up the social ladder had been responsible in part for their marriage. Lust and ambition. It had proved a deadly combination for Martha Browne.

Kit realized now that the king hadn't known that his wife was with child by another man, else he would not have sent him a discarded mistress, who was to bear a royal bastard, to take as a second wife. How could the king have known the whole story when it had been kept secret to protect the Trahern name? There was a macabre humor to the situation, Kit thought wryly. But it was not to be as easy as he had assumed, for Fancy was not particularly eager to remarry. He was, Kit laughed to himself each time he thought of it, too handsome for her taste. She did not, it seemed, trust handsome men. And given her history, she certainly had good reason. All his life he had been admired for being fair of face. Now to suddenly find himself being rejected for that handsome face was most humorous.

Fancy wanted to see Riverwood Priory. The marquis of Isham made arrangements with the dowager duchess to accompany her granddaughter when he returned to his home, which was some ten miles across country from Queen's Malvern as one went northwest toward Hereford. Fancy and Jasmine traveled by coach, accompanied by both Bess and Orane. The marquis of Isham rode alongside the vehicle as they went. The dowager's carriage was large, well padded, and well sprung.

Riverwood Priory was set on a rise just above a small branch of the River Severn. It had once been home to a religious order but had been confiscated during the reign of King Henry VIII. It was purchased by the Trahern family who lived nearby for their family seat as the house they inhabited was too small. It was similar in design to Queen's Malvern, being built of red brick with several soaring chimneys and covered with green ivy. It had many tall, leaded, paned casement windows. Coming from the main road, they drove through a small forest down a track that led to the house with its river view.

"How lovely!" Jasmine said as their coach drew up before the house. "A bit isolated, but that can be a good thing in times of trouble."

"It is an attractive enough house," Fancy said. "The interior, however, is apt to be woefully old-fashioned. Remember, Kit's mother died at his birth, and until the unfortunate Martha, whom I suspect was driven more by lust than housewifery, there was no woman in the house."

"You are probably correct," her grandmother said, "but an old-fashioned interior can be modernized."

"The marquis is not a rich man," Fancy replied.

"But I am a rich woman," Jasmine said quietly. "If you marry this man, I intend to see that you have every comfort you need, dear girl. And I shall see your father redowers you properly. Those monies we will invest, and they shall be yours alone."

"I have made no decision regarding Lord Trahern," Fancy answered.

Inside the house was indeed old-fashioned, but it had a lovely warmth about it, and the elderly servants were obviously devoted to their master. Orane and Bess quickly obtained all the gossip and with very little effort on their part. The marquis's servants were curious too, and so they were willing to chatter.

"The handsome milord tells the truth," Orane told her mistress. "The first wife was little better than a camp follower, and because he is a good man, he did not catch on right away."

"They say," Bess continued, "that she started the fire in her rooms in an effort to escape her confinement, so she might chase after her lover. But the blaze spread more quickly than she had anticipated, and so she died. The old nursemaid only escaped because she was pushed from the bedchamber when she tried to stop the lady. She died shortly afterward from the shock of what had happened, the other servants say."

"They were lucky the rest of the house was saved," Orane noted. "The marchioness's apartments, which were two rooms, and the salon below it were destroyed. The marquis said he won't rebuild them."

"I think he don't want the ghost of her having a place to haunt," Bess said. "If her rooms aren't there, she can't be there."

"Maybe she haunts the rooms that are the marchioness's," Fancy suggested mischievously. "The chamber where she was confined, Kit tells me, weren't those. He says he was so angry when he discovered her behavior that he put her in a part of the house that had not been used in some time. It was an original part of the priory where the nuns used to live."

"'Tis a wonder the nuns didn't haunt *her*," Jasmine said, laughing.

They remained at Riverwood Priory for three days. Fancy and her grandmother were shown the entire house by the marquis. Jasmine particularly liked the old Great Hall with its fireplaces and tall stained glass windows. Once it had been a church for the priory. Kit's ancestors had added the fireplaces when they had purchased the house.

"It is a good house for a family, and it is just waiting for one,"

Jasmine told her granddaughter as they returned home. "I knew little more about my second husband when I married him, and we were divinely happy, dear girl. You have already discovered more of Kit's character than you knew about Parker Randolph."

Fancy nodded. "I have. He is a good man, but I want something more than that, Grandmama. I want what my parents have. I want love."

"Then you are wise to wait until after your child is born," Jasmine replied calmly. "As for me, I like Kit Trahern, but the decision must be yours, Fancy. Yours alone."

"I do like him," Fancy admitted, slowly.

"That is a good beginning," her grandmother said.

Cynara and Diana arrived home on August first. Both looked very elegant and very sophisticated. They were full of court gossip. The three cousins hugged enthusiastically beneath the eyes of the elders.

"How gorgeous you both look!" Fancy said.

"How fat you look!" Cynara replied.

"*Cyn!*" Diana squealed.

"Well, she has gotten fat," Cynara answered.

"I am having a baby, remember?" Fancy responded, laughing. She linked her arms through her cousin's arms. "Now, come and tell me everything that has happened since I left," she said.

The trio sat down on a bench in the garden. It was a warm day for August, and Jasmine had said there would be a storm before night.

"Well," Cynara began, "Castlemaine rejoiced very publicly after your departure. She was certain that the king would come back to her bed, and she was very surprised when he didn't."

"He favors Nellie?" Fancy said.

"Very much so, and there are several highborn noses very much out of joint including one countess who shall remain nameless and who attempted quite brazenly to seduce him," Cyn replied archly.

"But not to be defeated," Diana continued, "Castlemaine put her cousin, the duke of Buckingham, up to approaching Nellie in an effort to spoil her position with the king."

"Nellie boxed his ears publicly!" Cyn said, and they all laughed.

"What did Buckingham do?" Fancy asked.

"He laughed, too, and begged Nellie's pardon, which she generously gave him," Diana told Fancy. "You were right, Fancy. She is a very amusing girl, and she is good for the king. He enjoys her saucy and irreverent ways, and she is wise enough not to deliberately make enemies."

"There are always some people at the court who get above themselves," Fancy said. "And some into whom much pompousness has been bred. They cannot, they will not, change. That is why someone like Nell Gwyn is refreshing. And she has a kind heart, as does His Majesty."

"Do you ever regret leaving?" Cyn asked her. "If you had remained, you could have eclipsed Castlemaine one day, Fancy."

"It only began," Fancy told her cousin, "because you said he was the finest lover in the world, and I was curious. I never sought to be a king's mistress, nor to remain one."

"But what will happen to you and your child?" Diana asked. Her lovely green eyes filled with concern.

"As you both know, the king has chosen a husband for me," Fancy said, "but whether I will accept his choice is to be my decision."

Her two cousins were immediately full of questions, which Fancy answered as she could. While they had seen him once, neither of them had ever met the marquis of Isham. They were both eager and curious to do so.

"He will be here on Grandmama's and Diana's birthday," she told her excited companions. "You will get to meet him then."

"Will you wed him?" Cyn demanded to know.

"I don't know yet," Fancy said.

"Do you like him?" Diana wanted to know.

"Yes, I do," Fancy admitted.

"Is he rich?" Cyn asked.

"No, not particularly," Fancy responded.

"Well," Cyn said, "the king might have chosen a rich husband for you. After all, you are having his child!"

"I don't need a very rich husband," Fancy said. "Grandmama says that we girls are all rich enough in our own right."

"Yes, that is so," Diana considered.

The marquis of Isham arrived and, looking at the three cousins, declared, "I know Fancy is without the family birthmark, but how on earth do people tell you other two apart? You all look like the lady in the hall above the fireplace."

"Diana's little mark is on the left, and Cyn's on the right," Fancy explained. "We also have different colored eyes. Diana's are green, and Cyn's are blue." Then she mischievously closed her own eyes tightly. "Tell me, my lord, what color are mine?"

"The blue of a Persian turquoise, as are your Grandmama's," he answered her without hesitation.

Fancy's eyes flew open with surprise. He had actually known! "How . . ." she began, but looking deeply into those eyes, he put a restraining finger on her lips.

"Because everything about you fascinates me, madame," he told her. "Why are you so surprised, I wonder?" Then removing his finger he kissed those lips gently, quickly.

"*I shall swoon!*" Diana murmured softly.

"*Bold*" was Cynara's low opinion. "*I like him.*"

"Well, mayhap one of them will be wed before year's end," the duke of Glenkirk said to his mother. He then turned to Diana. "Daughter, hae ye nae found a man to please ye yet? Surely there must be one good fellow I may call son-in-law at the Stuart king's court."

"Papa! This is not something that can be hurried!" Diana said.

"I saw yer mam and wed her the same day," the duke grumbled.

"Aye," Diana replied. "Because you wanted Brae, and that is no secret! Aren't you lucky that my mother fell in love with you?"

The duchess of Glenkirk laughed, and said, "Aye, Patrick, aren't ye lucky that I did?"

"I'll nae deny it," Patrick Leslie answered them with a grin. "Now, miss," he said to his daughter, "dinna think to lure me off the point. Hae ye found a man to wed?"

"She had a dozen, or more suitors, Uncle, who would gladly have her," Cynara said laughing. "She was so sought after that they called her *Siren*. She sent them all off but two in midwinter. Now my cousin cannot make up her mind."

"Telltale!" Diana said.

"Is this so?" Patrick Leslie demanded to know.

"Yes," Diana said.

"Well, then, lassie, the problem can be easily solved. Tell me who yer favorite is among these two laddies. I'll make yer choice for ye. 'Tis a father's duty to see his lasses wed and wed well."

"Grandmama!" wailed Diana.

"The women in this family make their own choices, Patrick, or have you forgotten that?" Jasmine gently reminded her son. "I am certain Diana will make her decision soon."

"Well," the duke huffed, "do I get to meet any of these fine lads before my daughter chooses?" He had forgotten what it was like being overruled by his mother. At Glenkirk he was never overruled, except perhaps by his wife, but she did it privately.

"We are not going back to court until December," Diana said. "You'll be back in Scotland by then, Papa."

"It's the Roxley boys, Uncle," Cynara said wickedly. "Twin brothers. A duke and a marquis. Uncle Charlie has invited them to visit. They live in northwest Herefordshire."

"I didn't think you had time to be bothered with my doings," Diana said sharply. "You spend so much time stalking after the earl of Summersfield, Cyn, it's a wonder you know what I do, or whom I favor."

"Summersfield?" Charlie, the not-so-royal Stuart, said. "He has a bad reputation, Cynara. I thought you were wiser than to chase after a man like that."

Cynara gave her cousin Diana a venomous look. "Now who's the telltale?" she demanded to know.

"Family," Fancy said softly to the marquis of Isham, "isn't it wonderful, my lord? What think ye now of a family of women?"

"Very dangerous, madame," he said and grinned.

The summer ended, and autumn came again. This year Fancy was not homesick for Maryland. Indeed, she hardly thought of it at all anymore. Her life was in England. While Diana and Cynara remained her companions, she found more and more of her time being taken up by Kit Trahern. He spent more of his time at

Queen's Malvern these days than he did at Riverwood Priory. The Leslies of Glenkirk had gone north to Scotland again, but before they departed, leaving behind their second daughter, Mair, Patrick Leslie had taken his niece aside.

"Yer a clever lass like most of the women in this family," he said to her. "The Stuarts hae nae brought luck to the Leslies, but yer nae a Leslie, nor was yer mam. Ye like this king for ye hae said it. If he thinks this marquis of Isham is the man ye should wed, then lassie, wed him! A lass is nae good wiout a husband, and ye hae the wee bairn yer carrying to consider. Better it grow up in a house wi 'a man to call its da. Though he hae been gone lo these many years, I still miss my father." Then the duke of Glenkirk had kissed his niece. "I like the laddie," he told her.

And her uncle Charlie, the not-so-royal Stuart, liked Kit Trahern as well and made no pretense about it. For that matter, her entire family liked him. But hadn't her family in Maryland liked Parker Randolph? Well, perhaps her father had had his reservations, but when her mother had said if she loved the Randolph boy, and he her, then they should wed, Kieran Devers said no more. Of course Parker hadn't loved her. What he had loved was her dowry, and the knowledge he thought would bring him more of her family's gold.

Kit Trahern, however, had made no declaration of love toward her. He had said that he would wed her because it was his duty to obey the king's wishes. It might not be very romantic, but at least he was an honest man, Fancy thought. Parker Randolph had swept her off her feet with sweet words and passionate kisses that had left her both breathless and aflame. She had since learned that men who kissed well could generally leave you breathless, and knowledge had the tendency to bank the fires of passion. Her uncle Patrick's words weighed on her. Every child did deserve a father, and while the king was more than willing to accept his responsibility in the creation of this child, he would not be there to love it or raise it. But the marquis of Isham could be if she would just give him her approval.

On a late October night she sat alone with her grandmother in the old family hall. "Is it wrong to want to be loved, Grandmama?" she asked Jasmine. "I know I must put my child first in this matter, but can we not both get what we need?"

"Ahh," Jasmine said. "You wonder if you should wed the marquis."

"Should I, Grandmama?" Fancy asked.

"What I think does not matter, my dear child," Jasmine told Fancy. "But perhaps this will help you to make up your mind. Are you aware that Kit has fallen in love with you? I have watched it happen over these last few months, but you have been so concerned with yourself, and your past, that you have not seen it happening. Nonetheless it has."

"Kit Trahern is in love with me?" She was surprised. "How can he be in love with a woman ripe and about to deliver another man's child, Grandmama? You are surely mistaken." She suddenly felt very distraught by her grandmother's revelation. Though she did not want to believe it, why would Jasmine say it if it weren't so?

"My dear, I haven't the faintest idea of why he is in love with you. That is something you would have to ask him. I have lived in this world for seventy-eight years now, and I still do not pretend to understand the human heart, Fancy. But I know love when I see it, and Kit Trahern is in love with you."

"Oh my!" was all Fancy could say. But did not her own heart feel lighter with this knowledge? She trusted her grandmother more than anyone else she had ever known. If Jasmine Leslie said the man was in love with her, then it must be so. But what was she to do about it?

"Tell him how you feel," her grandmother said in reply to Fancy's unspoken question.

"Tell him what?" Fancy fenced.

"That you love him, too," Jasmine answered her.

And the simple truth spoken by the old woman burst upon Fancy Devers. She did love Kit Trahern! "I don't know how," she admitted to Jasmine.

"You will find a way, my child," Jasmine assured her.

On the morning of the fourteenth of November, Fancy Devers went into labor with her child. She laughed aloud with the knowledge that it was exactly nine months since she and Nellie had entertained the king together on the Valentine's night. She told her grandmother the story now, and Jasmine laughed, too.

"What a pair of naughty wenches you were," Jasmine chuckled.

Fancy's labor was relatively easy until late in the afternoon. The sun had already set, and the pains now began in earnest. Her aunt and her grandmother remained with her, but her uncle, Bess, and her cousins were forbidden her bedchamber less the sight of her labor frighten them. Orane arrived to help, announcing, "The marquis is in the hall, and pacing back and forth with your uncle as if he had planted this seed himself." And the Frenchwoman laughed. In the hour before midnight, Fancy finally birthed her child.

"It is a girl," Jasmine said, smiling. "A fine wee girl!"

"Is she all right?" the exhausted young woman asked. "Let me see her, Grandmama!" She could hear the baby's cries.

"You must pass the afterbirth first, and while you do, we will clean her free of the birthing blood, and make her presentable for her mama," Jasmine said.

Finally the birth concluded, Fancy was washed with warm perfumed water, put into a fresh clean night robe trimmed with lace, and settled back upon her pillows. Jasmine herself placed the swaddled bundle into her arms. Fancy looked down at the baby girl. Her eyes were very dark blue and would probably be black one day like her father's, but other than that there seemed little to remind her mother of the king who had created the infant. The baby had a headful of dark hair. She looked directly at her mother as if to say, "So here we are at last." Orane had gone into the hall to tell those assembled of the birth.

Now they came, her uncle Charlie, Cynara and Diana, Diana's little sister, Mair, who had recently joined the household. They cooed and exclaimed over the baby, but Fancy's eyes went past them, seeking someone else. And then he was there. Jasmine shooed her family from the bedchamber as Kit Trahern sat down on the edge of Fancy's bed and taking the baby in his arms looked down at her.

"What are we to call her?" he asked Fancy. "Is she to be Charlotte or Anne or Jemima?"

"What was your mother's name?" she asked him.

"I never knew my mother. She died at my birth," he said.

"But what was her name, Kit?"

"Christina," he said. "I was named for her."

"Lady Christina Stuart," Fancy said. "Do you like it?"

"Aye," he nodded. "I like it."

"Stuart for he who gave her life, and Christina for the father who will raise her," Fancy told him. "I love you!"

"I know," he replied quietly.

"*You know?* How could you know? I didn't know! Not right away," Fancy cried.

"I knew. I don't understand how, but I knew," he told her.

"You love me, too!" she said, her teeth catching at her lower lip with nervousness as she spoke.

"Aye, I love you, Fancy Devers! I have since the first moment I laid eyes on you, though I shouldn't have," he said.

"*Why not?*" she demanded.

"Because I had a beautiful wife who betrayed me, who carried another man's child. You are a beautiful woman who was a king's mistress and was to bear that man's child. What madness to fall in love with such a woman." His silver eyes met her turquoise ones. "But love you I do, my darling."

"I know now that I never loved my first husband," Fancy said to him. "And I never loved the king. Not in the way I love you, Kit Trahern, but understand that the king will always be my friend. I don't want you to be jealous, or misunderstand. If we wed . . ."

"*When we wed* . . ." he corrected her, placing the baby back in her arms.

"I will always be faithful to you, Kit," Fancy promised him.

"And I to you, Fancy," he reassured her. "Now, I think that December first would be a grand day to marry. Do you?"

"Aye, my lord, I do," she agreed, and then they kissed, as Lady Christina Stuart watched them from the crook of her mother's arms before yawning and slipping into slumber.

Part Two

ENGLAND, 1667–68

SWEET SIREN

Chapter

8

For Diana Leslie, the year 1663 was a year of firsts. The wars in England were over. The Commonwealth was toppled. The king was restored to his rightful place on the thrones of England, Scotland, Ireland, and Wales. And for the first time in her life, she met her father's family, discovered she had many cousins, and determined that her speech was strange. It was the first time in her life that she perceived ladies wore shoes every day, and not just to kirk, or church as it was called in England.

In all her almost eleven years, Diana Leslie had only been off her father's lands to visit her mother's Brodie relations at Killiecairn. The Brodies were a noisy, quarrelsome group of clan folk, but they were also kind and plainspoken, especially Una Brodie who was her aunt. Una always seemed to find a fresh-baked scone or oatcake for her Leslie niece. Una told wonderful stories about Diana's mother when she was a little girl. She always ended these tales saying, "Yer nae in the least like Flanna Brodie, who was as naughty a lass as the divil makes. Nay, my wee Diana, yer the best little lass I hae ever known. It canna be the Brodie in ye. So it must be the Leslie and the Gordon in ye."

It had been four years since she had last seen Una Brodie, for in the summer of 1663, Diana Leslie, her parents, and her seven siblings left her childhood home at Glenkirk Castle to travel south into

England. It had been many years since Patrick Leslie, the duke of Glenkirk, had ventured from his holding. His wife had been out of their eastern Highlands only once before to Scone. Their children had never been.

The further south they traveled the more crowded the roads became with people, carts and animals. The eight offspring of the duke gazed with surprise at the first towns they had ever seen, then in utter amazement at the great city of Edinburgh with its castle, which was many times the size of their own Glenkirk. Their great-grandmother's second husband, the earl of Bothwell, had once been imprisoned in that fortress. He had escaped, and scaled his way down the sheer cliffs to safety. He had, their father told them, been called the uncrowned King of Scotland. His first cousin, King James VI, was very afraid of him.

"Why?" young James Leslie, the duke's heir asked his father.

"Well," Patrick explained, "puir King Jamie hae been taken from his mam. He was raised by the gentlemen of the kirk, and their wives. He hae been taught to be a-feared of his own shadow, the better for his keepers to control him. Bothwell was everything puir Jamie wasna. He was tall, and handsome. He was clever. He was educated far in advance of his time. And he was gallant. The puir king was none of these. His royal keepers convinces Jamie that the earl of Bothwell was his enemy. He nae was, but finally he was put to the horn in Edinburgh, and exiled. My grandmother joined him. They lived happily every after," the duke concluded with a smile.

Diana Leslie was never sure her father was telling them the complete truth, or if he was simply telling them a tale to keep them all amused. Like the story she had always been told of Bothwell's bones being put with her grandmother's bones in the same coffin returned from Italy, and buried in some secret place on the Glenkirk lands. She, and her elder twin brothers had been looking all of their young lives for that grave, but they had never found it.

And suddenly they were over the border into England. It didn't appear at first to be much different from Scotland. After some days of travel they arrived at Queen's Malvern, and another first. Diana met her paternal grandmother.

Diana remembered how warmly her grandmother's family had welcomed them. They had settled into an English summer, which had been unlike any summer Diana had ever known. Another uncle, Henry Lindley, the marquis of Westleigh, had come from an estate called Cadby with his wife and brood to meet them. Henry Lindley was the eldest of her grandmother's five sons. It was all a bit overwhelming, Diana thought, remembering all the names and how exactly she was related to everybody. They had been at Queen's Malvern for the month of July. In mid-August, the Leslies of Glenkirk would be returning north to Scotland.

Diana had made the first real female friend she ever had that summer. Her cousin, Lady Cynara Stuart, was only two months older than she was. Everyone remarked how much alike they looked and pointed to a portrait in their grandmother's favorite room, the old family hall, that the two girls resembled. It was of their grandmother's grandmother, a lady named Skye O'Malley.

And then there was the Mughal Mole. Their grandmother had it. So did Diana and Cynara. The only difference being that Diana's mole was beneath her left nostril above her lip, and Cynara's was beneath her right nostril above her lip. Cynara knew all the family gossip and was more than delighted to share it with Diana.

And then just before Diana's eleventh birthday, a date she discovered that she shared with her grandmother, the most wonderful thing happened. Her grandmother announced to her parents that she wanted Diana to remain with her at Queen's Malvern. Her father had naturally protested, but her mother had said yes. Flanna Leslie spoke more eloquently than Diana had ever heard her speak before. Unlike the noble Leslie women who had come ahead of her, Flanna, born a Brodie, was a plainspoken country woman. But when she had finished speaking, Jasmine Leslie had told the duchess of Glenkirk that while she did not have elegant manners, she had what many did not. She had a nobility of spirit. And Jasmine continued, she was glad Flanna was her son's wife. And so the matter had been settled that summer of 1663, that summer of so many firsts.

Lady Diana Leslie—for that, she had been told, was her rightful title and she would use it from now on—watched as her parents and siblings departed Queen's Malvern several days before her eleventh birthday. She stood in the driveway before the house waving them off and thinking the shoes on her feet pinched, but that she would get used to wearing them. She had already learned to say *have, had,* and *has* in place of *hae,* and the word *not* instead of *nae,* and *cannot* instead of *canna.* Her family's vehicles disappeared in a cloud of dust which evaporated in the breeze.

"I cannot wait to meet the king," Lady Diana Leslie said, and her grandmother had laughed aloud.

The first day of her new life had begun. Then four summers later, Lady Diana Leslie and her cousin Lady Cynara Stuart had stood with the duke and duchess of Lundy and their grandmother in the drive of the house once more. This time they had awaited the arrival of another cousin. When she had finally arrived, they were all surprised to discover she looked like them too, except she did not have the Mughal Mole and her eyes were a wonderful turquoise blue just like their grandmother's.

Cynara, who had bright blue eyes like her beautiful mother, was somewhat put out by this fact, but Diana, with her green Leslie eyes was not. "I like the difference," she said to Cynara. "It makes us each unique despite our many similarities."

"You always manage to find the good in a situation," grumbled Cynara. "I think her eyes so striking that all the gentlemen at court will see only her. We shall die old maids!"

"We shall have each other," Diana teased, a twinkle in her lovely eyes, and a grin upon her face.

"'Oddsfish!" Cynara swore the king's favorite oath. "That is the most cheerfully depressing thought you have ever had, Diana!"

As it turned out their new cousin, Fancy Devers, immediately became their friend. There was a sadness about her, Diana considered, and of course there was the gossip. Diana discounted the gossip, for she could only base her assessment of her cousin, Fancy, upon their personal relationship which was quite fine. And Diana trusted her grandmother's judgment. She knew that Fancy Devers would not be with them if her grandmother had not investigated the situation, and decided that it was all right.

They were to go to court. Diana and Cynara had been taken briefly the previous year, and introduced to the king and the queen. Then they had come home, for while some parents were willing to allow their fourteen-year-old daughters at court, the duke and duchess of Lundy, and the dowager duchess of Glenkirk were not. Cynara was annoyed.

"To return home to the country to study more French, and poetry when we might be dancing, flirting, and going to masques is so intolerable," she grumbled.

"I am content to have another year at home," Diana said. But now that year was up. Grandmama had chosen specific colors for them to wear, gowns were being fashioned, and frankly Diana was as excited as Cynara. They had traveled down to London, settling into Greenwood House, which belonged to the family. Immediately their beautiful and mysterious cousin, Fancy, had attracted the king's attention. She was as quickly a royal mistress. Lady Diana Leslie, who had just the day before been only one of a number of young women joining, or visiting the court, suddenly found herself in a more prominent position on the social scale than she might have wished. Cynara, however, was delighted.

"People thinking to get to Fancy through us will see we are included at all the best parties," she crowed.

"You will only accept invitations that I approve," Jasmine said, much to Diana's relief.

While Fancy Devers found herself tossed swiftly to the top of the court's social tree, her two cousins were absorbed into a coterie of young men and women very much like themselves. They had been approved by their dowager grandmother as fit companions for Diana and Cynara. There were some among the court's young people Jasmine considered too wild to associate with her granddaughters. Three of the approved group were in fact cousins that they had never known about. Cynara's eldest sister Sabrina had married just such a cousin, John Southwood, the earl of Lynmouth. John descended from their grandmother's grandmother, the fabled Skye O'Malley, and her second husband, who was called the Angel Earl for his beauty. They had been well known at the court of the great Elizabeth Tudor.

Kathryn Blakely, called *Pretty Kitty* by the gentlemen of the court, was a cousin. Her line came down through Skye O'Malley's second daughter, Deirdre Burke, and her husband, Sir John Blakely. Kitty had hazel eyes and chestnut brown curls. Cecily Burke, known as *Ceci*, was another cousin. Her line of descent was traced through Padraic Burke, Deirdre's brother, and his wife, Valentina St. Michael. Ceci was sixteen and had red-gold hair, with violet eyes. She was considered an unusual beauty. Two other young ladies were part of their group. Drucilla Stanton, who was called *Wily*, for she was very clever, was an ash blonde with sky blue eyes. Coralyn Mumford, known as *Slim*, for she was both tall and slender, was a pale blonde with gray eyes.

Greenwood was next door to Lynwood House, which belonged to the Southwood family. They permitted any cousin visiting the court to make it their home. Both Kitty and Ceci were residing there along with a third cousin, a handsome young gentleman, Jamie Edwardes, the young earl of Alcester. Jamie descended through Skye O'Malley's eldest daughter, Willow, and her husband, James Edwardes. He came immediately upon their arrival in London to pay his respects to Jasmine, for he was well aware of who she was.

"I hope for your good advice in seeking a wife," he told her.

"You shall have it whenever you desire it," she told him. She shook her head. "I am astounded to say this, but I knew your great-great-grandmother," she told him. "Willow Edwardes was my aunt. She was much older than my own mother, who was the youngest of my grandmother's children, but I knew her well *and* the earl for whom you are named."

"There have been three Roberts before me," he said with a smile. "I am the first James since that time. My father and grandfather were both killed at Worcester. I was just six when I came into my own. As my mother was wise enough to avoid politics, keeping to herself until the king was restored, we managed to hold on to our estates."

"I am relieved to hear it," Jasmine said. "I can but imagine my aunt's dismay at the thought of strangers taking over her home. Or worse, strangers ignoring the family graveyard, and allowing it to become overgrown."

The young earl of Alcester chuckled. "I never knew her, of course, but stories of the countess Willow still survive, I assure you, madame. I, too, am amazed to learn that you actually knew her."

Jamie Edwardes had a host of young gentlemen friends. There were Lord Edward Charlton, called *Neddie*, and Sir Michael Scanlon, a handsome Irishman they all called *Mick*. There was Baron Mayhew, Sir Gage Foster. Lord Rupert Dunstan, the younger son of the earl of Morly, and Niles Brandon, the earl of Dunley, called *Bran*, and like Jamie a man who had inherited as a child. The last of the earl of Alcester's troupe of gentlemen friends were Damien *"Damn"* Esmond, the duke of Roxley, and his almost identical twin brother, Darius, the marquis of Roxley, known as *Darling*. They were not yet in London but had written to Jamie that they were coming soon.

"Well," Jasmine noted dryly, "it's a good start."

"If our girls cannot find husbands among that bunch," Barbara Stuart said laughing, "then they are certainly not trying. Two earls, a duke, a marquis, and a baron! Every lass should have such a choice."

"They are suitable, every one of them," Jasmine agreed. And all of Jamie's friends were fixated upon Diana, but the dowager kept that thought to herself. There would be time for Cynara. While Diana might believe she was just up to London to have fun, Jasmine knew that her Leslie granddaughter was ready for marriage. The only question was which one of these presentable gentlemen would capture her young heart? Or would they? She watched as Diana threw herself into a round of dances, masques, and parties as the holiday season began in earnest while the lord of Misrule ruled.

To Jasmine's surprise, the elder of her Stuart granddaughters, Lady Sabrina Southwood, the countess of Lynmouth, came up to London with her husband several days after Christmas. They had decided some months ago to reestablish the fabulous Twelfth Night masque that the earl's famous ancestor, Geoffrey Southwood, and his son, Robin, gave each year. Sabrina had found all the memoranda and missives pertaining to this famous event packed in an old trunk. The masque had been held in the days of the Great Elizabeth and in the days of King James I.

"We have been working for over a year to restore this event to its former luster," Sabrina said proudly. "The king and the queen have agreed to come. Isn't it exciting?"

"I thought you preferred country life." Jasmine remarked.

"Ohh, I do, Grandmama," Sabrina said, "but once I had found all the information regarding the Twelfth Night masque, I could not resist having it and bringing it back to its glory. We're going right home again afterward. Besides, I wanted to meet Kitty and Ceci, and young James Edwardes. So did Johnnie. Your grandmother and her offspring were very prolific. There are so many cousins that we don't know. Do you like these girls?"

"Aye, I do," Jasmine answered. "This is very slight notice, however, Sabrina. How are the girls to have proper costumes made on such short notice? It is really too unfair of you." She was irritated. Costumes took planning.

"No, Grandmama," Sabrina said smiling. "The costumes are all in the attics here at Lynmouth House. I will wager you will find some in the Greenwood attics too if you look. We have but to bring them out, refit, refashion, and restore them. It can be done quickly. The difficult part will be deciding which to wear. I found them the last time we were in London. They are really quite beautiful, very imaginative, and some are most daring," she laughed. "I cannot help but wonder who wore them." She put an arm about Jasmine's shoulders. "Perhaps some of them will even bring back memories for you."

"Mayhap," Jasmine replied, and there was a small smile on her face. She and her last husband, Jemmie Leslie, had caused quite a stir at one of her Uncle Robin's Twelfth Night galas. Of course it was before they were married. *Long before.* And then she had wed the father of her eldest three children, Rowan Lindley, the marquis of Westleigh. What had she worn that night? God, it was so long ago that she wasn't certain she remembered.

"Come over tomorrow," Sabrina said cheerfully. "Bring my little sister and the cousins. Kitty and Ceci are already very excited. I can hardly remember what it was like to be *that* young," she laughed.

"You are only twenty-six, Sabrina," her grandmother said. "'Tis I who cannot remember what it was like to be *that* age or your age for that matter!" Jasmine chuckled.

"A Twelfth Night masque? How quaint," Cynara said loftily.

"Do not be scornful," her grandmother scolded her sharply. "Your own great-grandfather, King James, said it was the most wonderful party that he had ever attended. High praise indeed, my girl, for your great-grandmother Queen Anne was noted for her skill at giving masques and plays. I can remember the galas at Lynmouth House very well."

"Were the costumes really marvelous, Grandmama?" Diana asked.

"The costumes were wonderful, my child," Jasmine replied. "I cannot wait to see what is in those trunks that Brie has found."

The countess of Lynmouth had invited her cousins' two friends, Drucilla Stanton and Coralyn Mumford, to join them. Now seated in the beautiful Great Hall of Lynmouth House the seven young women waited expectantly as the trunks were brought into the room by a line of liveried footmen. Each of the chests was carefully deposited before the assembled girls who all leaned forward excitedly. The countess nodded to her servants, and the lids of the trunks were raised to a chorus of *"ahhs!"*

"Wait!" Jasmine commanded them. "These garments are delicate and must be handled with great care, my dear girls." She reached into a trunk and drew forth a sheaf of blue and green silks. *"My God!"* she ejaculated softly, laying them across her lap and reaching for a pair of silken wings edged in gold paint. "My mother wore this at the Lynmouth Twelfth Night gala," she told the wide-eyed girls. She set the wings aside and leaned forward once again. "Let us see if my grandmother's costume is here also. Ahh, yes!" She pulled out a handful of mauve and purple silks with matching wings edged in silver.

"Your grandmama was our common ancestor, Skye O'Malley, wasn't she, madame?" Pretty Kitty Blakely asked.

"Yes," Jasmine said.

"What do these costumes represent, Grandmama?" Diana wondered.

"My mother and my grandmother were *moths*. My half brothers were all in reds and golds as was my grandfather de Marisco. I have always remembered that night in great detail for it was my first fête at Lynmouth. I distinctly remember my grandfather saying that at his age he should have been permitted to wear his black velvet suit. You see, my dears, the gentlemen that night were garbed as *flames* to my mother and grandmother's moths."

"How wickedly clever!" Cynara said, and her tone was admiring.

"What did you wear, Grandmama?" Diana asked.

"I had just come a few months prior from India. I wore the garb of my native land. I am certain it is here somewhere," she told her audience. "Let us look further, but do be careful."

Forewarned, and amazed by the treasures in the chests, the girls brought forth the garments cautiously, spreading them out with meticulous care over the chairs and the settees in the hall. The trunks empty at last, they gathered around each costume, marveling over the jewels, beads, and exquisite décor of each garment, all of which was so subtly pleasing to their eyes. None of them had ever before seen gowns like those now displayed.

"I will wear this!" Cynara said suddenly.

"Nay, my pet, you will not," her grandmother overruled her. "This is the costume I wore that night. It is for Fancy to wear."

"But why Fancy?" Cynara demanded, not willing to give up yet.

"Because it matches my eyes," Fancy answered spiritedly. "It was made for that express purpose, Grandmama, wasn't it?"

Jasmine nodded.

Cynara sulked for a moment, but then her eye lit upon another garment. It was black velvet and silver, and from the style, it was very, very old. But despite its obvious antiquity, the gown was in perfect condition. Cynara held the bodice up. It had a deliciously low square neckline. The sleeves were slashed to show silver lace inserts, and the wrists were also edged in silver. Cynara looked further. The gown had two skirts, and there were black silk stockings with silver lace rosette garters sewn with tiny diamond brilliants.

"Then I shall wear this," Cynara said.

"It is very old fashioned," Ceci remarked. Her hand was on a spring green satin gown.

Jasmine looked carefully at the garment Cynara had chosen. "It is surely close to a hundred years old," she told them. "This is the kind of gown that was certainly worn at the court of the great Elizabeth. You will need a farthingale beneath it."

"What's a farthingale?" the girls chorused as one.

"It is a type of petticoat, shaped like a bell, and fortified with a succession of hoops made from whalebone," Jasmine explained to them. "I never particularly enjoyed wearing them, but they made our gowns look so very fashionable at the time. You shall probably all need them except for those of you who choose to go as moths," Jasmine finished with a smile. "I'm certain if the gowns still exist, the farthingales do too, but they may need repair."

They spent the entire afternoon seeking out the costumes and the accessories that they would wear. In the end it was decided that Cynara would have her black, Fancy, her grandmother's exotic native dress, and Diana a magnificent ruby silk and velvet gown. Ceci had chosen the gown of spring green that suited her so well. Pretty Kitty had decided to be the blue-green moth while their friend Coralyn agreed to be the purple-and-mauve moth. Drucilla had found a beautiful sky blue dress that had pleased her and complimented her delicate coloring.

A dressmaker was hired. She arrived with three assistants. The next few days were spent in altering the garments for the gala. Fancy's costume needed no alteration at all. Cynara's needed the bodice taken in for the gown's previous owner had obviously been better endowed than the fifteen-year-old was. Diana's gown was altered in both the bodice and the waist.

"There are advantages to being a moth," Pretty Kitty said smugly.

And the slender Coralyn Mumford, called Slim by the gentlemen, agreed with a laugh.

"We must all make an entrance," Diana advised them. "You must come and dress at our house," she told them all. "There is little fun in just being there if one cannot cause a stir upon arrival. I wonder if most of the court will dress in costume or simply in their usual finery. However they come, we shall be unique!"

Jasmine smiled at her granddaughter's infectious excitement.

The guests began arriving at Lynmouth House in early evening. They came by coach and by barge along the river. The king would arrive at nine in company with the queen. They would come via the river. The driveway leading to the house and the lawns bordering the river were ablaze with lanterns. Servants had been hired just for the occasion to help guests from their coaches, from their barges, and off with the capes and cloaks. Lynmouth House no longer kept a large staff.

The young earl and countess of Lynmouth stood at the top of the three wide stairs that led down into their ballroom graciously greeting their guests. The dark-haired Sabrina Stuart Southwood was wearing a rather wild assortment of flowing draperies in savage hues of red, gold, and orange. About her neck were rubies, and rubies dripped from her ears. Her long dark hair was unbound and dressed with strands of tiny garnets, yellow topaz, and thin gold chains.

"I am *fire*," she told those who asked. Then she would twirl slightly, the colors of her costume blending so cleverly it was hard to tell where one shade began and another ended. And when she twirled, her red silk stockings with their garters covered in twinkling red garnets flashed daringly.

The young earl wore a costume that had also been found in the many chests. It was cloth of gold and twinkled with golden beryls. Atop his head he wore a sunburst. "I am the sun," he said gravely. He was a country gentleman and unused to such finery.

Many of the guests had, as Diana predicted, come in their court finery for they didn't have the means to have a costume made. They did, however, carry elegant little masks. Consequently the seven young women made quite an impression as each was announced. Pretty Kitty and Slim Mumford danced with each other down the steps into the ballroom, their delicate wings seeming to flutter. Drucilla Stanton was much admired as she glided down the short staircase in her sky blue silk gown, the skirt's center panel sewn with pearls and moonstones creating the effect of small puffy clouds. Across the gown's front were little jeweled pins representing birds in flight. Atop her head Drucilla wore a headdress of fluffy white lawn and lace, giving the effect of a cloud topped by a jeweled rainbow.

Ceci Burke was also admired in a gown of spring green satin, its underskirt displaying a meadow full of colorful yellow and white windflowers. Across the skirt playful silver lambs gamboled. In her red-gold hair was a small golden bird's nest with its bejeweled inhabitant.

The gentlemen, as well as the ladies, were intrigued by the rich, ornate, and elegant costumes that had come out of a group of ancient trunks and were so very old. Many were quite envious that these lovely girls had taken all the attention this evening from other, more important members of the court.

And then the king's new mistress, Fancy Devers, entered and there was a gasp of surprise. Fancy wore a traditional Mughal *jaguli*. The high-waisted dress was fashioned from turquoise silk shot through with threads of beaten gold. The long, tight-fitting sleeves had two-inch bands of gold at the wrist, which were also sewn with tiny diamonds, pearls, and Persian lapis. The graceful skirt was edged with a band of gold, and the banding on the high round neckline matched that upon the sleeves. The dress, fastened at both the neckline and the waist with a large diamond button, nonetheless had a narrow opening that allowed a tantalizing glimpse of Fancy's pretty breasts, quite visible when, with her palms pressed together, she bowed.

On her feet Fancy wore heelless slippers of kid that had been covered in thin sheets of beaten gold. They were sewn all over with little diamonds making it appear with every step as if her feet were filled with lights. Her hair had been braided into a single thick plait woven with strands of pearls and lapis strung on thin gold wires. About her ankles were anklets of dainty gold bells. On her arms were delicate gold bracelets of silver, gold, and bejeweled bangles. She wore sapphires in her ears and about her throat.

But before the assembled court could fully enjoy Fancy's beautiful costume, Cynara was pausing a moment at the top of the stairs.

"I am night," she announced, and then descended into the ballroom in her black velvet and silver lace gown. Her skirts belled out over her farthingale in elegant fashion. The black brocade underskirt carried silver, diamond, and pearl embroidery representing stars, moons, planets. There were silver lace rosettes studded with tiny diamonds on her high-heeled black shoes. Her breasts swelled dangerously over the top of her low neckline. Seeing his daughter in so sophisticated a costume, the duke of Lundy felt suddenly uncomfortable. When had Cynara grown up? She was but two heartbeats away from becoming a woman. He hadn't noticed it until tonight. His wife put a comforting hand on his velvet-clad arm, understanding his surprise.

Finally Diana made her entrance. Her gown represented a ruby. The deep color of the gown was a rich and sumptuous red. Its underskirt was silk, sewn all over in a swirling ornate design with tiny rubies and gold thread that twinkled with each step she took. The overskirt was of a heavy velvet, the slashings in the velvet sleeves showing the matching silk of the underskirt, and repeating the design of tiny rubies. The neckline was daringly low. Diana wore her hair in an elegant chignon, set on the nape of her neck. The chignon was decorated with delicate red silk flowers. Her hair was parted in the center, and two small lovelocks dangled on either side of her face. About her slender neck Diana wore a necklace of large rubies and the matching gemstones hung from her ears. She swept the assembled guests a deep curtsy, and then glided down the three steps into the ballroom.

"I say, Jamie," Edward, lord Charlton, said to the earl of Alcester, "if your cousin, sweet Siren, ain't the most beautiful creature in this room, may I go blind!"

His boon companion, Sir Michael Scanlon, nodded in agreement.

"How can you single Diana out, Ned? She, Cyn, and Fancy are practically identical in features but for the Mughal Mole, and their eye color," the earl teased his friends.

"Well, Mistress Devers is rather involved right now," Ned replied meaningfully, "ain't she? And I would just as soon not tangle with the not-so-royal Stuart's lass. She's as prickly as a thornbush," and again Sir Michael agreed silently.

"There are other differences," Lord Rupert Dunstan, younger son of the earl of Morly murmured. "The king's Fancy has the most beautiful breasts I've seen in some time. Round and full. The lovely Cyn Stuart has high, cone-shaped bubbies. Sweet Siren's are like dainty little apples or perhaps peaches."

"You are a connoisseur then of fine titties," Mick Scanlon noted.

"Indeed," Lord Dunstan drawled. Then he looked at the assembled, and asked, "Can any of you think of anything finer than caressing a handful of sweet, perfumed flesh?"

"Beware the not-so-royal Stuart, or the magnificent dowager Jasmine hear you, Rupert," said the earl of Dunley, Niles Brandon.

Lord Dunstan grinned. "Agreed! We need to keep on their good side if any of us is to have a chance with the fair Siren."

His companions murmured their agreement, and then as one stepped forward to greet Diana as she reached the bottom of the steps.

Diana took her cousin, James Edwardes's hand, smiling sweetly at the rest of them. "My lords, how you flatter me," she said, "but I know I am not the only lady in the room tonight. You shall make the others jealous of me if you do not pay them some court."

"Alas, sweet Siren, all we can see is you," Sir Michael Scanlon said in his soft and lilting Irish brogue. "Why, lass, you are as fair as a Killarney morn in spring."

"Why, Mick, that is the dearest compliment I've been given today." She blew him a kiss and smiled sweetly. "But I would still have you gentlemen not make such a to-do over me. This room is filled with beautiful females. I cannot dance with all of you at once now, can I?" She cocked her head to one side. "But which of you first?"

They looked eagerly at her. Hopefully.

"I think you, Cousin," Diana finally said, and they groaned in disappointment, but she soothed them saying, "I will not play favorites, my lords. *At least not yet.*" Then she gave them another winning smile and turned away with the earl of Alcester.

"Y'don't think she'll marry him, do you?" Baron Mayhew asked.

"He's her cousin, Gage," Ned Charlton replied.

"Cousins wed, and her family is known for keeping a tight rein on their fortune," Gage Foster noted.

"She'll marry for love, and no other reason," Mick Scanlon predicted, and he smiled knowingly.

"How can you say that?" Rupert Dunstan asked.

"Because she's a Celt, lads. You all think of her as English, but she isn't. She was born in the eastern Highlands of Scotland, and until four years ago lived there. You can still hear the faint ring of it in her now very cultured voice. And the look of her is pure Irish. The blood of our wild tribes is in her veins, too. And do not forget her grandmother, the dowager Jasmine, who spent her early years at the court of her father, the Indian emperor. Sweet Siren, the delicious Cyn, and the mysterious Fancy will all wed for love, my lords, and for no other reason. Now the only question is, can they love one of us?"

"Well," Niles Brandon, the earl of Dunley noted, "Sweet Siren and the prickly Cyn are dukes' daughters. I can't believe that their paters would let them wed with just anyone. Love is all well, and good, but a duke's daughter needs a title to call her own, and I got a fine title, and a good house to offer the right girl."

"And a mountain of gambling debts," Mick Scanlon chuckled.

"Gentlemen are supposed to have gambling debts," the earl of Dunley replied huffily. "My title goes back to the first William. How old is yours, *Sir* Michael?"

Mick Scanlon laughed. "Hardly old at all," he said, "but at least I have no debts."

"That's because you have no money," Rupert Dunstan teased.

"Too true," Mick admitted. "But I have a fine house that with a small fortune could be enlarged to become a great estate, for God only knows I have land. It's rocky, and not good for much, but it's mine."

"So like the rest of us you have come for a rich wife," Lord Charlton said. "Well, 'tis the way of our world, and good luck to us all. There would, it seems, be pretty girls enough to go around."

"But none with fortunes like the dowager Jasmine's three fair granddaughters," the earl of Dunley noted. "And when the king's Fancy is once again free to choose a husband she will be more than well dowered, for the king is not known to be mean with his lovers. And if she should have a child, well, lads, then of the three I should think Mistress Devers would have even more value than Lady Diana."

"You are a cold-hearted devil, Niles Brandon," Mick noted.

"I'm a practical man, and no romantic, 'tis true," the earl agreed affably, "but then so are the rest of us, for all we may deny it. After all a pretty heiress likes to hear pretty sentiments, don't she? It seems little enough for a lass to ask, or a man to give."

"And while we have been debating the finer points of courtship," Mick said with a chortle, "Ned, Gage, and Rupert have hurried off no doubt to obtain dances from the fair Siren. Come along, Niles, lest we be left out entirely. We ain't the only ones looking to that lovely lass." And he hurried off, the earl behind him.

"The Duke of Roxley. The Marquis of Roxley," the majordomo intoned as he announced the two gentlemen at the head of the stairs.

Diana Leslie, still surrounded by her would-be suitors, looked up curious, and her heart stopped for just the briefest second. Standing atop the steps were two gentlemen, identical, or so it seemed, in features. Their handsome faces were ovals. Their cheekbones high, the long noses straight. They carried themselves gracefully, moving with assurance as they descended the steps. They were tall, with long legs, and broad shoulders. They had auburn curls, but she could not see their eyes, and she wanted to very much. They were dressed as Harlequins in black and white, and they wore the most fashionable high-heeled red shoes.

"Who are they?" Diana whispered to her cousin Jamie.

"Damien and Darius Esmond, better known here at court when they bother to come as *Damn* and *Darling*," he answered her.

"Introduce me!" Diana hissed at him. She had never before seen such handsome men. They were gloriously, marvelously beautiful!

"I don't know them well enough," James Edwardes said.

"If you do not introduce me this instant," Diana said, "I shall go up to them, and introduce myself, Cousin," she threatened.

"You are impossible," he told her. "Are you not satisfied to have conquered the heart of every young man at court? Charlton, Scanlon, Dunstan, Mayhew, or Dunley, you could have any of them."

"I don't want them, Jamie. They are your friends, our friends. Damien and Darius Esmond are the first gentlemen I have seen who interest me. Unless they are lacking in intellect or wit, of course."

He sighed. "Very well then, Cousin. Ah, I see Mick is already with them. He is their cousin, and that will give me the opportunity I seek to introduce you."

They moved across the room, and seeing them approach Sir Michael Scanlon said to his handsome cousins, "Here is Alcester with his beautiful cousin. She is Lady Diana Leslie, but we call her Siren."

"Her gown is magnificent," the duke of Roxley said, "and she wears her rubies well."

"Rubies suit her," the marquis of Roxley noted.

"Jamie," Mick said as the young couple reached them, "you have met Damn and Darling, I am certain."

The earl of Alcester bowed. "I have," he answered. "It is good to see you back at court, gentlemen. May I present my cousin, Lady Diana Leslie, the duke of Glenkirk's daughter."

Diana curtsied, and the gentlemen bowed.

"I have not seen you at court before, Lady Diana," the duke said to her. His voice was deep and rich. It sent a shiver down her spine. And then he smiled.

Diana thought her bones were melting, but she replied in a quiet voice that forced them to lean forward to hear her, "It is my first Season at court, my lord. I am here with my cousins, my aunt, my uncle, and my grandmother."

"You know Lynmouth?" the marquis asked her. His voice was as deep and smooth as his twin brother's.

"We are cousins, my lord," she answered him, her knees feeling as if they were jellies. "We descend from a common ancestress who lived in the time of the great Elizabeth."

"I'm another cousin," the earl of Alcester said, clarifying his position in Diana's life.

Suddenly the music stopped, then the majordomo' voice boomed out: *"His Majesty, King Charles II, and Her Majesty, Queen Catherine!"*

The royal couple came slowly down the staircase, escorted by the earl and countess of Lynmouth. Twin thrones had been set up for them at the far end of the ballroom. They passed between a line of bowing and curtsying courtiers as they made their way toward their seats. The king was garbed richly in a cloth-of-gold suit sewn all over with sparkling paste gemstones. It suited his dark complexion and his black curls. The queen complimented him in a cloth of silver gown, a long strand of large pink, black, and white pearls about her slender neck. Once they had been seated, the earl of Lynmouth signaled his musicians, and they began to play once again.

The dancers came slowly back on the floor once again as the king and queen watched them. The king enjoyed dancing, and eventually he would join the court. The young queen preferred to watch.

The duke and his brother bowed to Diana as one, and she laughed. "I cannot dance with both of you at once," she said.

"Why not?" the Duke of Roxley said laughing back. Then he and his twin led Diana out onto the floor, each holding her by a hand. The duke on her right, the marquis on her left. They began to dance, first one leading her in the figure, and then the other.

"Do you do everything together?" she asked of them as they danced. She was finding the situation most amusing.

"Almost," the marquis said with a wink, and then he chuckled as she blushed, suspecting her thoughts, and adding, "Sometimes we even do *that* together, my lady."

"Ohh, you are very wicked!" she cried, and she felt her cheeks hot with her excitement as the thought of doing *that* with either of them filled her brain.

"Just look at her," grumbled Slim Mumford as she watched her friend dancing. "Not one, but two partners!"

"And the handsomest men in the room," Pretty Kitty lamented. "Either one would make her a fine catch."

"Leaving the other for us," Ceci said bluntly. "We'll have no chance at catching a husband, any of us, until Diana is spoken for by one or another of the gentlemen we know. They are all besotted with her and can see none of us."

"I can't be jealous of her," Drucilla Stanton said. "She is so damned sweet, and she is generous too. She didn't have to ask us to share in her family's bounty from those trunks. We are the most admired girls here tonight even if the gentlemen we fancy can see only their Siren." She twirled slightly. "These costumes are wonderful. Don't you wonder who wore them once? I know I do."

The dance ended, and laughing breathlessly Diana walked arm-in-arm with the duke and the marquis of Roxley. "How can people tell you apart, or can't they?" she wondered.

"There is a way," the duke told her. He stopped. "Study us both, fair Siren, and see if you can tell. Most can't for they do not look at us closely enough. Can you?"

Diana looked carefully at each of the young men before her. Every feature matched, and then she saw it. "You have different colored eyes!" she exclaimed. "Yours," she said to the duke, "are a light blue with almost a hint of silver in them. And yours," she turned to the marquis, "are a deep ocean blue."

They grinned at her and nodded in unison.

Diana laughed again. "Heaven help the poor lasses who marry you, my lords," she told them.

"Well, you shall be one of them," the duke told her bluntly, "for my brother and I decided it the moment we saw you, fair Siren. We intend to both court you. You will have to decide which you prefer. Light blue eyes, or dark blue eyes." Then he took up her right hand, and kissed it even as his twin took her left and saluted it as tenderly.

Diana blushed prettily. "My lords, you are overbold, I think. We have just now met. I know nothing of you, nor you of me, and yet you would court me with marriage in mind? Perhaps on closer acquaintance, we shall find we do not like each other at all."

"Are you not a little in love with us already?" the marquis teased her. "We are said to be very handsome."

"Ahh, but there, my lords, is the crux of it. My cousin, Fancy, who is a widow, has warned us about handsome men. She says they are more often than not blackguards."

"Your cousin sounds like a wise woman," the duke replied. "We should like to meet her one day."

"You may meet her tonight if you choose," Diana told them. "She is there, dancing with His Majesty. She is his good friend," Diana murmured.

Her pert answer caught them both off guard. They gazed towards Fancy in her exotic costume as she danced with the king. Diana giggled mischievously. "Did you think the cousin giving such sage advice an old lady, my lords?" she teased them.

"You look alike," the duke noted.

"Not quite," the marquis said.

"We are said to resemble that common ancestress of ours. My cousin, Cynara too," Diana told them. "Now, my lords, can you tell the difference between us?"

"You have the most charming little mole, and your cousin, Fancy does not," the duke replied.

"And your other cousin, Lady Stuart, has her little mole on the opposite side from you," the marquis added.

"You are very observant, my lords," Diana said.

"Dear boys," Mick Scanlon now joined them, "you are being most selfish with the fair Siren's company. They have begun a lovely country romp, my dear, and I believe it is our dance."

"Indeed, Mick, and it is," she agreed. She curtsied to the duke and the marquis of Roxley. "Good-bye, my lords," she said, and tucking her small hand in Sir Michael Scanlon's arm, she moved off.

"She is very beautiful," the duke said. "She will make a wonderful duchess, Darling."

"I rather think she will be a magnificent marchioness, Damn," his twin replied with a smile.

And together they stood watching as Diana danced with Mick Scanlon, her ruby red skirts swirling about her.

Chapter
9

"Come on," the earl of Alcester called to his cousin Diana.

It was early February, and the King's Canal in St. James Park had frozen over quite solidly.

Diana and Cynara had spent the night in their cousin's apartment at Whitehall. It wasn't the most comfortable arrangement; they could not share Fancy's bed for obvious reasons. Instead they slept on settees in her salon. Fancy's serving woman, Bess Trueheart, was kind enough to serve them as well when she was not busy looking after her mistress. Cynara was only just stirring, but Diana had risen an hour before. Fancy was still sleeping.

Bess had brought Diana a basin of warm water, a cloth, and a towel. While the girl quickly bathed, for despite the fireplace the room was cold, Bess brought forth her clothing. Diana had slept in her chemise and was shivering as she pulled on her silk drawers, called *calecons* by the French who had invented them. She gratefully drew on half a dozen petticoats, the first being a fur-lined silk garment, the others atop it of soft white flannel. She donned a Holland waistcoat lined with rabbit fur to keep her chest warm, for her chemise would not be enough. Bess handed her a pair of knit silk stockings and then another pair of wool. Her skirts and the matching bodice were wine red velvet. Her dark leather shoes had comfortable round toes.

"Where are you going?" Cynara asked sleepily.

"Jamie is taking me sliding on the King's Canal," Diana said.

Cynara rolled over, and gazed out the windows which were now undraped. "It looks cold out," she said.

"If the canal has frozen over, of course it is cold," Jamie said as he stepped into the salon. "Come on!"

Bess draped a wine velvet cape lined in dark marten fur over Diana's shoulders and handed her a pair of dark, fur-lined leather gloves.

"You have fun, m'lady," she said with a smile. "Wish I could go too, I do!"

The earl of Alcester hurried from the apartment with his young cousin in tow. "Everybody is going to be there," he said.

"I've never been sliding," Diana said.

"It's great fun!" Jamie told her. "I have had a pair of sliders made for you. Bess loaned me one of your shoes for size."

"Why, Cousin, how kind you are!" Diana exclaimed.

They hurried into the courtyard of Whitehall Palace where the earl's coach awaited them. Outside the air was chill, but inside the comfortable vehicle, it was warm and cozy. The footman put a fur robe over their laps, and beneath their seats two small charcoal braziers burned, heating the carriage. They were driven the brief distance between Whitehall and St. James Park where the palace of St. James was also located. They walked together to the canal, a footman walking behind them carrying the two pairs of sliders. There were several marble benches set about the narrow canal, and finding one empty they sat down. Kneeling, the footman removed their leather shoes and fitted the sliders over their stockinged feet.

"Careful now," Jamie warned as they stood up, and moved across the frozen ground. He stepped gingerly onto the ice, then turned, offering Diana his two hands.

Cautiously she accepted his aid and placed her feet one at a time upon the ice. "I don't know if I can do this," she said nervously.

"Of course you can!" he said enthusiastically. "The two runners on each of our sliders are sturdy, and I shall hold your hand, little cousin. Indeed I shall be the most envied man here today for I see many of your suitors," Jamie teased her with a smile. "Come on now, sweet Siren. Naught ventured, naught gained."

"Is it like walking?" she asked raising one foot, and then the other. "That doesn't seem like much fun, Jamie."

He chuckled. "Nay, silly, you slide your feet along the ice. Do you think you can stand alone while I show you?"

"I . . . I think so," she replied, her upper teeth worrying her lower lip.

He let go of her gloved hands and glided over the ice of the long canal. "See? Like this." He glided back to her and, taking up her hand, said, "Ready, Cousin?" Then he began to move his feet, and Diana followed suit.

Soon they were gliding gracefully down the long canal.

"Ohhh!" she cried delighted. "This is wonderful, Jamie!"

Very quickly several of Diana's suitors were gliding near them, attempting to catch her eye, boldly calling out to her to glide with them, but refusing to play favorites she remained with the earl of Alcester to their disappointment.

Finally after a time he said to her, "Are you brave enough now to attempt gliding on your own, Cousin?"

"I . . . I think I can," she said, "but do not leave me, Jamie." Tentatively she let go of his hand and glided away from him. It was wonderful! It was almost like flying, she thought excited. Then suddenly her feet seemed to lose control of themselves, and she began to career out of control. "*Jamie!*" she shrieked at him, but before he might answer her desperate summons the duke and the marquis of Roxley came up by her side, each taking an arm, and glided off with her.

"Oh, my lords," she said to them, "Thank you!" Her heart was still pumping with a mixture of excitement and fear.

"A disaster averted, eh, sweet Siren?" the duke said smiling down into her small upturned face. He had such beautiful light blue eyes, she considered dreamily.

"You are new to gliding, of course," the marquis said. "We saw it the moment you stepped upon the ice."

Diana turned to look up at the marquis. *Oh my,* she thought! *His eyes are as blue as the sea, and as deep as the night.* But she managed to answer in a cool and composed voice, "You are correct, my lord. It is my first time wearing gliders. Have you glided before then?"

"Indeed we have," the marquis replied. "Our home is in the north where the winters are colder than warmer. Our mother's brother is married to a lady from Holland. She taught us how to glide when we were small boys. It is a grand sport that both ladies and gentlemen can play at together, which of course makes it more fun, sweet Siren."

"Hollanders glide, too?" she asked.

"It is practically a national sport in the winter when the canals freeze over. I am told they glide from village to village rather than walk or ride. Their canals are longer and more natural than this lovely neat and orderly canal the king has built," the duke said.

"I am told the king swims here in hot weather but allows no others, even his favorite ladies, to do so," Diana answered.

"Your cousin is the king's new friend, isn't she?" the marquis asked, and his brother shot him a ferocious look of disapproval.

"You need not answer such a rude query," he quickly told Diana.

She stopped upon the ice and said quietly, "It is a fair question, my lord, and I am glad to answer it. Yes, Fancy is the king's new mistress, for let us elucidate her position at the court honestly. She is a widow, however, and the dearest, kindest girl I have ever known. Now, my lords, if you will return me to my cousin, the earl of Alcester, I should be grateful."

"We have offended you," the marquis said, and there was genuine regret in his voice. He turned so he might face her and bowed as he glided backward to her amazement. "I most humbly apologize, sweet Siren. Can you forgive me? Will you not hold my blunt speech against me? I can sometimes be a bit of a fool."

"Too true," his twin murmured beneath his breath, and Diana laughed.

"I forgive you, Darling, because of your beautiful sea blue eyes," she told him, and she smiled her radiant smile.

Darius Esmond clutched at his heart, and pretended to stumble backward. "*I have been forgiven!*" he cried dramatically.

"I shall take it all back if you do not behave yourself, my lord," Diana promised him. "Do you enjoy making a fool of yourself?"

"Let me answer that," the duke replied. "Yes! Be warned dear sweet Siren, though we may look alike we are not. I am the more sober of the two of us."

"Except when you are in your cups, Brother," the marquis responded with a laugh. "He does really like his wine, don't you, Damn?"

"I think I may be forced to punch you in your rather handsome nose," the duke announced.

"Then I shall leave you to settle your differences, my lords," Diana said, disentangling herself from their grip and gliding off to join Jamie at the other end of the canal. "Good-bye!" she called as she coasted down the ice toward the earl of Alcester, but she was hard-pressed not to laugh again. It was obvious that the twins were in a competition for her attentions. Were they serious, or was this just another case of sibling rivalry on their part? Time would tell. "Here I am again, safe and sound," she told Jamie as she reached him.

"I see Damn and Darling are seriously vying for your favor, dear cousin," he observed. "Which do you prefer?"

"I haven't decided yet," Diana said, "and I wonder if indeed I ever can. They are both so charming and so amusing."

"And so eligible," her cousin replied. "Either would please your grandmother and your parents."

"But I do not know if I am ready to marry, Jamie. This is my first Season at court. I find it wonderful, and there is so much I do not know and have yet to discover. I want to have fun, Jamie!"

"The purpose of a respectable girl coming to court," he said, "first and foremost, is to find a suitable husband, little cousin. In times past our families made the matches for us. We had not the luxury of choosing amongst our peers. But nowadays our choices are usually acceptable to our families. When I set my sights upon a young lady, I shall ask your very wise grandmother's advice in the matter. If you are seen to be having too much fun, or remain too long with the court, your good name will be compromised, Diana, even if nothing can be proved against you. The ladies of this court are not always good examples of chastity. A gentleman prefers to marry a girl who is modest, and whose reputation is spotless," he concluded.

"Yet you think naught of jeopardizing a lady's name, not you in particular, dear Jamie, but the gentlemen of this court," Diana observed. "You cannot, I fear, have it both ways."

"Which is why many gentlemen go home to wed with their childhood sweethearts more often than not," he told her. "Come summer when you return to Queen's Malvern, you should have narrowed the field of gentlemen about you, Cousin. Mayhap you will even choose a husband by that time. But if you return to court in the late autumn with no choice made, you are no longer considered new and fresh for there will be a whole new crop of young ladies arriving. You will be considered sophisticated, and you will be fair game to the roués, men like *The Wits*, who debauch pretty creatures like you on whims. Several lasses from good families have been ruined by those men. The king will not lift a hand to interfere for many are his friends, and he finds them amusing."

"They write most scurrilous poetry," Diana said. "There is already one about Fancy killing the king with her rabid colonial appetites."

"I am shocked that you have heard it," he said, disturbed.

"Everyone has heard it, even Grandmama. She laughed and said the meter was clumsy. Then she told us that *The Wits* always write naughty rhymes about the king's mistresses. Or anyone else they consider fair game, or for that matter anything that takes their fancy."

"Begin to consider your suitors more carefully, Cousin," he advised her with utmost seriousness.

"Your supervision and solicitude of my reputation is most kind, dear Jamie," Diana said as they glided to the edge of the canal. "I think you are much like your ancestress, the countess Willow, in your care of me. She was famous within the family for her good manners, and attention to the standards of acceptable social behavior. Grandmama has spoken often of it." Then she shivered. "I am suddenly freezing," she told him. "Gliding is cold sport."

"Come," he said, "we'll get off the ice, and warm ourselves by the fire. The chestnut vendor is there, and there is nothing nicer than hot chestnuts on a cold day. Ho, Master Syms! Chestnuts, if you please, for my lady cousin!" Jamie called to the royal chestnut vendor who was licensed by the king to ply his wares within the park. He could always be found by the canal whenever it froze, and the gliders appeared upon the ice.

By the time they had removed their gliders, and the footman had replaced their shoes upon their feet, the chestnut vendor was ready to serve them. They walked around to the other side of the canal where a large bonfire blazed, and the chestnut seller had set up his cart. Upon it he had a small charcoal brazier where he roasted the nuts. He handed them each a small wrapped paper of his product, and the earl gave him a coin. The peddler nodded his thanks before they walked away. They stood by the roaring fire warming themselves and eating the hot chestnuts, which were crisp and sweet.

"I cannot feel my feet," Diana said popping a nut into her mouth.

"Neither can I," he admitted, "but it has been my experience that cold feet warm up eventually." He chewed vigorously on a nut.

"I loved gliding, but I don't ever think I shall be warm again," Diana decided. "Can we come tomorrow, Jamie?"

"I cannot," he said regretfully. "I promised to spend the day with your grandmama."

"*Oh.*" The look on her face was pure disappointment.

"Perhaps you could get Cyn to come with you," he suggested.

"*Cyn?*" Diana laughed. "Hunting is her sport. She has no other. Dogs and horses are her passions. She is a true lady of the court and hardly arises before noon. Some days it is close to three or four in the afternoon before we can get her from her bed. No, Cyn would neither like gliding, nor the early hour we chose for it."

"Hallo!"

"Mick! Have you come to glide?" Diana asked Sir Michael Scanlon.

"I was on the ice but you didn't see me for you were much too busy with the Esmond twins," Mick said with a grin. "You look sad, sweet Siren. How can I cheer you and take that unhappy look from your beautiful green eyes?" he asked.

"Will you bring me gliding tomorrow, Mick? Jamie has not the time for his cousin. He would spend the day with Grandmama," she said.

"Your grandmama is a fascinating lady, my dear, and given the opportunity I should spend the day with her myself," he replied with a wide grin, "but as I am not invited, I shall gladly be your escort tomorrow. Is eleven o'clock too early for you?"

"Ten o'clock is better," she responded. "Ohh, thank you, Mick!" Leaning over she gave him a quick kiss upon the cheek and smiled.

He put his gloved hand up to touch where her lips had brushed his face, and said, "I shall be the envy of every gentleman in the court, sweet Siren. I have heard no rumor that you have ever bestowed a kiss on any eligible man since you have come. I am not worthy of your hand, my dear, for you are a duke's daughter, but I shall be admired tomorrow for my good fortune in having you as my partner on the ice." He bowed to her, and taking up her small gloved hand he kissed it.

Diana blushed prettily. "Thank you, sir, 'tis a lovely compliment you have bestowed upon me. You shall have my second dance this evening as well for your kindness."

"'Odsfish, lassie, you will start a rumor when I am seen not only dancing with you this evening but gliding with you tomorrow." Then he grinned at her. "What fun, dear girl!"

Diana laughed. "Aye," she agreed mischievously.

"Oh, lord," Jamie said. "You have found a playmate, Cousin, every bit as naughty as you can be." He turned to Sir Michael Scanlon, "Now, Mick, I must rely upon you to make certain that Diana does not find herself in difficulties. Will you promise me that you will guard her as carefully as if she were your own dear sister?"

"'Tis a great deal you ask of me, Jamie Edwardes," the big Irishman said in sorrowful tones, shaking his dark head. "But I will certainly promise to keep our sweet Siren from trouble. I shall watch her far more carefully than my sister Maeve, for I cannot stand the wench!"

"Why not?" Diana asked him.

"She is too damned much like me," he answered her grinning, "and now that she is wed she is producing brats just like her."

They laughed.

Then Diana said, "Cousin, I am yet frozen. Take me back to Greenwood, please. I need a hot bath and some of Grandmama's tea."

"You do not like chocolate?" Mick asked.

"It is too thick and bitter," she replied. Then she smiled up at him again. "Good-bye until this evening, Mick Scanlon."

The earl of Alcester escorted Diana back to their coach, and as it left St. James Park, Diana leaned from the window, and waved.

"Do you see how she favors the Irishman?" Darius Esmond grumbled to his twin brother. "What the hell does he have that we don't?"

Damien Esmond, who had been watching Diana, said quietly, "She holds no tendre for him."

"She kissed him, for God's sake!" Darius said jealously.

"A peck upon the cheek. One friend to another," the duke of Roxley told his brother. "She thinks of him as a friend, a cousin, a big brother, even as Alcester is. There is naught in her eyes for Mick Scanlon. Try not to let your temper make a fool of you, Darling."

"You really think there is nothing there?" the marquis of Roxley asked his twin.

"I do," the duke said. "It is between us that she will have to choose, but I would not have it come between us. Will you accept that the best man will win, and leave it at that?"

"Of course, Damn, for I am the best man," the marquis responded. "I truly hope that you will not be too disappointed."

The duke laughed. "I hope that *you* will not be too disappointed," he replied with a wide grin.

Then arm-in-arm the two brothers glided down the ice of the King's Canal as Mick Scanlon was surrounded by his friends, all demanding to know what had transpired between him and the divine sweet Siren.

Arriving at Greenwood House, Diana found Cynara already there, and looking both sleepy and disgruntled. "I thought you would still be at Whitehall," she said by way of greeting.

"The king decided to break his fast with Fancy so I was forced from my settee and sent packing," Cynara said sourly. "You would think if he enjoys her company so much she would have a bigger apartment. At least one with a small dining room. She could ask."

"She won't, for she is really too modest," Diana said, "and besides you know how tight space is at Whitehall."

"Where did you go?" Cynara asked. "Hello, Jamie," she greeted her cousin from her place by the fire in the hall.

"Tea and some of the wonderful little meat pasties," Diana told the servant at her elbow. Then she turned to Cynara. "Jamie took me gliding on the ice at the King's Canal. I told you before we left, but you were obviously too sleepy to remember. It was wonderful! I am going tomorrow with Sir Michael Scanlon."

"You don't have a passion for him, I hope. He is entirely unsuitable," Cynara said sharply.

"Mick is a friend, like our cousin," Diana answered. "Jamie can't take me because he has promised to spend the day with Grandmama."

"You look frozen," Cynara observed.

"I am!" Diana admitted enthusiastically, "but you were right, Jamie, I am beginning to feel my toes again. Gracious, my poor feet are both burning and tingling."

"It sounds highly unpleasant," Cynara decided.

"It was fun," Diana insisted. "No matter the cold. Would you like to come with me and try it? Everyone was there."

"What you mean is all your suitors were there," Cynara chuckled.

"Well," Diana admitted, "they were, but I only glided with our cousin and the Esmond twins."

"Ah-hah!" Cynara looked distinctly interested. "And why did you single them out, dear coz?"

"I didn't. I lost my balance and was about to fall when they glided up and rescued me from a most ignominious mishap," Diana explained.

"How fortuitous!" Cynara purred. "And you remained with them?"

"For a short while until they began squabbling over me," Diana responded. "Then I was sure enough on my gliders to glide back to Jamie. We left the ice, and warmed ourselves by the bonfire, and had hot roasted chestnuts. Mick joined us, and agreed to escort me tomorrow."

"A duke and a marquis are excellent candidates for your hand," Cynara said seriously. "Don't you agree, Jamie?"

"Indeed," he said cheerfully. "Wouldn't mind having either of them in the family, Cyn. Both have fortunes enough so that we can be assured that they ain't after Diana's boodle. Neither has any bad habits of which I know."

"Darling says that Damn likes his wine," Diana noted.

"He slanders his brother to gain your favor over his elder," Jamie said with a laugh. "If anything Damien Esmond is a bit too sober."

A servant arrived with a plate of meat pasties, half a wheel of hard yellow cheese, a bowl of apples and pears, and a pot of hot tea. The three cousins poured the tea and ate the repast that had been put before them, drinking the fragrant beverage they had all grown up knowing. The tea came from a distant cousin who owned a tea plantation on the island of Ceylon off the coast of India. They weren't quite certain who it was, but their grandmother knew.

"This is a pretty picture," Jasmine said coming into the hall. "How pleased my grandmother would be to see her descendants so loving toward one another. Cynara, give me a saucer of tea, dear girl. And what have you been doing this day, my Diana?"

Diana launched into a recitation of her adventures in gliding at the King's Canal while Jasmine drank her tea smiling and nodded, even laughing once or twice at the lively recitation.

"But do you approve of her going with Sir Michael Scanlon tomorrow, Grandmama?" Cynara demanded when Diana had finished.

"Of course," Jasmine said. "He is a respectable escort if Jamie cannot accompany our Diana."

Diana stuck her tongue out at Cynara. "Busybody!" she said.

"This tea is delicious," the earl of Alcester said quickly, in an attempt to change the subject. "Which relative sends it to us, madame, for I am certain that you would know."

"I do," Jasmine said. "His name is Robert O'Flaherty. He descends from my grandmother's second son, Murrough, who was a sea captain. Grandmama had two sons by her first husband. The first inherited his father's lands in Ireland. His descendants are still there. The second, like Grandmama's own father, was called by the sea, as were the sons and grandsons who followed him. Robert O'Flaherty's father sailed on the East Indies run. He fell in love with Ceylon and with one of the daughters of a local rajah. They married. He gave up the sea and learned to raise tea. It is the first son of this union who so kindly remembers me, and the rest of his family on the other side of the world," Jasmine said.

"We seem to have relations everywhere," Jamie noted.

"My grandmother had six living children who all wed and produced many offspring. Remember, my dears, that Skye O'Malley was born in the year of our lord, fifteen hundred and forty. The king upon the throne then was the Tudor, Henry VIII, the great Elizabeth's sire. We have had three kings and two queens, and a usurper queen since that time until our own King Charles II. My grandmother's first son was born when she was barely fifteen. Her last child was born in the year fifteen seventy-three. Almost a hundred years ago. We seem to be a prolific family, and all the offspring since then have produced in great numbers. It is to be expected that many, like my own dear Fortune, Fancy's mama, would seek their destinies elsewhere."

Jamie nodded. "That would answer my concern," he said. "Do you miss your daughter, Fortune, madame? I mean, after all these years."

"Aye," Jasmine said, and she sighed, "and all the grandchildren I shall not know, but I am grateful she sent Fancy to us. I have learned over the long years that we have been separated how the mother who raised me at my father's court—her name was Rugaiya Begum—must have felt after I left India. I was so young, and we never saw each other again." Jasmine wiped a tear from her eye, and laughed softly. "Now I begin to reminisce like the old woman I am," she said, mocking herself gently.

"No! No!" Diana said. "We love hearing stories of our family," and even Cynara nodded in agreement.

"Well," Jasmine replied, "that is enough for today. You were up early this day, my darlings, and if you are to sparkle tonight at court you must nap now. Jamie, go home to Lynmouth House, and do try not to take up too much of Ceci's time, unless of course your intentions are honorable," she told him with a twinkle in her eye.

He actually blushed, then laughed. "I do like her, madame," he said. "She is a gentle and most sensible girl."

"She is a most suitable prospect, James Edwardes, but you must love your wife. Do not choose a girl for practical reasons only. Even my Aunt Willow loved her husband dearly," she advised him.

"I have not forgotten we are to spend tomorrow together," he said to her.

"You are taking me to the theater," she answered him. "I shall give you your dinner first, however."

"And I shall take you to supper afterward," he promised.

"Where?" she demanded of him.

"At Lynmouth House, of course," he said laughing. Then he arose, and kissed her hand. "Farewell, madame. Farewell, Cousins." And he was gone from the hall.

"So he is interested in our Burke cousin," Cynara said.

"A fact you will manage to keep to yourself," her grandmother said. Then she turned to Diana. "And you, my dearie, has any gentleman taken your eye yet?"

"I would wager on the Esmonds," Cynara said.

"But there are two of them," Jasmine noted. "Which one of the two do you favor, Diana?"

Diana sighed deeply. "There is the problem, Grandmama. They are both very handsome, and very charming, and very amusing. The duke has the most beautiful light blue eyes, but the marquis has wonderful deep blue eyes. Yet they are so alike otherwise that it makes it difficult to separate them. Still they are very different as well. I do not know what to do. Or perhaps I should turn my attentions to the other young men who court me, for I do not honestly know if I could ever make a choice between Damien and Darius Esmond."

Cynara rolled her eyes in a most unsympathetic fashion at her cousin's declaration. "You have got to stop being so nice," she said, irritated.

Jasmine was hard put not to laugh, but she could see that this conundrum posed a real problem for Diana. "I think," she suggested to her granddaughter, "that perhaps you should concentrate on finding their differences to see which pleases you more. You know what you like about them. See if there is more to them than meets your eye, dear girl. Then you will be able to discern which you like better of the pair if indeed you do. Perhaps neither of the Esmonds is for you, Diana. Are there any others among the young men surrounding you who please you?"

Diana shook her head. "Perhaps, Grandmama, I am not meant to be wed. In another age I might have considered a convent."

"In another age a beautiful young heiress like yourself would already be wedded, and bedded with at least one child tugging at your skirts. You would have been considered a great prize. Besides, if I remember your father's history, I do not believe there has been a nun in the Leslie family in several centuries. Glenkirk women seem not well suited for a religious life. Now, the two of you go and rest. If you expect to be at your best tonight then you must not have dark circles beneath your pretty eyes. Cynara, I hear you have been gambling."

"Aye, but I do not lose, Grandmama," came the reply.

"Be a bit more discreet in your habits, dear girl," was Jasmine's answer.

The two cousins retired to their bedchambers. Diana gave instructions to her serving woman to have a hot bath ready in early evening so she might bathe before she went to court.

"You'll take your bath now," Molly replied sternly. "I can't have you going out on a cold winter's night still overheated from your tub, my lady."

"Then I shall wash my hair now as well," Diana decided.

She bathed in rose-scented water, rose being her favorite fragrance. Drying her long dark hair by the fire, Diana considered her grandmother's advice. She had to divide the Esmond twins in order to see what each of them was really like before she could make any decision. She wondered what it was about her that had made them her suitors. She hoped it wasn't because she was considered one of the court's *catches* this Season. She would insist if they wished to continue to court her that she be able to see each without the other. That was the only way she was going to be able to separate them. Her hair dry at last, Diana lay down to rest and quickly fell asleep.

That evening dressed in a deep rose velvet gown with dainty silver ribbons on the sleeves and delicate silver lace at her wrists, she went to court to dance and play at cards with her friends. A footman took her velvet cape, which was lined and trimmed with gray rabbit's fur. Almost at once the twins were at her side, both talking at her at once, and an irritated Diana stamped her foot at them.

"Be silent, Geminid!" she scolded them.

Surprised they grew silent, both looking at her.

"I will permit you to court me," she said quietly, but in a voice that brooked no argument. "However, you will each court me separately. I will do nothing with you both together again. If you cannot bear to be parted from each other, then perhaps neither of you should seek a wife. A marriage is between two persons. A husband and his wife. It is not between a husband, his brother, and the wife. Do you both understand me, my lords?"

"'Odsfish, madam," the duke exclaimed. "You are most direct. Are we together so aggravating then?" The light blue eyes studied her.

"My lord, to be frank, yes! I mean no insult to either of you, but together you are simply overwhelming. I do not know if you seriously seek to court me, or if you are so used to competing with each other that courting is a game. But for your eyes, you are identical to my eye, yet I know there are vast differences between you. I will marry no man I do not know and love. How can I get to know either of you, or come to love one of you, if indeed it comes to that, if you are both attempting to attract my attention at the same time," Diana told him.

"Courtship is indeed a game, madam," the marquis replied.

"All games have rules, my lord," Diana quickly responded.

"And what are your rules?" the duke asked. He had to admit that he found her candor refreshing. They had underestimated her, it was now quite obvious.

"You may each have two days a week of my time," she began, "although Sunday I will keep to myself."

"Which days?" the marquis queried. Now his deep blue eyes were dancing speculatively.

Diana drew a small coin from her gown's inner pocket. She flipped it into the air, catching it neatly, and placing it covered upon the back of one hand. "Call it, my lords!" she told them.

"Tails!" the duke said quickly.

"Why should you get to call first?" the marquis demanded.

"Because I am the elder, and I have always gone first," Damien Esmond told his twin, "but if you want tails I shall be generous and give it to you, Darling."

The marquis eyed the duke speculatively. After a long moment he said slowly, "No. I shall be satisfied to have heads, Damn."

Diana uncovered the coin. "Heads, it is," she said holding out her hand to show them. "Very well, Darius Esmond. Which two days of the week will you have for yourself?"

"Monday and Thursday," he replied. "And today is Thursday!"

"We will begin this game next week," Diana told them. "Until then neither of you is to behave as you have been, or I shall call our play off," she warned him.

"Yes, my lady," he said, grinning.

Diana turned to the duke. "Which days will you have, my lord?"

"Friday and Saturday," he said quietly.

"That is not fair!" his brother cried.

"What is unfair about it, Darling?" Diana asked. "I offered you each two days each week of my exclusive company. The only restriction I placed upon you was that I should not let you have Sundays. You chose first, and took Mondays and Thursdays. Do you wish to change your selection now, sir?" She looked at him so disapprovingly that the marquis of Roxley shook his head in the negative.

"Nay," he said. "I will stand by my decision."

Diana threw them both a brilliant smile. "Then it is settled, my lords. It is to be hoped that after all of this difficulty that I find at least one of you promising."

The two men began to laugh for neither had expected such honesty from the girl known as Siren. Her frankness intrigued them, and they found themselves more fascinated by her than ever before.

"Will you dance with us tonight, madam?" the duke asked.

"If I may dance with you one at a time," she said. "I will have no more of your childish competing, my lords."

"Agreed!" the marquis said, speaking for them both.

Diana danced with each in turn and then left them to join her friends who were seated chattering and gossiping.

"What were you talking to the Geminid about?" Ceci asked. "Did you know that you actually shook your finger at them?" she giggled.

"I find their rivalry annoying," Diana said. "I told them if they would court me, they must follow my rules."

"'Odsbodkins!" Pretty Kitty swore lightly. "Only Siren would dare to tell her suitors how to court her," and she laughed.

"Well, they had to be brought under control," Diana replied "They are like a pair of squabbling lads. I could tolerate it no longer."

"What rules did you lay down?" Slim Mumford asked Diana.

"Basically that they must court me individually, and to that end I gave them each two days a week in which to do it. That way I have two days free for my other gentlemen," she smiled. "And, of course, Sundays I shall devote to the Lord," she finished piously.

Her friends laughed.

"Clever," Wily Stanton noted, "but I suspect that Sundays you shall devote to resting," she chuckled, and the others laughed again.

"It is to be hoped," Pretty Kitty said, "that you will choose one of your suitors soon, dear cousin, for none of the rest of us will have a chance until you do."

"Ohh, but that is not fair!" Diana cried. "I mean none of you any harm. Men can be so difficult! I told my grandmama that if this were another time I should seriously consider a convent!"

"What did the dowager Jasmine say to that?" Wily Stanton asked.

"That if this were another time, I should have already been married off by my family to the best advantage, and no nonsense about it," Diana told them. "Thank heavens we live in modern times!"

The others nodded in agreement.

"Has anyone seen Cyn?" Diana wondered aloud.

"Look for Harry Summers," Ceci said. "He is rightly named *Wickedness*. I am surprised that the not-so-royal Stuart hasn't put a stop to his daughter's pursuit of that rogue. They say," and she lowered her voice so that her friends had to lean forward to hear her words, "that any girl who spends too much time with him is considered ruined. You should speak with her, Siren. You are closest to her of all the girls. She is my cousin too, though not to so near a degree, but I don't want to see her reputation in tatters. If *The Wits* get wind of her behavior, they will begin writing their scurrilous rhymes about it you may be certain."

"Cynara can be stubborn and sometimes difficult," Diana replied, "but she is no fool, Ceci. Believe me, there is nothing that I can say to her that would change her course."

"Does she want to wed him?" Pretty Kitty asked. "They say he has had numerous heiresses tossed at his head but vows he will never wed any woman. I think him a misogynist."

"Any man who beds as many women as he has claimed is hardly a misogynist," Wily Stanton murmured.

"You don't think he has . . ." Ceci said nervously, looking about the group.

"As I said," Diana murmured, "Cynara is no fool. If the earl of Summersfield desires the cow, he shall get only a quick hint of her cream, I promise you."

The others giggled.

"I do not think Cyn would enjoy hearing herself referred to as a cow," Pretty Kitty chuckled.

"Oh lord!" Slim Stanton said, and she straightened up in her chair, dabbing at her curls with a quick hand. "Here come all of your eager swains, Siren."

"Well," Ceci said dryly, "she can only dance with one of them, and that does leave the rest for us." She smiled brightly as the gentlemen approached, as did the others.

Chapter

10

There were few secrets at the court of Charles II. Consequently the arrangement between the beautiful Lady Diana Leslie, known to them all as sweet Siren, and the duke and marquis of Roxley was very quickly public knowledge and fodder for a group of the king's friends called *The Wits*. Diana knew that they had obtained their information through Fancy's friend, the actress, Nell Gwyn. One of Nell's former lovers, Charles Sakeville, Lord Buckhurst, was a prominent member of the group.

With one exception, that of George Villiers, the duke of Buckingham, *The Wits* consisted of well-born young men born just before, or shortly after the Battle of Worcester, during the last of England's civil wars. They had no ties or memories of England before Cromwell, but their families were quietly loyal to the Stuarts. By the time Charles II was restored to his throne the members of *The Wits* were half-grown. Now, several years after his restoration they had joined the court, and been brought together by their penchant for writing scandalous rhymes, drinking, and wenching. The king found them amusing, as did the court. Even those scourged by them found them amusing.

No king's mistress, no prominent lady, or gentleman, no one who caught their attention was safe from their scurrilous doggerel. Fancy had been the topic of their verse but once, referred to as "*a beau-*

teous, but murderous wench, who spread her legs on the royal bench." But
Nell, who was considered one of their friends, prevailed upon Lord
Buckhurst to cease their attacks, explaining that Fancy Devers was
"a good lady," and nothing like the termagant Castlemaine.

"Well, praise God for that," George Villiers, the duke of Buckingham said. The king's contemporary, he was somewhat older than
his companions but had managed to become one of them for he was
most clever. He also had a foot in the camp of a more serious group
of gentlemen, the men who advised the king.

The Wits, sometimes called *The Merry Gang*, also consisted of such
notables as John Wilmot, the earl of Rochester; Henry Jermyn; John
Sheffield, the earl of Mulgrave; Henry Killigrew; Sir Charles Sedley;
and two well-known playwrights of the day, Sir Charles Etherege
and William Wycherley. They amused themselves with poetry,
plays, and literature when they were not writing unprintable rhymes
about the prominent members of the court who caught their collective eye. Some of them were considered eccentric in their ways, and
those not closely associated with them sought to keep out of their
way.

Now, however, the situation between Lady Diana Leslie and the
Esmond twins had caught their attention. They learned that she
had christened them the Geminid. They were referred to as such
among her friends, a group of very pretty and smart young girls. But
not only was this tender beauty being pursued by the Roxleys, a
whole group of other gentlemen were eager for her favor and her
hand. They considered seducing her, ruining her reputation, and
then seeing which among her suitors would have her for her father's
wealth. It was the kind of vicious and immoral trick that they were
capable of, for they were really quite a group of reprobates when
they chose to be. Here again, however, Nellie Gwyn prevailed on
them not to carry out their wicked plan.

"It ain't her fault she's such a dear," she told them.

"Surely she isn't as nice as is claimed," the earl of Mulgrave said,
cocking a skeptical eyebrow.

"She's nicer," Nellie said. "Siren is just one of those girls who is
exactly what she seems. Kind and generous to a fault. If you criticize

someone, she can always find something good to say about them. If you lot mistreated her, debauched her, the king would see you all ruined. She is, after all, the not-so-royal Stuart's niece, raised these last few years in his own house. And you know how the king feels about the other Charles Stuart. He loves him."

"Hardly know the fellow," Henry Jermyn said. "He's rarely at court."

"No," the duke of Buckingham replied, "he isn't. Charlie doesn't like life at court. He far prefers his home at Queen's Malvern. He has come this Season with one purpose in mind: to marry off his nieces and his daughter. But, gentlemen, he is the king's close friend as well as his cousin. Had Prince Henry lived—had he been allowed to wed with Jasmine Lindley as she was known in those days—this Charles would have been seated on England's throne today, and not the one whose royal bottom warms that seat. Charlie has never wavered in his devotion to his family. He was with us in our fight against Cromwell and his ilk. He was in exile with us. His first wife was killed by Roundheads, and after hiding his children with his brother, the duke of Glenkirk in Scotland, he was separated from them for ten years. The king knows his sacrifices and loves him for it. But more important, Charlie has rarely, if ever, requested a favor from the king. Misbehave with any female member of his family, and your heads will all roll. Nellie speaks the truth when she says Lady Diana Leslie is naturally sweet. She is. Attempt to tamper with her innocence, and not only would the king revenge her, but her father, the duke of Glenkirk, would be down from Scotland like an avenging angel. Trust me, my lords, you don't want to find yourselves at the pointed end of that gentleman's sword."

"But we may write little verses about her situation, mayn't we?" William Wycherley asked. "The situation is simply too delicious for us to ignore, Buckingham."

"Write about the situation, but do not tarnish the lady's good reputation, Will," the duke advised.

"Why, Buckingham," Henry Jermyn remarked, "how solicitous you are of the young lady."

"Her grandfather was a friend to my father long ago," the duke said quietly. "I did not know him, but my mother often remarked upon it for at one time they were rivals for the same lady, yet they remained friends. That lady was she whom we know as the dowager Jasmine, the not-so-royal Stuart's mama."

"How about this?" Sir Charles Etherege said with a smile.

> *Just like a siren of old,*
> *Delightful, so sweet, never bold.*
> *Has a lady we know,*
> *An abundance of beaux.*
> *Just what has she got?*
> *That pretty young Scot,*
> *To set those poor fellows a-gog?*

His companions laughed, declaring a fine beginning, and the duke of Buckingham nodded his approval. It was amusing but not cutting. They would hone their collective wits upon the situation but not the lady involved.

Very quickly Sir Charles's rhyme was making the rounds. It was to the court's vast amusement quickly followed by another.

> *The Geminid, they both would vie*
> *To catch sweet Siren's emerald eye.*
> *Who will the dear wee lassie choose?*
> *Will the duke or the marquis lose?*

Even Jasmine found the rhymes funny. "They are not usually so kind to their victims," she told Diana. "I think you may thank Mistress Gwyn for prevailing upon them. They were not so easy with your cousin, Fancy, as you well know."

"She should, I suspect," said Cynara, who was just the tiniest bit jealous, "thank the duke of Buckingham as well."

"How clever of you to consider that, Cynara," her grandmother replied, "and you very well may be correct. Buckingham's father was a good friend to Jemmie and to me."

"Why is the court so fascinated with Diana?" Cynara asked.

"Because she intrigues them, my dear," Jasmine answered. "Even you love her. Every once in a while, someone comes along in this world who is just so sweet and so good that she is impossible to resist. That is our Diana. But your cousin is not satisfied to bask in the glow of her niceness, Cynara. She is intelligent, as you are. Her manner of solving the problem she had between the Esmond twins is to be admired, but it is also a remarkable and unusual solution. That is why it has attracted so much attention."

"The other girls hope she chooses soon. As long as she is undecided as to who will be her husband, none of the rest of them has a chance, except for Ceci, of course. I do believe that Jamie is falling in love with her, Grandmama, and she with him. How simple it seems to be for all of them," Cynara concluded.

Jasmine said nothing, for she knew that Cynara would take no advice from anyone right now regarding Harry Summers. Her Stuart granddaughter would have her way in the matter. And Jasmine thought ruefully, Was that not the way it had been for her in her youth? She instead now concentrated on Diana and her suitors.

Darius Esmond, the marquis of Roxley, began to visit Greenwood House each Monday and Thursday. His brother, the duke, came on Fridays and Saturdays. What had seemed an ideal solution in fact made more difficulties, for on Tuesdays and Wednesdays Diana found herself besieged by her other suitors.

"I am exhausted by them all," she half-sobbed to her grandmother after a month had gone by.

"Are you at all interested in any of the others?" Jasmine asked.

"They are all very nice," Diana sniffed, "but nay, Grandmama, I would not marry any of the others. Mick, of course, knows that, and we have become friends, but as for the rest of them, no."

"Then tell them," Jasmine advised sensibly.

"*Tell them?*" Diana looked perplexed. "I would not hurt their feelings, Grandmama," she said. "How can I possibly tell them?"

"You invite them all here, and when they have gathered, you say, 'My lords, your friendship means much to me, but I cannot love any of you for I am in love with the Geminid, though which one I love more I have yet to discover.' You then tell them that it is their duty to find wives, and that there are many suitable girls at court from which they can choose. That, dear child, is how you tell them."

"They will be offended," Diana cried.

"Indeed they will be offended when you finally decide between your duke and your marquis, after having kept them on your line for months, my dear Diana. Set them free now, child," Jasmine counseled her granddaughter. "Consider, first though that if neither the duke nor the marquis pleases you, would one of these others?"

Diana shook her head. "No," she said again. "Ned is a dear fellow as are Gage and Rupert, but like Mick, they are not really my equals. Bran, being an earl, would be suitable, but he is so cold-hearted a man. I could never love him, or be happy with him, Grandmama."

"You are not being influenced by Cynara, are you?" Jasmine wondered. "You should not judge your suitors on their social standing. All of these gentlemen are eligible, Diana, and your parents would be happy to accept any of them as long as you are content with the match. You are a wealthy girl, my child. None of your suitors can equal what you will have one day. Not even the Roxley Geminid."

Diana shook her head again. "Nay, it is not that," she said. "Ohh, Grandmama, I do not know what to do! I like them both so very much! How am I going to choose between them? I am not certain I can."

"The time will come," Jasmine told Diana, "when you know in your heart that it is right to choose. And you will."

In early March, Diana, taking Jasmine's advice, called her other suitors together and dismissed them as gently as she could. "You are all the dearest gentlemen," she assured them, "but I am not a girl to tease and flirt unless my heart is engaged. I think of you all as I do my brothers, but I cannot picture any of you as my husband. I would not keep you buzzing about me like so many bees about a flower, especially when there are so many other beautiful and eager flowers in the gardens, my lords, for you to buzz about. My grandmother has reminded me that you each have a duty to wed and breed up heirs. I must eventually choose between Damn and Darling for that is where my heart is leading me. Will you all remain my friends? *Please.*"

They were disappointed, but they had all seen the handwriting on the wall long since. Lady Diana Leslie had been more honest with them than many a girl would have been, and they could not resist her charming plea to remain friends. Each gentleman kissed her hand and vowed they would honor her request. Then they departed Greenwood House, the last to go being Sir Michael Scanlon.

" 'Twas nicely done, lass," he told her.

"They were exhausting me, and Grandmama suggested it was the only way," Diana's slim hand smoothed her garnet silk skirts.

"And have you decided between the Geminid, Siren?" he asked.

She shook her head. "Not yet. They are so much alike, even when apart, that it is impossible to make a decision."

"Do you love them then, lass?" he queried.

"I adore them both!" she cried.

"Do they kiss alike?" he wondered.

She blushed. "I do not know. We have not kissed."

"*What!*" Mick Scanlon's tone was scandalized. "What the hell is the matter with those lads?" he demanded to know.

"I think perhaps they both fear to offend me, and lose my favor," Diana admitted, blushing.

He tilted her small heart-shaped face, and said with the utmost seriousness, "Then, my dear, dear, sweet Siren, it is up to you to take the initiative with those two. What a pair of fools they are!"

Now she laughed. "Do not be so hard on them, Mick. This is very serious business, this courting." Then she pierced him with a look. "Am I mistaken, sir, are you showing an interest in my friend, Mistress Wily Stanton? Now that I have set my suitors free, they will be carefully considering the other eligibles at court. Drucilla is a very pretty girl and has a small but most respectable dower."

"I'm interested," he said with a grin, releasing her chin, "but it's those sky blue eyes of hers that attract me, along with her sensible nature. Do you think she would accept me, Siren?"

"She would be a fool not to, Mick. It's true she's an earl's younger daughter, but you've got a respectable house for a wife. It is respectable, isn't it?" And when he nodded, she continued, "And I have heard from Jamie that you have no debts and are careful never to lose more at cards than you can afford to repay. Her dower isn't large enough to attract many for she is the youngest daughter of five. I expect her father would welcome your suit, provided you had Wily's permission to approach him first."

"But would she live in Ireland?" he wondered. "It's unlikely I can afford to come back to court once I leave it," Sir Michael Scanlon said. "I did not come until this year because I could not afford to come. I will have to return home this summer."

"Where is your home?" Diana asked him.

"Outside of Dublin," he answered her.

"I have heard tell that Dublin society is a most congenial one," Diana noted.

"Aye, it is!" he said. "I can afford Dublin society."

"Then pursue the lady, Mick. What is the worst she can say to your suit? No. It is not such a terrible word," Diana said smiling. "Can you love her? I think a man should love his wife, although I know that such a view is considered infantile and foolish."

"I *already* love her," he said softly. "That is why I so fear her rejection, Siren."

"Oh, Mick," Diana replied, "do not waste another moment in fearful contemplation. If your heart is involved, then you must certainly woo and win her. And you will, I am certain!"

"You are the kindest girl!" he told her, and he kissed her upon her rosy cheek. Then he bowed a most courtly bow. "I must go else the others be jealous that I remained with you despite your dismissal of them. They will spend at least a full day and a night in deepest mourning."

"'Odsfish, Mick, I hope not," she told him laughing.

"Oh, they will," he assured her. "It will be all over the court by nightfall that you have sent them off and intend to concentrate all your effort on the duke and the marquis. Well, I am off, my dear lassie. Farewell, and wish me well in my endeavors."

"I do, Mick!" she promised him.

When he had gone, Diana sat herself by the fire and considered their conversation. She must tell Drucilla Stanton of Mick's interest. It would really be a very good match for both of them. Wily had worried about her small dowry, knowing she would be overlooked in many instances because of it. She had a maternal Irish grandmother, and Dublin society was known to be most merry. Mick was handsome, although the oldest of their group of friends. Still, he was well liked and a good fellow. Yes, it would be ideal if they wed, and she would tell Wily so this evening when they met at court.

Then she began to consider what Mick had said to her regarding Damn and Darling. She had twitted them about doing everything together, but it was obvious that they did. Neither of them had done more than dance with her, hold her hand, and chat. The few differences she had elucidated between them so far were hardly worth mentioning, and certainly nothing that would cause her to favor one over the other. The duke seemed a bit more sensible than the marquis. The marquis, however, had a quicker wit when it came to jests. *But neither of them had kissed her!* Nor had they attempted to fumble her. Was Mick correct? Should she invite an attempt at passion?

Jasmine came into the salon. "You are alone? Your covey of suitors has left? I saw that Sir Michael remained behind."

"We are friends, Grandmama; we talked. I have dismissed the others as you suggested and will now concentrate my efforts upon finding out whether it is light blue eyes or deep blue eyes that I can love." She laughed. "But I have a problem you must help me with, Grandmama."

"You know I shall," Jasmine answered the girl. "What is it?"

"The Geminid have never kissed me. They have not even made an attempt to kiss me! Mick says I must initiate the kissing myself for he thinks the duke and his brother fear to offend me and lose my favor. So neither will act upon his desires. What am I to do?"

"Exactly what he says," Jasmine responded, half-laughing. "What a pair of fools your twins be, my dear child. In my youth the gentlemen were not so delicate, and sensitive of our nature. They would use whatever means necessary to win fair maid, and if that meant overwhelming her with passion, they did so!"

Diana sighed. "Then I must encourage them to act upon their desires. Obviously this is the only way I shall be able to make a decision at all, Grandmama. But I have never been kissed."

"You have seen it done, haven't you?" Jasmine asked her.

"Oh, yes," Diana responded.

"You are certain?" her grandmother said nervously. If Diana was going to encourage her two suitors in their desires, it would be best that she knew what she was doing.

"I've seen Fancy with the king," Diana replied innocently. "It looks most exciting, Grandmama, and both my cousin and His Majesty are very enthusiastic in their kissing."

"It might be wise," Jasmine suggested, "to be a bit more restrained when you kiss for the very first time. If the passion is there, you will naturally become more zealous. On the other hand, if there is no spark of desire, then you will know that the gentleman is not for you."

Diana nodded. "I think," she said, "that I shall not go to court this evening, Grandmama. The duke is coming tomorrow morning to visit me, and as he is the elder, I will start with him. If I go to Whitehall this afternoon, the gossip, Mick assures me, will already be circulating. Everyone will know that I have declined the advances of Lord Charlton, Baron Mayhew, Lord Dunstan, and the earl of Dunley. They intend to play heartbroken, Mick says, but I suspect by tomorrow evening they will be prowling like alley cats. Being so eligible, a number of mamas and daughters will be trolling for them as quickly. Mick is interested in Wily Stanton. What do you think of that?"

"'Twould be a good match if she is wise enough to take it," Jasmine said. "Now, about you, my dear child. I think you are wise to remain at home today. I could wish that Cynara were as wise."

"Do not worry about Cynara, Grandmama. She knows what she wants, and she will get it in the end, I vow," Diana replied.

"I have dealt with some rogues in my time, Diana, but I like not what I hear about the earl of Summersfield," Jasmine answered. "He has a cold heart. Perhaps too cold to warm again."

"Cynara will have her own way, Grandmama. If that means she

must suffer a broken heart before she finds her true love, then perhaps that is what must happen to her, but I hope not."

Diana spent a quiet afternoon alone. She had not had such a lovely private time in weeks, she realized. She knew now that she missed the country far more than she had previously admitted to herself. She walked in the riverside garden of Greenwood House, spying the first signs of the spring to come. There were already patches of bright purple and gold crocus. There were clumps of daffodils, their green shoots several inches high and showing their slender buds. Two gardeners were at work, their spades turning the soil in the flower beds and then mincing it fine. The roses had already been trimmed, and looking closely Diana could see the minuscule red shoots beginning to show forth. The willows by the river were displaying the beginnings of their yellow-green. It was a perfect March day framed by a blue sky and a cheerful yellow sun. The river was as smooth as glass as it waited between the two tides. She sat down upon a small marble bench and watched the water as the gulls soared high, then swooped down seeking their dinner.

She sat for some time, unable to tear herself away, until suddenly she was very cold. She arose and returned to the house, asking her servant, Molly, to arrange a bath. She would soak her chills away. While she waited, she slipped down to the kitchens and was welcomed by the cook, an apple-checked woman who always seemed dusted with flour. The cook beckoned her in and sat her down at the long wooden kitchen table where the servants ate their meals. She plunked a mug of hot tea before the girl and a slab of fresh bread, smeared with butter and jam. When Diana had finished, she thanked the cook and hurried back upstairs where the last of the footmen was filling her bath, which had been set before the fire in her bedchamber.

Molly helped her to undress.

"I am going to soak for a while," she told the servant. "Tomorrow is to be a special day, Moll. I am going to kiss the duke, for I am tired of waiting for him and for his brother to kiss me. Either they love, or they don't."

"Does your grandmama know what you plan?" Molly asked.

"Oh, yes," Diana said, climbing into her tub and sinking down into the hot water with a grateful sigh. "She approves."

"Well, you just be careful, m'lady. All this kissing, and what comes with it can lead a lass into difficulties," Molly warned her young mistress. "You ain't Mistress Fancy, or that proud baggage, your cousin, Lady Cynara. You're a good lass, and I know you want to make your family proud. The duke will be real pleased when he comes this summer if you have chosen a good husband."

"I know," Diana said, "but I am not certain I am ready to choose even if I like kissing my suitors," Diana admitted to Molly. "I rather enjoy the court and all its diversions, Molly."

"You're going to be sixteen soon, m'lady, and if you don't mind my saying so, the bloom begins to come off the rose quickly after a lass reaches sixteen. 'Tis time you were wed."

Diana wanted to giggle at Molly's stern warning, but she refrained from doing so and hurting her maidservant's feelings. Molly loved her and wanted her happiness. Diana sank down in the perfumed water and said, "Leave me alone now, Molly. I will call you when I am ready."

Molly curtsied, and gathering up her mistress's laundry and other garments, she hurried from the room.

Sixteen. She had forgotten her birthday was coming about again. Was Molly correct? Did the bloom come off the rose or begin to after a girl reached that age? The king certainly seemed to enjoy younger lovers to my lady Castlemaine who was now in her late twenties. *But I am not ready to marry quite yet,* Diana thought. *I should rather be an old maid than an unhappily married woman. Yet I do love Damn and Darling. Either would be a good match for me. But I must love one more than the other, or I cannot be happy. If I simply pick blindly, and then discover afterward, that I have chosen wrongly . . .* It was a horrific thought, and Diana shuddered in the hot bathwater. Maybe she should send both twins away and begin afresh. But she knew all the eligible young gentlemen at court, and it was the duke and the marquis of Roxley who attracted her. Was there someone at Queen's Malvern? One of her cousins, perhaps, who could make her happy, and save her from this terrible decision? No, there was not.

How could a girl love two men at the same time? she wondered. But she knew. They looked alike. They behaved alike. It was simply impossible to separate Damien and Darius Esmond. Or was it? There had to be something that made each man an individual. Some one thing that appealed to her more than the other, dividing the twins into distinct personalities that would allow her to make a choice between them. *But what?* Kissing them seemed as good a place as any to begin, and she was rather looking forward to it for she had never before been kissed by a suitor. She knew how it was done for she, Cynara, and Fancy had spent hours discussing the merits of kissing, and men who kissed. But she had never experienced a kiss though the other two certainly had. Fancy because she had been married, and Cyn because she was daring.

I am not as adventurous, Diana thought, *but I can be if I want to be.* Realizing the water was beginning to cool, Diana took up the wash-cloth and completed her ablutions. Standing up, she stepped from her tub and reached for the towel warming on the rack by the fire. Drying herself briskly, Diana wrapped the towel about her and walked across the bedchamber to where Molly had laid out her clean nightgown. Tossing the towel aside, she donned the garment, tying the little pink ribbons at its neck. Then she climbed into her bed to keep warm.

Molly brought her a tray of supper containing a thick vegetable pottage, several slices of pink country ham, bread, sweet butter, and a goodly wedge of sharp cheddar. When Diana had finished all of the repast, including the small mug of the last of the October ale that had been stored in the house's cellars, Molly plunked a dish before her mistress containing a large apple baked with cinnamon and sugar and surrounded by a lake of thick sweet cream.

"Now you eat every bit of that up," she said, knowing there was no need to admonish her young mistress to do so. Baked apples were Diana's favorite. "And here's another glass of that nice sweet wine your grandmama likes in the evening too." She set a tiny crystal goblet down on the tray.

"You are spoiling me," Diana said with a smile.

"A lass who is going to begin kissing games needs all of her strength," Molly said with a mischievous grin.

"Then I must certainly finish this all up," Diana agreed, as the last of the wine slid down her throat. "I think I may develop a taste for this wine, Molly. It is delicious!"

"Your grandmama's ships bring it from Portugal," Molly said, "where our good queen comes from, m'lady." Molly then removed the tray from her mistress's lap, and brought her a silver ewer in which to bathe her hands and face, as well as the special little boar's bristle brush with the carved silver handle that Diana used for cleaning her teeth. Many ladies, Molly knew, used a tiny bundle of twigs, but all the women in the dowager's household had these special brushes that they used with a mix of finely ground pumice stone and mint oil. Molly didn't hold with most foreign customs, but she liked this one for her mistress always had fresh-smelling breath unlike many others.

When Molly had taken the basin and its accoutrements away, Diana snuggled down into her bed and was quickly asleep. Molly put another log on the fire, and tiptoed from the room. Soon a spring rain was beating upon the bedchamber windows, but Diana never heard it, for warm and well fed, she slept the sleep of the innocent. She awoke to a fine spring day. Seeing the sunlight streaming through her window, she knew that the duke would take her riding in St. James Park. The ice on the royal canal had melted almost two weeks ago, and the sliding season was over. Some of the young people at court were playing tennis already, but Diana thought it an over-rough sport.

Molly came in with her breakfast tray, asking, "What shall we wear today, m'lady? If you are to be kissed by a duke, it should be something special." She set the tray down upon her mistress's lap.

"We'll be going riding," Diana told her servant. "He said on the next fine day we had together, we would ride in the park."

"Then the crimson velvet habit it shall be, m'lady," Molly said. "Now eat up your breakfast. Cook did those eggs you are so fond of and there is lovely lamp chops with them."

Diana ate heartily. She had, as her grandmother noted, a healthy appetite, yet she never grew plump, which infuriated Cynara who had to watch every morsel she put in her mouth. When the tray of food had been devoured, and the last saucer of tea drunk, Diana set the tray aside, and arose from her bed. Relieving herself in her chamber pot, she washed her face and hands. Next she brushed her teeth again for her breath should be sweet when she kissed the duke. Picking up her hairbrush, she began the requisite one hundred strokes. When she had finished, she dressed with Molly's aid.

"I've polished up your buskins," Molly said, pulling the black leather boots up over her mistress's white silk stockings. The boots came to Diana's calf. They had a flap that folded over from their top.

Diana stood up now, her red skirts falling gracefully about her. "Just a veil for my head, I think, Molly," she said.

"Lace or silk gauze?" Molly asked.

"The silk, I believe. There is a piece that matches my gown, I think. Yes, that is it," Diana said taking the veil and draping it over her hair.

"If he don't kiss you without encouragement, I'll be surprised," Molly said, handing her mistress a pair of red kid gloves embroidered with little pearls.

"Send around to the stables," Diana said, "for my black mare. Is Grandmama up yet?"

"Aye, and she will want to see you before you go," Molly said.

The two young women hurried out, Molly heading down to the stables to order her mistress's horse be saddled, and Diana to her grandmother's apartments.

"How absolutely lovely you look!" Jasmine greeted her grandchild. "I always wore red well, too, and so do you with that clear skin of yours."

"Molly says if he doesn't kiss me without encouragement, she will be disappointed," Diana said with a smile, and she sat down on her grandmother's bed.

"The young men in your generation need a wee bit of encouragement," Jasmine replied. "They are not quite as daring as in my day. Yet given a signal to advance, I have no doubt they are just as passionate as when I was a girl, Diana. The nature of men does not change, my dear child," Jasmine remarked with an answering smile.

"How can I love two men at the same time, Grandmama?" Diana burst out. "And do I really want either of them for a husband? I know that I didn't want the others."

"You love them both because there is little to distinguish between them," Jasmine answered her. "As for whether one or the other will suit you better, time will tell you that. But, Diana, my darling child, you must not marry simply because it is expected of you. *You must marry for love.* I always did."

"Not the first time," Diana said. "I remember you saying your father arranged your marriage to Prince Jamal Khan, Grandmama. You never met the prince until the day you wed him."

"That is true," Jasmine said, "and I was fortunate in that I came to love Jamal Khan. That is why I made certain that I loved my next two husbands first."

"You had three husbands, and a Stuart prince for a lover, Grandmama. Which did you love best?" Diana asked Jasmine, hoping that her grandmother's answer would give her the answer that she sought.

"I loved them each in their own way, in their own time, Diana. I did not have the difficulty that you are having."

"But you knew my grandfather and Fancy's grandfather at the same time, didn't you? It is whispered that you had an affair with Lord Leslie before you married the marquis of Westleigh," Diana remarked.

"Jemmie Leslie and I had a brief encounter after a Southwood Twelfth Night fete. We were discovered by my stepsister who fancied herself in love with Jemmie. I can still remember the earl of BrocCairn, who was my stepfather, demanding that Jemmie and I wed. I refused. I had no intention of forcing any man into marriage."

"But why?" Diana began.

"Because both Jemmie and I were lonely at that moment in time. We were both widowed. We were not children. But I knew the marquis of Westleigh far better then. My grandmother could see he wanted to marry me and arranged it. I quickly forgot about Jemmie

Leslie for I adored Rowan Lindley until the day he died. As for your Uncle Charlie's papa, Prince Henry was a charming boy, and I very much enjoyed being seduced by him. I loved him, too, but I could not tell him."

"Why not, Grandmama?" Diana asked.

"Because our circumstances would not allow for a marriage between us. I believed if Hal knew I loved him, his family would not be able to get him to wed with their choice, whoever she would have been. But he died before anything could be arranged. At least he lived to see his son," Jasmine said, and her voice trailed off.

"It was because of Uncle Charlie that old King James made you marry my grandfather, wasn't it?"

Jasmine laughed. "Indeed it was, but I led your grandfather a most merry chase first. I suspect he might have never found me had it not been for my own grandmother, Madame Skye. Still, she would not let him bring me back to England until she was certain we were both madly in love with each other. And then the king almost ruined it again, but you know all the stories, Diana, for I have told them to you."

"And I love them!" Diana declared. "You have lived the most fascinating life, Grandmama."

"My grandmother lived a more exciting one," Jasmine said with a chuckle. "And I do not know the half of it, for there were some things she would not share even with me."

There was a light knock on the bedchamber door, and Orane popped around it. "The duke is here for Lady Diana," she said.

Diana arose from her place on the edge of the bed. Her cheeks were suddenly very pink with her excitement. Then she suddenly grew pale. "What if I do not like his kisses, Grandmama?" she said.

"Well, my darling child, it will solve the problem for you, will it not?" Jasmine answered.

"But what if the marquis kisses the same, and I do not like his kisses?" Diana fretted.

"Then Diana, you will begin again," Jasmine replied, "but it is unlikely that you will dislike either of their kisses. You will just have to decide which you enjoy more. Now, run along."

"I can't even decide if I like light blue eyes or dark blue eyes," Diana wailed softly. Then she sighed. "I cannot believe I am being such a ninny, and am so indecisive. I must regain a hold of myself, and make an intelligent decision."

"Of course, my darling," Jasmine said, and she waved her granddaughter out of her bedchamber. Gracious, she thought as the door closed behind Diana, such a fuss over this matter. Her granddaughters seemed more concerned with the status of their future husbands than of falling in love. But it was the age, of course. *I think I am glad I grew up when I did,* she considered. *How I would like Fancy, Diana and Cynara to simply be overwhelmed by their passions as I once was. Was several times in fact.* She chuckled. Then she wondered if her darling girls even suspected what falling in love was like? Of course not. They had had little chance for it. Except Fancy, her beloved daughter, Fortune's, youngest child. Fortune had fallen in love, but it had been with the wrong man. But perhaps the wrong man was better than no man at all.

She arose from her bed, and walked bare-footed across the floor of her bedchamber to the windows. From one she could see Diana as she stepped into the duke's coach. Her black mare was tied behind the vehicle. St. James Park was not near Greenwood House. She looked more closely at the duke of Roxley. He was certainly a handsome young man. She wondered why he had not married sooner. There was much she didn't know about him, but she thought perhaps now she might investigate. And Sir Michael Scanlon would be just the fellow who could help her, Jasmine reflected. She wanted no more tragedies in her family. At least not if she could help it.

"Orane!" she called to her serving woman. "Orane, come and help me dress!"

Chapter

11

Damien Esmond, the duke of Roxley, climbed into his carriage, seating himself opposite Lady Diana Leslie. He smiled at her. "You are looking especially lovely today, sweet Siren," he said. "Red is a color that suits you."

"So Grandmama says," Diana replied. "You may kiss me, Damn."

"*What?*" Surely he hadn't heard her a-right.

"You may kiss me," she repeated, and leaning forward Diana closed her eyes while pursing her lips.

He kissed her upon her rosy cheek.

Diana's emerald eyes flew open. "Are you my cousin then?" she demanded to know. Her tone was offended and most indignant. "I hope that your brother can do better when I offer him the opportunity to kiss me next we meet, my lord Duke."

'Oddsfish! She had meant it. The duke wasted no time on explanations. Reaching out he yanked her into his lap and kissed her hard. "Is that better, madam?" he demanded of her as he looked satisfied into her startled young face.

"*Oh, yes!*" Diana managed to murmur before he was kissing her again, his lips taking hers more tenderly this time, and she sighed with her own delight. So this was what kissing was all about, she thought muzzily, and sighed again softly.

She had never been kissed before, he realized. She was not playing the tease. She simply wanted to experience kissing, and she had chosen him to be her first lover. Damien Roxley knew then and there that he didn't want to share his sweet Diana with anyone else, even his twin brother, Darius. He lifted his auburn head and said passionately, "Marry, me, Diana! Cease this foolishness, and marry me. I adore you! I will make you happier than any woman has ever been, I swear it!" And the light blue eyes bore into her, demanding an answer.

"I can give you no answer yet, Damn," she told him honestly. "You are the first man I have ever kissed. I think it only prudent that I offer Darling the same advantage as I have you. I love you both for your wit and your charm, but I have not yet the experience a girl needs to make such a momentous decision."

"But . . ."

Reaching up, she stopped his speech with a gentle hand. "If you win me, if I choose you over your brother, is it not better that you gain me for a wife fairly, my lord?" She attempted to sit up.

"I will win you fairly," he declared and kissed her again, but this time his big gloved hand smoothed itself daringly over the small swelling of her breasts. He groaned softly. "I *must* win you, my darling, for the thought of any other man having you, even my brother, sets me into a frenzy!" Then he released her, helping her to reseat herself on the carriage bench opposite him, noting her cheeks were now quite pink.

"You quite overwhelm me, my lord," Diana told him, and her face felt hot with her blushes. What kind of a Pandora's box had she opened demanding he kiss her back? Were all men's kisses this exciting? she wondered. Did she even want the marquis of Roxley to kiss her now? *Yes, she did!* She needed some sort of comparison between these two twin brothers. It would not do to choose the wrong husband.

They rode in silence to St. James Park, and when they had arrived the duke leaped from the coach and helped her to dismount. A groom, who had ridden behind the vehicle, untied the duke's silvery white gelding and Diana's dainty black mare. They mounted and began their ride meandering through the greenery, meeting friends and acquaintances as they rode. For a time they continued in silence, and then Diana said, "Tell me about your home, and how is it that there are two titles for Roxley, my lord?"

"There have been twin brothers in my family for many generations," he began. "In the time of Edward IV, we supported the Lancastrian cause of the Tudors. The first Tudor king, Henry VII, often said without our aid he might not have won his throne. He said no one family, especially one of such little importance, should have such power in their hands. That it was dangerous to the throne. So he elevated the then marquis of Roxley to a dukedom, which in itself was unusual as most dukedoms were possessed by royalty back then. He then gave the second-born of that generation's twins the title of marquis of Roxley. Until my brother and I were born, the titles remained in separate families, but the last marquis of Roxley died without heirs of either sex in the first of the Civil Wars. Our father immediately applied to the first King Charles to retain his title of marquis for my brother. It was granted as our uncle had died in the cause of the late king who yet held some power. During the Protectorate, our family remained on our estates like so many others. Our mother had died giving birth to us, and so our father's main concern was making certain that Darling and I grew to adulthood in safety. But he died when we were fourteen. Because our estates, which adjoin each other, are isolated and because our few servants were loyal to the Esmond family, we managed to maintain our cloak of invisibility so that the authorities in the region did not learn that two young noblemen were without proper supervision. We raised our cattle and grain, paid our taxes, and did not complain when the government confiscated our livestock to feed their troops." He smiled at her. "It allowed us to hold on to what was rightfully ours when others lost everything. The king had promised that in exchange for his restoration, he would not confiscate estates that had been appropriated and commandeered from their rightful owners during the era of the Commonwealth. Had we lost Roxley, it would not have been returned to us. Being mere lads, we had not openly supported the king so we would have been given nothing to replace our losses. We are not an important family as is yours, sweet Siren."

"Where is Roxley?" she asked him, for she had never bothered to ask either of her suitors. Now it was important as she was bound to wed one of the twins and live there. Would she be near family?

"In the northwest section of Hereford. My brother and I raise cattle for meat. And we have some fine apple orchards. Our cider is quite famous throughout the county," he explained.

"Then neither of you is a wastrel," Diana said. "I could not wed with an idle man. My family has merchant vessels that trade all over the world. The enterprise was begun by my great-great-grandmother and continues to this day. The O'Malley-Small trading fleet is well known and prosperous. Many of my cousins are involved to this day in her venture. Our wealth depends upon it."

"Are you?" he asked, not really expecting that she would say that she was.

"Of course," Diana answered him. "All the women in my family have been taught how to manage our wealth. If you or your brother would have me to wife, Damn, you must understand that marriage will not change that. My wealth will remain in my hands. It has always been that way with the female descendants of Skye O'Malley, for that was my great-grandmother's name. She was the countess of both Lundy and Lynmouth, Lady Burke, and the duchess of a Mediterranean kingdom called Beaumont de Jaspre among others."

"'Oddsfish, madame! How many husbands did this great-great-grandmother of yours have?" Her revelation was both fascinating and intriguing.

"Six," Diana said. "The two I have not named were not particularly noble. Her first husband was the son of the master of Ballyhennessey in Ireland where she was born. Her second was a Spanish merchant in Algiers. My cousin Jamie descends from their daughter." She smiled. "I did not know her, but my grandmother did and speaks highly of her. She had six children as well as six husbands and was a contemporary of the great Elizabeth."

"'Odsfish!" he said again, not knowing what else to say.

Diana laughed. "It is a great deal to take in all at once, my lord. My family can surely be considered unusual. One of my own ancestors was an Ottoman sultan. Does it change your desire to court me?"

"*No!*" he exclaimed, but grew silent after that. He needed time in which to absorb all this fascinating information. Their kisses, it seemed, had opened up a flowing font of information. Never before had they spoken so intimately, their previous conversations being polite small talk. Suddenly he was seeing her in an entirely new light. They rode for a time, finally returning to the place from which they had started. The duke lifted Diana from her saddle, and their eyes met. Unable to help himself, he wrapped his arms about her and kissed her again.

Diana melted into his arms until remembering that they were in a public area she pulled away from him. "My lord," she gently admonished him, "'tis too common a place. If we are seen, we will be the talk of the court by evening. I should not like that."

Nodding, he assisted her into his carriage and joined her. The vehicle moved away, departing the park and making its way back through the city streets to Greenwood House. Within, Diana and the duke kissed more and more passionately. His hand caressed her bosom, and she trembled at his touch, yet she was thrilled by it too. He felt himself rigid with his burning desire, but she was a virgin. And she was not yet his and his alone. But she would be, he promised himself. This was one battle that his twin was not going to win.

Diana emerged from the duke's coach when they reached Greenwood House. She was rosy with her blushes. Wordlessly he escorted her to the open door, kissing her hand, and bowing politely as he did so. "Will you come to court this evening?" he asked her low.

"Yes," she nodded softly. Her heart was hammering with her excitement. She was only just beginning to understand what love was all about. "You will be there too?"

"Aye!" he responded with such enthusiasm that she blushed again.

"I will save three dances for you, my lord," she told him, and then turning hurried into the house.

"You will save all your dances for me!" he called after her.

She turned and laughed. "No, my lord, I won't," she said as the servant closed the door behind her. Then Diana hurried to find her grandmother. *"I have finally been kissed!"* she announced as she entered the library where Jasmine sat reading by a window.

The dowager set her book aside and asked, "Did you enjoy it, Diana?" She smiled, and beckoned the girl into a chair opposite her. "And was it more than one kiss?"

"Oh yes!" Diana enthused. "So many, Grandmama, that I cannot number them." She paused as if considering, blushed, and then said, "And he caressed my bosom as well, Grandmama."

"Indeed," Jasmine replied dryly. "I am happy to learn that the duke's passions can be aroused. He has been so polite I feared that perhaps he had no passion in him at all. You must not wed a passionless man, my dear child. It makes for an unhappy union."

"If his brother is as ardent," Diana said, "I shall again be faced with the same quandary, Grandmama."

"It has been my experience," Jasmine said with a smile, "and before I wed your grandfather I had much experience, that no two men are alike where love is concerned. The marquis will be an entirely different kettle of fish, I guarantee you. But at least then you shall be able to begin to make a choice between them. Or no choice at all mayhap."

Diana dressed carefully for her visit to court that evening. She wore a gown of pale rose petal silk trimmed with cream-colored lace, the sleeves decorated with a line of turquoise blue bows. The neckline was deeply scooped, and the satin overskirt was a slightly deeper pink. Her ebony hair was dressed from a center part into wide side ringlets with a single shoulder ringlet. About her slender neck was a choker of pink pearls.

As it was a lovely evening, and there was no breeze, Diana and Cynara decided to take the family's barge to Whitehall. Cynara was in defiance of her grandmother's suggestions, wearing a gown of black silk with a shockingly low scooped neckline. The black lace collar, which was sprinkled with miniscule sparkling diamonds, made a futile attempt at modesty. The tiny gemstones twinkled from her lace cuffs as well. There was a brilliant diamond bow pin in the center of the black lace collar that demanded inspection of her swelling breasts.

"Did Grandmama see you before you left?" Diana asked her cousin. "And will your parents approve of you wearing such a gown?"

"I did not have time to see Grandmama," Cynara said.

"You mean you knew she would make you change into something more suitable. You are a duke's daughter, Cyn. You are a virgin, and yet you behave as if you are not. Your reputation will be in shreds if you are not more circumspect. *The Wits* are already circulating a bit of doggerel about you. *She chases, yet he would run, but will he finish what she begun?*"

Cynara laughed. "At least I am now noticed. Between our cousin Fancy and her relationship with the king and the spectacle you have made with all your suitors, I have been ignored! Tonight I shall make the earl of Summersfield dance to my tune for he treats me shamefully."

"You pursue the most unattainable man at court, and you are surprised that he pays you little heed?" Diana said. "Why can you not just find a good man who will love you, Cyn?"

"Love my dowry more than likely," Cynara replied bitterly. "Nay, my dear and sweet cousin, I want the earl of Summersfield. He is the only man at court who I would truly believe loved me for myself and not my wealth. He has wealth of his own and is not known to be an avaricious man. There is no other who will do for me. Now, tell me, have you yet decided between your duke and your marquis?"

"I let Damn kiss me this afternoon in his coach," Diana confessed.

Cynara laughed and clapped her hands. "Then you have at last experienced your first kiss," she said. "And did you like being kissed, Cousin?"

"Very much!" Diana admitted with a mischievous grin. "I shall let the marquis kiss me too when the occasion arises. I need a way to pick between the two of them, and Grandmama says no two men are alike when it comes to passion."

"Grandmama would certainly know such things," Cynara chuckled.

Their barge moved up the river with the incoming tide. The lights of London twinkled on either side of them. New buildings were springing up everywhere in the wake of the great fire that had destroyed a good part of the city several years back. Finally, they reached Whitehall. Their barge bumped the stone quay and was made fast by a palace footman. The two young women were helped out of their transport and made their way up the embankment to the palace where the nightly revelry was already under way.

There was to be a masque that evening featuring the king's three mistresses. My lady Castlemaine, under protest, was to have the role of the Winter Queen. She would be vanquished by Springtime, played by Mistress Nellie Gwyn. When Barbara Villiers learned of what the playwright Wycherley had planned, she threw one of her famous tantrums. She was finally calmed, and advised by her cousin, the duke of Buckingham, that to refuse a prominent role in the first major pageant of the spring season would be very foolish. It would also leave her open to even more ridicule.

"Play your part with charm and elegance, Barbara," George Villiers said to his cousin. "Everyone knows it is over between you and the king. Instead of allowing yourself to be an object of the court's pity, let them admire your good sense in stepping gracefully aside and taking a new lover. The king has made you a rich woman, my dear."

"Go to hell!" she raged at him.

"If you decline the role, someone else will be found to play it, but the court already knows you have been chosen to be the Winter Queen. You will be a laughingstock if you refuse now," the duke said.

"I will be a laughingstock if I do play it," she countered. "It too closely mimics my situation."

"You can't change that," George Villiers said. "You will find a way to make it all palatable. If you do not, Barbara, I will withdraw my support of you. Do you understand me, Cousin?"

"I hate you!" she snarled angrily.

"But you will accept the role," he stated.

"What other choice do I have," she muttered.

So now my lady Castlemaine, garbed in silver and white, her gown sewn all over with tiny crystals, gracefully danced her part as the spectacle opened before the seated court. From a silver bag, she tossed little silver snowflakes into her audience as the court musicians played a sprightly tune. She spoke her lines clearly, praising the cold and snow of the season, declaring that she would never let go her grip upon the earth that she might reign forever. These words were said through gritted teeth.

"What part is Fancy to play?" Diana asked Cynara in a whisper.

"She is April, princess of the Flower Fairies," Cynara whispered back to her cousin. "'Odsblood, Castlemaine has beautiful hair!"

Now the tenor of the music began to subtly change, becoming lighter and gayer. Springtime appeared, ready to vanquish winter. Mistress Nellie, garbed in flowing silks in at least a dozen shades of green, all of which were most flattering with her auburn hair, danced onto the stage. There was a gasp from the audience. It was very obvious that Nellie was quite naked beneath her strategically sewn gown and her most shapely legs were bare. The king was distinctly heard to chuckle his deep rich laugh as Nell set about to vanquish her rival.

The Winter Queen was supposed to cower at the appearance of fair Springtime. Instead she glared at her rival whose elegant body was untouched by childbirth and whose bouncing breasts thrust so boldly beneath the sheer silk of her costume.

"Begone, oh wicked Winter!" Nellie cried in her clear and pretty voice. She danced around my lady Castlemaine.

The Winter Queen threw a handful of her silver snowflakes at Springtime, but Springtime just laughed.

"Your part here is done!" she said, and several in the audience snickered audibly. William Wycherley had a wicked sense of humor, and he did not spare Barbara Villiers one bit.

Barbara was furious, but she knew as her cousin had advised that she had no choice but to retire gracefully. *"I am vanquished! Alas, and woe!"* she said. *"But my time shall come again,"* she added to the playwright's script. Then she danced from the stage.

"Not if Springtime lasts forever!" Nellie quickly cried her own ad lib.

"Here! Here!" a number of young gentlemen in the audience added, and there was a smattering of clapping.

Springtime next introduced April, princess of the Flower Fairies, and her court: Daffodil, Narcissus, Daisy, Bluebell, Gillyflower, Lilac, Mary's Gold, and Rosebud. Each flower fairy had a male partner in a similar garb and together they danced from the stage, and through into the audience, and back up onto the stage again, led by Springtime and April holding hands. Springtime was garbed in lavender and violet silks.

The pageant concluded with Nellie declaring: *"Let Springtime reign forever!"* The curtain fell to much clapping from the spectators.

"That was wonderful!" Diana declared to Cynara. "Weren't the costumes just beautiful? And isn't Nellie bold? I would not dare to wear anything so revealing in public."

"Ahh, but would you wear something as daring in private?" the marquis of Roxley asked as he came up behind her. He slid an arm about her narrow waist and dropped a kiss upon her bare shoulder.

Diana pulled away and turning, scolded him. "I did not give you permission to handle my person with such familiarity," she said.

"But you gave my brother permission, didn't you?" he said angrily.

"He told you?" She was suddenly outraged.

"Nay, sweet Siren, you have just told me. Damn is not a man to boast over a lady's favors, but I saw the change in him when he returned to our Spartan quarters this afternoon. I recognized the look, for I have worn it enough times myself," he finished.

"I cannot distinguish between my Geminid," she said. "And, besides, it is past time I was kissed, Darling." She looked at him directly thinking as she always did what beautiful deep blue eyes he had. "Would you like to kiss me, sirrah?" she demanded of him saucily.

Cynara giggled at the look of surprise upon the marquis of Roxley's handsome face. "Well, my lord, my cousin has asked you a fair question. What is your answer?" she teased him mercilessly.

He actually blushed, but then a wicked look came into his eye, and taking Diana by the hand he said, "Come, sweet Siren, and we shall find a hidey-hole where I will let you compare my kisses to my brother's."

Diana's heart began to beat a quick tattoo. She had not expected to compare the brothers' kisses so soon. "It is Friday," she protested. "Your brother will be waiting for me for this is his time you steal."

"When you kissed Damn, you changed the rules, sweetheart," he told her. Then he stopped and drew her into an alcove. He looked down into her beautiful little heart-shaped face. His lips brushed her brow, her cheeks, the tip of her nose. "You have the greenest eyes," he murmured so softly she just heard him. "And you do have an adorable mouth." He ran a finger over her lips. "It is absolutely meant for kissing, sweet Siren." Then he brushed her mouth with his once, twice, three times before his lips kissed her a long, slow kiss that left her breathless.

"*Oh, my!*" Diana exclaimed. Closing her green eyes, she gave herself over to his embrace, realizing as she did so that Darius Esmond was indeed every bit as passionate as was his elder twin, Damien. He leaned his long body against her, and she felt his desire for her. She pulled away. "We must cease, my lord. *Right now!*"

"I don't want to stop," he groaned. "You intoxicate me, my sweet Siren. I am utterly and completely bewitched by you! I must have you, my adorable girl. *I must!*"

Diana pushed him firmly away, saying as she stepped from the alcove, "You flatter me, my lord, but you also insult me if you think I should allow my passion to overwhelm me at this point. You and your brother both seek my hand in marriage. Therefore the choice is mine to make, and I will not be forced to it. You claim that I have changed the rules, but I tell you I have not. Friday and Saturday belong to your brother. He shall have them." Then she walked away from him and back into the crowd of courtiers.

He watched her go, his dark eyes narrowing. The game was at

last becoming more serious. Did he really want a wife? *Now?* But she was beautiful and she was rich, and the thought of besting his sibling was just too much for him to resist. For the sake of his marquisate, he must take a wife sooner or later. He and Damn were now twenty-six. It really was time. And Lady Diana Leslie came from a fecund family. She would be certain to give him a nursery full of sons and daughters. But it was beating his brother at this game that really proved the most tempting, Darius Esmond considered. *And he would beat him!*

Diana sought out her friends, her mind filled with confusion. She joined Jamie, Ceci, and Wily at the card table, but she played badly and lost too much. She was furious at herself but paid her debt immediately. Her cousin saw her state of mind though she hid it from the others. He arose from the card table and held out his hand to her.

"Come and walk with me in the gallery," he said with a smile. "I am weary of the cards for now, sweet Siren."

He led her into a long gallery filled with the most magnificent paintings hung on a wall covered in red silk brocade. They strolled in silence for a time, and then Diana spoke.

"Kissing but adds to my confusion over the Geminid," she told him. "Why do I have to pick a husband now, Jamie?"

"You don't," he said quietly. "You must only marry for love, Diana. The women in our family always have, you know. Our mutual ancestress made that wise rule over a hundred years ago. Her daughter, my great-grandmother, Willow, met my namesake at the court of the great Elizabeth. She was one of the queen's maids-of-honor and asked her permission to marry the earl of Alcester. The queen, who didn't like seeing others about her wed, was fond of my great-grandmother and gave her blessing to the union. It is said the lady Willow ruled her family with an iron hand, and they loved her for it. Marry for love, dearest cousin. *Only for love.*"

"But that is the problem!" Diana wailed. "I love them both! The more I try to separate Damien and Darius Esmond, the more alike they appear to me. I thought that kissing might make a difference, but I like kissing them both! What am I to do, Jamie? What on earth am I to do?"

"Perhaps instead of concentrating upon your feelings, Cousin, you should learn how each of them considers you," he said. "If you love them both, then it would be wise for you to find out which one of them loves you more than the other. That should be the twin you marry," he concluded.

She stopped. She turned. She grasped him by his broad velvet-covered shoulders. *"Jamie!"* she cried. *"That is brilliant!"*

"Indeed?" he replied with a grin.

"No, it is!" Diana told him. "The twin who loves me best will share himself with me, will try to learn my feelings, not simply to win in this silly competition with his brother, but because he loves me. Really loves me. I have driven myself to distraction worrying about which one of the two to choose. But I don't have to any longer. I shall enjoy the rest of my time here at court, and let them worry about the situation between us." She grinned at him. "And when the season ends I shall give the twins a single task to perform. And whoever pleases me the most I shall wed, for whoever completes the task well will be the man who loves me."

"But you will love him," Jamie said.

"I already love them both. Sometimes I wonder what it would be like to have them both as my husband."

"Surely not at the same time," he replied, a bit shocked by her girlish revelation.

Diana grinned again. "Why not?" she demanded. "If men can keep more than one woman, why cannot a woman have more than one man? Can you imagine the court, *The Wits*, if I married one and took the other for my lover? Perhaps that is the answer to my dilemma, Jamie."

"It most certainly is not!" he said sternly. "Must I speak to your grandmama about you, sweet Siren?"

"Nay, I will behave, Jamie, but I cannot help but think it," she responded with a small chuckle.

He laughed in spite of himself. Such bawdy notions were not the kind of thoughts he would have considered the sweet and gentle Lady Diana Leslie to have. "This new and naughty side of you is most intriguing, my dear cousin," he told her.

They returned to the court, and it was there that the duke found them.

"I am relieved," he said, to discover you in the company of your cousin and not my brother," he told her.

"Oh," Diana answered him. "I have already been in your brother's company, but as I reminded him, this is your night, my lord."

The duke led her silently into the dance, and they pranced to the lively music, moving in and out of the figure as it wove itself about the floor. When the music had ended, and before another dance might begin, he led her off into a corner, seating her and then hurrying off to bring her a goblet of chilled wine. Returning to her side they sat quietly for a time. Finally he said, "Why were you in Darling's company?"

"He wanted to kiss me as he had decided you already had, my lord. I am not certain I appreciate you wearing your heart on your sleeve so openly."

"Did he kiss you?" the duke demanded, a hint of jealousy in his voice.

"Of course," Diana answered him. "I was not reluctant, as I really must find some difference between you, if not to choose, then for my own peace of mind."

"You do not dissemble with me, even to spare my feelings," he noted dryly.

"It is not in my nature to lie, my lord," she told him. "Did you think that having kissed you, I would not kiss him? If I am to choose a husband, I think I must have some small experience in passion other than in one man's arms."

"Hmmm," the duke considered. "I am not certain that I like that idea, my adorable Siren."

"Now, my lord, play fair," she teased him. "I know I cannot be the only woman you have ever kissed. Why should it be different for me?"

"You are a girl!" he said quickly.

"That does not mean I must remain a complete ninny where love is concerned, my lord," she returned.

"Did he caress you?" the duke demanded to know.

"I have said we kissed, and that is all I will say," Diana snapped at him. "I am not suggesting an ultimate consummation, but I should have some small knowledge of passion before I wed."

"I will kill him!" the duke cried, jumping to his feet so suddenly that his chair tipped over.

"Well," Diana pondered, "that would certainly solve my problem, Damien, but then the king would be forced to hang you, and I should be a widow before I was a bride."

"Is it your intent to drive me mad?" he demanded of her.

"I haven't decided yet," she said sweetly.

"Perhaps I will kill you instead," he grumbled, but he was beginning to find humor in the whole situation.

She stood up, and pressed herself against him. "How shall you do it, my lord?" she taunted him wickedly.

He wrapped his arms about her. "With kisses," he growled, and then his lips were on hers, and she was suddenly floating.

His arms tightened around her. His kisses demanded, and Diana suddenly found herself dizzy with the pleasure that was enveloping her. "Oh, Damn," she murmured against his big mouth.

"*What?*" he whispered in her ear, sending a shiver down her spine.

"It is too lovely," she found herself admitting.

"Aye," he agreed, "it is."

They stood looking at one another, wrapped in an embrace, and Diana began to wonder if she didn't far prefer light blue eyes to deep blue ones. Yet when the marquis had kissed her, she had soared too. The obvious answer was that kissing someone you loved was delicious, and she did love them both.

He loosed his grip upon her saying, "This is hardly the place for kissing, sweet Siren. It is almost two o'clock of the morning. I shall take you home, but be warned that tomorrow is Saturday, and I shall come early to be with you."

" 'Tis the shank of the evening, my lord," Diana said mischievously. "Besides I cannot go home yet as I came with Cynara, and we used Grandmama's barge. If I know Cyn, she will not yet be ready to depart," Diana explained to him.

"Then it is fortunate I have my carriage," he countered.

"What of your brother?" she asked him.

"He has a horse," the duke said. "Now, shall we take my vehicle, or leave it for Cynara, and go via the river?"

"If we take the barge you will have no way of returning to your quarters, my lord. I will not ask Grandmama's bargemen to make another round trip. We must use your carriage. I shall tell Cynara that I am leaving so she does not worry."

"And I will meet you in the courtyard," he replied.

They separated, the duke going to call for his coach, and Diana to tell Cynara that she was leaving.

"Ahh," Cynara teased her, "a romantic ride home in the duke's carriage, Cousin. Perhaps now that you have begun kissing it will help you to make a decision."

Diana blushed, and hurried off. He awaited her in the court, and helped her into his carriage. The vehicle moved off, and she thought she heard shouting behind them. "Stop the coach, my lord!" she said.

"Why?" he asked.

"Someone is calling to us," she told him.

"It is not important," he assured her.

"Stop this instant, my lord!" she said, but she didn't have to order him for their carriage was already coming to a halt.

At once the door was yanked open. *"Get out, Darling!"* the duke commanded his brother, reaching in to yank his sibling from the vehicle. Then he hit him a blow, knocking him to the cobbled pavement before climbing into the coach. "You never play fair when you think you might lose, do you?" the duke said. Then he pulled the coach door shut, commanding his driver to move on leaving his brother on his rump, rubbing his handsome jaw.

" 'Oddsblood!" Diana swore. "I didn't know, my lord."

He nodded curtly, then said, "You couldn't see his eyes in the dark, nor could you see beneath his cloak that he was not dressed as I am. Somehow, though, he knew we were leaving. One of the king's little pages came to say His Majesty wished to see me at once. Fortunately your cousin Fancy, who was with His Majesty, realized almost at once what was afoot. I came as quickly as I could."

"My hero," Diana murmured, unable to help wondering what a carriage ride with the marquis of Roxley would have been like.

As if he knew her thoughts, he drew her into his arms and kissed her deeply. All thought of Darius Esmond disappeared instantly. Diana purred with pleasure as Damien's lips moved over hers, tasting her, drawing forth the sweet nectar of her soul. Reaching up she caressed his handsome face with a gentle hand, and he smiled down at her.

"You understand that I am going to make you my wife," he told her. "Unlike my twin, this is no longer a game I play, Diana. I am falling in love with you. I can imagine no other woman in my heart, in my bed, bearing and mothering my children. Only you, sweet Siren."

"I am overwhelmed by such a declaration, my lord," she told him honestly. "But you must give me time to consider."

He nodded agreeably. "As long as in the end it is me you choose, my darling," he said. Then before she might answer he bent to kiss her again, and Diana willingly gave herself up to his embrace. Their kisses deepened in intensity. His hand began to caress her young breasts. His long fingers trailed over the tops of her bosom, then suddenly plunged beneath her neckline to cup a single breast.

Diana gasped, surprised. "My lord," she protested softly.

"Nay, sweetheart," he whispered back, "I will not hurt you, but I must touch you. *Please!*" He held her little breast tenderly, now and again fondling it, his thumb reaching out to brush the nipple.

She could feel her own heart hammering wildly. She had never before been touched in so intimate a fashion, but for some reason she did not want to stop him now. Her blood flowed like boiling honey in her veins, making it almost impossible for her to even move. She closed her eyes, and let the sensations overwhelm her.

"My God," he groaned low, "you are so very, very sweet, my

Diana. I must stop else I seduce you and shame us both. I cannot win you by foul means, my adorable one." Reluctantly he drew his hand from her gown, a small smile touching his lips when she sighed with open and obvious reluctance. "Sit up," he instructed her, gently moving her from his lap and his embrace. "I cannot promise to remain the gentleman when I am in such close proximity to your precious person."

"I never . . ." she began, but he stopped her mouth with two fingers.

"I know," he said. "I am the first man to kiss you, the first to touch you, sweet Siren. I know. Would that I be the only man to touch you. Do you understand?"

She nodded, and her eyes filled with tears. "I cannot promise you that, my lord, for to do so would say I had already made my decision, and the truth is that I have not. I have told you that I do not lie."

"I know," he said, and there was sadness in his voice.

"All maidens play at kiss and cuddle before they settle down, Damien. It is part of our growing up. But should I choose to become your wife, you will never have to worry about my fidelity. I will be true although I know it is not the fashion at court for a wife to be faithful to her husband."

"I don't want to live at court," he told her. "I want to live on my estates where I have always lived. I have made no secret of that, Diana."

"And I don't want to live at court either," she assured him. "Well, my lord, here is something that we may agree upon."

He chuckled. "Indeed, madam, indeed," he replied.

"Do you like children?" she ventured, curious.

"I will love as many as you choose to give me, Diana," he answered her with a smile. "I have enough wealth to dower daughters and send our sons, but for my heir, safely out into the world. Aye, I like children."

"I am very rich," she told him.

"So I have been told," he said mildly.

"I have said I will control my own wealth. I ask you again if the thought of it disturbs you."

"Nay, it doesn't," he said.

At that moment the coach came to a stop. They had arrived at Greenwood House. The duke escorted Diana to the door where the majordomo was waiting for her.

"Good night, madam," he said. "Today has been most informative for us both, hasn't it?"

She nodded. "Until tomorrow, my lord," she told him, and turning entered the house, a small smile upon her lips.

Chapter

12

The court always enjoyed the month of May at Greenwich. The dowager duchess of Glenkirk had taken a house on the river for that time so that her granddaughters would have beds in which to lay their heads on the rare occasions they returned home to her. With the longer days, the court seemed more and more intent on having its pleasures. Fancy had been the reigning *maitress en titre* for the first half of the month, but then Mistress Nell arrived from London, which had served Fancy's purposes as she was now with the king's child and planning to retire from the court sometime in June.

I will be glad to get back to Queen's Malvern, Jasmine thought. *I am too old to be traipsing about like this with a trio of nubile young girls in tow. Fancy will be settled soon with her child. The king, being generous, will provide for her, but I am here to advise her in that matter. And my sweet Diana.* Here Jasmine smiled. Where had the child ever inherited such an amiable character? *It certainly isn't from our side of the family,* she considered ruefully. *We are all hellcats. It must be from her grandmother Gordon's line that such niceness flows.*

I believe I know now which of the Roxley boys I would have her wed, but I will say nothing for that decision must be Diana's alone. If only she will make it. I have never known anyone to create such a fuss over choosing a husband. Actually either one of them would suit, but I shall be curious to see

*which of them she chooses, and pray God it is sooner than later! Patrick will
not be pleased to learn she is still not set in her mind on a husband.*

And Cynara. Here the dowager duchess frowned. Of all her flock
of grandchildren, Cynara was the most like her as she had been in
her youth. Willful. Headstrong. And inclined to make foolish decisions, particularly where a certain gentleman was concerned. *I cannot stop her though*, Jasmine thought sadly. *She will make her mistakes.
She will be hurt. Her parents will be furious. But I will be here for her. I
will do whatever I can, whatever I must to see this dearest-to-my-heart
grandchild happy.*

"Grandmama?" Diana came into the small riverside garden.
"Why do you look so unhappy? Are you all right?"

Jasmine put the dark images from her and looked up smiling at
her granddaughter. "Sometimes old women have sad thoughts, my
dear child. Seeing you, however, brings the joy back into my heart.
How pretty you look, Diana. What plans do you have for today?"

"'Tis another picnic, Grandmama," Diana responded, sounding
just a trifle bored. "At least this time it will not be held at the palace
but rather out somewhere in the country. A suitable meadow has
been discovered. The farmer was paid to move his cattle for the day.
The meadow has been thoroughly scoured for cowpats. Even now
the royal servants are on their way so that when we arrive the carpets
will be spread upon the grass, and the feast laid out and awaiting us.
I do not recall our picnics at Queen's Malvern being this grand at
all." And she laughed.

Jasmine laughed with her. "It sounds to me, my child, as if you
are becoming tired of court life and all its pretensions," she noted.

"I am, Grandmama! I long to go home to Queen's Malvern, but I
have promised Cyn that I will remain with her until mid-summer,
and she has promised me that she will come home then too."

"Thank God!" Jasmine said.

"You are worried about her, aren't you?" Diana replied. "I am too.
The earl of Summersfield has surely earned his sobriquet *Wickedness*.
He is so dark and brooding. Unlike any other gentleman at court. I
think he frightens me, although Cyn does not see it. She but sees a
challenge, and you know how she likes challenges."

"She will go her own way, Diana," Jasmine observed, "and there is nothing you or I can do to stop her. But tell me, dear child, are you any closer to making a decision between your duke and your marquis? The family is acceptable. They have their own wealth, although nothing like yours. Their lads are within a comfortable traveling distance of Queen's Malvern. Are they still so indistinguishable?"

"Not quite as much now, Grandmama," Diana admitted.

"What differences do you see, then?"

"The duke is a bit more serious, but I think that may come from being the elder, even if it is only be seven minutes as he has told me. The marquis is a bit more reckless, but that I believe comes from feeling he is the lesser twin, but he really isn't. He is just himself."

"You obviously still like them both equally," Jasmine observed. "How will you choose? Have you thought about it?"

"I have, Grandmama. I am now well acquainted with both Damn and Darling. The question is how well do they know me? A man should know well the woman he is to marry. He should not be driven simply by beauty and his lustful desires. Perhaps that was all right in your day, Grandmama, but not in this modern age," Diana declared seriously, and her grandmother was hard put not to laugh.

"In other words you will choose the twin who you believe knows you best," Jasmine said.

"If I cannot make my decision any other way that would seem to be the sensible thing," Diana replied. "I adore them both."

"And they make love equally well," Jasmine teased gently.

Diana blushed, but she bravely answered, "Aye."

"Well," Jasmine admitted, "I certainly was never faced with such a problem as you have, Diana. If you wish my counsel, I am glad to give it to you, dear child."

"I am not ready yet, Grandmama, but I will make no decision before I have had my summer at Queen's Malvern. I should like to ask the Geminid to come and visit us at our home. And my parents will be there too."

"You must speak with your uncle," Jasmine said, "but I think it a splendid idea, dear child."

Molly came into the garden, and said, "Your two swains is here, my lady. Your mare has been brought from the stable." She curtsied.

"Tell their lordships that I shall be with them anon," Diana told her servant. Then she turned to her grandmother. "Do I look all right? I didn't choose to wear a riding outfit for it is warm today." She pirouetted for the older woman.

"You look lovely. Very fresh and springlike," Jasmine said, admiring her granddaughter's simple gown of lilac silk with its low scooped neckline and lightly boned bodice. The full sleeves had deep ecru lace cuffs. She wore no hat, and her hair was dressed in ringlets and curls. "Go along now, and have a wonderful day," Jasmine finished.

With a smile and a wave, Diana left her grandmother in the garden and hurried through the house to exit the front door where her two suitors awaited her, admiring her gown as a groom helped her into her saddle. Diana straightened her skirts prettily over the pommel, and threw the duke and marquis a brilliant smile. "Are we ready?" she asked them. "Is it not a glorious day, my lords?"

They agreed. Then the trio gently encouraged their mounts forward. Outside the gates of her grandmother's house, they found more of the court mounted and following along to the picnic site. There were several upholstered open carts decorated with garlands of flowers. Nellie and Fancy rode in one and were chatting amiably together. They waved at Diana, and she waved back, moving her horse alongside of them.

"You are not riding?" she said.

"Nellie is not used to being mounted," Fancy replied with a wicked smile. She was wearing a gown of teal blue silk, and her companion was garbed in bright grass green silk. Both gowns were extremely low cut, the scooped necklines revealing generous expanses of creamy swelling bosom. Both were lavishly trimmed with fine French lace. The two young women wore matching felt hats with tall crowns, broad brims, and decorated with snowy white plumes.

"Oh, I'm used to being mounted," Nellie riposted with a wicked grin, "but I ain't used to spreading meself atop a horse, being city bred."

"You are terrible, both of you," Diana laughed.

"I see you have your two admirers in willing tow," Fancy noted.

"And a riper pair I ain't never seen!" Nellie remarked, smacking her lips with approval.

"Why, Mrs. Nell," the marquis said, "we did not think you had ever noticed us." His dark blue eyes were dancing with merriment.

"You would be surprised what I see," Nell told him, and she wagged a finger at him while giving him a broad wink.

Darius Esmond actually blushed.

"Why, Darling, what secrets do you keep from me?" Diana asked him, cocking her head to one side.

"Why none, dear Siren. My life where you are concerned is an open book," he vowed.

"Now there is a gentleman for you," Nellie teased him further. "He is careful in his answer, is he not?"

"Madame! Give over, I beg you," the marquis pleaded with her. "I am naught but a man and cannot help it."

"Before Mrs. Nell sends my brother into a deeper bog," the duke spoke up in mild tones, "he is embarrassed, dear Siren, because he lost rather heavily at the cards recently. Darling is not used to losing, are you, Brother? Could this be a hint of things to come, I wonder?" The duke's light blue eyes were dancing with his amusement.

"Oh, pooh!" Diana responded. "Everyone loses heavily at the cards at least once a Season. *But no more, if they are wise.* Are you wise, Darling? I could not consider marrying a man who was not."

The marquis looked extremely uncomfortable, but he nodded. "I have paid my debt, have I not, Mrs. Nell? But my brother will have to kindly sponsor me and pay my way if I am to remain at court as long as we intend," he said.

"*And will you, Damn?*" Diana asked him. "I could not consider marrying a man who was not generous to his family."

"As much as I should enjoy an advantage with you," the duke said, "I would not consider it sporting. My brother and I will remain with the court together. But he will refrain from gambling."

"Why how loving they are to each other," Nellie purred.

"And because they are I invite them both to come to Queen's Malvern while I am home this summer," Diana said. "It is my uncle's, the not-so-royal Stuart home and he is going to ask you properly. Depending upon when you come, you may get to meet my family," Diana said. "I hope that you shall come." She smiled at them.

"I'd be surprised if they didn't," Nellie teased.

"Go along, Cousin," Fancy advised, "before Mrs. Nell gives your swains apoplexy," and she laughed at the looks of relief upon the identical faces of the duke and the marquis of Roxley.

Laughing Diana moved away from the flower-decked cart, her suitors in her wake.

Finally they came to a lovely green meadow filled with wildflowers. There were daisies and bluebells dotting the field, along with multicolored poppies. On one edge of their picnic ground, there was a stream bordered by weeping willows. Royal servants had already spread Turkey carpets, both large and small throughout the area for the court to sit upon. There were two large pits filled with coals over which roasted both venison and wild boar. Net bags had been set in the flowing stream. They were filled with bottles of wine, and oysters that had been brought fresh from the sea that very morning.

"Quickly," the duke said. "There is a lovely spot by the bank that is perfect. I see your cousin Jamie nearby, and all of our friends."

They dismounted, and a waiting groom took their horses. The trio hurried across the meadow to join their group.

"Come along!" Pretty Kitty waved to them. "We have saved you the best spot. It is just large enough for three." Seated next to her was Niles Brandon, the earl of Dunley. Of late they had taken a great interest in one another. It was expected that a match would soon be struck between the two young people. Although the earl was a bit stuffy, Kitty had the ability to make him laugh, which she did often.

"Another earldom in the family," Jasmine had remarked when Diana had mentioned the possibility of such an alliance.

Jamie Edwardes had proposed to his distant cousin, Cecily

Burke, and been accepted. He would speak with her parents when he escorted Ceci home to Clearfields Priory. Jasmine had been particularly delighted with this match.

"How pleased my grandmother would be to see descendants of her daughter Willow and her son Padriac wed," she said smiling when she had learned the news.

The last of their friends, Coralyn Mumford, called Slim for her slender figure had caught the eye of Lord Rupert Dunstan, the younger son of the earl of Morly. The old earl had traveled up to London, which he rarely did now, to meet and approve of his son's choice. There remained the matter of gaining the permission of Slim's family in Glocestershire, well-to-do landowners who would be delighted with their daughter's success at court.

Lord Charlton and Baron Mayhew had dropped away when it became obvious that there was no hope of winning the heart of sweet Siren, or the other girls. Now the four couples, with Diana and her Geminid, sprawled lazily in the late May sunshine upon the carpets that had been laid upon the meadow grasses. Along with the rest of the picnickers, they were served roasted venison and boar and capon. The oysters were brought from the stream along with the wine. There was freshly baked bread of several varieties. There was cheese: cheddar, Stilton, and Brie from France. There were cold asparagus in a delicious vinegary dressing and pickled beets. Then came tiny iced cakes and strawberry tartlets with thick clotted Devon cream. Sated at last, and relaxed with good wine, they lay on their backs watching the dappled sunshine through the delicate graceful branches of the willows that lined the embankment by the stream.

Diana closed her eyes and sighed. It was the most perfect day, she thought happily. Her right cheek was kissed. Then her left. She kept her eyes closed enjoying the sensation. Lips met her lips in a passionate but tender kiss. It was the duke. He wore a sandalwood scent as the marquis wore violet. Now she smelled violet as Darius Esmond kissed her a rather demanding kiss, and Diana suddenly realized that there was a difference between the two. Damien seemed to consider how she would feel, but Darius just took. The mouth was removed from hers, and she opened her eyes to see if she was right, and indeed she had been. She remained strangely silent considering.

"Let's go wading," Jamie suddenly said. "The streambed is sandy here, and it is getting hot."

There was a murmur of agreement. Boots, buskins, and stockings came off. Skirts were tucked into waistbands as hand in hand they stepped down the narrow embankment into the stream. There were squeals of surprise for the water was very cold, but they remained, stamping and splashing each other with abandon.

From his carpet, his two favorite mistresses by his side, the king watched them, amused. The queen did not like picnics and so had not come. Charles Stuart, the king, was at his most relaxed, his white silk shirt open, his black curls tumbling about his shoulders.

"When I was their age," he remarked, "I was engaged in a struggle for my kingdom, and my life. It does my heart good to see our youth at play, my pretty pets."

"Enjoy them while you may, Your Majesty," Fancy replied. "But for my cousin, Cynara, they are now all matched. They will not likely return to court for some time to come for they will be too involved starting families. Still, when the hunting season is over, a whole new crop of pretty faces and handsome lads will descend upon the court, for is not that the way of it, Your Majesty?" She smiled at him.

"And will you be content to remain in the country with your child, my dear?" he asked her. His dark eyes searched her face.

"I am more than content with my decisions, Your Majesty," Fancy told the king.

"'Odsfish! She sounds almost as amiable as her sweet cousin," Nellie teased. "I'll not be content to be retired to the farm."

"My dear Nellie," the king laughed, "no farm would have you, nor would they even know what to do with you should you go. You must, I fear, remain in London by my side."

"In your bed is more like it," Nellie chuckled, and her two companions laughed at her quick wit.

Now the royal servants began to pack up all the evidence of the picnic. Diana and her friends came from the stream and began to dry off their legs with cloths provided by the servants. The gentlemen eagerly rolled their lady loves' stockings back on again, slipping their garters up their legs on soft milky thighs, daring to stroke the tempting flesh until scolded. Boot and buskins were donned once more. They mounted their horses and began their return to Greenwich.

On May twenty-ninth the king celebrated his birthday at Whitehall Palace, where the foreign ambassadors might come and pay him tribute. The celebrations began in the morning as the tower cannons were fired to salute to His Majesty's natal day. The festivities continued with a service at Westminster Abbey, and then for the entire day, concluding with a great party in the evening. The king was now thirty-eight.

Jasmine had chosen to go to the evening festivities to wish the king a happy day, and year to come. She and Fancy would soon be leaving for Queen's Malvern, although Charlie and Barbara would remain behind for another month until it was time to bring Diana and Cynara home for the summer and autumn. It would be her last appearance at court for she was not likely to come again. It was just too difficult traveling at her age, and she smiled to herself as she thought it, recalling her long journey from India so many years ago. *Sixty-two years ago*, she grimaced. Where on earth had all that time gone?

She had bathed. Now Orane was helping her to dress. Jasmine had chosen to wear an elegant gown of violet satin with the overskirt looped up and held with silver bows to reveal an underskirt of lilac silk brocade. The puffed violet sleeves of the gown were lavishly trimmed with silver lace. The neckline was lace trimmed as well. She wore a fine silver gauze veil that was tucked into her neckline for modesty's sake, and she could not help but laugh, remembering her younger days and how proud she was of her bosom. Her earbobs were of amethysts, diamonds, and pearls. She wore a rope of perfectly matched pearls, each pearl the size of her thumbnail. In the center of her neckline was a broach of diamonds, amethysts, and pearls. The heels of her violet satin shoes were studded with diamonds.

"Madame is yet magnificent in her appearance," Orane pronounced as she finished helping her mistress.

"There was a day when I was called extravagantly beautiful," Jasmine chuckled.

"You still are," Orane said quietly. "But beauty is for the young, madame. Magnificence, ah, that comes with age, *non?*"

"Despite my old-fashioned hairstyle?" Jasmine laughed.

"The chignon suits you, madame. It is far more elegant than all those little corkscrew curls the young girls wear today. And for the ladies of a certain age to copy the children is foolish. *Non,* madame. You are as you have always been, elegance personified."

"Well, then, Orane," her mistress said. "Give Elegance her cloak, and see if my granddaughters are ready to leave."

Orane handed Jasmine the lilac silk garment, curtsied, and hurried off on her mistress's instructions. Jasmine stood in front of the long mirror in her bedchamber, staring into it. For the briefest moment she saw herself as she had been the night she had met her mother, Velvet, for the first time. Her gown had been scarlet. She had had a great barbaric necklace of rubies about her neck, and red roses in her hair. She was Yasaman Kama Begum, the Mughal's sixteen-year-old daughter, come to England, to a family she hadn't known existed until a few years before.

But now she was an old lady who had not thought of herself as the Mughal's daughter in many years. England was her home as India, Scotland, and France had once been. She had lived all her life but those first sixteen years here on this side of the world. She was the matriarch of a large brood even as her grandmother, Skye O'Malley, had been before her.

"I miss you, Grandmama," she whispered softly to herself, "and I miss you, my Jemmie."

Orane's gray head popped around the bedchamber door. "The young ladies are ready, madame, and eager to get to Whitehall," she said. "Let me put on your cloak, and I have your gloves."

Jasmine noted as they entered their coach that her two grand-daughters in deference to her were wearing their chosen colors. Cynara in scarlet and Diana in a soft blossom pink. She smiled.

"You have your gifts for His Majesty?" she asked.

"Yes, Grandmama," they chorused, holding up gaily wrapped packages.

Jasmine settled back into her seat to enjoy the ride. She closed her eyes, knowing that she would get little rest the remainder of the evening. Her granddaughters were silent, and she almost laughed aloud. That they had no gossip to tell her about their lives spoke volumes. Diana, she suspected, was close to making some sort of a decision, but she had said quite plainly that she would not speak until after the Roxley twins had visited them at Queen's Malvern. As for Cynara, she had made her decision the first moment she had seen Harry Summers. The difficulty was that the earl of Summers-field did not know it.

They reached Whitehall, which was ablaze this night with lights as the court descended upon the palace by coach and river barge to congratulate the king. This was not just his birthday, but the eighth anniversary of his return to England's throne from exile. The duke and duchess of Lundy were awaiting Jasmine's coach as it drew up in the courtyard. Once the door was opened, the duke helped his mother from her vehicle.

"You are looking particularly splendid tonight, Mama," he told her with a broad smile. "I told His Majesty that you would be coming, and he is delighted. He says he has not seen nearly enough of you while you have been with the court this year."

"I am too old to be with the court at all, Charlie," Jasmine said tartly. "Only for the girls I should not have come, and you know it. This shall be my last appearance before I return to Queen's Malvern to live out my days."

"I cannot believe that you will retire so meekly," he teased her grinning.

"I retired years ago," she chuckled. "I expect there were many here who were surprised to learn I was even still alive." And she laughed.

"True," he agreed with a chuckle.

She took his arm and, with Barbara and the two younger girls following, they entered the palace, moving past crowds of courtiers, and other well-wishers until they arrived at the great Banqueting Hall where the king and the queen sat ensconced upon their gilt and red velvet thrones.

"The Duke of Lundy," the majordomo's stentorian voice boomed. *"The Dowager Duchess of Glenkirk and Marchioness of Westleigh."*

They swept into the room hearing the majordomo behind them announcing, *"The Duchess of Lundy, Lady Cynara Stuart; Lady Diana Leslie."*

Charlie casually proceeded past the line of people waiting to pay their respects to the king. He led his mother directly to the foot of his royal cousin's throne. The king's black eyes lit with pleasure as he saw Jasmine and her family before him.

He stood. He stepped down from the dais, and taking both of her hands in his, he kissed them. "Madame, you honor me," he said smiling at her. "It is so good to see you once again. You came to court, and yet I hardly knew you. Now my cousin tells me you are to return to your home with Fancy."

She gently drew her hands from his and, stepping back just slightly, curtsied deeply to the king, thinking as she did that her knees were not what they had been. "Your Majesty honors me," she said, smiling gratefully as he helped her to arise. "I came to court only for my granddaughters' sake as you well know."

"We will speak together before you leave us," the king said low. "Come now, and greet the queen." He led her over to the second throne where his wife sat sedately. "My dear, here is Charlie's mama to pay her respects to you."

Jasmine curtsied to the queen as the king stepped back up onto his throne and began to greet his other guests. "Your Majesty," she said.

"My husband is disappointed that he has not seen more of you," the queen told Jasmine.

"I am, alas, too old for all the Society of the court," Jasmine replied to Queen Catherine. "In my youth I cut quite a figure here, in the time of King James and Queen Anne, but I am an old woman now, Your Majesty. I long to return home to Queen's Malvern if the truth be known. I will be leaving shortly with one of my grand-daughters. The younger two will remain another month before being escorted home by my son and his wife."

"Is it true," the queen queried Jasmine, "that you have had three husbands, madame?"

"Indeed, Your Majesty, yes, and my grandmother had six hus-bands. My father was the Grande Mughal Akbar of India, and I lived my youth there. My first husband was a Kashmiri prince. He was, unfortunately, murdered by my half brother, who was my father's heir. My second husband was Rowan Lindley, the marquis of West-leigh. My third was the duke of Glenkirk, James Leslie."

"Forgive my curiosity," the queen said prettily, "but there are so many stories about you that I do not know what to believe."

Jasmine laughed softly. "Aye, Your Majesty, I imagine that there are many stories, and most made up by those who have never known me, let alone set eyes upon me. For the sake of my good name, however, I would tell you that I was a widow when I knew Charlie's father."

"Three husbands," the queen said shaking her dainty head. "You are obviously a strong woman, madame. I find one husband is far more than I can manage!" And her warm brown eyes twinkled.

"Stuarts are not easy men, Your Majesty," Jasmine replied softly. "And I have that on the very best authority." Then seeing that their conversation was over, she curtsied again to the queen and moved away.

" 'Odsfish, Siren," the marquis of Roxley said. "Your grandmama is certainly thick with the royals."

"The Stuarts have always been kind to her," Diana murmured.

"I would be kind to you," he said, bending to whisper it in her ear, kissing the small curl of flesh as he did so.

She shivered deliciously. "Are you flirting with me again, Dar-ling?" she asked him.

He nodded. "Aye, I am," he told her.

"I am not ready to make my decision yet," she said.

"So you tell me each time I even allude to the subject," he returned. "I am near to kidnapping you, Siren, so that your decision would be made, and I might marry you."

"Do not ever presume to make my decisions for me, Darling," she warned him. "The Leslie women can be very difficult when provoked."

"I should like to provoke you!" he growled, slipping an arm about her supple waist.

"You do," she told him, "but perhaps not quite in the way that you desire, Darling. Do not, I beg you, press me further." She removed his velvet-clad arm. "I am no man's possession, nor will I ever be."

"But if you are wed," he protested, "you become your husband's possession. That is the law, both God's and man's, Siren."

Diana turned to face him, laughing. "How old-fashioned you are, Darling. This is not the dark ages in which we live. These are modern times, my lord. You may possess a horse, or a dog, but certainly not another human soul."

"What about slaves, but then you are right, Siren. Slaves are not human," the marquis said.

"My family does not believe in slavery," Diana told him with the utmost seriousness. "My uncle in the New World will not keep them but rather frees them. My own grandmother came from India with three servants she freed from slavery before they even left the shores of that foreign land. Those we call slaves are just as human as we are, Darling. Did not God create them too? In His image? Is God then a slave, my lord?"

"You think too much," he told her, and promptly kissed her pretty lips. "I should far rather speak to you of love, sweet Siren."

"Go away," she told him. "I am very displeased with you," she said.

"But why?" he demanded.

"If you do not know, then I cannot possibly explain to such a dunderhead," she replied, and turning she moved away from him.

She felt a hand upon her arm, and turned back to scold him, but found instead that she was looking into light blue eyes, and not dark. "Damn!"

"What has my brother done to upset you, Diana?" he asked her. "Shall you force me to call him out?" he teased her.

"He does not understand, I fear, and sometimes I think I may be forced to smack him for he can be so stupid," Diana said bluntly. Then she explained to the duke.

He listened to her patiently as he escorted her across the room to a more secluded spot, and seated her, sitting himself opposite so he might look directly at her. When she had finished the duke said, "My brother does not understand many things, Diana. He has never before been to court and is more at home on his lands. He is not at all wise to the ways of the world in which we live, I fear."

"You have never been to court either until this year," Diana said to him, "yet you seem to understand what I am saying."

"Have you not yet discovered the difference between us, Diana?" he asked her quietly. "After knowing us these past months, have you not yet discerned the variance in our characters?"

And then it dawned upon her. "*You have an intellect!*" she cried. "Darling does not."

"Precisely," the duke answered her. "And it was ever thus. He was a poor student in the classroom. I was not. While the times necessitated we remain on our lands, I spent my time learning as much as I could. Our tutor was an elderly gentleman who did not hold with Puritan ways, and so he taught us the way he had always taught the young gentlemen in his charge. I learned eagerly. My brother spent most of his time finding creative ways to escape the schoolroom so he might go hunting or be out in his fields. While I know much of what he knows with regard to our lands, I respect them. But Darius *loves* his lands. Because we are closer than most brothers are, and because we are so alike in face and form, everyone assumes we are alike, but we are not."

"Of course," Diana said. "I should have seen it long since."

He laughed. "I am pleased that you have *finally* seen it at all," he told her. "Now, my dearest sweet Siren, you must decide not just between light blue eyes, and dark blue eyes, but the real substance that separates Damien and Darius Esmond." He arose, and offered her his hand. "Shall we rejoin the rest of the court now, Diana?"

He had given her something very serious to consider, she realized. She told her grandmother of the conversations that she had had with both of the twins. They were sitting in the gardens of Greenwood House several days after the king's birthday, and just before Jasmine and Fancy were to return to Queen's Malvern.

Jasmine's still beautiful eyes watched the river as she spoke. "So now you have a distinct choice between the two," she said. "Do they still interest you as possible husbands, my child?"

Diana nodded slowly. "I love them none the less, but now I must decide whether I want a husband of charm and wit, but little else to recommend him; or a man with both charm, wit, and an intelligence that I both admire and appreciate. Do I want a husband whom I can easily manage because he is not as clever as I am? Or do I want a husband who is my equal and even possibly wiser than I?" She chuckled. "It is an intriguing conundrum, Grandmama. I would seem to be actually no better off now than I was four months ago."

"And the passion?" Jasmine inquired.

"Both seem to possess it, but in what true measure I cannot know for certain if I am to remain a virgin until my marriage, Grandmama," Diana told her. "With Darling there is much enthusiasm, but with Damn I sometimes believe he is holding back his emotions for whatever reason. Would it be that way if we shared a bed?" Diana wondered aloud.

"Perhaps the marquis approaches you as he would anything he truly enjoys, but his brother, the duke may hold his affections for you in check for fear of frightening you," Jasmine suggested to her granddaughter.

"But why would he do that?" Diana asked innocently.

"My dear child," Jasmine said, "I refuse to believe that you are so dense as to not know that the duke of Roxley is desperately in love with you, but he is a gentleman, Diana. He will neither voice his

sentiments, nor use his experience in the sensual arts to win you un-
fairly if it is his brother you prefer. He will not tamper that way with
your inexperienced heart."

"You like him," Diana said softly.

"I like them both for they possess good qualities," Jasmine told
the girl. "You will not get me to make your decision for you, my
dearest girl," she laughed.

"Uncle Charlie has asked them to Queen's Malvern this summer.
I will make my final decision then, Grandmama."

"When will they come?" Jasmine inquired.

"Sometime before the end of August," Diana said.

"Good! Your parents will be with us, and I think they should
meet your two suitors. Your mother is a practical woman, Diana, and
you have inherited that from her. She will trust any decision that
you make. Your father, however, is a completely different matter. He
will want to meet and pass judgment on your young swains, although
frankly I do not know what he could find wrong with either of them."

"He will make a choice between them you may be certain, Grandmama," Diana chuckled with a grin. "And he will be extremely annoyed with me if I do not choose his choice."

"Let no one influence you, my darling girl!" her grandmother
pleaded. "Especially my Patrick. You are the one who must live with
the husband you choose, and not your father."

Now Diana laughed. "Grandmama, I think that you know that
my father cannot force me to anything. I am a true Leslie woman. I
have a very strong will of my own. The Leslie men have never been
as strong as the women. Look at our history."

"That is true," Jasmine agreed, suddenly relieved. Diana would
indeed make her choice all by herself.

"I have one more test for my Geminid," she told her grandmother.

"And that is?" Jasmine queried her.

"When they come to visit me, each must bring me a gift. Their
choice of that trifle will decide their fates," Diana explained.

"You would make your decision based on their largesse?" Jasmine was shocked by her granddaughter. She might have expected such a thing from Cynara, but certainly not from Diana.

"No! No!" Diana quickly reassured her elder. "I believe I have already made my decision, Grandmama. I merely wish to confirm my judgment in the matter."

"Which have you chosen then?" Jasmine asked her excitedly.

Diana shook her head. "No, Grandmama, I shall tell no one that, not even you. What if something happens in the meantime to change my mind? And it might."

"The blood of both the Ottoman and the Mughal runs hot in your veins, my child. You have devised a clever stratagem worthy of your ancestors," Jasmine said admiringly. "And you have surprised even me," she told her granddaughter with a smile. "They call you *sweet*, but I think in doing so they have all underestimated you. And that may be to the good. Men are never quite comfortable with a woman who has an adroit mind and a skillful manner. Better they believe you sweet. Whomever you choose, Diana, I am now confident that you will rule him and your family wisely."

"I will miss you, Grandmama," Diana said, putting her dark head on Jasmine's shoulder.

"Of course you will," Jasmine agreed, "but you will be home soon enough, my child. Enjoy your last days here at court for once you are wed, your duty will be to produce an heir for your husband as soon as you may. Only when his nursery is full will you be able to return to court to enjoy its diversions again."

"I don't know if I want to come back ever again," Diana said. "I have been fortunate to escape the true wrath of *The Wits*. Because I am known to be virtuous and have a close connection to His Majesty, none would dare to tamper with me. Still I have seen too many married women eschew their vows to play the whore. Good women who are tempted into adultery because their husbands are as well. They believe what is sauce for the gander is also sauce for the goose. I do not want to fall into that trap. I do not want a husband who could do so. I will remain at home, visiting among my various family once I am a wife."

"It is not a bad fate," Jasmine agreed.

Several days later the dowager and her granddaughter Mistress Devers departed London for Queen's Malvern.

"Now that Grandmama is gone I may wear what I choose to wear all the time," Cynara exulted. "Do you not think I am wonderful in black and diamonds? Grandmama left us some of her jewelry to wear."

"I think it is a good thing that we are going home soon," Diana told her cousin. "You are beginning to gain a reputation."

"I want a reputation," Cynara said. "How else can I make Harry sit up and take notice of me? Only if he thinks I am as wicked and as daring as he is, will he become truly interested. Being the duke of Lundy's daughter does not intrigue him as it does so many others interested in my connections and my fortune. If I can make this man love me, he will love me for myself, and no other reason. I shall never have to doubt him, Diana. I shall never have to be afraid of losing him ever. That is what I want, and it is what I shall have."

The rest of June passed, and then the not-so-royal Stuart announced to his family that they would depart for Queen's Malvern in mid-July. They would not go on the royal summer progress, which was to begin then, but rather leave for home. Cynara was not happy, but she had no choice in the matter. And to make things even worse, the duke and marquis of Roxley were to travel with them part of the way.

"Just what we need, those two jackanapes dancing about Diana," she grumbled to her maidservant, Hester. But advised sharply by her mother to behave herself, Cynara put a smile on her beautiful face, riding out from Greenwood House on the day of their departure with her cousin and the two young men.

Diana could hardly contain herself. She had had enough of the court. It had been exciting, but the city now stank even through the pungent spicy scent of her pomander, and riding in St. James Park was just not as much fun as riding over the hills surrounding Queen's Malvern. She was anxious to see her family who would probably be in Worcestershire before she was.

They had said good-bye to all of their friends, all of whom were to marry in the near future. They had already attended the nuptials of Sir Michael Scanlon and Lady Drucilla Stanton, whom they called Wily. Her father had given his permission. As the Irishman wanted to return to Ireland as soon as possible, the wedding had been celebrated promptly so Mick and his wife might travel together. It had been a small but tasteful celebration. The newlyweds had stayed at Lynmouth House on their wedding night, and in the morning before they left, Wily had told her friends with a broad wink, "I made no mistake in taking Mick for my husband." Then she grew weepy to their surprise. "You'll come to Ireland one day to see me, won't you? I hope you will."

"Now, woman," her bridegroom said seeing a problem about to develop, "don't go weeping on me. We've a long way to travel this day, and I'm not about to do it with a howling female." He gave her a quick kiss on the lips and smiled into her eyes.

"I'm fine," the new Lady Scanlon sniffed, and after hugs all around the couple departed.

Their cousins, James Edwardes, the earl of Alcester, and Cecily Burke were to marry in the next four months. So was their cousin, Pretty Kitty, who would become the countess of Dunley upon her union with Niles Brandon. Lord Rupert Dunstan, younger son of the earl of Morly was to wed with Coralyn Mumford, the charming Slim. Their wedding date had not yet been chosen, but they all promised that whenever it was, they would all be there, but for the Scanlons. It but remained for Lady Diana Leslie to make her choice. The friends did not speak of Lady Cynara Stuart, for they feared for her eventual fate.

The duke and the marquis left their traveling companions several days before reaching Queen's Malvern, turning onto a road that led northwest into Herefordshire. They would come to Queen's Malvern at the end of August. The night before they departed the duke of Lundy's party, Diana called them into the private parlor the duke had booked for his family. It was empty except for the lovely girl.

"Sit down, my lords. We must speak." She poured them each a small goblet of wine, fully aware that their eyes were following her every move. Handing them the wine, she stood between them. "I am almost ready to make my decision between you both," she said, "but before I do I would set you a small task."

Damien and Darius Esmond looked at her expectantly.

"When you come to see me at the end of August, and to meet my family, you will each bring for me one perfect gift. It is important to me that the man I wed know me well before we are joined together for eternity. Let us see just what you have learned about me during our association, my lords. Do you understand?"

"What do you want, sweet Siren?" the marquis asked.

"No, Darling, that is up to you," she told him.

The duke remained silent.

"But you are a girl of means, sweet Siren," the marquis persisted. "What could either of us possibly bring to you? Can you give us no hint?"

"Therein lies the puzzle, my lord," Diana told him.

A small smile touched the duke's narrow lips, but he continued to remain silent.

"I shall find the perfect token, and win you, sweet Siren!" the marquis of Roxley vowed. He turned to his brother saying, "I will win, Damn! I have always been better with the ladies than you." His dark blue eyes danced with both excitement and triumph.

"We shall see," the duke finally broke his silence. Then placing his untouched goblet of wine upon the small table he arose, and taking Diana's hand in his, he kissed it. "You have set me a labor of Hercules, Diana. I shall have to consider very carefully what to do."

"I am certain that you will, my lord," she told him, and she smiled. "Travel with God's blessing, my lords," she said. Then curtsying, she turned and left the little parlor.

Chapter

13

Patrick Leslie, the duke of Glenkirk, had passed his half-century mark two and a half years earlier. He was a big man, but he had not grown portly in his later life as so many men of his generation did. He was comfortable in his manner of living as few men were. Unlike the Leslie men, and women who had preceded him, Patrick Leslie was content to remain on his own lands in the eastern Highlands of Scotland. Had his mother not been living, he would have been pleased to remain at Glenkirk forever.

But she was living, and she was as lively as she had ever been in her long life, much to his annoyance. He thought that a woman who had just celebrated her seventy-eighth birthday would have become more sedate in her manners and her speech; but his mother had not. He loved her dearly nonetheless, and now he sat with her in the old family hall of Queen's Malvern.

"What do ye think of these two young bucks Diana would decide between, Mama? Are they worthy of my lass, or are they a pair of fortune-hunting laddies and weak as water." His dark green eyes scanned her visage.

"The family is good. I have checked carefully. I allowed your daughter no unsuitable associations, Patrick," Jasmine told him.

"I dinna think ye would, Mam. Yet my brother's lass is gossiped of among the servants, or so I am told by my valet," the duke replied.

"Cynara is not your concern, Patrick," his mother told him sharply. "I trust her to behave properly, whatever is said about her. I will consider her fate after I know Diana is safe. Either one of the Roxleys will make her a loving husband. I have my own thoughts on the matter, of course, but I have kept them to myself, and I will continue to do so. This decision must be entirely Diana's, so after you have met them, Patrick, do not, I pray you, attempt to influence her."

He laughed. "I just want her happy," he told his mother.

"She will be, and especially because she has struggled so hard with this decision," Jasmine noted.

"What hae been so damned difficult for the lass, I would know?" he asked his mother.

"Well, for one thing, Damn and Darling look alike," Jasmine began.

"*Damn and Darling?* Jesu! Save me from those precious names the court gives to each other! They hae Christian names, I assume?" the duke said.

"Damien and Darius Esmond," she replied, her mouth twitching with her suppressed mirth.

"'Tis nae much better," he grumbled. "Dare I ask what they called my lass and her cousins?"

"The King's Fancy. Sweet Siren and Cyn," Jasmine said.

Patrick Leslie grimaced. "I suppose it could hae been worse," he muttered. "So these laddies are twins, and look alike. With twin brothers, and marrying a twin, she'll surely hae twins herself. What else?"

"Well, until she could separate them each from the other so she might know them individually, it was difficult to distinguish between them at all, Patrick. She fell in love with them both."

"*Jesu!*" he swore again. "Hae the lass no sense, Mam?"

"Do not be fooled by your daughter's sweet disposition, Patrick," his mother advised. "Diana is a clever and intelligent girl who has gone about this difficulty in a careful and workmanlike manner. She will make the right choice, and you will be pleased."

"*Jesu!*" he said for a third time. "Whatever happened to the days when a man and a woman were swept away by passion alone?"

"I don't seem to recall your being swept away by passion when you met Flanna," his mother remarked. "It was her lands you wanted and not her. Still you came to love her and are fortunate in your wife, my son. Your daughter will be happy in her marriage too."

"I must trust ye, Mama, but then I always hae, and ye hae nae disappointed me yet," the duke told his mother.

"I am glad of that, Patrick," his mother replied dryly.

Diana and her cousin had not meant to overhear the conversation between their grandmother and the duke of Glenkirk. They had been entering the hall to sit by the fire and gossip together, when Cynara had sensed something was being said they they might want to hear. She had stopped them, and by the time Diana realized that they should not be eavesdropping it was too late to reveal themselves without revealing their guilt. When their elders' talk turned to another subject they crept from the family hall, and went out into the gardens.

The duchess of Lundy had added a charming marble summer house at one end of the gardens near the lake. The girls now hurried there to watch the sunset, and chatter.

"I cannot believe I once sounded like my parents," Diana noted. "Each summer they come, and I am surprised to hear them. I am a Scot by birth, and yet I sound so English now. I suppose Mair will sound like us in a few years' time." She turned to Cynara. "Your parents are really wonderful to let her come, and live with Grandmama."

"They say children make a house alive," Cynara said quietly. "Since my half-sister, Brie, and her brood live down in Devon; and neither of my half-brothers has shown any inclination to marry yet, there are no children here at Queen's Malvern any longer. What is it your parents call them? *Bairns!*"

"Yes," Diana said. "Bairns."

"I like your parents," Fancy said. "I am so glad they have come to England. My mother used to tell me how when they lived at Glenkirk they would all come down to England in the summertime like their grandmother, the countess of BrocCairn. It's a nice tradition. I like tradition." Her hands rested protectively over her belly.

"My instinct tells me that you have already decided between the duke, and the marquess," Cynara said wisely. "Tell us who it is to be, cousin."

Diana shook her head. "No," she said. "I do believe I have made the decision, but until they come I will not say. He whom I have picked will hear it first from me, and not you, Cynara. You cannot alas, keep a secret," she laughed, and Fancy laughed with her.

"I can too keep a secret!" Cynara protested.

"Well, you won't have to keep this one, because I shall not share it with you," Diana said, still laughing.

The duke and the marquis were scheduled to arrive the last week in August. The Leslies of Glenkirk would be returning north shortly afterward and were anxious to meet the man who would be their daughter's husband.

"Make up yer flighty mind, lassie," the duke warned his eldest daughter. "I'll nae miss grouse season for ye."

"I promise, Papa," Diana said.

"And yer nae to interfere, Patrick Leslie," the duchess of Glenkirk chided her husband. "Yer mam knows best, and she hae told us Diana will do the right thing."

"Ye've gotten bossy in yer middle years, woman," he told her.

Flanna Leslie swatted at her husband affectionately. "I hae always been bossy where ye are concerned," she told him.

"Aye," he agreed drolly. "Ye surely hae."

Diana's suitors arrived. The duke mounted upon a large dappled gray stallion with a black mane and tale. His brother, the marquis, upon an equally large coal black gelding. Their dark auburn hair gleamed in the late summer sun. Their blue eyes were warm as they looked on Diana.

"They hae a good eye for horseflesh," Glenkirk remarked.

"And for a lass," his brother of Lundy added.

The brothers laughed.

The two guests dismounted, and introductions were made all around as they were ushered into the family hall to be offered some refreshment after their journey. The brothers could not help but gape a bit at the large family gathered. Diana's five brothers were big Highland ruffians, even the youngest who was just seven; and they were proud of it, they liked to brag. The smallest sister was much like them, but the girl introduced as Mair seemed more like Diana. She curtsied prettily to the two visitors.

As small talk was made, Mair sidled up to her oldest sister, and whispered, "I hope ye nae hae chosen the marquis."

"Why?" Diana asked softly, intrigued by her sister's query. "Has Cynara put you up to this in order to discover my choice first?"

"Nay," the young girl said quietly, "but I'll nae say until ye hae said, and then mayhap nae at all."

Diana ruffled her sister's red-gold hair. "You are a funny little lass," she said. "I have missed you."

"And now that I am here," Mair teased, "ye are to choose a husband and leave Queen's Malvern."

"You will love it here," Diana told her sister, "and I will not live so far away that we cannot visit easily. Besides, Grandmama, our aunt, and uncle will spoil you deliciously."

"Do ye ever think of Glenkirk?" Mair asked.

"When I first came to England, aye, but not often now," Diana admitted. "It is no longer my home. Soon even Queen's Malvern will not be my home."

The main meal of the day was served. Diana sat between her two suitors at the linen-covered table in the duke of Lundy's fine dining room. They had had scarcely a moment to speak with Diana for her father was busy quizzing them both on their dwellings, their domestic arrangements, and their incomes. At one point he fixed the two young men with a hard look. Diana, remembering that look from her childhood, knew there was a difficult-to-answer query about to emerge from her father's mouth. She closed her eyes and instinctively held her breath.

"Hae either of ye a mistress?" the duke of Glenkirk demanded, "and I dinna mean some silly milkmaid or serving girl ye amused yerselves wi' now and again as any healthy man is wont to do. I mean a woman that ye keep in her own establishment. *Well?*"

"Nay," the twins answered as one, the duke of Roxley having the grace to flush slightly, but a small muscle in his face twitched with his obvious irritation at such an indelicate question.

"Dinna think me rough wi' ye," Glenkirk said by way of an apology, for he had seen the duke of Roxley's aggravation. "This is my eldest, and much loved daughter that ye seek to wed, my lords. Now then, hae ye any bastards for which ye need to account?"

"I may have sired a child or two," the marquis said slowly.

"Do ye nae know?" Glenkirk demanded.

"My brother has three children," the duke said. "I have one, a four-year-old daughter. Her mother was my gamekeeper's child. We grew up together. Her name was Anne Flemming. She died giving birth to our daughter, who is called after her. Annie lives with her grandparents, in their cottage. I see to all of her needs, my lord. I will not deny my own even for the sake of a wife."

Glenkirk nodded, a small smile touching his lips, but then he turned to the marquis. "Did ye lie to me, laddie, or are ye just a careless fellow?" he said dryly. "A man should at least know how many bairns he hae gotten, no matter the side of the blanket."

"The last was born just before we came to court," the marquis excused himself. "I have only seen the little fellow once or twice. I thought of my other get, two girls, my lord. If it seems that I was not truthful with you, I tender you my regrets for I would not lie to the man who is to be my father-in-law. 'Twould hardly be very politic."

"As my lass hae nae made her decision yet, *Darling*," Glenkirk murmured wickedly, "whether you and I are to be related remains to be seen."

"Enough, Patrick," his mother finally said. "Did you not tell me and Flanna that you would trust my judgment in this matter? And did I not tell you that the Geminid, as Diana has cleverly christened them, are both suitors for your daughter's hand?"

"Yes, *please* give over, Papa," Diana said, totally mortified by her father's questions. "A gentleman is expected to have shown a small bit of indiscretion prior to his marriage. It is most forgivable."

"Well, then," her father said belligerently, "will ye please tell us yer decision in the matter of these two laddies, and put us all out of our misery!"

"I am not certain that it is the right time," Diana considered. "After all, they have just arrived today. Can I not visit with them both for a while before I must say my choice?"

"*No!*" her cousins and her siblings cried with one voice.

"Fer mercy's sake, Diana, gie over, and get on wi' it!" her older brother Angus, the earl of Brae, said irritably.

"Aye," his twin brother, Jamie, their father's heir echoed.

"First, I must see what gift each has brought me," Diana finally answered. "You do remember the task I set you before we parted last, my lords?"

Darius Esmond leaped up and, pulling a flat white leather box from inside his coat, said, "I am assured that these are perfect, even as you are perfect," he told her. He proffered the box.

Diana opened it slowly, and within upon the silk lining rested a strand of exactly matched pearls. They were all identical in size and the color of heavy cream. They were beautiful, but they were an uninspired gift. He had just assumed that like most women she would want jewelry, but she had jewelry, and the hope of inheriting more from her grandmother one day. Saying nothing to him, she closed the box and turned to Damien Esmond. "And you, my lord?" she asked. "What have you brought me?"

"*Nothing,*" he said quietly. "You are a wealthy girl, Diana. You already have everything that you could possibly want, including my heart. However, if you would have something of me," he stood, and pulled a pink rose from one of the table arrangements, "then take this with all the love I have for you, in that heart which you now hold in your two dainty hands." Placing a kiss upon the rose, he proffered the flower.

"Thank you," she said softly. "How well you have come to know me, Damien. It is you I will marry, and no other." She turned to face the dark blue eyes so sorrowfully watching her. "Your gift is lovely, Darling, but it was not the gift I wanted. I wanted your heart, not another jewel. Had you understood that, you would have been the man for me, but you did not, and are not. Are you too disappointed? I would not hurt you."

"Yes," he admitted slowly. He had lost the game, and he really wasn't very good at losing, but he had indeed lost.

"You will recover," she assured him with a small smile.

"I suppose," he muttered. How could he have been so damned dense as to have not understood her? But then he was not, had never been a man of great intellect as his elder sibling was. *And like Diana was.* He sighed. "You are a perfect match," he told them with a sigh.

"Must you recover your heartbreak so quickly?" she asked him in slightly aggrieved tones. "I wonder that you loved me at all."

"I did, but now I understand not enough, sweet Siren," he admitted to her. "You have chosen the right man." Graciously he held out his hand to his brother. "You have won fairly," he told the duke as they shook hands. "But now I must find a wife of my own."

"Ye will hae to wait five years, my lord," a young voice from the end of the table said seriously, and they all turned to look at Mair Leslie.

"*Why?*" Darius Esmond asked the young girl, amused.

"Because I will nae by old enough until then to marry ye," Mair told him bluntly. "I am nae my sister, all confusion over who she should wed. The first time I laid eyes on ye I knew I wanted ye for my husband. Ye hae no idea how I feared my sister would choose ye."

"Sit down, ye bold baggage!" her father roared, outraged.

Mair Leslie sat meekly back in her chair. She had said what she wanted to say, at least for the moment.

"She's coming home to Glenkirk when we leave here," Patrick Leslie said furiously. "I'll nae leave her here to play the coquette!"

"Dinna fret yerself," Flanna, duchess of Glenkirk soothed her husband. "Yer mother will see that she behaves herself, will ye nae, madame? 'Tis the last lass ye'll lose to England, my lord, for Sorcha will remain in our Highlands."

"She's too young," Glenkirk muttered. "Diana was eleven when we left her. Mair will only be ten this autumn."

"This is not the place to discuss this," Jasmine interrupted her son and his wife. "Your eldest daughter has just chosen her husband. We must celebrate and make plans."

Patrick shook his head as if the clear it of cobwebs, and turning to the duke of Roxley said, "Yer pardon, my lord. If ye would truly hae my lassie, then I am glad to accept ye as my son-in-law. We will discuss the business of it tomorrow, eh?"

"Agreed," Damien Esmond said nodding his auburn head. "Now, I think, with your permission, I shall take your daughter into the garden so we may discuss our future together." At the tip of Glenkirk's head, Damien arose from his place at the table and held out his hand to Diana.

She took it smiling, and together they left the duke of Lundy's fine dining room. As the doors closed behind them, the duke swept Diana into his arms and kissed her until she was breathless and laughing.

"I adore you!" he said, his light blue eyes filled with his passion for her. "I died a thousand deaths thinking you might choose Darius. I would have had to kill him then, you realize."

"I chose you weeks ago," she told him. "Even before we left court. Darling is a dear fellow, but I could never really find any serious subject on which we might converse. Why is it you are so well educated, and he is not?"

He took her hand, and they exited the house into the gardens to walk. "I have told you. Darius never enjoyed our studies. He is a man of the earth. His estate is magnificent, and 'tis all his doing, for he oversees every detail of it. He loves his horses and his dogs. He takes pride in his cattle herds. I, on the other hand, prefer my books, although I have never neglected my estates. For me that is the chore, and he has always generously helped me with it," the duke told her.

"Yet you look alike, but for your eyes and you have much the same wit," Diana noted. "It was so difficult to separate you until I could get you each alone," she admitted.

"I am glad that you were clever enough to come up with that stratagem," he said. They strolled hand in hand, and he asked her, "Is your little sister always so candid? I am not certain that she has frightened my brother," he chuckled.

"I have only seen her summers in the past five years," Diana replied, "but it is her character that once she sets her mind on something she will not rest until she has obtained it. Mayhap Darius should be frightened."

"She is clever like you," the duke noted. "A young, clever wife might be just what my brother needs. It is unlikely that Darius will return to court again. He can't afford it. Your sister might be just the lass for him when she is old enough. She will, I suspect, grow up long before he does," the duke laughed.

"Did you invite me into the gardens to speak about possible future matches between our families, my lord? Or did you lure me out here to make love to me?" Diana inquired of him flirtatiously.

He stopped suddenly and drew her down onto the green lawn behind a row of tall hedges. She lay upon her back as he leaned over her saying, "I sense a wanton in you, Diana. I want you to be wanton for me and me alone." His lips brushed her lightly, teasingly.

"I am not certain I know how to be wanton," she whispered. "I do not believe I have ever been wanton before, Damien." Her heart was beating very quickly, and there was a distinct feeling of nervousness in the pit of her belly as his eyes smoldered down at her.

"Were you a good student?" he murmured, his lips brushing her brow softly.

"Yes," she answered slowly.

"Good," he murmured in her ear, "because I am going to teach you to be wanton. *Very wanton.*" His slim fingers toyed with the lace that edged the low neckline on her rose satin gown.

"Oh, Damien, should we be doing this?" she asked him. He was drawing the neckline of her gown down, down, until suddenly her breasts were exposed to his eager eyes.

He stared. While he had fondled her before this, he had never seen her as God had so beautifully and exquisitely fashioned her. "You are perfect," he groaned, his voice thick with emotion. "*And you are now mine!"* His dark auburn head dipped, and his lips kissed the nipple of each breast, turning the tender flesh into taut nubs.

The elegant fingers stroked and caressed the smooth, firm globes of her young bosom. Diana shivered, but not from fear or cold, rather from the pleasure his touch gave her. His lips skimmed over the soft swell of her breasts. His hot kisses grazed her skin. Then his mouth closed hungrily over one of her nipples, drawing hard upon it. She gasped with surprise, a liquid fire poured through her rendering her so weak with delight that she was unable to move or even speak for a moment. Then her hand reached out to touch his head, trailing through his silky locks, caressing the nape of his neck. Finally he lifted his lips from her breast, his blue eyes warm with the love he felt for her.

Diana took his face between her two hands and kissed him with gentle lips upon his narrow mouth. Then her lips touched his cheeks, each in turn, his chin, his nose, and his eyelids. "I love you," she said simply. "I will be anything you desire me to be."

"Be my wife," he said. "My sweet, wanton wife."

"Yes!" Then she unbuttoned his coat, aiding him as he struggled to divest himself of the long garment. Now her fingers undid the lacing on his white silk shirt, opening it so she might run her hands over his smooth broad chest. She pulled him down so that their naked flesh touched and cried out softly at the sensuous contact as his hard flesh crushed her breasts.

Now his mouth was taking hers again, but this time his kiss was fierce and demanding. She kissed him back, her small tongue daring to flick along his lips until he caught it, and drew it into his mouth, his own tongue caressing hers passionately. The heat generated between their two eager bodies threatened to explode into a conflagration. Diana finally pulled her head away from his.

"We must stop!" she told him.

"I know," he groaned, and began kissing her again.

Her head was spinning as she drew away a second time. "I am going to swoon, Damien. Never have I felt like this before! You must help me. You are the more experienced."

"Once again," he laughed weakly, "you ask a Herculean effort from me. This time to cease our lovemaking. Very well, my adorable Diana, I shall do your bidding, but it is not easy. You have allowed me a small glimpse of paradise. Now I am eager to have it all." He sat up and began relacing his shirt. Then leaning over he drew her gown up, lightly kissing the swell of her bosom as he did so. Standing, he picked up his coat and put it back on.

Diana rose to her feet, and helped him button the garment. "You are quite in order again, my lord," she told him, her hand pushing back an errant lock of his hair. "Am I?"

"Turn around," he instructed. "Ahh, good," he said, brushing her free of any grass, "there are no green stains upon your gown. It is a lovely gown, my darling. I shall always remember you in rose satin and ecru lace on the night you agreed to marry me."

"You are the most romantic gentleman," Diana said, turning about again to smile at him.

He took her by the shoulders and looked deep into her eyes. "You know I love you. You have agreed to marry me. *When?*" he asked.

"I have always wanted a winter wedding," Diana responded. "I like the month of December, don't you? Fancy's baby will be born by then, and Cynara will not yet have returned to court. I must have them both with me when I wed you."

"What of your parents?" he inquired.

"They will return from Scotland. Papa will grumble, but they will come. There is no time now. Glenkirk will *nae* miss his grouse season," she laughed up at the duke. "He has already told me that."

"Then December it shall be," Damien agreed. "We can fix the exact date another time after we have spoken with your grandmother. She is, I can see, the real power in this family."

Diana nodded. "She is. You are very wise to recognize it."

They walked together through the gardens of Queen's Malvern, and back into the house where they announced to their family that they would marry in December.

"Ye canna wait until next summer?" Glenkirk teased his daughter.

"*Papa!*" Diana feigned outrage.

"So yer mam and I must get on our horses, and trek down from Glenkirk in some raging winter's storm wi' the chance we may not get here at all, or if we do, not be able to return north until spring. The thought of leaving yer brother in charge frankly, my lass, scares me to death."

"Ye would put Jamie in charge of Glenkirk?" Angus Gordon Leslie demanded to know.

"Aye, he's the heir," Patrick Leslie said to his son.

"But I'm an earl, Papa," Angus protested.

"Yer Brae, laddie, nae Glenkirk. Besides, yer namesake will be wisely guiding ye both in our absence," the duke reminded the second-born of his sons. "Go to yer own holding, Angus. 'Tis where ye should be now."

"Why can we nae come wi' ye, Da?" Jamie asked his father.

"Because if ye come, then Angus will want to come, and the rest of yer brothers, and Sorcha too. Yer mam and I must travel hard, for the winter will be all around us. We will hae nae time to coddle any of ye. Ye'll remain home. What difference does it make? Ye've met your sister's man, and ye'll see them next summer."

"When Diana will have a fat belly, I'm sure," Angus teased his sister wickedly.

"*Angus!*" Jasmine and Flanna chorused together.

"I hope I do!" Diana told her brother spiritedly. Then she stuck her tongue out at him.

"Yer certain she is old enough to wed, are ye?" Glenkirk said to her mother.

"She's sixteen now, my son, and 'tis just the right time for a girl to take her husband," Jasmine told him with a satisfied smile.

Diana took the rose Damien had given her to bed with her, placing it on her pillow where she might smell its fragrance as she dreamed of her lover. "I shall keep it forever," she declared.

"Then you had best press it between the pages of a book," Cynara advised. "I'm glad you chose the duke. Darius is a great deal of fun, but there is little to him other than his passion for his lands. Imagine little Mair saying she wants to marry him one day. Hardly a consolation for losing you, I think."

"I shall make Darius a good wife when I am grown," Mair said stoutly. "Dinna gie yerself airs, Cousin. When I see what I want, I take it. From all the gossip I hae heard, we are much alike, Cynara."

"I cannot believe she is only going to be ten," Cynara said testily.

"Mair has always has a wise head," Diana laughed. "I recall our mama calling her *'my wee old woman.'* Does she still call you that, little sister?"

"Aye, she does," Mair admitted.

Molly came into the room. "What?" she said. "You are not all abed yet? Dolly!" She called to her younger sister who was to be Mair's servant. "Come, and put your mistress to bed. She is too young to be up so late. Can you not do your duty? If I do not see an improvement in your behavior, I shall ask our mistress to find another more suited to take care of Lady Mair."

"Aye," Cynara laughed as Dolly hurried in to shepherd her young mistress to her bed. "The Lady Mair will be a marchioness one day, Dolly. You had best take good care of her so she'll take you with her when she marries Darius Roxley."

"I suppose I can develop the expertise to get along wi' the proud bitch," Mair murmured to Diana before she left the room.

Diana's hand flew to her mouth to keep from laughing.

"What did the little wretch say?" Cynara asked.

"Something rude," Diana said, chuckling. "'Tis of no matter, Cyn. You will have little to do with my sister once you return to court next winter."

A shadow flitted across Cynara's beautiful face, but it was quickly gone, and she said, "I cannot wait to return! I love the court! It is so filled with excitement. There is always something new to do there. I am never bored at court as I am here at Queen's Malvern."

"We have had little time to talk together since you came home," Diana said quietly. "Do you still seek to pursue Harry Summers?"

Cynara nodded.

"Yet he offers you no encouragement, not even a tiny sign that he cares for you," Diana continued. "I cannot bear to see you hurt, Cyn. We have been friends since our childhood. I love you every bit as much as I love my sisters. Is there no one else to please you?"

Cynara shook her head. "Nay. I must have Harry or die!" she said with such conviction that Diana shivered.

"Do not say such a thing, I pray you, dearest!" she cried.

Realizing that she had frightened Diana, Cynara put her arms about her cousin. "'Tis just a saying, sweet Siren. There is no need for you to worry. I will kill Harry before he kills me." And she laughed. It was a mocking sound that had no real mirth in it.

Worried, Diana spoke with Fancy, who said, "I will try to reason with her. If anyone knows the harm a wicked man can cause, it is certainly me. Were it not for the king's loving kindness, I should have gone through life believing that all men were wretches."

"I like Kit Trahern," Diana sold softly. "He is a good man. You will marry him, of course, Cousin."

"We shall see," Fancy evaded. "Let us concentrate on Cynara. My problems are small compared to hers, I fear."

A few days later Patrick Leslie and his family departed for Scotland. He was satisfied with his daughter's choice of a husband. The duke of Roxley, Patrick had to admit to himself, was the perfect husband for Diana. Together the two men had sat in the library of Queen's Malvern and hammered out the marriage settlement. Damien Esmond had signed without question the legal document that would allow his wife to keep and manage her own fortune. He was more than pleased with the dowry the duke of Glenkirk settled upon Diana. It was far in excess of what he had anticipated. He had not realized how wealthy this family was, for they did not flaunt their riches.

"You would not be foolish to wait for Mair Leslie to grow up," he advised his brother. "Her father tells me he will settle a similar amount upon her and the youngest daughter when they are grown. Do you think you can keep out of trouble for the next five years, Darius?"

The marquis of Roxley laughed. "Probably, as long as I remain on my estates. Unless someone comes along, and I fall impossibly in love, Mair Leslie will suit me well. She likes the country, and I am surprised how much she knows about horses despite her youth."

"Think more of her and less of yourself, Brother," the duke advised his sibling. "Had you taken the time to know more about Diana, you might not have lost her."

After the Leslies had gone, the duke and his brother remained at Queen's Malvern for several weeks. The marquis of Isham joined their group, and together they picnicked, and all but Fancy rode. The summer was ended, and the autumn was beginning to show itself in the trees and in the days, which were growing noticeably shorter. Finally the dowager decided it was time for Diana to pick her wedding day that the preparations might begin.

"December thirty-first," Diana said, looking to Damien for his approval.

He nodded. "We will marry as the old year ends and start our new life together as a new year begins," he said. "Aye, 'tis a good choice, Diana."

They turned to Jasmine to learn her opinion.

She nodded. "It is very symbolic, my dears. I fully approve. Tomorrow, however, the Geminid must go home. You may spend December with us, but I do not want to see you before then."

"Grandmama!" Diana protested. "Should I not at least go to pay a visit to my new home so I may ascertain what needs to be done to make it habitable for a bride? It has been years since a woman was in residence at Roxley. I will need to interview the servants, perhaps hire more, and pension off those who are too elderly now but remain out of habit. It cannot wait until after I am wed. I would spend a cozy winter in honeymoon with my husband."

Jasmine was pleased to see her granddaughter was already taking her future duties seriously. "Very well," she said. "We shall pay you a visit, my lord, the first week in November."

"I shall expect you then, madame," the duke answered her formally.

"May Damien and I have some time together now, Grandmama, as he is to go tomorrow?" Diana asked politely.

"Run along," Jasmine told her granddaughter, watching as the two lovers made their way from the old hall.

"How I wish Cynara could find such happiness," Barbara, duchess of Lundy, said to her mother-in-law. "She is utterly miserable most of the time and longs to return to court and her pursuit of Harry Summers." She looked closely at Jasmine. "You have been amazingly silent in this matter, madame. What do you know?"

"They call him *Wickedness* at court, but you know that. His reputation is said to be bad, but his family is quite an excellent and old one. While he is called a reprobate, I have yet to actually discover why it is he is deserving of this reputation, but I will, Barbara. I assure you that I will."

"I cannot allow my only child to be harmed," the duchess said. "You know what her early childhood was like."

"Cynara cannot be stopped in midflight, Barbara. She is very much a Stuart. They are passionate and reckless people. She will learn by experience and no other way. She will either tame the earl of Summersfield, or he will tame her. Either way she will not be happy otherwise. If it ends badly, she will have no one to blame but herself. Cynara is a resilient girl. She will survive, Barbara, but we will nonetheless do our best to protect her from herself and from the earl of Summersfield." Jasmine reached out and patted Barbara's hand. "It will all work itself out eventually. That much I have learned in my long life. Whatever is meant to happen will happen. It is that simple."

"But you have said you do not intend returning to court," the duchess pointed out to her mother-in-law.

"Indeed I do not, Barbara, but you and Charlie will be there," Jasmine said. "And you will write to me, so I may advise you."

"When did Cynara ever listen to me?" the duchess lamented.

Jasmine laughed. "All daughters demand independence, but they cry for their mothers in the midst of childbirth."

Barbara Stuart laughed. "I did not cry for mine, but then she was dead. I was glad, however, that my faithful old Lucy was with me when Cynara was born," she noted. "I see your point, madame. You are telling me to let Cynara find her own path, but to be there when she stumbles and needs me."

"Exactly," Jasmine smiled, and nodded. "Ah, Barbara, look into the garden. Are not Diana and Damien sweet? How I prayed she would choose him, and not his brother. A few moments with each of them, and I knew the answer, but then I am a wily old vixen," she concluded. And her eyes grew misty with memories.

In the gardens Diana strolled with her betrothed. They held hands, and for a time did not talk. Finally she said, "I hate it that we are to be separated now, Damien. I shall have no one to kiss, and cuddle me, my lord. Now that I have grown used to it, I am certain to miss it. If gentlemen can tumble for a chambermaid, I do not know why ladies cannot kiss the footman."

"*Diana!*" Then he laughed. "You are really quite outrageous, my darling girl. If I did not know what a prankster you can be, I should be quite concerned."

"Why would you think me jesting in this matter?" she asked him, green eyes wide, feigning innocence. "It is quite a serious question and deserves an intelligent answer, my lord."

He stopped. He turned her about, and kissed her a long, hard kiss. "Would a footman kiss you like that, madame?" he demanded.

"I do not know," she said sweetly. "I have never kissed a footman. Shall we call one, and put him to the test?"

Grasping her by the wrist he turned her over his knee, and gave her a spank. "No, madam, we will not!" he said in outraged tones.

Diana pulled away from the duke and pushing him hard sent him sprawling backward into a green boxwood. "Bully!" she taunted. Then she turned, and scampered away into the garden's maze, daring him to follow and find her. "Come and get me!" she called.

He insinuated himself into the maze quietly. "Where are you, my darling girl?" he called. Then he listened closely to pinpoint her exact location.

"*Over here, Damn,*" she cooed in seductive tones, and then Diana moved quickly around a corner, and cheating, slipped through the greenery into another whorl of the maze. She bit her lip to keep from giggling. She and Cynara had played together in this maze for years.

Then to her surprise Cynara was by her side, fingers to her lips in a gesture of silence. She nodded, and disappeared back into the greenery. "Damien," she called. "Where are you?"

Diana moved deeper into the hedge puzzle, calling to him,

"Come, my lord, can you not find me?" She heard him stamping through the maze, becoming confused.

"Over here!" Cynara called.

"No, over here!" Diana cried.

Was he going mad? The duke stopped, and listened. Her voice came from here and then as quickly from there? What was going on?

"Yoo-hoo!" to the right of him.

"Yoo-hoo!" behind him.

And then he realized that Cynara must also be in the maze with them. A crafty look came into his eye. While the cousins did often sound alike, there were distinct differences in their voices. He made it a point to listen more carefully when the next alluring call came.

"Where are you?" Cynara said mischievously. She was so close to him she could see him through the boxwood.

Immediately Diana took up the cry. *"Come to me, Damn! Can you not find me?"* And she giggled.

There she was, the little vixen, the duke realized. He followed the teasing sounds of her dulcet tones until at last he saw her, standing in the center of the maze. Carefully he crept up behind her even as Cynara called from the opposite end of the garden labyrinth. Softly, softly he moved until reaching out he clapped a hand over her mouth to still her cry of surprise. His big hand fondled her breasts and he whispered in her ear, kissing and touching it with the tip of his tongue as he did so.

"You are a wicked little wench," he murmured, "and if we were already married, my sweet Siren, I should have you on your back with your skirts about your ears. But we are not wed and will not be for several months. So instead I shall just tease you, all the while reminding you that I am leaving in the morning and will not see you for some weeks. Now, kiss me, Diana Leslie, for I long for your sweetness." Then spinning her about, he took his hand from her mouth and kissed her, his lips playing over hers until she was weak with her pleasure.

She clung to him because she knew that her legs would not hold her at this moment. One kiss blended into another until finally, lips raw, they eased from the embrace. "I am satisfied now," she told him, her green eyes dancing, "that no footman could kiss me the way that you do, Damien Esmond. You have, I fear, ruined me for another lover."

"Then you cannot return to court ever, madam, for to have a duchess of Roxley be so unfashionable as to love her husband would simply not do. This is a dark secret that we must keep to ourselves." He was smiling down at her, and its effect was to but render her weaker.

"I cannot stand," she said softly. "If I let go of you, I shall collapse. I am quite sure of it." The small heart-shaped face looking up at him so desperately sent his heart into spasms of love for her.

"Then I shall have to carry you out of the maze, Diana," he told her.

"Damien?" She sighed as he picked her up in his arms.

"Yes?"

"Can we not remain here and just make love?" she wondered.

Now it was the duke who sighed. "I should like it, my darling, but no. The first time I make love to you, Diana, it will be in a flower-filled chamber with the glow of candlelight illuminating your beauty. You will be my wife, and the child who will be born from the passion we create that night will have been conceived honestly from our love for one another. I love you, Diana. I would honor you in this way. Do you understand what I am saying to you?" He kissed the tip of her nose.

She nodded, but he thought he detected a hint of disappointment in her emerald eyes, and he was flattered. She was an intelligent girl, a beautiful girl, but she was also an innocent. When she looked back upon the first time they really made love, the memory would be wonderful as it should be.

"Very well then," he said to her. "Now please tell me how the hell to get out of this puzzle."

She sighed again. "Turn left first," she said as she began to direct him. Then she called, "Cynara, I am caught."

"I know," Cynara said, stepping from around the curve in the green boxwood. "Actually, Grandmama sent me to fetch you two. 'Tis getting dark, and the evening meal will soon be served. My lord," she said to the duke, "your brother was no better at finding his way from our maze. My cousin, Mair, lured him in this morning. She has a way with her, however, the little wretch. The marquis found the whole situation very amusing, although I know I should not have. I actually think he might miss her when you are gone back to your home."

"Then perhaps my brother will marry Mair Leslie one day," the duke said. "But, I believe, they should become friends first."

"How old-fashioned you are, my lord," Cynara replied.

"Aye, I am, Cyn," he told her. "Most men are no matter what they may say. Remember that when you return to court this winter."

Cynara was silent as they exited the maze back into the garden, and then she said, "I suspect that your advice is sound, my lord. I shall remember it."

"Remember this also, Cynara Stuart. You will always be welcome at Roxley Castle, not just for your cousin's sake, but for mine as well."

"Thank you, my lord," Cyn responded, her blue gaze meeting his, and she gave him a small smile.

"You have a castle?" Diana squeaked from the shelter of his arms.

"'Tis just a small one," the duke answered her. Laughing at her honest surprise, he carried her back into the house.

Chapter
14

The duke and the marquis of Roxley departed the following morning for their respective homes. Diana was beginning to get used to the fact that she was to live in a small castle. It was known as Roxley Castle. The marquis's home was called Roxley Hall. Mair said a hall would suit her quite well when she married Darius one day. She was reminded that Darius Esmond had neither proposed to her as she was just ten, nor had he even accepted the idea of a match between them one day. Mair smiled with an almost feline look, saying it would all come about in its due course; and for the next few years she must devote herself to learning how to speak English properly and become a fine English lady like her sister and her cousins. No one argued with her as they had quickly realized that arguing with Mair Leslie was a futile pursuit. She might look like a Leslie, but she had her mother's character.

The various harvests had all been gathered in, the last being the apple and pear orchards. Apple cider and pear wine were made for the winter. The rest of the fruit was carefully stored in cold dry cellars until needed. The trees were turning soft colors. The days were growing shorter. The nights longer and chill. Their work for their master completed, the duke of Lundy's tenants began making repairs to their own roofs and chimneys in preparation for the winter. The miller was kept busy grinding grain into flour, his millstream wheel turning from dawn until dusk. The pigs were slaughtered. Ham, bacon, and sausage were made. Sides of beef were hung with the venison and game birds in the cold pantry.

October was about to become a memory. Fancy had grown rounder and plumper with her expected child. She was making peace with herself and with Kit Trahern, to the family's relief. Diana and Jasmine were to depart for Roxley on November first. They had asked Cynara to come with them for she had been like a tigress of late, irritable, riding her horse at breakneck speeds across the country-side in her unhappiness. It was hoped that a visit to Roxley with Diana and her grandmother would prove a pleasant diversion for Cynara.

Roxley was a full two days' journey from Queen's Malvern. They overnighted in a comfortable inn the first night, reaching their desti-nation close to sunset on the second day. As the duke told them, his castle was not a large one. A fortified dwelling built in the thirteenth century as a marcher fort, Roxley was, despite its four square towers with their battlements, more like a comfortable manor house. Constructed of grayish brownstone, it had dark gray slate roofs. It was set upon the crest of a small hill with an ancient stone chapel at its foot. In the surrounding fields herds of cattle and flocks of sheep browsed peacefully, giving testament to the duke's modest wealth.

"It is so isolated," Cynara noted as they approached the castle. "You will certainly have to make your own amusement here, for we have not passed another substantial dwelling for miles. I wonder where the Hall is. I suppose we will see Darling. I shall enjoy teas-ing Mair. She so wanted to come."

"I suspect a newlywed couple will welcome the solitude," Jasmine told Cynara. Then she turned to Diana. "It is lovely, my dear child, isn't it? I can just make out the gardens in the rear. We shall see tomorrow the condition they are in."

Their coach drew up to the front door of the dwelling, and the duke was there to meet them. He helped Jasmine from the carriage, kissing her hand as he did so. He helped Cynara from the vehicle, kissing her hand as well. Finally he helped Diana out, and without a word he enfolded her into his arms and kissed her.

"Welcome home, my sweet Siren," he said to her.

Diana's eyes filled suddenly with tears, but they were tears of joy. "Ah, Damien, I am so happy!" she half-whispered. "Happy to see you again. Happy to know you still love me and happy to see the place where I will spend the rest of my days and raise my children."

The duke kissed her gently again. His heart was filled with his happiness. Had he not thought it unmanly, he might have wept himself. As it was he had to blink back his emotions. Putting an arm about Diana, he walked her into the house. When his guests were settled in his Great Hall, warmed by the fire, with goblets of good wine in their hands, Damien Esmond said, "Diana, madame, I should like to make a small change in our wedding plans. It would mean a great deal to my tenants to see me married here at Roxley. Would you consider it? While I do not currently have a cleric in residence, there is a lovely old chapel on the castle grounds where, if it would please you, I should like to have the ceremony performed."

"While I had always expected to be married at Queen's Malvern," Diana said slowly, "I can understand your wish to have the ceremony here. We could bring our chaplain, could we not, Grandmama?"

Jasmine nodded. "And it would certainly be a bit easier for your parents," she considered.

"But will Fancy be able to travel? I will not be wed without both of my cousins by my side," Diana said.

"I foresee no difficulty there," Jasmine told her granddaughter.

"And if she cannot travel," the duke promised Diana, "then we shall be wed in your uncle's house."

"Then I most certainly will agree!" Diana responded.

"We shall have to depart immediately, a day or two after the Christmas celebration," Jasmine said. "Rohana and Toramalli will be disappointed, but they are simply too frail any longer to do much more than doze by the fire. I wonder that they yet live. Still, they will understand if you come at Christmas, Damien, and they may see you again."

"To that I will most readily agree, madame," the duke replied.

Dinner was served in the hall at an old-fashioned high board.

"I have not yet a fine dining room like your son, madame," the duke explained, "but if Diana desires she may do whatever she wants with the house."

"As you know," Jasmine told him, "I have always preferred our old hall. I fear my age makes me old-fashioned, but Diana is young and will, I have no doubt, enjoy modernizing your castle just a wee bit. It will keep her amused while she waits for your first child."

"*Grandmama!*" Diana blushed prettily.

Cynara laughed. "Grandmama's correct, sweet Siren. What else will there be for you to do in this sequestered place? I shall think of you this winter when I am back at court playing and keeping my figure."

After the meal was over, and a reasonable amount of time had elapsed, Jasmine insisted that she and Cynara must be taken to their rooms so they might get some rest after their journey. Cynara was about to protest, but a look from her grandmother set her quiet and nodding in agreement. Diana, who had seen the by-play between the two, giggled softly, but as silently blessed her grandmother for her discretion. She watched as the two women left the hall after bidding them good night.

The duke arose and walked across the hall to seat himself in a large comfortable upholstered chair. "Come, and sit with me, sweeting," he invited her, and Diana eagerly complied, curling up in his lap happily.

"I have missed you," she told him. "I never thought November the first would arrive and then another two days of travel to reach you. While Grandmama must have a coach now, I rode most of the way. I often got so far ahead of the carriage a mounted footman had to be sent ahead to fetch me." She smiled up at him. "Are you shocked that I am so impatient to be with you?"

His light blue eyes regarded her seriously, and then he said, "It took you long enough to decide what I knew from the moment I laid eyes upon you, Diana Leslie."

"Villain! You never said you loved me until I agreed to marry you!" she cried. "Besides, I am not certain of the sincerity of love at first sight."

He chuckled, then tipping the heart-shaped face up to his, he kissed her, tenderly at first, his lips moving gently over hers; but as Diana met his rising ardor with her own, Damian's kiss grew more demanding. One kiss followed another. Her dark lashes were like small black butterflies upon her pale cheeks. She sighed with contentment when he began to carress her breasts, his hand slipping beneath the neckline of her gown, unlacing the silken ribbon holding her chemise closed, moving past that delicate garment to cup her warm flesh. He could feel his own desire growing. Indeed it threatened to burst through his breeches. He was astounded that a young, and really quite inexperienced virgin could arouse him so quickly, and so thoroughly. Reluctantly he withdrew his hand from her delightful bosom, his mouth moving away from hers to place a chaste kiss upon her smooth brow.

Diana's eyes flew open, sensing the change in his passions. "Why have you stopped?" she asked him nervously. What had she done to displease him? she fretted silently.

"I had not realized that my love for you, my wish to have absolutely everything you can offer me, here and now, was quite as great as it is, sweeting. I will not take your virtue from you before we are wed, Diana. Your cousin, Cynara, once accused me of being old-fashioned, and I am. But as I told you several weeks ago, our coming together must be perfect."

"There is no such thing as *perfect,* Damian. If you believe that then you will be disappointed," Diana advised him. "And you shall never have my virtue from me. My virginity, yes, and joyfully, but never my virtue. If I tempt you, however innocently, although I do not mean to tempt you, my lord, then we shall cease our love play. And we shall not practice it again until we are well married. Will that satisfy you?" she asked him which utmost seriousness.

"No," he quickly responded, "but it will be as you have said because I find my determination crumbles when you are near me."

Diana slipped from his lap, straightened her gown, and she curtsied to him. "What a lovely thing to tell me. Good night, my lord. I shall ask a servant to show me to my chamber."

In the morning Diana and her grandmother inspected Roxley

Castle. It was a very comfortable establishment with a small group of dedicated servants who were obviously devoted to their master. There would be no need for now to replace anyone or hire more staff. Jasmine nodded.

"This speaks well of Damien," she told her granddaughter, very pleased. "Bide your time once you are mistress here. Learn as much as you can from the housekeeper and the majordomo. They appear to be most deferential, but I am here with you now. When you are alone, make certain their attitude remains respectful. Do not allow them to take advantage of your youth. They have had their own way for some time, but time will tell if their hearts are good."

They met the head gardener, a man of indeterminate years named Bennett, who happily showed them about. Diana was pleased to find the gardens at Roxley were old-fashioned, filled with rose-bushes, flowering bushes, and evidence of summer flowers, now almost all faded and gone. It was not like the newer fashioned gardens to the south, all greenery and sculpted into fantastical shapes. Diana was relieved and told Bennett so. He, in his turn, showed open pleasure at her delight in his handiwork.

"Do you think there might be a place near to the house to put in a small herb garden next spring?" Diana asked him.

"I has just the spot," Bennett replied, smiling.

Darius arrived, full of mischief and amusing chatter. He tried to tease Diana into admitting that she had made an error in judgment and must change her mind and wed him. But he also evinced a mild disappointment that little Mair had not come with them. "The little wench makes me laugh," he said casually. "And she doesn't judge me or compare me to my brother."

"I never judged you," Diana quickly remarked. "As for comparing you with Damien, it was nigh impossible to tell you apart when I first met you both."

"But you can now?" he said, surprised, and interested. "How? And do not tell me the eyes, sweet Siren."

"The timbre of your voices is different," Diana told him. "Damien's is slightly deeper, while yours is more musical."

"Well, I'll be damned!" he exclaimed, surprised again by her clever evaluation.

"Oh, I hope not, dear brother," she said wickedly.

He laughed. "If your little sister grows up to be as adroit and as charming as you are, sweet Siren, I very well may marry her."

"She will be delighted to hear how reasonable you have become with her absence," Diana murmured sweetly.

And they all laughed.

Jasmine was pleased to see how easily Diana fit into Damien's family and relieved that Darius held no grudge against her granddaughter for choosing his brother. If she had worried to herself about anything, it had been that, but she now saw she had no cause for concern. The next morning they departed back to Queen's Malvern, and upon reaching her home the dowager sent messages to the various members of her family that Diana's marriage would be celebrated at Roxley Castle instead of Queen's Malvern. It would be a small wedding at any rate given the time of year the bridal couple had chosen. But better it be held in December so Diana might get about the business of giving her husband an heir and affixing her position in her new family solidly.

A trousseau was to be prepared, but hardly had the local seamstress gotten underway in her work than Fancy decided to have her baby. Of course neither Diana nor Cynara were allowed into the birthing chamber for fear of frightening their delicate virgin sensibilities. Diana was annoyed.

"What twaddle!" she told her cousin. "I quite clearly remember being with Mama when Mair and the bairns who followed her were born, and I was even allowed to cut the birthing cord for Sorcha. It looks like a pig intestine," she noted.

"It sounds terrible, and that is disgusting," Cynara murmured faintly. "I am just as glad to remain clear of the whole thing. Look at how shapeless Fancy has become with her child. I have heard the ladies of the court say that once you start having children you never get your figure back again. I want to fascinate Harry until we are old and gray."

"If you can get the earl of Summersfield to the altar," Diana remarked, "he will expect you to give him an heir sooner than later. I cannot wait to have Damien's seed growing within me!"

The door to Fancy's bedchamber opened, and a serving woman rushed out with an armful of bloody linens, while another rushed in with a fresh stack of laundry, followed by a second servant struggling with an infant's cradle. The door slammed shut, but they could distinctly hear Fancy swearing fiercely.

"My God! All that blood! Is our cousin dying?" Cynara asked, eyes wide.

"Birthing is a bloody business," Diana said. "And the pain can be fierce, too. With Mair my mother pushed her out of her body with incredible ease, but with Sorcha, her last, it was hours before the little wretch was born. My mother swore just like Fancy then," Diana giggled. "Cyn! Why are you so pale? You aren't going to swoon on me, are you?" Diana reached out to steady Cynara who was swaying. "Here, sit down, Cousin, before you fall down. What is the matter with you?"

"Your mother pushed a baby out of her body?" Cynara whispered, as if she could barely say the words.

"Of course," Diana replied. " 'Odsfish, Cyn! How did you think babies were born? Someone must have told you something. I cannot believe that such a sophisticated girl as yourself didn't know how babies are born."

"It is not a subject that ever came up," Cynara said, "and I have no siblings born after me. I don't know what I thought, Diana. For mercy's sake, enlighten me. I feel enough of a fool as it is. I wait outside of our cousin's chamber hearing her cries, seeing all the blood, and the hustle bustle of servants while you speak casually of pain and cords that look like pig's intestines."

"The baby is pushed from the same place the manhood enters into our bodies. We have talked about that enough," Diana said in matter-of-fact tones. "It enlarges to allow a manhood inside, and when the baby wants to be born, it enlarges itself even more. It's all quite natural."

"It sounds awful!" Cynara replied. "I think it is a fortunate thing that Grandmama insisted we remain outside." She stood up, her legs still shaky, but she steadied herself on the arm of her chair. "I am going down into the hall to await the arrival of the king's brat. Are you coming with me, Diana?"

"Very well," Diana agreed cheerfully. It was unfortunate that Cynara didn't understand, but she would eventually.

They spent the evening with the men of the household and Mair. Cynara played chess with Kit Trahern who had been pacing back and forth for hours. Mair had fallen asleep in her aunt Barbara's lap and the duchess of Lundy herself dozed lightly. Diana sat quietly playing cards with her uncle until finally Orane entered the hall to announce that Mistress Devers had birthed a daughter, and both mother and child were fine. They might come and see the baby now.

They filed into Fancy's bedchamber. Diana thought her cousin looked beautiful though tired. A small swaddled bundle was tucked into her arms, and she proudly displayed her newborn daughter for all to see, but her eyes were already going past them, seeking out the marquis of Isham.

"She looks like the king," Jasmine said.

"Not the nose, thank God!" Diana put in.

"And she's fair, not swarthy like His Majesty," Cynara noted.

"So another generation has produced another not-so-royal Stuart," Charlie noted dryly, and his family laughed.

On the following day Fancy announced that she and Kit had decided to wed on the first day of December. "Do you mind that we have chosen the same month in which you and your duke will wed?" she asked her cousin. "If you do, I suppose we could marry on the thirtieth of November."

"There is hardly enough time for December the first," Diana said. "What of your trousseau and a wedding gown? And, of course, I do not mind. I think it rather charming that one of us shall wed on the first day of December, and the other on the last day of that month," Diana responded generously.

"I already have enough clothes to last me a lifetime," Fancy said. "And I do not need an elaborate gown in which to say my vows with Kit. I had one when I wed with Parker Randolph. None of the tradition or beautiful clothing prevented me from disaster. And besides, I am yet a bit thicker in the waist than I would prefer."

"Where do you want to have the ceremony?" Jasmine asked.

Fancy looked to her aunt and her uncle. "May we be wed here at Queen's Malvern in the old chapel, please?" she asked.

"I would not have you married in any other place," the duke of Lundy said generously to his niece and his duchess agreed.

Lady Christina Stuart was baptized when she was but three days old in the same chapel in which her mother would shortly marry. Charles Frederick, the not-so-royal Stuart, stood the baby's godfather. He was her great uncle, but they were also joined by another bond. The infant's godmothers were her two cousins, Lady Diana Leslie and Lady Cynara Stuart. The child cried at the appropriate moment as the holy water was laved over her dark head, and she was pronounced Christina Margaret Mary Stuart, a now spotless Christian of the Anglican Church.

On the first of December in the chapel of Queen's Malvern, a holy spot that had seen many a family wedding, Mistress Frances Devers was married to Christopher Trahern, the marquis of Isham. Her grandmother, who would not hear of her grandchild appearing in anything less than a fine gown, managed to provide a satin dress the color of heavy cream, lavishly decorated on the sleeves, and at the neckline with fine French lace. She had warned the marquis in advance, and he appeared before his bride in a matching satin suit. The bride carried a nosegay of multicolored late-autumn roses and dried lavender tied with a cream silk ribbon.

In the duke's fine dining room afterward, a wedding breakfast was served before the couple departed for Riverwood Priory. Jasmine had insisted that her granddaughter hire a wetnurse for Lady Christina. She explained to Fancy that having done her duty to the king, it was now time for her to do her duty by her husband. He must have full access to her charms and should not have to share them with an infant.

"You will nurse your other children, if you so desire. I have done both, and found I love the children who nursed at my teat no more or less than those who did not. I will keep Christina here at Queen's

Malvern with me for a short time. You must prepare a nursery for
her, and then we must attend Diana's wedding. After that, you may
have your daughter."

When he learned of it, Kit Trahern thanked the dowager.

"A bridegroom is entitled to his bride's company alone, at least in
the first month," Jasmine told him with a twinkle in her turquoise
eyes. You both need time together, and an infant is a great deal of
trouble no matter how good, and Christina is a good child."

So the marquis of Isham and his wife, the marchioness, left for
their home at midday, and on the following day the preparations
began anew for Diana's wedding to Damien Esmond. A coterie of
servants was dispatched to Roxley Castle to help the duke's people
prepare. The seamstress and her assistants sewed diligently on
Diana's wedding gown and her trousseau.

"I don't know why you need so many new clothes," Cynara said.
"Who will see them in your isolation?"

"Grandmama insists," Diana said. "She will do the same for you
one day, too, Cyn. Are you really going back to court immediately
after my wedding?"

"The festivities have already begun, and I am not there. Who
knows if some cow-eyed creature will come this winter, and try to
steal Harry from me? I could not bear it, Diana. *I could not!*"

"How I wish you had not fixated on that man," her cousin
replied. "Can you not find a nicer gentleman to love? One who will
be grateful that you have chosen him. One who will love you?"

Cynara sighed deeply and then said in a burst of candor, "It
would be easier, wouldn't it, and I should probably not be so
damned unhappy, but there it is. I love Harry Summers. If he died
tomorrow, my heart would go with him."

"But he has such a dreadful reputation, Cynara. We are all afraid
he will seduce you for the mere sport of it," Diana said.

"You don't know him as I do," Cynara insisted, "and it is more
likely that I will seduce him than he me," she laughed softly.

Two days before Christmas the duke and duchess of Glenkirk arrived from Scotland.

"I thought to see you at Roxley," Jasmine said to her son and daughter-in-law, surprised.

"We feared waiting too long lest the weather impede us," the duchess said. "'Twas simpler to leave earlier and come here. We will return directly home from Roxley."

"And we hae nae shared a Christmas together in many a long year, Mam," the duke said to his mother, putting an arm about her. "Ye dinna mind, do ye, Barbara?" he asked his sister-in-law.

"You know you are always welcome here," Barbara said.

Mair came forward and curtsied to her parents prettily. Her gown was neat, her hair was combed, and she wore slippers upon her feet. "Welcome back to Queen's Malvern, my lord, my lady," she said. Her speech was already more English than Scots.

Flanna Leslie nodded, well pleased. This daughter was going to do every bit as well as her eldest daughter.

"She is a quick learner," Barbara told her sister-in-law, "and she is a joy in my house. I will be glad for her company this winter while Cynara is back at court."

"Yer nae going back?" Patrick Leslie said, curious.

"Charlie is going," Barbara said. "He will keep an eye on Cynara. I prefer remaining here as I did before last year. Charlie often goes up to London alone without me. No one will think the worse of me for it."

"I dinna think I should let yon wild lassie go to the king's court wi'out me," Flanna said softly.

"I am not indifferent to her," the duchess of Lundy told the duchess of Glenkirk in low tones. "But whatever her fate she must meet it head-on. If she is to gain wisdom through heartbreak, then so be it. She will listen to nothing we have said to her, Flanna. Short of locking her in a stone tower, I don't know what else to do."

"What does the dowager say?" Flanna queried.

"What I have said," Barbara Stuart responded.

Flanna nodded. "The old woman hae good instincts. I pray they hae nae failed her in the matter of yer lass."

They celebrated Christmas in the old hall of Queen's Malvern with a Yule log, groups of flickering candles, and bunches of holly and pine, as well as a ball of mistletoe hung over the entry. Charlie's new dining room was overlooked in favor of the high board. There was roast goose and salmon that Patrick had brought from Scotland, along with a Christmas pudding made with raisins and spices, flour, and suet. They began their celebration at midnight in the chapel, exchanging presents afterward. Jasmine's ancient servants, Toramalli and Rohana, were carried into the hall to celebrate with the only family the two old ladies had ever known. Everyone was amazed that they yet lived for they were a full ten years older than Jasmine herself.

On the twenty-seventh of December, they departed on the two-day journey to Roxley Castle. The weather was cold, but it was clear. Although the ground was frozen, there had been only one light snow in mid-December. Jasmine rode in her comfortable carriage with Barbara Stuart, but Flanna, her daughter, and her niece rode their horses along with the gentlemen. Fancy and Kit would meet them at the inn on their first night of travel.

And they were waiting when the party from Queen's Malvern finally arrived in late afternoon, the sun already set. Fancy was radiant in her happiness and immediately asked after her daughter. The marquis of Isham could not, it seemed, stop smiling. They had never seen him this way.

"They are so in love now," Diana said softly to Cynara. "Do you remember how harsh and dour he first was?"

"Perhaps then there is hope for me," Cynara said quietly.

Diana's heart constricted. She felt almost guilty being so happy when her cousin was so sad. Why had she and Fancy found their true loves so easily while Cynara's lot appeared to be so difficult.

Flanna seeing her daughter's face and guessing the reason for it, put an arm about Diana and gave her a hug. "She'll find her way, lass. 'Tis nae for ye to be unhappy, too. Yer to wed wi' a fine man. Ye love him, and yer content. 'Tis yer fate. Hers is whatever it is meant to be, and we can, nae one of us, change it. Only Cynara can make her happiness. And she will one day. She is a Stuart. They are nae unhappy souls for long, for they will hae their own way in life."

"I know," Diana replied to her mother, "but here I am happy, and Fancy obviously so; then there is poor Cynara."

"Is the man she hungers for worth the trouble?" Flanna asked.

"I honestly do not know, Mama. They called him *Wickedness* at court, but I have never known the reason why, nor does anyone with whom I have ever spoken. He is very handsome. Tall and saturnine in appearance. There is something mesmerizing about him, and yet he frightens me too. I do not believe I ever spoke a word to him, nor even heard him speak. Yet the first moment Cynara saw him . . ." Diana's voice trailed off.

"Tomorrow we will arrive at your new home," Flanna said. "Ye must think only of yerself and yer wedding now, my lass. Cynara loves ye, and she would hae it nae other way, I am certain. The dowager says ye hae already paid a visit to this wee castle. Do ye like it?"

"Ohh, yes, Mama!" Diana said. "It is beautiful, but nothing at all like Glenkirk. In fact once you walk through its doors, you find yourself in a cozy place. It isn't grand at all. And the gardener's name is Bennett. He is a lovely man, and we are going to put in an herb garden near the house next spring."

Flanna smiled. She had turned her daughter's dark thoughts away from Cynara and back where they belonged—with her new home and her husband-to-be. Cynara was Charlie and Barbara's problem. And the old dowager's. If anyone could make Cynara's dreams come true, it was her grandmother.

They arrived at Roxley late the following day. Just three days remained until the wedding. The duke immediately asked Jasmine to oversee and make certain that all the arrangements had been done properly and to her satisfaction. On the morning of the twenty-ninth of December, the dowager and her chaplain, the Reverend Master Prosper Tanner, visited the small church, called by the duke a chapel, that stood at the foot of the castle hill. The small building would just barely contain the family and guests, but it had been swept, scrubbed, and polished within an inch of its life. The altar was of golden oak, a raised and carved scene of the Last Supper upon its frontal. The altar was covered by an embroidered lace and linen cloth that had been bleached snow white. There were a pair of fine silver candlesticks flanking a crucifix of gold and silver. There were three windows on each side of the chapel and one behind the altar. The stained glass in them was very old and showed scenes from the Bible.

"I am astounded that these were not destroyed during the Commonwealth," Jasmine said.

The Reverend Master Tanner nodded his head in agreement. "'Tis a miracle," he said. "God still gives us miracles, my lady."

"Meaning no offense," a voice said, and a man shuffled into their view. He bowed stiffly to Jasmine. "When we heard that the Roundheads was coming our way, m'lady, we removed every one of these windows and hid them all about the estate. The altar was put in one of the duke's barns beneath a pile of hay. The rest all secreted in various hidey-holes. We even hid the pews in our cottages. It looked to Cromwell's men that our wee chapel hadn't been used in years. As it be stone, and there was naught to burn, they let it be and moved on. I have brought flowers for the altar. The duke has a small greenhouse. We'll have flowers for the wedding, I promise you." He bowed again.

"Thank you, Master Bennett," Jasmine said, "but I must correct you. Reverend Tanner was right. There was a miracle that saved this chapel. You, and the others like you who loved the duke's family, were the miracle, sent by God to keep this small house of his safe from the destruction of wicked and ungodly men."

"The lass is like you," Bennett remarked cordially. "Always a good word, and at the right time." Then he gave her a third nod of his head, and moved off with his flowers to decorate the altar.

Jasmine and her chaplain departed the building, walking back up the hill to the castle.

"I hope you will encourage Lady Diana to influence her husband to offer a living, however small, to some deserving young clergyman," the Reverend Master Tanner said. "It is a shame to have such a dear wee church unused, and alone."

Jasmine nodded. She had no doubt that her chaplain had some

worthy young gentleman in mind, a relative, no doubt. She would take the matter up with Diana, however. Her family should have its own minister especially as they were so isolated, far from any town, or even a good-sized village. She left her chaplain, and hurried on to the kitchens to see what yet needed to be done. The kitchen staff, however, had everything well in hand, they assured her ladyship. There was little else, Jasmine realized, that needed her. The chapel was ready. There were flowers, and food. Diana had a wedding gown, and a wardrobe. The guests were settled comfortably. They had but to wait for the last day of the year.

It came, of course, dawning sunny, cold, and dry. Jasmine was up early to oversee Molly as she dressed the bride. Diana's wedding gown was of off-white velvet. It had a deep, low neckline with a wide lace collar the same shade as the gown. The sleeves were slashed, and showed creamy satin. They were decorated with small bows studded with seed pearls, and they dripped with delicate lace from elbow to wrists. The gown was simple, its bodice plain but for its lace collar, and a small heart-shaped diamond brooch, a wedding gift from the groom to his bride. The skirt fell in graceful folds, with but a hint of train.

Diana had bathed at first light, and now she stood in her gown, Molly brushing out her long, dark hair, which Diana would, according to an old-fashioned custom, wear loose to signify her innocence. Her cousins now entered her bedchamber to bring her a small nosegay of dried white heather, dried lavender, and a single pink rose.

"The duke clipped it himself," Fancy said. "'Odsblood, he is a romantic fellow!" She and Cynara were garbed in gowns of garnet red velvet, similar in style to the bride's.

The clock on the mantel struck ten o'clock.

"It is time to go," Jasmine said. "Cynara, Fancy, you come with me. Molly, get your mistress's cloak and help her into the coach. Then you come with her, for there is a place for you at the church."

The carriages bearing the bridal party descended the castle hill to the chapel. The road down was lined with the duke's tenants, farm workers, and servants. They waited patiently, for the duke and his new duchess would return on foot from the chapel, and they should get to see them in their finery then.

They reached the church. Patrick Leslie, handsome in his green plaid kilt, handed his daughter from her vehicle. His mother and his wife went inside while Fancy and Cynara brushed imaginary wrinkles from their cousin's gown. Then from just inside the door to the chapel came the strains of a bagpipe.

Diana looked to her father, her eyes filling with tears. "Ohh, Papa," she sold softly.

"Ye dinna think I should allow my eldest, my dearest lass, to be wed wi'out a proper Leslie escort, did ye?" he said, a smile on his handsome face. He brushed a tear from her cheek. "Now, now, lassie, there is naught to cry about. Come along, and let us get ye wed wi' yer man. And by this time next year, I expect to be celebrating wi' ye as I dandle my first grandchild upon my knee."

They entered the chapel, Cynara and Fancy going ahead as the duke of Glenkirk brought his daughter to the foot of the altar where the duke of Roxley and his brother awaited them. The groom stepped forward, but looking into his face Diana saw dark blue eyes. Grinning she pushed him back and drew Damien Esmond forward with a giggle. Behind them bride and groom heard their family chuckle. Even the Reverend Master Prosper Tanner allowed himself a small smile.

"You will not escape me so easily now, my lord," Diana whispered.

"I have made my bed," he solemnly told her, "and I shall be content to lie in it," he murmured back, causing her to blush.

"Dearly beloved," the minister began, and Diana's heart soared with happiness as she realized that her dreams were not ending. Rather, they were just beginning. She caught Fancy's eye, and Fancy nodded approvingly. She looked to Cynara and was rewarded with a tremulous smile that told her Cynara was content and happy for her.

Damien Esmond took her hand in his as instructed by the minister. Diana almost wept with the beauty surrounding her, and the gladness that filled her very soul. Joyfully she repeated her vows to the man she loved, almost weeping as he repeated those same vows back to her. And then it was finished.

"I now pronounce ye husband and wife," the Reverend Master Tanner said. *"Those whom God hath joined, let no man put asunder."* They knelt, and he blessed them. Finally the duke and the duchess of Roxley arose and led their guests from the little chapel, back up the hill to their home. They passed through the throng of their retainers lining the road and cheering. The winter sun shone down on them all as the duke invited everyone to join them in the hall for a toast. The well-wishers fell in behind the bridal party, the castle servants running ahead to prepare.

It was a wonderful party attended by both high and low, who mingled together at the tables set up below the high board where the duke and duchess sat with their immediate family holding sway. Jasmine was well pleased by the meal served. Each place below the high board had a wooden plate and a pewter spoon and goblet. There was beef that had been roasted packed in rock salt and fine venison and roast boar. A dozen turkeys, and another dozen of capons stuffed with dried fruit, sage, and bread were served. There were oysters that came from barrels that had been filled with ice and snow to transport them from the coast. There was trout and salmon on silver salvers decorated with watercress. There was pickled eel and creamed cod and prawns steamed in wine. There was duck and rabbit pies with brown gravy flavored with red wine and leeks. There were beets and carrots and braised lettuces, along with creamed onions. There were breads, both brown and white, crocks of sweet butter, and several cheeses. Cider and ale were served below the board. Wine above it.

A bridal cake iced in white sugar with a spun-sugar prince and princess was brought into the hall upon a great silver charger, carried by six kitchen boys who struggled to bring it to the high board, and place it before their master and mistress. Seeing it brought a great cheer from the assembled. A cake carver, hired for just this occasion, was brought forward, and began to section the sweet so that all might enjoy it.

Sated with good food and drink, the guests sat back as the Leslie piper played. Charlie, the not-so-royal Stuart, and his brother, Patrick Leslie, danced between a pair of swords that had been set upon the floor.

"They have done this at many a family wedding," Jasmine told Damien.

"They shall dance at our wedding one day, Darling," Mair Leslie said to the marquis of Roxley, and to everyone's surprise Darius Esmond nodded his head solemnly in agreement.

When the duke of Glenkirk sat back down again, the marquis said to him, "My lord, we must talk before you leave us."

"She is a child yet, sir," the duke of Glenkirk said.

"She won't be forever," the marquis replied.

"I promise ye nae to match her wi' anyone else until she is old enough to decide if ye are really the one she wants," Patrick said. "Ye hae my hand on it, but know that the choice will always be hers."

"Agreed," the marquis said and shook Patrick's hand.

Jasmine shook her head wonderingly. How easy it was for her Leslie granddaughters. Would that it could be that simple for Cynara.

It had been arranged that Diana would discreetly depart the hall with the least fuss in order to prepare for the bedding ceremony. She did so, her two cousins coming with her. Molly was awaiting them. They helped the maidservant divest the bride of her clothing, sponged her with rose water, dried her off, and put her in a soft lawn nightgown adorned with lace. Molly brushed her hair out a final time, and then the three helped the bride into her bed.

"We're just in time," Molly said. "I hear them coming now."

The door to the ducal bedchamber flew open, and the family crowded in, pushing Damien Esmond, now in a silk nightshirt, ahead of them. He climbed into bed next to Diana. They were handed a cup of wine to share. Then the Reverend Tanner spoke a final prayer, praying for their fruitfulness. After a ribald jest or two, the guests trooped out, closing the door behind them.

The duke arose from their bed and walking across the chamber, threw the bolt hard. "I'll not have Darling playing any further tricks on us," he said, climbing back into bed with her.

Diana, however, taking no chances, took up the taper stick by the bed, and held it up to his face so she might see the color of his eyes. "I do not trust your brother either," she said, satisfied by the light blue eyes laughing back at her. She blew out the taper and set it back upon the bedside table.

"Are you afraid?" he asked her. "You must not be."

"Nay, I am not afraid. My grandmama has explained everything that I will need to know. Are you afraid, Damien?"

"Only of disappointing you, Diana. I am not a virgin as you are. I am experienced. You must tell me if I lust too quickly after you, my darling wife."

"Damien," she said laughing softly, "I think it is past time for talk. Please kiss me, and then whatever happens between us is certain to be nothing but good. I know it! My papa says he wants a grandchild by this time next year. That being the case, had we not best get to it, my dear lord?"

"You are amazing!" he said admiringly and he drew her into his arms.

"I know!" Diana agreed sweetly. Then she gave herself into his keeping, because that was how it was when you loved someone, and was loved back.

Part Three

ENGLAND, 1669–70

CYN AND WICKEDNESS

Chapter

15

"**D**amn, Cyn!" Lord Barton of Barton's Court swore. "You are the luckiest girl I have ever known. You always win! In fact, I don't know any other girl who dices with gentlemen *and* on her hands and knees, too."

"Dicing, Willy, is hardly a proper lady's game, or so I have been told by those not as fortunate as I am," Lady Cynara Stuart said. Then she laughed. "But I am not a proper lady at all. Not like my cousin Diana, and not even like my cousin Fancy."

"Proper ladies ain't apt to have as much fun," Nellie Gwyn said, joining them. She grinned mischievously, then took up the dice cup, and shook it several times before rolling the ivories onto the floor where they were playing. "Ohh," she said disappointed. "I have not made my point. Oh, well, the king will pay the debt for me as he always does. Are you through fleecing these poor fellows for the night, Cyn? There is going to be dancing shortly." She arose from the floor.

Cynara considered a long moment, and then she, too, arose. "Why not," she agreed. "I am bored with gambling now." She shook out her black silk skirts and linked her arm in Nellie Gwyn's. "Come along, Mistress Nell. I am certain there is some mischief we can cause if we think about it a moment. What do you think of the

latest crop of dewy-eyed virgins come to court? Have any of the little darlings caught His Majesty's eye?"

"He's quit virginity after Frances Stuart," Nell laughed.

"I heard that lady broke his heart," Cynara noted.

"She did, but generous of nature the king forgave her when she
married the duke of Richmond," Nell replied. "Are you going to
Newmarket to the races? We're leaving soon, His Majesty says."

"My father has a house there and a rather good stable," Cynara
replied. "Aye, we'll go. Perhaps my mother will even come with my
grandmother from Queen's Malvern. Grandmama won't come to
court any longer, but she does love racing so Papa may cajole her
into coming to Newmarket. Nell, I can only ask you this. Will Harry
Summers be there? I know how everyone teases me for my pursuit
of him. He persists in ignoring me, which but makes me look the
fool, and I hate that."

Nell reached out and took Cynara's hand, drawing her into an alcove and sitting down with her upon a marble bench there. "Cyn,
listen to me. Harry Summers is spoiled for any woman, and especially one like you. Do you know why they call him Wickedness? He
stood by, and he watched his own father die a horrible death. He
would not send for a physician, so eager they say was he for his father's title and lands. I have friends, who like you, have been taken
in by his handsome face and that brooding air of mystery that surrounds him. They have suffered for it, I promise you. You are a
duke's daughter. You are related to His Majesty by a bond of blood.
You don't have to crawl to a man like Wickedness. Lord, lass, there
are any number of men here at court who would have you."

"They would have me for my wealth, Nell. They would have me
for the very things you speak about. Because I am my father's
daughter, and because I am the king's cousin. *Any man*. But I don't
want just any man. I want one who will love me for myself. Harry
doesn't care that I am rich, or who my father is, or that I am a royal
relation. So if one day he loves me as I love him, then I will have
found the right man, and not just any man, Nellie."

Pretty Nell shook her head sadly. "You are a romantic fool, Cyn,
and that is something none would think of you. You love him? God

Almighty help you, for no one else can. And how can you love a man you barely know? I think I should get the king to make a decent match for you before you ruin yourself. Look how well he did for Fancy."

"Don't you dare!" Cynara cried. "You ask how I can love him? Do you not see the sadness in his eyes, Nell? He has suffered. I see it. Once my mother had that same look in her eyes. I remember it well." Cynara paused a moment, and then she said, "I doubt anyone here at court knows. Mayhap a few souls, but it is not common knowledge. I was born nine months after the battle of Worcester. My mother was a respected widow who lived in an isolated house well away from town. She and my father had grown up together. She became his mistress after her husband died. He and Siren's father were ordered by the king from Worcester even as the battle was beginning. It was important to the king that my papa get to safety. He feared that if the cousin bearing his name were killed or captured, the Roundheads would make the most of it."

"And those knowing no better would think they had killed the king himself!" Nellie said, immediately understanding.

Cynara nodded. "Aye. So Papa and Uncle Patrick rode off. They went to Mama's house, arriving at dusk. They neglected to hail the house, and Mama shot my uncle through the shoulder before Papa could say it was them. Uncle Patrick stayed hidden at my mother's for several weeks until the furor had died down, and he might return north to Scotland, his shoulder healed. My father spent one night, the night I was conceived. The next day he departed for the coast and France. I was born the following June.

"My mother had a local Puritan lordling who was her protector. He assumed at first I was his bastard. He feared what his wife would say, and he feared the scandal. He fretted that his Puritan masters would punish him, but Mama convinced him she wanted nothing of him. My mother told him the child she carried was not his, but the offspring of one of a group of cavaliers escaping Worcester. They had, she explained to Sir Peter, invaded her house and raped her. She suggested that it might be better they not see each other again."

"And he agreed?" Yet Nell wasn't surprised. "How like a man to run from responsibilities. How could your mama be so certain you wasn't this man's child?"

"She fretted about it in the beginning, she told me," Cynara said, "but then decided since Sir Peter had no children with his wife, and my papa had several children, that I must be a Stuart. As soon as I was born she knew for certain her fears were groundless. Not only do I look like my papa, but I have a family birthmark. 'Tis called the Mughal Mole," Cynara explained, and she pointed to the tiny dark mark between her upper lip and her nose on the right side of her face. "My grandmother Leslie has the same mark. So do a number of her grandchildren. Siren has it, but on the left side of her face."

"So your mother waited for your father, and that is why her eyes were so sad," Nell said.

"Aye, but it was more than that. There was no way in which my mother could communicate with my father. She could not tell him that he had a daughter. In the eight years that they were separated, he was only able to get messages to her three times. The first two came by word of mouth. Spies slipping into the country for a purpose. Mama did not know who these men were. And they knew nothing about her but that she offered them a hot meal and a safe bed in return in her barn. The messages they offered my mother were impersonal. And each time these men said the same thing. *The duke of Lundy tenders his regards to Squire Randall's widow.* He said later that it was the only way he could let her know he was still alive and well.

"In the months just before the king was restored, my father was able to send a written letter to my mother. She still has it, though some of the writing is gone, for she cried many tears on the parchment." Here Cynara smiled, and so did Nell. "He wrote to her of his life since his escape from England. He wrote of his children safe in Scotland with his brother. He wrote that he loved her, and hoped she would consent to be his wife when he returned, which he would with the king. And he would bring his mother, and his youngest sister, who was now widowed. My mother asked the messenger if he had been paid to return with a message, and was told he had. So she wrote a brief missive to my father telling him that she would happily wed him, and that she had a surprise for him when he finally returned to her."

"She didn't tell him about you?" Nellie laughed. "Your mam has a rather wicked sense of humor, Cyn. Did you know about yer father?"

"Oh, yes," Cynara said. "From the time I could understand my mother always spoke of him. She knew he would make everything all right when he returned, but it meant a great deal to her that before even knowing about me, he offered her marriage. And it was over two more years before they were wed, although I did meet my father before then. When Papa finally returned to Queen's Malvern he could not send for us, for he wanted to put his house in order again. There was not a great deal to do for Becket, our majordomo, and his wife had kept the house safe. Then the king wanted Papa back at court, and then when he returned home again his sister, my aunt Autumn, was suffering melancholy so Papa decided to take her to court. She became the king's mistress during one of Castlemaine's breeding periods."

"I had heard Fancy wasn't the first in your family to warm His Majesty's bed," Nellie said. "So when did you finally meet your father?"

"Well, the first time he came back from court, and was on his way home to Queen's Malvern, he stopped to reunite with my mother. It was then we met. I will always remember it. I saw him coming, and ran to tell my mother a stranger was approaching. Mama looked, and suddenly she was running towards the man. He jumped from his horse, and they kissed. She said something to him, and he turned towards me. We stood staring at each other for a long moment. I thought him the handsomest man I had ever seen," Cynara reminisced. "Then he held out his arms to me and enfolding me in his embrace, he kissed the top of my head and my cheek. When he finally looked at me again I could see tears in his eyes. 'What has your mother called you, my daughter?' he asked me. 'Cynara Mary, Papa,' I replied. 'Welcome home.' We went into the house together, and my parents fell into each other's arms weeping. I had never seen grown people cry. In fact, other than Lucy and Mama, and a passing stranger, I had seen few people at all," Cynara explained.

"Which is why you like the court with all its excitement," Nellie observed nodding. "So when did your parents wed?"

"Well, after Papa and Mama had reunited, he wanted her to come to Queen's Malvern right away, but she said no. Not until they were properly wed. So Papa left us, and my two half brothers and my half sister, who had been living at Glenkirk with my Uncle Patrick and his family, came to Queen's Malvern to be reunited with him. He told no one about Mama and me. He wanted to surprise them as Mama had surprised him. But between his other children, and my aunt Autumn, and his service to the king, and then my half sister Sabrina got married to a cousin of ours . . ." she stopped and laughed.

"He was so upset for every time he attempted to set a date with Mama, something else interfered. Finally just before my eleventh birthday he came to our house on the hill. He had legal papers with him that he explained to Mama and me legitimized me as his daughter. Then he told Mama we were leaving immediately for Queen's Malvern where the Anglican priest awaited us. They would be married on the morrow and he would allow nothing to interfere this time. He said my grandmother, who now knew about us, was furious that he had delayed so long; that we could come back for our possessions later, but he and Mama would marry tomorrow, or she would damned well know the reason." Cynara laughed again, and Nellie joined in her merriment.

"So," Cynara continued, "we left the only home I had ever known and went off to Queen's Malvern. When we arrived, my grandmother was waiting. She took one look at me and said to my father, 'Well, really, Charlie, you might have said something sooner!' Then she turned to me and said, 'I am your grandmother, child. Welcome home!' She hugged me, and the very next day, June first, two days before my eleventh birthday, my parents were finally married. And I have never again seen that look of sadness in Mama's eyes that I now see in the eyes of Harry Summers," she concluded.

"He needs me, Nell. One day he will see it, and I will have no other to husband me but him."

The king's mistress sighed softly. "'Tis as I said earlier, Cyn. You're a romantic fool. I'll help you where and when I can, for like your two cousins you have treated me well and been my friend. 'Tis the least that I can do. And in answer to the question you asked me, aye, the earl of Summersfield will be at Newmarket. He has a very fine stable of horses, Cyn. Perhaps that will be your route to his heart." She patted her friend's hand, and stood up. "Come along, now. The king will be waiting for me."

Cynara arose. "My tale was for you alone, Nell," she said.

"Of course," Nell agreed, and together the two young women hurried to the ballroom where the dancing was already in progress.

Looking about, Cynara espied Harry Summers standing and watching, a cynical look upon his handsome face. She swallowed hard. For over a year, she had tried to attract his notice. She sat next to him when she could; went where he went. Nothing had gained his serious attention. There was naught to be lost by being bold, she suddenly decided, and glided across the room toward him, her heart racing. Reaching the earl, she smiled up at him, for he was very tall. "I have come to ask you to dance, my lord," Cynara said. And she held out her hand to him.

"Why not, madam," he answered. His voice was deep and as smooth as cream and set her pulses pounding. He looked down at her. For a moment she thought she saw an admiring light in those icy green eyes of his, but it was quickly gone, if indeed it had been there at all. He took her small hand in his big one. "Why do you always wear black?" he demanded of her.

"Because it sets me apart from all the other little virgins here at court," she told him boldly. "And it suits me. Notice how creamy my skin is against black."

"And are you indeed a virgin, madam?" he asked boldly.

Cynara felt her cheeks grow warm, but her own blue eyes never left his eyes. "I am, my lord. Why on earth would you think otherwise?"

"The women in your family are rather careless in their morals," he said coldly, his fingers tightening upon hers.

Cynara was genuinely shocked by this remark. "Why would you say such a dreadful thing, my lord?" she asked. "My family is highly respected."

"Your cousin and, I believe, one of your aunts played the king's whore for a time. Your other cousin dangled herself before all the young gentlemen at court last winter. Then she made a great to-do about choosing a husband. Your grandmother has a rather interesting history, and your mother did not wed with your father until you were already half-grown."

"My cousin and aunt were both widows when they engaged the king's interest. My cousin Diana wisely and most cleverly sorted out the men who wished to make her a wife, choosing the one man she found who knew, understood, and loved her. My grandmother was the daughter of a great potentate, my lord. There are other lands and other religions and other kings besides England upon the face of this earth. She was also a widow when Prince Henry fell in love with her. You may recall, my lord, that England was embroiled in a revolution for any number of years. My parents were wed in all but law for those years. And when they were finally able to do so, they stood before the church and said their proper vows. Considering your own family's history, my lord, I have nothing to be ashamed of at all. *Oww!* You are hurting my hand!"

"Be grateful, madam, that is all I am hurting," he said threateningly. "Do not mention my family's history again in my presence!"

"Then we are even, my lord, for you will not speak disparagingly of my family! You will remember that I am related to the king."

"How can anyone forget it, madam? You never permit them to," he mocked her.

"Let us speak on another subject," she suggested.

"*Horses?*" he proposed. She was extraordinarily beautiful, he thought. Was she really still a virgin? He would like to discover that for himself, but even if she wasn't, he doubted that he would be disappointed. No man would ever make love to Cynara Stuart the way he would.

"You are going to Newmarket, I expect," she said casually. "Will your horses be racing this season?"

"Of course," he told her. "My animals are the ones to beat. I have a stallion the king has been trying to buy from me for two years now. He breeds up champions on my stable of well-bred mares." He smiled a cold smile at her. "You would probably like him. He is wild, and all black, but for a white star on his forehead."

"I ride a black stallion," Cynara said. "The beast you refer to originally came from my father's estate. I believe you purchased him several years ago, raced him, and when no one could beat him took to breeding him instead. He descends from a horse called Night Wind."

The earl nodded. "Do you like riding?" he asked her.

"I do," Cynara told him.

"We will ride together at Newmarket and tomorrow then," he said. Now why on earth had he suggested they ride together? He had never before asked a woman to ride with him.

"I hope you are not a man who thinks a woman should ride seated sidesaddle, decorously trotting," Cynara remarked. "I find that sort of riding dull. I wear breeches, and I ride hard, my lord. It is far more exciting."

"Is it?" He actually laughed a short sharp laugh.

"Yes," Cynara said. "It is. Now, my lord, I asked you to dance, and dance you will." She drew him into the line of dancers forming up upon the floor. The music began, and she was surprised to see him execute the dance's patterns and figures with great skill. Cynara had never seen him dance before. He always stood on the sidelines watching. She laughed as holding hands they ducked and slid their way beneath an arch of upraised hands and arms. She couldn't believe that bearding him had actually been this easy. She should have done it last year instead of attempting to gain his attention by all sorts of girlish stratagems and pining when he did not notice her. The dance finally came to an end, and they walked together from the floor.

"You are graceful, my lord, and have a leg as nicely turned as His Majesty's," Cynara told the earl of Summersfield.

He stopped and, taking her by her shoulders, looked down into her heart-shaped face. "You are as bold a baggage as I have ever met," he said, his voice suddenly rough. "Do you know how much I want to make love to you, madam?"

Cynara thought that her heart would burst through her chest at his words, but she coolly said, "You are as insolent and impudent a man as I have ever met, my lord. If you would have the cream, you must buy the cow. I have been told you are not in the market for a wife at the present time. I, on the other hand, must eventually wed if only to please my family. I do not believe it would be wise for me to dally in carnality under such circumstances, do you?"

He bent and kissed her lips. Cynara tasted his mouth on hers and struggled to remain standing. He grazed his knuckles down the side of her face. "I enjoy a challenge, madam. And I mean to have you before any other who may desire you. You do understand that?"

Her head was spinning, but she focused her eyes onto his face and said coolly, "Do you always win, my lord? I do, as anyone can tell you. I am considered quite lucky. Now if you are, too, then we have already arrived at a standoff. On the other hand perhaps you might make me a suitable husband, and I shall have you!"

He laughed softly. "You are brave, Cyn, I will give you that. Had I approached any other young woman as I have you, she would have long ago swooned. You do look a bit pale, however."

"I am pale all over, my lord," she teased him.

A single finger thrust into her gown, and he peered down. "Aye, Cyn, you certainly are. And soft, too."

She snatched his hand away, her cheeks now flaming. "Too brazen, my lord! Much too brazen! I am quit of you now!" She turned from him.

"I did not think you were a girl to run away," he called after her, and she heard the mockery in his voice.

Cynara whirled about. "And I did not think you were a man to make a fool of himself in a public venue, my lord."

"Well said, Cyn," he replied. "I shall call for you tomorrow afternoon, and we will take our first ride together in St. James Park."

For a moment she was tempted to tell him to go to the devil, but instead she heard her voice coolly asking, "What time?"

"Two o'clock," he responded.

"Very well," she said, and then turned from him again. He had kissed her! He had touched her! True, it hadn't been a very deep or passionate kiss. It had been more exploratory, as if he were attempting to ascertain just how far he might go with her. She wondered that herself. And that hard finger that had pushed between her breasts. She had been overwhelmed by the most incredible feeling. She had wanted to take her gown off and let him touch her all over. She shivered at such a daring thought. From the moment she had seen him, Cynara Stuart had known she wanted Harry Summers. Her Stuart blood was running hot. She was suddenly very aware of it, and of everything she had always heard about her family. Now, facing herself for the very first time in her life, Cynara wondered just what it was she really wanted.

She didn't want to embarrass her family. While she enjoyed the admiration of gentlemen, she knew now that she didn't want to be a courtesan or any man's mistress. She realized that she wanted just what her cousins had. A husband. A home. Children. It was quite a shock to find she wasn't that different from them at all. And she had fallen in love with the wrong man to boot. But the streak of wildness that ran in Harry Summers's veins ran in hers as well. He didn't want a wife, but she now wanted him as a husband. And just how was she going to accomplish that? He was a puzzle to solve. For him, she knew that she was a prize to be taken. They were going to play this game until one of them won it. But which one? The earl would be no easy opponent.

I always win, Cynara thought. Then she looked across the room to where Harry Summers stood lounging against one of the room's decorated pillars. Their eyes met and held for a long moment. Then gaining a mastery over herself again Cynara looked away, a small mocking smile upon her lips. *There! Let him wonder,* and she giggled to herself.

An arm was slipped through hers, and Nellie said, "The queen is taking up all of the king's attentions tonight. There is just the faintest rumor that she is breeding again. Let us hope it is true, and that this time something comes of it. I saw you dancing with Wickedness. How did that come about? Has he finally noticed you?"

"I asked him to dance," Cynara said. "He accepted."

"You didn't!" Nell was surprised but also delighted.

"We are going riding tomorrow afternoon in St. James," Cynara continued. "I decided that I could wait no longer for him to notice me. He is brazen and far too bold, Nell, but he excites me."

Now Nell Gwyn grew serious. "Be careful, Cyn, do! Harry Summers is a risky lover at best. If he would kill his own father, God only knows what the man would do. Make certain he always remembers that you are the king's kin. Perhaps that can protect you."

"I have already mentioned it," Cynara laughed. "He says I let no one forget it. Am I really that bad, Nell?"

"You're proud of your blood, and why not?" Nell demanded to know. "When I give the king babes, I will always see they know who they are and remind others who might not be as kind to them otherwise. Look how well Castlemaine's brats are received, even now that she is no longer in favor with His Majesty. My children will have the same advantages."

"Are you?" Cynara ventured softly.

"Not yet. I be a careful girl," Nell said. "It is not the time yet, especially as the queen might be."

"Cynara." Her father was by her side. "It is late, and I think 'tis time for you to withdraw." Then he turned to the king's current favorite. "How are you, Nellie? As impudent as always, I hope."

"I could not be otherwise, my lord duke," Nell said, sweeping Charlie a deep curtsy that revealed her bosom quite clearly. There was a wicked smile upon her lips.

He admired her treasures with a grin, but then remembering his daughter was by Nellie's side, he grew serious again. "You are not selling currently, Nellie," he teased her.

"Not at the moment, my lord," she replied saucily, "but perhaps one day you will be my Charles the Fourth." It was a joke the duke appreciated for by coincidence all of Nell's lovers had been named

Charles. She arose from her curtsy, and with a friendly smile left them, but suddenly she turned, saying to Cynara, "Remember, Cyn, to be careful tomorrow."

The duke of Lundy took his youngest child by the arm, and they moved across the room in order to excuse themselves. "What did she mean?" he asked his daughter.

"I am going riding with the earl of Summersfield tomorrow afternoon in St. James," Cynara said. "Nell worries too much."

"I do not approve, Cynara, but I will not forbid it for I know to do so will but make you more determined to be with this man," the duke said. "I do not understand your fascination with Harry Summers. His reputation is most foul."

"What has he ever done to deserve such notoriety, Papa?" Cynara asked her parent. "He is dark and brooding. He seems to have few friends here at court. Indeed I do not know why he is even here at all. He stands and observes but rarely takes part in any activity that I can see. You may as well know, but 'twas I who asked him to dance tonight," Cynara finished defiantly.

Charlie was forced to laugh at this revelation. "'Odsblood, Cynara!" he said to her. "You are a Stuart, and no mistake about it."

"You have not answered my question, Papa," Cynara said.

"It is said he murdered his own sire for his title and his lands," the duke began. "He consorts with courtesans openly and quite apparently without shame. Nell could tell you if you asked. He is a gambler, although I have heard he is a lucky one and pays the few debts he incurs. But most important, he has said publicly that he will never marry. Your future concerns me, Cynara. You are my youngest child, and I love you. I do not want this man to break your heart, for he has no heart of his own."

They had reached the twin thrones where the king and Queen Catherine sat. The duke and his daughter made their obeisance to the monarchs, and the duke begged leave to withdraw with his child.

"Are you growing old, Charlie?" the king teased his cousin. "I can remember a time when you and I would remain up the entire night and see the sunrise together."

"Your Majesty knows I am almost twenty years his senior," the duke reminded the king. "I should not be here at all but for my daughter. Her mother and my mother do not think it wise she comes to court unchaperoned. She is, I fear, very much a Stuart."

"You do well to listen to the women in your family, my lord," the queen said. She turned her gentle gaze on Cynara. "Did I not see you dancing with the earl of Summersfield tonight, my child?"

"Yes, madame, I asked him to dance," Cynara said and made another curtsy to the queen.

The king laughed knowingly. "We shall have to keep a stern eye upon you, my lovely young Cousin. I suspect we must find you a husband, eh, Charlie?"

"I will pick my own husband, Your Majesty," Cynara replied boldly. "It has been the right of the women in my family for as long as anyone can remember."

"And you have already picked, I suspect," the king murmured low, looking directly at Cynara.

"Yes, Your Majesty, I have," she said, her eyes lowered for she knew the king did not like anyone looking directly at him.

"Cousin," the king continued to speak softly, "this man has a bad character, I am told. Are you aware of it?"

"Like my cousin, Fancy, much is said of the earl of Summersfield," Cynara defended, "but what has actually been proven of him, Your Majesty? Even here at court he keeps his distance but whether from preference or because he is truly ashamed of what is said about him, I do not know. But there is something in his eyes that bids me explore further," she finished bravely.

"A true Stuart," the king replied shaking his dark head. "Both gallant and foolish. Do not get your heart broken, my dear. Your father and I are too old to fight a duel over your honor. Now go home, and sleep on what has been said."

They bowed again, and were dismissed. Together father and daughter walked from the ballroom and through the palace to their quarters. There Charlie bid Cynara sweet dreams, and watched as she entered her bedchamber where her serving woman, Hester, awaited her. He heard the maid's greeting as the door closed behind Cynara. Charlie walked across the salon of his apartment, and poured himself a dram cup of Glenkirk whiskey. Then seating himself before the fire he began to sip it slowly. He wished his wife were here. Or his mother. He was not certain if he was capable of coping with his daughter, but he knew that either one of them would be up to the challenge that Cynara offered. One, or preferably both of them, must come to Newmarket for the racing season.

While Cynara's interest in the earl of Summersfield had been but a girlish fancy at first, his impatient child was now determined to have her own way with the man. And what was her way? Certainly she didn't think she could seduce him into marriage. *Or did she?* He had to admit that this younger of his two daughters was wild, and he blamed himself for all the years he had been away with the king in exile. Had not even been aware of her existence. He remembered how Barbara had given herself to him when she was sixteen. He remembered how angry his family had been that he would seduce her. How they had said she was not the girl they expected him to marry one day. How they had married her off to Squire Randall. But Barbara had been a merchant's daughter. Cynara was his daughter. A Stuart whose blood was mingled with that of the king's, as was his. He needed his wife. He wanted his mother's advice.

The duke of Lundy went to his desk and drew forth a sheet of vellum. Sitting down, he sharpened the quill and dipped it into the inkpot. Then he began to write to Barbara, begging her to meet them at Newmarket, his mother, too. Cynara, he explained, had now engaged the interest of the earl of Summersfield. He did not feel he could cope with her wild behavior. He needed his women to aid him in protecting their child. When Charlie had finished his missive, he folded it, dripped sealing wax on the parchment, and sealed it with his ring. He would send it off on the morrow to Queen's Malvern.

Cynara awoke the following morning excited and yet contemplative. She called to Hester, her maidservant, to arrange a bath for her.

"If you're going riding this afternoon why not bathe afterward?" Hester demanded to know. She was twice Cynara's age, and had been with her since Cynara arrived at Queen's Malvern. Her parents were Becket, the majordomo of Queen's Malvern, and his wife, who was the housekeeper.

"I will have two baths today," Cynara said stubbornly. "I wish to be fresh when I meet the earl, and I will be refreshed again this evening before I go to Whitehall."

"The footmen here ain't as cooperative as at Greenwood House," Hester grumbled.

"Then remind them that I am the king's kin!" Cynara snapped. She didn't want to be argued with now. She wanted her bath so she might smell sweet when they met this afternoon. What was she to wear? She considered her wardrobe carefully, for she had several riding outfits. The midnight blue velvet. Yes! She would wear the blue, which always brought out the color in her eyes. "See that my black boots are polished," she called to Hester. "And I want the black felt hat with the ostrich plumes brushed."

Hester came and stood in the door of Cynara's small bedchamber, her hands on her ample hips. She was a handsome woman with light brown hair visible beneath her white linen cap and intelligent hazel eyes. "And will you be wearing just the boots and the hat?" she demanded to know. "Or shall I get something else out for you to wear as well?"

Cynara began to giggle. The thought of the earl of Summersfield's face should she appear in just her riding boots and hat made an amusing picture. Last year one of the king's courtiers had walked five miles stark naked to win a bet. "The midnight blue riding outfit," she managed to gasp before dissolving into full-blown laughter.

"Don't know why I put up with you, m'lady," Hester said, but her own eyes were twinkling with amusement.

"Because Grandmama makes you, I expect," Cynara replied pertly. "Besides, you're a Becket, and Beckets have always served at Queen's Malvern, even keeping it safe in the era of the Roundheads."

"Aye, that we did, m'lady," Hester replied. "I was just a little girl, and then half-growed, but my parents told me what was going on as we worked together in secret to keep the house safe for the duke's return one day. My father always said he and the king would come back."

"And they did!" Cynara said. "I always love the stories your parents tell about how the ghosts of the previous tenants drove out that ridiculous Puritan couple. Did you ever see the ghosts, Hester?"

"Once when I was sent to the hall to dust it, I saw *her*," Hester said, her eyes growing large with her memory. "It was the lady in the portrait, and she glided through the hall as truly as she was really there. I remember being so amazed to see her. I knew she wasn't real because of her gown being so old-fashioned. Then just before she exited the hall she turned, and looked directly at me, and she smiled! You smile a lot like her, m'lady."

"*Skye O'Malley*," Cynara said softly. "My great-great-grandmother."

"Aye, that 'twas her," Hester said. "Now I can't stand here telling you tales if you want to make the royal footmen go to all that trouble of bringing you your bathwater."

"I want my bath!" Cynara said, determined not to yield.

"Then I'll get the lads started. Brush the tangles out of your hair, and pin it up so it don't get wet," Hester said, handing her mistress the silver hairbrush as she hurried out.

Cynara untied her lawn nightcap and laid it aside. Slowly she undid the single plait into which she braided her hair each night and began to brush it out. One, two, three, four. She began to count the requisite one hundred strokes, leisurely pulling the bristles through her long sable hair. She had beautiful thick hair that was much admired, and she took great pains with it. Cynara's hair was always clean and shining in an era when men used perfumes to cover a great lack of personal care.

She had noticed the previous evening when she had danced with the earl of Summersfield, that Harry Summers wore no scent, yet he had had no body odor about him. Nor were his teeth yellowed, and when he spoke he seemed to have all of them. And when he had briefly kissed her, his mouth was fresh. It showed not simply a healthy respect for his body, but a lack of vanity. *I don't care what they say about him*, she thought. *I know he is a good man, and I know he is the man for me. I must, however, try not to be impatient. I know that I will be seventeen in June, and will, by eighteen, be considered a spinster, but I don't care! I want Harry Summers, and I will have no other!*

Cynara climbed from her bed, laying the hairbrush on her dressing table. She pinned her dark tresses up with several tortoise-shell hairpins and then used her chamber pot. She washed her hands and face afterward in the chassed silver ewer Hester had left out for her. She could hear the footmen outside her chamber pouring the hot water into her brass-bound oak tub. Finally Hester reentered the room.

"Yer bath is ready, m'lady, and yer pa has gone off to ride with his friends. You'll not be disturbed. I'll go fetch you something to eat as soon as yer settled. Are you hungry this morning?"

Cynara nodded as she came from her bedchamber to climb into her tub. "Aye, I am," she admitted. "Anticipation seems to increase my appetite greatly." She settled herself in the scented water.

Hester shook her head. "From what I hears, and believe me, m'lady, the servants hear more than anyone else here at Whitehall, this earl of yers ain't too respectable a fellow. You sees him as a challenge to beat, but he's a dangerous man. What if he seduces you, and yer no longer fit for a decent gentleman?"

"What if I get him to marry me?" Cynara countered.

"They say he ain't the marrying kind," Hester retorted.

"No man is until he finds the right woman," Cynara expounded. "That is what Grandmama says."

"Well, yer grandmama is a wise woman, 'tis true," Hester said, "but given what is said about this earl, I don't think even she would approve of him."

"Get my food," Cynara told her serving woman.

"*Humph!*" Hester replied, and disappeared through the apartment door, closing it with a sharp bang.

Cynara sat back and closed her eyes, enjoying the hot water and the exotic scent of the gardenia oil perfuming her tub. Her cousins favored rose and jasmine and heather, but Cynara loved the rich smell of the gardenia. Her family's shipping company imported it from the Far East. It was brought into India from China, but few Westerners were currently trading with China or Japan. She laved the oily water over her shoulders with her cupped palm and sighed. There was surely nothing as lovely as a hot bath.

She heard the door to the apartment open, and assuming it was her father she called out, "Papa! You did not ride long this morning." As there was a screen set about her tub, she could not see him. "Hester has gone to fetch me some food. Will you remain and share it with me, or must you join the king?"

"I am not your papa," the earl of Summersfield said, and he stepped around the lacquered screen. "Good morning, madam. I must say you are looking most fetching in your tub."

Cynara cast a swift look down to be certain that nothing was showing that ought not be showing. It wasn't. "My lord," she said in what she hoped passed for a nonchalant voice, "are you not in the habit of knocking? If you did, I did not hear you."

"I did not expect to find a lady at her toilette, madam, but rather some dragon of a serving woman guarding the portals."

Cynara laughed. "The dragon has gone to the kitchens."

"And your papa is out riding," he noted.

"What, my lord? Do you think because I am alone to force your will upon me and thus avoid the necessity of our acquaintanceship?" Cynara mocked him boldly. To be bold and unafraid was the way to conquer this man's heart, she sensed.

"And if I lifted you up from this tub . . ." he began.

"I should slip from your hands like a greased piglet, my lord," she told him. She swished her hand in the water, and then held it out to him. "See? I am quite slick with oil."

He took her hand and, turning the palm over, bent his dark head to kiss it, his eyes never leaving hers as he did so.

Cynara fought to contain the shiver that raced down her spine.

"Your scent is intoxicating, madam. What is it called?" he asked, releasing her hand from his grip.

"It is oil of the gardenia flower and is brought to me from China, my lord," she answered him.

"You are quite spoiled," he responded. The corners of his mouth fought to remain straight, but he had to admit to himself that he found her not only wildly beautiful but amusing. He had never before met a woman like Cynara Stuart, but then she was just another variety of whore. All women were, even those who still remained virgins, if indeed she was telling him the truth. Still he had heard no gossip about her, and the king's own whore, Mistress Nellie, was quite fond of her. Harry Summers liked Nell Gwyn. She made no pretense of being other than what she was. All other women did, it seemed.

"Of course I am spoiled," Cynara surprised him by saying. "I am a Stuart, related to the king by a bond of blood. I am a duke's youngest daughter. Surely, my lord, you did not believe that I should be an unspoiled little featherhead? I am sorry to disappoint you, but I most certainly am not."

The earl of Summersfield laughed. "I have expected nothing of you, madam, but perhaps I should."

"If you please me, my lord, I shall make you my husband one day," Cynara said brazenly.

"I seek no wife, madam, and you would be wise to heed my words," was the reply she received.

"No man seeks a wife, my grandmama says, but they all eventually end up with one. Do you have good jewels? I have only the best. See my ring? 'Twas given me by my grandmother, the dowager duchess of Glenkirk. The ruby is called the Tear of Kali, who is the goddess of birth, death, and destruction in India." She held out the hand he had so recently kissed, displaying the tear-shaped ruby.

Harry Summers found himself momentarily disarmed. Cynara, he was discovering, was a mixture of sophistication and an odd sort of innocence. Unable to help himself, he took the hand she displayed and began to nibble each finger in its turn, slowly, deliberately.

Cynara's blue eyes grew wide. She could feel her heart pounding wildly. "My lord, I am too young and inexperienced to be entertaining a gentleman in my bath," she told him. "Why have you come?" She actually felt the pulse in her throat jumping and wondered if it was visible to his eye.

"I came because I thought that perhaps you would have changed your mind about riding with me this afternoon. I doubt that your father approves of me, given my reputation," he said bluntly.

"My father does not know you, *Wickedness*, and while he has expressed his reservations that I would spend time with you, he trusts me not to bring shame upon the family name. *And I will not.*"

"Perhaps your father is so busy here at court that he does not really care," the earl suggested cruelly.

"It is obvious, my lord, that you do not know my papa," Cynara defended her parent. "But you will eventually. Now, my lord, I believe it would be prudent if you took your leave of me. I do not want my Hester finding you here and raising a row. It would surely result in my father's forbidding me your company."

"And if he did?" the earl said softly.

"Then I should have to disobey him, Wickedness," she answered as softly.

He bowed to her. "I will come for you at two o'clock, madam."

"I will be waiting," Cynara responded.

Then he turned and was gone quickly from the duke's apartment. Cynara took up the flannel cloth, soaped it, and began to wash herself. Would a gentleman discovering a lady in her bath have departed immediately? Not at this court, Cynara grinned to herself. She had never in all her life imagined that she would sit calmly in her tub verbally sparring with the earl of Summersfield. She hoped that no one had seen him enter or leave, lest it get back to her father. He had seen nothing that he shouldn't, and there was surely no harm done. Finished, Cynara arose from her bath and wrapped herself in the drying sheet that Hester had left on the rack before the fire. Stepping onto the carpet, she walked slowly back to her little bedchamber wondering why she had waited all this time to approach him. Had she been daring enough last year when she just mooned after him and struggled to be near him, perhaps they would now be wed. *But next year,* Cynara considered. And she laughed.

Chapter

16

What was he getting himself into? Harry Summers wondered as he departed the duke of Lundy's apartments. Whatever was said about him, and he knew he was a subject of gossip, no one had ever connected him with a woman of good family. He had always made it his habit to consort only with lowbred women. He was not his father, whoring with his neighbors' wives. He was not his mother, disregarding her marriage vows. He satisfied his lust with women who were exactly what they said they were. *Whores*. And yet all women were the same no matter their rank. The only thing that separated Cynara Stuart from the others was her virginity. *For now*. Married she would become what they all were, but she would not cuckold him. It would be some other poor fool, but not Harry Summers, the fifth earl of Summersfield.

Still, he found himself tempted by her. She was outrageously beautiful and unlike all the other pretty misses come hunting for mates. There was nothing demure about her. All last winter she had stalked him. And when the spring came, she had always found a way to be near him even if he neglected her. And now this winter she had obviously grown tired of being ignored by him and last night had asked him to dance. He should have made an end of it then and there. He should have refused her, but no. He had danced with her and invited her riding. He had come this morning to her father's apartments with the full intention of canceling their rendezvous this afternoon. But there she was in a perfumed tub, visible only from her creamy shoulders to the top of her sable black hair. And engaged once more in a verbal battle with her he had been unable to call off their appointment.

It was the fact she was untouched. It had to be. What else lured him onward? This was a dangerous game he was becoming engaged in, for the duke of Lundy would not take lightly a man who seduced his daughter. And there was the king to consider as well. Everyone at court knew that Charles Stuart, the king, was deeply fond of and very loyal to Charles Stuart, duke of Lundy. The not-so-royal Stuart might have been king under other circumstances. He had followed his cousin into exile and done everything he could to aid him, for he was a wealthy man. He had often gone without himself to see that the king had food and clothing and some coin in his pocket. Charles Stuart, the king, did not forget his family, nor did he forget a genuine kindness. Debauch the duke's daughter, and Harry Summers could find himself headless.

But it was she who was the aggressor. And was he not man enough to contain his own emotions? What was the harm in an innocent little flirtation? *But would it be innocent?* Cynara was like a young panther on the prowl. He recognized all the signs for he was no fool where women were concerned. Would she be content with a flirtation? He somehow did not think she would, but he realized he could not prevent himself from being with her. Perhaps a familiarity with Lady Cynara Stuart would breed a contempt of her. He wondered why now in his twenty-sixth year of life he should suddenly find himself interested in a girl of respectable family. He shook himself hard. He was not interested in Cynara Stuart. Intrigued, perhaps, to see just how far she would go but absolutely not interested.

"I want no wife," he muttered aloud.

The object of his interest was even now considering the clothing she would wear that afternoon. Would he admire her in her midnight blue velvet breeches and jacket? Would he be shocked that she rode astride? Well, she had mentioned it the evening before. If he had actually been listening instead of considering the ways in which he might seduce her, he would not be surprised. Hester had finally returned with a heavy tray which she had set upon the mahogany sideboard in the salon.

"Did I spy someone coming down the corridor from this apartment?" she asked Cynara suspiciously.

"I don't know," Cynara replied innocently. "There was no one here. Perhaps a guardsman or some other servant? What have you brought me? I am ravenous." Cynara walked across the salon in her chemise and her bare feet. She began lifting the silver covers on the dishes. "Ohh, poached eggs!" she exclaimed. "I hope they did them with that delicious marsala sauce the royal kitchens do so well. And lamb chops?"

"Sit down," Hester said. "I'll bring you a plate. Best eat it while it's hot. I'll have the men clear the tub away afterward."

Cynara's appetite had always been very good, which was a great annoyance to her mother who was forced to watch her weight and could not always indulge in the foods she loved. She ate two eggs with her favorite sauce and two plump lamb chops, shoving out the marrow from the bone with her fingers and licking it off. There was a dish of fresh-cut pineapple from the royal greenhouses. Cynara particularly liked this exotic fruit and its juice. There were dainty little breads called rolls, sweet butter, and a cherry jam. And Hester brewed a pot of tea from the duke's private stock for her mistress. Finally sated, Cynara pushed her chair back and said, "I will nap for an hour. Then call me so I may dress and be prompt. I suspect the earl thinks he will be forced to wait upon me. I would surprise him."

"I'll call the footmen and have your tub removed," Hester said.

"Remind them I'll want it refilled tonight at five-thirty," Cynara replied, "and do not frown at me, Hester. I'll not go to the evening's entertainment stinking of my horse!"

"Never knew a girl who was such a one for bathing," Hester muttered. "Were you like this when you was small?"

Cynara nodded. "I have always loved a hot bath," she said. She slept quickly and soundly. But when Hester touched her shoulder, Cynara was immediately awake. She arose, splashed water from her silver ewer on her face, and brushed her teeth with her special brush, rinsing her mouth with the mint water afterward. Then throwing off her chemise, she began to dress herself with the carefully laid out garments. She drew on a silk shirt with a ruff of lace that would spill from her jacket like a waterfall. The lace on its cuffs would show at her wrists. She pulled on her white silk boot hose and then her midnight blue velvet breeches. The breeches came to her knee and fastened with large carved silver buttons, a style that was Cynara's own design. Most breeches had silk, or satin bands, but Cynara's legs were so slender that banded breeches rode up on her leg.

Hester frowned as her mistress buttoned the breeches. "I think it is shocking that you will wear no *calecons*," she said.

"Who is to know?" Cynara teased the older woman, "if I don't take them off, or you tell them."

Hester shook her head. "You are determined to live up to that name they call you, m'lady."

"Cyn? I rather like it. The earl's sobriquet is *Wickedness*." Then she chuckled mischievously and sat to put on her boots.

"Bad to the bone you are!" Hester scolded. "Yer poor mama and the dowager Jasmine will weep over you yet again, m'lady."

The duchess Barbara had installed a full-length mirror in the ducal apartments. Cynara now stood before that mirror admiring herself in the clear glass. "No one gets my boots as well polished as the palace bootblack," she said, observing the high sheen on her black riding boots. She sat down at the dressing table, and Hester began to brush her hair out before styling it into a chignon, which Cynara preferred when riding. "Now, my hat," Cynara said, placing the shallow-crowned black felt chapeau upon her own dark head. Its broad brim and the two graceful ostrich feathers adorning it gave her a very dashing appearance. Cynara arose and returned to the mirror. Hester handed her her white kid riding gloves, embroidered with seed pearls, and her leather crop. Cynara preened. "He will not be able to resist me," she said in satisfied tones as she twirled before the glass.

"You just remember who you are and behave yourself, m'lady," Hester said. "Yer papa don't want no scandals over you!"

Before Cynara might answer her servant, there was a brief knock upon the apartment door, and Hester ran to open it as Cynara emerged from her bedchamber. The servant bowed the earl of Summersfield into the room. He gave her a brief nod of his head, and then his eyes went to Cynara filling with his admiration as they beheld her.

"Your riding apparel is most stylish, madam," he said as he bowed and kissed her outstretched hand, noting she was wearing her ruby ring.

"Thank you, my lord. Shall we go? Hester, you did remember to order my horse from the stables?" Cynara cocked her head to one side.

"As always," Hester said sharply, then she added, "And what time can I tell yer father, the duke, to expect you back?"

"When I arrive," Cynara laughed and swept out of the door of the apartment followed by her companion.

"She loves you dearly to make such a point of mentioning your papa," the earl chuckled. "I think if she dared she might have inquired as to my intentions, madam."

"Which are quite dishonorable, I have not a doubt," Cynara teased him, laughing.

"You are not afraid of me, or of what people say, are you?" Again her boldness surprised him although he did not know why. It was certainly unusual in a virgin. *If she was a virgin.* And why did that truly concern him? the earl wondered. It concerned him because the thought of anyone but him tampering with that divine beauty sent thoughts of violence swirling about his head. What sorcery was this that she had practiced upon him? She was a girl. *A girl ready to become a woman.* And once she was, she would be like they all were. Greedy. Deceitful. Dangerous.

She noted his silence as they walked through the jumble of corridors that connected the various sections of Whitehall and finally out into the main courtyard where two grooms stood waiting patiently for them to arrive and claim their horses. Pulling on her gloves, Cynara said nothing, but she was curious as to what he was thinking. That it concerned her she had not a moment's doubt. She waved the mounting block aside, instead commanding the groom, "Cup your hands." She vaulted into her saddle neatly, smiled a quick thanks at the grooms, and gathered her reins into her gloved hand. The black stallion danced nervously as he felt Cynara's weight upon his back, but she soothed him with soft words in his large cocked ear.

The earl's equally dark chestnut stallion leaned his long graceful neck out and attempted to nip at the flank of Cynara's mount. The black beast turned aside sharply and snorted a warning to the other animal who whickered a challenge back.

"One of us," said Harry Summers, "is going to have to ride a mare or a gelding in future. 'Twill be hell keeping these two creatures apart today. They are already disputing each other."

"Do you have another animal?" she inquired sweetly.

"I never knew a lady who preferred such a horse," he told her as they turned out of the palace courtyard and onto the street.

"His name is Fluffy," she told him.

"You named a great beast like this *Fluffy?*" The earl began to laugh heartily.

"Well," she explained, "his formal name is Mughal's Shadow, but when he was born he had the sweetest, fluffiest whisk of a tail and so I called him Fluffy. He was a birthday gift from my grandmother on my twelfth birthday. His mother came from Grandmama's stud in Ireland. He descends from Night Wind and Night Shadow."

"He's quite handsome," the earl remarked.

"If you have any good mares, I would gladly loan him to you for breeding purposes. Fluffy does like a pretty mare, don't you, boy?" She leaned forward slightly and patted the stallion's neck, and the stallion snorted and tossed his head as if he understood her perfectly.

They turned into St. James Park now and were soon riding along beneath the just-budding trees. They walked along demurely, nodding and greeting the courtiers that they knew. Finally Cynara issued a challenge to her companion, and they raced down a wooded path for a mile or two before drawing up to a stop. She slid from her mount.

"Let us tie our horses to a branch so they may rest awhile, and we will walk," she suggested.

He concurred, and they began to travel along the early spring greenery. Here and there small patches of bright yellow daffodils clustered in tight groups. Cynara gathered some up.

"Is it permitted to pick the king's flowers?" the earl asked.

"I am a Stuart," Cynara replied as if that were the answer to everything. "My cousin would hardly deny me a few blossoms."

She looked like the subject for a painting, standing there against an ancient oak in her midnight blue velvet, clutching a sheaf of golden flowers to her bosom. He moved in closer, pressing her against the trunk of the tree. There was a small smile upon her lips that said, *You cannot resist me, can you?*

"I can't!" he agreed aloud with himself, and then his lips met hers in a fierce kiss. He didn't ask. He demanded.

She was being pressed hard against the tree trunk. She could feel the rough bark imprinting itself upon the velvet of her jacket. While Cynara considered herself sophisticated, she did not in fact have that much experience with kissing, or any other form of lovemaking. Her heart raced. She was suddenly lightheaded, but then instinct took over. She pressed herself against him, and her lips softened beneath his passionate onslaught. He actually groaned against the lush mouth that gave back all he silently asked for and more.

Her arms wrapped themselves tightly about his neck. He could feel the softness of her breasts giving way against his hard chest. He was dizzy with the exotic scent of her body. *Gardenia.* Yes! That was the flower her perfume was made from. His lips could not stop kissing her, or, it seemed, could she cease kissing him. He ran his tongue along her mouth. She copied him instantly. He could feel his male member, now arousing itself, and growing hard within his breeches. In another minute he was going to throw her to the ground, and if he was executed for violating the king's cousin, then so be it. He didn't care! *He had to have her!*

It was getting out of hand. Cynara sensed the desperate desire in both herself and the earl. She must be the one to stop it and quickly. Her hands went against his broad chest, and she pushed hard against him. "No more, my lord," she said huskily. *"No more!"* She moved quickly around and away from him, turning to walk back to where their horses were tethered. She was amazed that her legs could hold her, let alone move her away from him.

He gritted his teeth in frustration although he knew she was right. He could not move for several more minutes. Mounting his horse in his current condition would prove impossible. "Are you then a cock tease, madam?" he demanded of her, half-angry, but at whom his anger was directed—her or himself—he was not certain.

"Are you a cunt tease?" she challenged him back. "Or do you assume I feel no desire being a mere woman?"

He laughed, his anger diffused by her frankness. She was right. Men always assumed that good women did not feel lust while *bad* women did. "You will have to wait for me," he told her. "I am in no condition to ride with you right now."

"Why not?" she asked.

"Because my cock is as hard as an iron bar, my dear Cyn. You have roused it with your kisses and the soft give of your titties," he told her bluntly.

She turned and came back. "Ohh, let me feel it!" she said excitedly, reaching out to run her hand along the visible bulge in his breeches, her blue eyes wide, and quite fascinated.

He leaped back as if scalded. "*No!* Listen to me you damned vixen, you had better be a virgin because if I learn you are not, I may kill you. If you touch me, it will make it worse. *Go away!*"

"How would you possibly be able to discern if I am a virgin, my lord? *Or not.* Without a more intimate knowledge of my person," Cynara taunted him, moving back from his reach.

"Because I intend bedding you, madam!" he growled.

Cynara laughed and with a wave of her hand turned about again. "Farewell, my lord," she said. "Do not worry about me. I can mount my own horse without aid, and I do know my way back to the palace." And she laughed again sensing his frustration. "I believe I have won this round too, Harry Summers," she told him. Then she mounted Fluffy and, kicking the horse into a trot, rode away. She was, she realized, humming beneath her breath. She wished she had known before what fun the earl of Summersfield could be. And while she had little to compare him with, she also suspected that he was a marvelous kisser. She would certainly be kissing him again very soon. Perhaps tonight.

But at court that evening there was no sign of the earl of Summersfield. Cynara was annoyed by his absence and found herself losing at the cards. Finally with a small sound of irritation she arose from the table, paid her debts, and returned to her father's apartment. She had told Hester earlier that she would not need her services again that evening. Her early years in her mother's isolated house had taught her how to dress and undress herself. Angry she yanked her clothing off, letting it lie where it fell. Hester would be upset with her in the morning, but Cynara didn't care. Where had he been this evening? How dare he ignore her after their ride this afternoon?

The object of her ire was at that moment in the bed of his favorite whore, a woman who despite her thirty years, was still exciting. She lay beneath him now gasping with the surprise and shock of his lust. She had never known him to be like this.

"Jesu, 'arry! You 'ave battered me nigh unto death," she told him frankly. She pushed him off her and looked down into his handsome face. "Who is she?"

"Leave it be, Lizzie," the earl said angrily

"You wasn't fucking me just now," Lizzie persisted. *"You wasn't!* So who was it you was fucking? It ain't often I 'ave a third person in my bed, nor 'ave you ever been so fierce with me."

The earl arose from Lizzie's bed and began drawing on his clothing. His look was both bleak and furious.

"'Ods bloody blood!" Lizzie exclaimed. "Yer falling in love, 'arry Summers. And for some reason you can't 'ave her. God knows an 'usband never stopped you. So what is it?"

"You don't know what you're talking about, Lizzie," the earl told the whore coldly. His fingers became all thumbs as he buttoned his dark velvet jacket, and he swore beneath his breath.

"The 'ell I don't," she said laughing. "If there is one subject I knows well and good, 'tis the gentlemen. *She's a virgin of good family!*" Lizzie cackled. "And if you wants her, you 'as to wed her proper. *That's it, ain't it?*" Her brown eyes were dancing with amusement.

"You know I will never marry, and you know the reason," the earl of Summersfield said.

"You ain't yer da, nor are you to blame for what 'appened," Lizzie told Harry Summers. "I knows what they calls you, 'arry, but you ain't a bad fellow at all. Why do you let them all believe you are?"

He gave her a brief sad smile. "Because 'tis easier, Lizzie. Easier than explaining that my father was a monster who raped my mother, was forced to wed her because she was carrying his child—me—and then spent the rest of their years together torturing her until he finally killed her. I remember it well, Lizzie. And I remember how I killed him when I was given the opportunity. I am not fit to husband a decent woman, let alone a duke's daughter."

"Why you insist on believing you killed yer da when the truth is nothing would 'ave saved him, I don't know," Lizzie said impatiently.

"He was helpless. He begged me to call the physician. I didn't. Instead I left him to die alone," the earl replied, his eyes haunted by the memory. "I left him, and spent the hours in which his life ended fucking his current mistress in the room next to his. He had to have heard us for she howled like a damned banshee each time I stuck it to her, the heartless bitch!"

"You was sixteen," Lizzie reminded him. "And you was angry, and rightly so. Devil Summers did the exact same thing to yer mam. He left 'er dying alone while he fucked his whore in the room next to hers. Turn about is fair play, I says," Lizzie concluded.

He laughed. Lizzie could always make him laugh. She was a sensible and practical girl. He reached into his velvet jacket and drew out two coins which he tossed her. "I'll be back," he told her.

"Until you gets all that nonsense out of your 'ead and marries that lass," Lizzie said wisely. "But I'll be 'appy to see you whenever you comes, 'arry Summers. Try not to break the lass's 'eart."

"*Cynara?* She's as hard as a bright diamond," he answered. "If she has a heart she keeps it well hidden, Lizzie."

"Every woman 'as a 'eart," Lizzie said wisely. "If she loves you, 'arry, you'll soon learn that."

The earl of Summersfield returned to the quarters he kept in a small but pleasant inn near Whitehall. His manservant, Browning, awoke from his slumber by the fireside and helped his master to undress. He could smell the lust on the earl and asked if he would like a bath.

"In the morning," the earl responded, and pouring himself a tumbler of Irish whiskey he climbed into bed. Browning returned to his own cot, and the earl slowly sipped the amber liquid in his crystal. He thought tonight of things he hadn't thought of in years. Of his mother, a wealthy merchant's daughter from Londonderry in Ireland, who had refused the rough advances of the earl of Summersfield, a visiting English nobleman. Devil Summers did not enjoy being made a public fool. He stalked Mistress Sophia Elliot silently until he caught her alone one afternoon and took his revenge, raping the innocent girl viciously several times and then leaving her for dead.

A cousin, who loved Sophia, found her, battered and bloody, beneath the trees by her favorite brook. He carried her home, and when she regained consciousness, she told her family what had happened. Her father, a prominent man, wished to avoid a scandal at all costs. He went to the lord mayor of Londonderry, his best friend, and told him what had happened. The lord mayor dispatched his personal guard to bring the earl of Summersfield to him. Devil Summers was given a choice. He could marry Sophia Elliot, or he could hang.

The earl protested at first. The wench wasn't worthy of his name. She had led him on, and only gotten what she deserved. But he knew that to be untrue, and so did everyone else. Master Elliot had resolved the matter by settling an enormous sum upon his only child, and by advising Devil Summers that Sophia would inherit all of his wealth one day. And so the marriage had been celebrated, and in all of Ireland it was said there was never a more unhappy bride. But by her wedding day Sophia was already showing signs of pregnancy in the secrecy of her family.

The earl immediately removed his wife back to England, and for the months she carried his child he was distant but respectful to her. Once his son had been born, however, his behavior reverted to the man she had first met. The countess was afraid of her husband and could not conceal her fear. He despised her for it. She strove desperately to keep out of his way, but he often sought her out when he lacked other amusements. He never again after the day he had violated her slept with her, but he particularly enjoyed punishing her with a variety of sexual toys he kept.

One of his favorite tortures was to tie her to a chair, and force her to watch while he committed adultery with any number of their neighbors' wives. He would lay his lover with the top of her head toward his wife, and then he could pleasure himself while watching his wife survey them. The first time she had refused to watch closing her eyes tightly. He had beaten her afterward in the presence of his lover for her defiance.

As the years went by, it became more difficult for his mother to face her neighbors in a social situation knowing what she knew about their wives. Her husband, nonpolitical in the regime of the Commonwealth, nonetheless behaved like a satyr, but if the authorities knew, they looked the other way, for their wives and daughters were involved. As long as there was no public scandal and all appeared well, his father was safe.

But then his mother's cousin had come from Ireland on business for his grandfather. He had visited and seen Sophia's continuing misery. He declared that his love for her had never died. He told her that when she had been first violated by the earl, he had begged her father to let him wed with her. Master Elliot, however, seeing an opportunity to better his family's connections, had insisted upon his daughter's marriage to Devil Summers. It had done him little good, her cousin said, for the earl had ignored his in-laws from the day after the marriage. He had never answered her father's letters or his requests for introductions to important men. Both her father and her husband had used Sophia Summers and then discarded her. Her cousin, however, had never forgotten her. He understood her not corresponding back to his letters.

But the countess of Summersfield had not known of the letters her cousin had written her. From the day she had married Devil Summers and come to England, she had assumed her family did not wish to know her any longer. No one had written to her. No acknowledgment had been made concerning the birth of her son. Finally after several years she had stopped writing to them, she told her cousin. Was she aware that her mother was deceased? he asked her. Sophia burst into startled tears, and Daniel Elliot put his arms about her to comfort her.

And in that fateful moment, their lives took a direction that would lead to disaster for them both. She hadn't meant for it to happen, Sophia later confessed to her fourteen-year-old son as she lay dying. She and her cousin had entered into a love affair. When Sophia found herself with child after all those years, the decision was made to run away together. But the coach in which they were making their escape met with an accident. Daniel Elliot was killed, and Sophia was brought home to recover from her injuries, but she did not. Instead she died miscarrying her child while his father entertained his latest whore and permitted no one to go to his countess's aid that her last hours be made comfortable. Harry Summers, however, had snuck into his mother's room to bid her farewell, to try to comfort her. Learning of it his father had dragged him from the death chamber, swearing. His mother had died alone and in terrible agony.

The following morning when her cries could no longer be heard, Devil Summers brought his son back into the death chamber. He yanked back the coverlet from the bed, and pulled up his wife's nightgown, which was black now with the drying blood. Reaching down between the woman's legs, he brought up a small, perfectly formed scrap of humanity, thrusting it beneath his son's horrified eyes.

"'Tis your half brother," he said, and then he laughed. "I would not have thought the bitch could still get a son. Now here's a lesson for you, my lad. All women are born whores, even your precious mother. Don't ever trust any of 'em!"

Harry Summers had run from the bedchamber to vomit the contents of his guts. His mother was buried that day, and that night while his father lay drunk, the earl's latest mistress crept into his son's bed, and Harry Summers became a man. And in the nights that followed, whenever his father slept heavily, the woman came to the son. At first he had been thrilled with what was happening to him, but then he grew disgusted with himself. He was no better than his father, he realized. The next time the woman came to his chambers, he sent her away.

"I can find my own women," he said cruelly, and he did. There were servant girls, and dairymaids, and farmers' daughters. They, he found, pleasured him freely. Then there were the whores, and they pleasured him for the coin he offered. And he had his pick from among the women his father kept for they were only too willing to entertain a young man with a strong and randy cock after his father had fallen into a drunken slumber. Once his father declared that his current mistress was the best fuck that he had ever had.

"You have had more experience, of course," Harry had said coldly, "but I find her merely satisfactory."

His father's mouth fell open in surprise at his fifteen-year-old son's declaration. Devil Summers knew his son futtered the females around his estate, but his own mistress. *"You've had her?"* he demanded to know, his dark eyes narrowing, his face flushing.

Harry Summers smiled disdainfully. "Of course," he said.

"You bastard!" his father snarled angrily.

"Nay, my lord, you saw that I was not, and I do thank you for it," Harry replied mockingly. "And did you not tell me that all women are whores? So why are you surprised that I availed myself of your whore? She was happy to have a younger and more talented cock for a change. You should not drink so much."

His father seemed to wither before his gaze, and Harry found that he was glad. He had never thought that he could wound his father, but he saw now that it was quite possible. From that moment on, he took every opportunity to injure Devil Summers, watching as his father grew sick and began to fade before his eyes. His old nurse seeing what he was doing admonished him, waving her bony finger beneath his nose.

"Yer wickedness personified, you are!" she said, and thus he had gained his sobriquet.

His father had died when he was sixteen, and Harry Summers had become earl of Summersfield. He kept mostly to himself. Unlike his father, he kept no mistresses but availed himself of certain whores. He managed his estates well, raising cattle and horses. Several years after the king was restored to his throne, Harry Summers came to court. As his neighbors had been there before him his reputation and his sobriquet preceded him. At court there were ladies only too willing to please and amuse him. And he had found Lizzie, who as it turned out, had come to London from Gloucester seeking her fortune.

And now he found himself in a quandary because of Lady Cynara Stuart. Lizzie said he was falling in love, but he was not. *He wasn't!* Was she beautiful? Aye. But so were many others. Was she tempting? 'Odsfish, she could tempt a saint, he thought! But Cynara Stuart was a girl one married, and he did not wish to marry. There was enough of his father in him to frighten him. He would never willingly do to any woman what his father had done to him. Better he keep to his whores.

The earl slept restlessly. He was not quick to rise, but finally he called for Browning to bring him a bath. He could yet smell Lizzie's violet water on his skin. The innkeeper's serving men brought him a large round oak tub, which was set up before his dayroom fire. They then filled it with hot water. When they had done, the earl stripped off his nightshirt and climbed in, smiling that his knees stuck above the steaming water. The heat sank into his flesh, and he actually began to feel better. He closed his eyes with a sigh.

"Browning, fetch me something to eat," he said to his servant.

He heard the door closing behind the man. A moment later, however, he heard Browning's voice most distinctly.

"Madam! You cannot go in there! *Madam!*"

The door flew open with a bang. The earl's green eyes opened to behold Lady Cynara Stuart. She whirled ferociously on Browning. "Go about your business!" she told him, and slammed the door shut again. "Well, my lord, and where were you last night?" she demanded of him.

"My dear Cyn, good morrow to you too," he said dryly. "I do not believe that my whereabouts are of any concern of yours."

"I thought you would come to court last night. I lost at the cards waiting for you, and I never lose!" she told him.

"Then perhaps your luck is changing," he suggested. "Now, my pet, either go away, or make yourself useful. Browning usually scrubs my back, but I am happy to have you do it."

Cynara stood her ground before his tub, and then to his surprise she began to unfasten her jacket. Removing it she laid it aside. Then she knelt by the tub, and taking up his brush, she soaped it and began scrubbing his long back vigorously.

"Jesu! Mary! You'll have the skin off me," he protested, but he could not take his eyes from her snowy breasts so very visible beneath the scooped neckline of her lace-edged chemise.

"It will take some scrubbing to rid you of the stink of violet water," she snapped. "You were with a whore!"

"An old and dear friend," he murmured wickedly. *"Ouch!"*

"You spent the evening fucking a whore when you could have been with me?" she said furiously, and she splashed water on his back to rid it of the soap.

"I would have only spent the evening with you, my dear Cyn, if I could have spent it fucking you. Such a diversion between us, however, is not possible, I fear," he told her. He took up the flannel and washed his face.

"Why not?" She was so tempting kneeling there by his tub, her heart-shaped face looking at him.

"You are not stupid, Cyn. Far from it. You are probably the most intelligent girl I have ever met or will meet. I can say it no more plainly. *I will not marry, and you are a girl who must be wed.* You are a duke's daughter, and a cousin of His Majesty. You are so damned desirable, but much to my surprise even I draw the line at seducing you though I should very much like to do so."

"Why will you not wed?" she demanded to know. "Do you think I have not heard the rumors, my lord?"

He had to make her go away. He could not bear much more of

this temptation. He stood up, the water sluicing down his lean hard body. Her eyes grew wide, but there was no fear in them to his surprise. Only admiration as her gaze warmed his skin and lingered on his male member. Then she got to her feet and, reaching out, took the drying cloth from the rack before the fire, wrapping it about his narrow hips.

"Did you think I would scream?" she gently teased him.

He nodded wordlessly and stepped from the tub, drying himself.

"Siren has little brothers who come each summer to Grandmama's. I should have to be blind to have not seen a male form before now with all those little boys running about," she told him. "They say you killed your father? How?"

"This is not the time . . ." he began, but she put her hand over his mouth.

"It is as good a time as any, my lord," she told him.

"I would not call the physician for him when he lay dying. Instead I spent the hours of his death fucking his latest whore in the room next to his so he might hear us."

Cynara was shocked, but she hardly considered it murder and was relieved. "If he was dying, the doctor could have done him no good," she reasoned. "Perhaps he might have eased your father's pain, but no more. Why did you use his whore in that manner?"

"Give me my shirt," he said, and pointed to where it lay on a nearby chair. "Because that was how he spent his time when my mother lay dying, Cyn. He would seek no help for her while she miscarried her lover's child, and the sounds of his rutting were the last she heard. I wanted him to know how she felt."

"Tell me about your mother," Cynara said. "Had he loved her?"

"She was the only child of a Londonderry merchant," the earl said. "My antecedents are hardly worthy of the daughter of the duke of Lundy."

"My mother's father was a Hereford merchant," Cynara told him. "We would, it seems, have something in common, my lord." She gave him the shirt and stood before him tying the laces.

His head began to spin with her closeness, but he couldn't seem to move. When she stood upon her tiptoes and kissed him, he groaned desperately.

"You want me," Cynara said softly.

"I want you," he admitted, "but I cannot wed you. There is too much of my parents in me, and I should make you miserable, Cynara. I have never felt this way about any woman, nor have I ever admitted to having a heart, but I do, it would seem. Do not torture me further, I beg you. If you continue to taunt me so, I cannot be responsible for my actions."

She reached up and touched his face with gentle fingers, rubbing the tips over his jaw line. "You need a shave," she told him.

"I think I may kill you," he said.

Now she stepped back, but she was not afraid. "With love?" she teased mischievously. "Go and put your breeches on, my lord. I will wait for you."

"Go home!" he cried, but he walked across the small dayroom and into his bedchamber to do her bidding. When he turned, she was standing in the doorway. She stepped into the room, and reaching out, he grabbed her, his mouth fusing with hers in a passionate kiss. Her arms wrapped themselves about his neck, and she sighed. The vixen sighed for she had gotten her way, he thought desperately. Harry Summers couldn't help himself. He pushed her back onto the bed, flinging himself atop her. He kissed her eyes, her nose, her cheeks, her chin. The little dark mole just below her right nostril fascinated him. He stared at it, and then he kissed it too.

He could feel her young breasts beneath his chest. He raised himself slightly, and with skilled fingers, he undid the ribbons holding her chemise closed. Her breasts were perfect little round globes of perfumed enticement. Adorable snares luring him to his doom. He kissed those breasts and buried his face between them. Her nipples thrust upward, daring him, and he accepted the challenge, kissing each in their turn.

Cynara cried out softly for she had never permitted such access to her person. But she wanted him to touch her and kiss her. Her heart raced with her excitement, and her breath came in tiny pants that seemed to mingle with his as his lips met hers again. He couldn't seem to stop himself from touching her, and she didn't want him to stop.

Then they heard the door to the dayroom open with deliberate noise, and the footfall of the earl's serving man as he brought his master's food. Harry Summers ceased his seduction immediately with a deep sigh. He arose from the bed, and drew her up with him.

Cynara retied her chemise ribbons. "You shall have to visit your old and dear friend again, I fear," she said wickedly. "Would you fetch my jacket, please. I would not shock your man."

"No, that would not do at all," he murmured dryly. "Save your shocks for me, my dear Cyn." He stepped from the room, returning a moment later with her garment.

Cynara carefully rebuttoned the jacket and attempted to make some semblance of order to her hair. "I shall see you at Newmarket, my lord," she said softly.

He took an errant lock of her hair, and gently put it in its place. He nodded. Then he said quickly, "You realize if we continue this that I am going to seduce you, Cynara."

She smiled at him mischievously. "Of course you are, my lord," she said.

"But I won't wed you," he said once again.

"Yes, you will," she told him. "Perhaps not right away, but one day you will wed with me, my darling Wickedness."

"You are a true vixen," he said despairingly.

"Aye, my lord, I am," she agreed, and then pushing past him, she departed his apartment, nodding at Browning as she went.

Chapter

17

The court prepared to decamp Whitehall for Newmarket. The king enjoyed the racing seasons, and visited in the spring, and again in the autumn before he hunted in the New Forest. In these first years of his restoration the royal forests had been well restocked with the game that had been slaughtered wholesale during the period of the Commonwealth.

Newmarket was located in the western part of the county of Suffolk. It was twelve miles from the beautiful university town of Cambridge where several of Cynara's cousins had studied. She had been there before. She very much liked the rolling heathland about the town. One could both walk and ride most comfortably. Her father had a stable at Newmarket as well as a fine brick house. Cynara was not surprised, but perhaps just a tiny bit irritated to find her mother and her grandmother awaiting them. She knew that her father had written, begging them to come. She frowned. It was easy to evade her father, and any questions he might think to ask especially when he was in the company of his royal cousin. That was not the case with her mother or her grandmother. But she would allow nothing to stop her pursuit of Harry Summers.

Dutifully she greeted her female relations, kissing them upon their cheeks. "Mama. Grandmama. This is a surprise," she said smiling.

"I am certain that it is," Jasmine murmured archly, and Cynara laughed. How well the two women understood each other.

"You look pale," her mother said. "Have you been getting enough rest?" The duchess Barbara was genuinely concerned for her only child.

"Mama, you know that one does not get enough of anything at court, food or rest," Cynara answered. "Still, it is quite wonderful!"

"Have you met any suitable young men?" the duchess inquired.

"My dear Barbara," Jasmine said exasperated, "if Cynara were interested in anyone other than Harry Summers, Charlie would not have asked us to come to Newmarket. Is that not so, Cynara?"

Cynara laughed again. Her grandmother's honesty and frankness did not upset her at all. Indeed she admired the old woman for it. "You are correct, Grandmama," she said. "I still pursue Harry Summers, but I do believe I am making a progress of sorts. We have danced, and ridden, and spoken at length now. We have arranged to meet here at Newmarket, and I understand he is already here."

"Oh dear," Barbara Stuart said, and the distress in her voice was more than evident. "Cynara, please believe me when I tell you that Harry Summers is a most unsuitable husband for you."

"Wickedness says he will never marry," Cynara informed them blandly, "but he is wrong. He will marry me eventually, I promise you. And he will want to wed with me when that day comes."

"He has told you he will not marry, and you yet chase after him? *Cynara!* Where is your pride? You who have always been so proud to be who you are, related to His Majesty, your father's child," the duchess of Lundy cried despairingly. "I can only believe that this man has bewitched you and intends to seduce you!"

"Of course he intends to seduce me, Mama," Cynara said calmly.

Jasmine's laughter was sharp with her amusement. She had always believed that this granddaughter, of all her grandchildren, was the most like her in character. And Cynara certainly was. Poor Barbara with her solid middle-class roots would not understand, but Jasmine certainly did.

"His father is said to have been a monster!" the duchess cried.

"And his mother like you, Mama, was a respectable merchant's daughter from Londonderry. I have been quietly ferreting out his background, but other than the most basic facts, I can learn naught."

"Do you want to know?" Jasmine asked the girl.

Cynara turned, and her eyes were shining as she looked to the dowager. "Ohh, yes, Grandmama! Yes, I do want to know for therein lies the key to Wickedness's reluctance to marry."

"That much is obvious," Jasmine replied. "The parents' union was an unhappy one. What you want to learn, my child, is why."

"You would encourage her in this madness!" the distraught duchess said. "Madame! I thought better of you!"

"My poor Barbara," Jasmine said, "you must understand that Cynara will not quit her desire to have the earl of Summersfield easily, if indeed at all. If this man is the man she wants, then we must aid her in order to prevent a tragedy. Even if you do not understand, you must trust me to see that all comes out happily. Have I ever before failed my family?"

"No, madame, you have not," the duchess answered, chastened.

"Cynara," her grandmother said, "do you love this man?"

The girl's face lit up, and she actually blushed. "Aye, Grandmama, I do."

"Does he love you?" was the next query.

"I think he may, but he struggles against it," Cynara replied. "I have not the experience to know if it is love he feels for me now or simple lust."

Jasmine nodded. "You are wise, child, to understand that," she told her granddaughter. "I wish to meet him."

"Not yet, Grandmama," Cynara responded softly. "It is too soon, and I would not frighten him away. Let me weave my web a bit tighter."

"Oh God!" the duchess half-sobbed, but Jasmine laughed.

"I will trust your judgment in this, child, but do not wait for a perfect time, for there will never be one," she said wisely.

Cynara put her arms about her mother, and kissed her brow. "I am not a fool, Mama," she said. "I am young, but no fool."

Young, but in love, and reckless, Jasmine thought, remembering her own youth, and how she had had a brief affair with her third husband years before they finally married. She would speak to Hester this very day. Hester would know much of her granddaughter's behavior.

"She's still a virgin, of that I am certain," Hester told the dowager. "She hasn't had much time with him alone that I knows of, m'lady. But then to be honest, she sometimes gets away from me."

"Orane will give you a bottle with a potion in it. Stir one spoonful in a cup of clear water each morning, and take it to your mistress. Tell her that it is a strengthening potion that I have sent. Make certain she takes a draught every day, Hester. Do you understand?"

"Yes, m'lady," Hester replied.

Well, Jasmine thought as she left the maidservant, *if she flings herself into his bed in her attempt to force him to the altar, she will at least be safe from children. I must seek information on the Summers family and learn what has set this handsome young earl so against the bonds of matrimony.* She called her personal serving man to her. He was the son of her now-retired captain.

"Young Hugh," she said. "I have a task for you. I need to learn all I can about Harry Summers, the earl of Summersfield. I know the basics, but I want to know the truth that lies beneath the obvious. Return to London, and speak with Jonah Kira. He will find out what I need to learn about this young man, including his financial position. If my granddaughter marries him one day, I must be certain it is not her fortune he seeks. Perhaps he plays difficult to obtain merely in order to entice her into a compromising position. I need to know these things as quickly as Jonah can gather the information."

"Yes, m'lady," young Hugh responded, and he left his mistress. Several days later he returned with the entire truth about the Summers family. Jonah Kira had included a missive of great length and great detail. He ended it by telling the dowager that while much was said denigrating the current earl, he could find no proof that Harry Summers was the villain he was said to be. The young man lived discreetly, had a favorite whore he treated well, and a most comfortable fortune of his own, inherited from his maternal grandfather. He had also inherited his grandfather's shipping fleet, which he personally managed. He kept his funds with the Kira banks in London, in Dublin, and in Londonderry. He gambled infrequently. Most important of all, there was no serious scandal about him that was current.

Jasmine considered all of the information that the Kiras had compiled for her. She had never known them to be inaccurate. She was impressed that despite a goodly fortune, the earl directed and controlled the shipping fleet that he had inherited. The O'Malley-Small merchant company could certainly use a new partner. She wondered how large his vessels were. Were they coastal traders that ran back and forth between England, France and Ireland; or were they vessels that traveled the wide world over? Having the information that she needed, she wrote to Jonah Kira thanking him and inquiring further about the earl of Summersfield's ships, their capacity, and sailing range.

The night before the races began, the king held a fete at his house at Audley End, which was located several miles from Newmarket in Essex. He had let the house originally from its owner who was finally this very year convinced to sell it for fifty thousand pounds to His Majesty. The great house which had once been the Benedictine abbey of Walden was granted by King Henry VIII to his faithful Lord Chancellor, Sir Thomas Audley. On Sir Thomas's death, the estate had passed to Thomas Howard, the second son of the duke of Norfolk. His bravery in England's defense against the Spanish Armada, and in his country's long fight with Spain brought him a baronetcy first and the earldom of Suffolk next. Having served Elizabeth Tudor well in war, he served her successor, King James I, as Lord Treasurer.

The house that King Charles II purchased had been built by Thomas Howard on the site of the original abbey. Four wings of limestone and brick were constructed about an inner court. A gallery extending two hundred and forty feet took up the first floor of the east wing. To the west, a large outer courtyard was formed with three extensions. The kitchens and pantries and storerooms took up the lower level on the north block. There were stables beyond the River Cam, which flowed through the great estate.

The third earl of Suffolk, James Howard, was burdened with

debts due to the great expense of running such a large establishment. The king was only too happy to purchase Audley End, which was every bit as large as several of his palaces. The Great Hall was a marvelous place to entertain the court. Its chief feature was an example of late medieval artistry, a screen, carved by Italian craftsmen. The court filled the Great Hall with music and noise. The duke of Lundy and his family entered unannounced, for Audley End was an informal place despite all its wondrous magnificence.

Almost immediately Cynara saw Harry Summers. Their eyes met, then he turned away to her frustration. She had felt the heat of their glances, and she knew that he had too. Why then did he persist in ignoring her?

"Pretend you have not been offended," Jasmine murmured to her granddaughter.

"Why does he do this?" Cynara whispered back.

"Because he is afraid. He has obviously recognized in himself the ability to love and the need to be loved. He struggles against these emotions, my child. You must be patient with him, I think," Jasmine told the young girl.

"I do not know what has happened to me, Grandmama. I have been hard-hearted all of my life until the moment I saw him."

"You have simply recognized, and accepted your own need to love and be loved, Cynara," Jasmine said quietly. "Trust me, and I will help you."

The Great Hall at Audley End had walls paneled in a warm wood. The windows were wide and tall. The ceiling was coffered with plaster between the wooden beams and decorated with both painted and raised plaster decoration. The floors were white marble, and in the center of each great tile was a diamond of black marble. It was a grand place. Embroidered silk banners belonging to the former owner hung from brass poles that jutted out from the walls. There were also portraits on the walls of previous earls of Suffolk, and their wives.

There would be no dancing tonight. Servants passed among the guests offering small goblets of wine. Some of the ladies and gentlemen had already disappeared into side rooms to play cards and dice.

Cynara, casting about for Harry Summers, could no longer see him. She swore softly beneath her breath, and then her grandmother's hand touched hers.

"Come, my child, and let us leave this cacophony and walk outside. The evening is warm, and the river soothing."

Arm-in-arm the two women departed the Great Hall, Cynara remarking, "It is hardly like our dear hall at Queen's Malvern, is it?"

Jasmine nodded in agreement. "I knew Thomas Howard, the younger, when I was at King James's court. He was a second son and forever proving himself. An annoying man. I am surprised to see what taste he has exhibited in the construction and decoration of this house."

They moved across the lawns toward the river, and as they approached the water they saw him standing, his back against a lone willow tree. They could smell the nearby stables. Cynara clutched at her grandmother's elegant hand, causing the older woman to wince.

He turned, hearing the light footfall. His handsome face was grave, and Jasmine knew immediately that she would like Harry Summers. The long face was an intelligent but tortured one. His green eyes, not quite the same green as her Jemmie's, lit with pleasure at the sight of Cynara, but then as quickly grew inscrutable.

"Wickedness! This is my Grandmama!" Cynara said quickly.

The earl of Summersfield accepted the hand offered him and, bowing, kissed it. "Madame, your reputation precedes you. I am honored."

"Which reputation, my lord?" Jasmine teased. "The good one or the bad one?" And she smiled at him.

He laughed, genuinely amused. "I am certain, madame, that far more has been reported of you than of me."

Jasmine nodded, and then she slipped her hand through his arm. "Indeed, my lord, I have lived a rather full and, at times, most exciting life. When one reaches my age, she has a tendency to look back."

"And looking back do you regret anything?" he wondered.

"No," Jasmine said. "I have lived as I chose to live."

"Do you not even regret running away from Lord Leslie?" Cynara asked her grandmother.

"I regret nothing," Jasmine repeated. "I needed the time it took him to find me in France for myself and my children."

The earl looked puzzled. "You ran away?" he said, curious.

"It is a long story," Jasmine chuckled. "Perhaps my granddaughter will tell you about it one day." She slipped her hand from his arm. "I think I shall return to the house now. It is not really warm enough for a lady of my years to be out-of-doors in early evening. And I am certain that you and Cynara have much to discuss." She moved away from them, turning but briefly to wave cheerily.

"*If* I were to ever wed," he said, "I would probably take you for your grandmother. What a wonderful woman, Cyn!"

"*When* you marry me, my dear Wickedness, it will be because you are madly in love with me and cannot do without me. I will only wed for love. I will have no man for wealth, for I have wealth enough. Or for a title. I am a duke's daughter. I will only marry the man who loves me unconditionally. *You!*"

"I am not in love with you," he said, almost angrily.

"Of course you are. You simply will not admit it," she replied with infuriating logic. "Grandmama says you fear to love because of your parents' unhappy alliance."

He grabbed her by her soft shoulders, his fingers digging cruelly into the soft flesh. "*I will not love you!*" he said in a fierce tone.

"*Yes, you will!*" Cynara replied, and then they were kissing, and one kiss melted into the other until they were both breathless.

His hands dropped from her shoulders, and he looked bemused.

"You have bruised me," Cynara complained at him. There were marks where he had held her and her lips ached, but whether from his lips, or the loss of them she could not determine.

"I can see the pulse at the base of your throat," he said. Reaching out, he touched it with the tip of his finger.

"You excite me," she responded.

"'Oddsfish, madame, you are bold!" he told her.

"What am I to say to such a remark, my lord? Would you have preferred that I stammer and blush like some little ninny?"

"Damn it, Cyn, what am I to do with you?" he asked her.

"I think you know the answer to that question, my lord, but you are not ready yet. There is still too much bitterness, cynicism, anger, and fear within you. It is to be hoped that in time my devotion to you can overcome the hurt done to you."

"I want nothing of you but your luscious body," he said cruelly.

To his surprise Cynara laughed and replied, "You may have it any time you choose, my lord. I am yours, and none other shall have me but you." The look of utter confusion upon his face made her laugh again, and she told him, "I believe I have won this round between us as well, my darling Wickedness."

With a smothered oath he flung himself away from her and walked back up the broad lawns to the house.

Cynara remained where she was, by the riverbank. There was a sudden ache in her chest, and she realized that she hurt for him. What was happening to her? For the first time in her life, she was thinking about someone else and not herself. Her grandmother had told her much of what Jonah Kira had reported about Harry Summers's early years. Well, they had both had rough beginnings, yet they had survived. But Cynara knew that her survival was due to her mother's great love for both Charlie, the not-so-royal Stuart, and for the child she bore him in secret—alone but for a single elderly servant, in the early summer following the royal Stuart's defeat at Worcester.

Her mother had told her often of those early days, and years. Barbara Carver, the widow of Squire Randall, had sheltered her lover and his brother after the battle of Worcester. Charlie had spent but a single night with her, but in that night Cynara had been conceived. By the time it was safe for the duke of Glenkirk to go north to Scotland, Barbara had a suspicion that she was with child. She said nothing. And then she and Lucy, her old servant, were alone again in her house on the hill, isolated and off the main track.

By December she could no longer fool herself and confided to old Lucy. The servant nodded, for she had suspected her mistress's condition. "We'll manage," was all she said, and Barbara almost wept with her relief, realizing now that she was not really alone. When the spring came again Sir Peter, her Puritan protector, had come to visit her. She had not seen him in seven months and had hoped that he would not come again. Seeing Barbara in the pale blue smock that modestly covered her belly, he blanched.

"It is not yours," Barbara quickly reassured him. She knew that Sir Peter feared his wife, and a bastard child by Mistress Randall could destroy his standing in the community and lessen his power as the local magistrate.

"You have an explanation, madame?" he demanded of her as if he had the right.

"After your departure last September," she told him, and she sat heavily, her head in her hand for effect, "some Cavaliers escaping the battle at Worcester forced their way into my house. Do not, I pray you, ask me what happened!" She sobbed dramatically.

"Oh, my poor girl," Sir Peter replied sympathetically. "How can I aid you?"

"You must keep my secret, sir," she said simply. "It is not my fault or indeed that of the poor child I carry. I will raise it alone as best I can."

"But someone is eventually bound to learn of what has happened to you, Barbara," he protested. "Give the child to a farmer's wife to care for so that your reputation is protected. If no one sees the child, they will not know of your shame."

"You have been kind to me," Barbara replied, "and I am grateful for your advice, Sir Peter, but you must never come here again lest someone think I have made up the story of my child's conception in order to protect you." She looked at him, smiling wanly. She knew him well. His good character meant more to him than anything else in his life.

He took up both her hands in his and kissed them. A surprisingly tender gesture, she thought, as she remarked to her daughter years later. "You are, as always, my dear Barbara, wise and loving. That you would consider me in your despair is most Christian. But you are right though I shall miss our little *visits*. If you should need any-thing, please send to me. I will do whatever I can to help you." He knew that she would most likely ask him for naught, and that he would never see her again. She could see the relief mixed with sadness as he rode away.

Cynara was born nine months to the day the king and his forces were beaten at Worcester. England was now firmly in the cold grip of Oliver Cromwell, and his Puritan allies; at Hilltop House, however, life went on as it always had, but for the addition of an infant into their midst. Barbara's tenants tilled the fields, tended the orchard, and brought in the crops. They asked no questions about the baby although they had their own thoughts. Grain was taken to the miller, ground, and returned as flour. Cider was made. One of her tenants paid his rents in sausage, bacon, and ham. Another hung a side of beef in her cold larder. She and Lucy tended their poultry flock, and each morning Lucy's granddaughter came to milk the cows so they might have milk, cheese, and butter.

Nothing was said about the baby now nursing at her mother's full breasts. But when her mother needed to be elsewhere on her lands, there was always a farmer's wife or daughter ready to watch over Cynara for a few hours. Her name defied them, however. *Cynara*. It was so elegant and drew attention to the fast-growing little girl. Why had her mother not named her something simple, like Jane, or Mary, or Elizabeth? They did not dare ask Mistress Randall, and all old Lucy would say was, "She will be a great lady one day for her sire is a great man."

But even in the country the Commonwealth brought hard times. By the time Cynara was four and running about, food was becoming harder to obtain. The miller demanded a greater toll of the grain that he might sell it to feed his large family. It was all Barbara could do to keep her poultry safe from the thieves now roaming the countryside. They took to bringing the chickens and geese into the house at night. One of her tenants gave her a dog saying he could not feed more than one beast any longer, and she would need a good watchdog. He was right. More often than not the barking of Lad sent strangers turning away from Hilltop House. Barbara and her servant took to eating one scant meal a day so that the child might have more food, what little there was of it.

Cynara's only company now was her mother, Lucy, and the dog,

Lad. She did not remember other children for it had been two years since she had seen any. The autumn she was four her mother began to teach her letters and numbers. Over the next few years, she learned to read, and to write, and to do her sums. Cynara was surprisingly good with her sums.

"There might be a bit of the merchant in you, my child," her mother said once.

But Cynara had also learned from Barbara who her father was, and she replied, "I am a Stuart, madame. We are not merchants."

Barbara had been forced to laugh then. "My father was a merchant, my daughter," she said, "and your father's grandmother was a great merchant queen. Your family's wealth come from trade."

"Then why are we so poor?" Cynara had demanded to know.

"Because these are hard times, and your papa is not with us," Barbara replied honestly. "Your father and I are not wed, Cynara, and he does not even know of your existence. But one day he will come back to us, and he will love you every bit as much as I do," Barbara promised.

So they had continued to live alone, isolated on that hilltop, rarely seeing anyone but Barbara's three tenants when they came to pay their rents. And one year they could not pay at all, and came hats in hand to tell the squire's widow.

"You must survive as best you can as will I," she told them. "One cannot get blood from a stone. Do your best. We will have good times again one day."

The three farmers departed, realizing as they went what a fine mistress they had who would let them off so lightly, even under these trying circumstances. The one with the pigs, however, returned several days later with a small ham and some bacon, saying his wife had scolded him for not at least sharing what little they had with so good a mistress. Barbara had thanked the farmer, and gratefully stored the ham and the bacon in her larder. She would have Lucy eke it out over the winter months.

Cynara never understood that they were in danger because of the blood in her veins; or that her mother lived in fear of the authorities learning about her child. A child who was related to the exiled king. And then the Protector, Oliver Cromwell, died. His son, a weakling, could not hold England. After eight years the king was sent for; negotiations settled; and Charles Stuart, the king, returned home to England, riding into London on his thirtieth birthday. And with him came his cousin, Charlie, the not-so-royal Stuart, who as soon as he was able rode northwest to his home, *and to the woman he had left behind.*

It was right after her eighth birthday when he came riding up to Hilltop House. Cynara, out in the fields playing, had seen him first. She ran quickly to tell her mother that a stranger was approaching. Barbara, her gun behind the front door, had looked out at the rider and recognized him immediately. Picking up her skirts she ran from her house, and down the path to meet him, crying his name as she went. Cynara had watched in amazement as the man jumped from his horse, and wrapping his arms about her mother, kissed her fiercely. Barbara was both laughing and crying at the same time. She engaged him in earnest conversation, and suddenly the man swung about to look at the child watching him. Their eyes met, and Cynara knew in an instant that this was her father.

With a sharp cry of joy she raced into his arms, crying, "Papa! Papa! You have come home to us as mama said you would!"

"I have indeed, little one," he agreed, and he kissed her cheek most soundly. "And what a wonderful surprise your mama had for me."

"What surprise, Papa? What surprise?" Cynara asked eagerly.

"Why you, Cynara Mary Stuart! You are my surprise, and your mama could not have given me a better gift than you, my daughter."

And from that day on Cynara had enough food to eat, and her gowns were no longer too short, or patched until they could not be patched any longer. And the house was warm that winter for the first time in Cynara's memory. No one's hands, or feet grew red, and chapped. And old Lucy died, which sent Cynara's mother into a spate of mourning, for the servant had been with Barbara since she married her first husband, Squire Randall. Cynara's father, however, sent a young serving woman from his own estate, to look after them.

"Will my father marry you, Mama?" Cynara had asked her mother that autumn before their old Lucy died.

"*Yes!*" the duke said as entering the house he overheard the child's question. "But first I must make my house habitable again, and my youngest sister needs me, for she mourns her husband who has died. I am taking her to court in hopes of cheering her up. But I promise you, Cynara, that your mother will be my duchess, if she will have me. What say you, Barbara Carver, my first and now last love? Again I ask, will you marry me, and be my darling wife?"

"Yes," Barbara had answered. "And tomorrow you will go and try to help poor Autumn overcome her malaise."

But before her parents were able to wed, there was the business of legitimizing his daughter. Charlie, the not-so-royal Stuart, would not allow the stain of bastardy to besmirch his youngest child. And then there was the business of his eldest daughter, Sabrina, marrying. One thing after another seemed to stand between the duke and his beloved until finally his mother put her foot down.

"Sabrina is wed. The boys are at court, and Freddie plans to go to university. Cynara is legitimized. The house is in good repair, and even Autumn is settled. Fetch Barbara and your daughter! Bring them home to Queen's Malvern. You will be wed before Cynara's eleventh birthday, Charlie, or I will know the reason!"

And so they were, as her grandmother had told her. Cynara smiled at the memory, looking out over the River Cam. It was beginning to grow dark now. She turned away from the river and walked back up to the house where there was still a great crowd filling the king's dwelling. She sought out her grandmother and said, "Can we go home now, Grandmama?"

"I see no point in remaining," Jasmine answered her. She looked at the girl. "Have you and Harry Summers said what you needed to say to each other tonight?"

"Yes," Cynara replied with a smile. "He is a very stubborn man, Grandmama, but I shall not give up."

Jasmine sighed. "He will not be easy, my child. But pursue him until you either bring him to your will or grow tired of the game. You will not be satisfied otherwise, I think." She arose. "Give me your arm, Cynara. These late hours the king keeps will be the death of me." She leaned lightly on the younger woman.

"Grandmama!" Cynara laughed. "It isn't quite nine o'clock of the evening. Surely you have kept later hours."

"A very long time ago," Jasmine chuckled as they made their way from Audley End outside to where a senior servant, seeing the dowager duchess of Glenkirk coming, called for the duke of Lundy's coach.

"Have you arranged to meet him again?" Jasmine asked Cynara when they were finally settled in the coach and on their way to High Manor House, the duke of Lundy's dwelling at Newmarket.

"Nay, he ran away from me, but I have already learned when and where he rides in the morning. We shall meet on the morrow."

"It was not necessary to pursue young men in my day. 'Twas they who pursued you," Jasmine said. "At the time I thought it annoying, but in retrospect, my dear child, there was a certain orderliness to such on arrangement. This modern world in which we live can be rather confusing," she decided.

"But you also had arranged marriages," Cynara noted.

"Indeed we did," Jasmine agreed, "but 'twas not such a bad thing. My grandmother would have never allowed Rowan Lindley to marry me if she had not been entirely convinced that he loved me. She wanted me happy, but she also knew that marriage was what I needed. She was a very wise woman, Madame Skye."

"But the king arranged your marriage with Lord Leslie, and you ran away from him," Cynara reminded Jasmine.

"Ohh, that was simply because Jemmie was being such a pompous fool. Grandmama finally sent him my way when she decided that I had punished him enough," Jasmine laughed. "And God only knows how happy I was with my Jemmie. I wish you had known him, Cynara. You should have liked him very much, and he you."

"Papa remembers him as his only father," Cynara told her grandmother. "I wonder if Prince Henry would have married you had he lived. I'll bet he would have defied the world for you!"

"I would not have married Prince Henry, Cynara, even if he had gotten down on his knees and begged me," Jasmine said quietly. "It was Hal's duty to wed with France, or Spain, or some other important alliance. He had to wed for the good of England. Princes and princesses are rarely allowed to follow their hearts, I fear."

"But you might have been queen of England, Grandmama!" Cynara cried.

"Cynara, even though I was the daughter of the Grande Mughal of India, the offspring of his last wife, Christianity does not recognize plural marriages. In this world I was considered bastard born. No one, of course, would have dared to say it aloud because my grandmother was a great lady with even greater wealth and the ability to cultivate power and powerful friends. That, and my own proud attitude, saved me from ignominy, Cynara. *I was the Mughal's daughter.* If the English were too ignorant to understand what that meant, I could certainly not be held responsible for their lack of knowledge. Neither my grandmother nor I ever permitted anyone to treat me as any less than I was. I can but hope that you will exhibit the same pride in your dealings with the earl of Summersfield. Still, as a princess born I fully understood the duty your grandfather, the prince, had to his family and to his kingdom. One reason King James and Queen Anne loved me so was that I did comprehend my duty far better than their son. Had he lived they knew I should have never asked him for marriage. Henry Stuart was born for an important alliance. It is tragic that he did not live long enough to make one and sire a legitimate heir."

"Did you love him, Grandmama?" Cynara asked boldly.

"Yes, I did, but I never told him," Jasmine answered.

"Why on earth not?" the girl cried.

"Because I could not break his heart, child. Because I knew that he would never be mine. I promised myself that when a match was made for him, and announced that I would leave the court and his life that I not intrude upon his marriage," Jasmine explained. "You see how poor Queen Catherine has suffered the Castlemaine woman. The creature, for all her pretensions at a respectable birth, is low and cruel. I could have never done such a thing had Hal taken a wife."

"I think you were very brave and noble, Grandmama," Cynara said admiringly. She had not heard this story before.

"You will, hopefully, not have to give up the man you love, my darling girl," Jasmine told Cynara. "You will have to be very clever to bring him to the altar, but you will win this game you play, Cynara. I know you will win him."

Cynara nodded, and she smiled. "I will, Grandmama. *I will!*" she said, and then she laid her head on her grandmother's shoulder as the carriage moved briskly down the road toward High Manor House.

Harry Summers had watched her go. She was the most beautiful and aggravating creature he had ever come in contact with, and her absolute assurance that they would marry defied him, confounded him, and yet it made him laugh. Did she love him, or was he merely a title? He knew it wasn't his wealth, for hers was greater. And how did he feel about that? Was it honorable to marry a woman who was richer than he was? And he had heard the marquis of Roxley gossiping recently about the legal document that his brother, the duke, had signed when he married Lady Diana Leslie. The duke, his brother said, had had to agree to allow his wife possession of her own wealth and the right to manage that wealth. Harry Summers expected it would be quite the same with Cynara. *Whoever wed her. But certainly not him!*

And yet . . . was he really his father? Cynara was certainly not his mother. His mother had been a gentle soul. Strong willed for she managed to live with his father, yet she had been soft. Cynara was not soft. If Cynara had married a man like his father, she would have probably killed him before she suffered as his mother had suffered. But did a man really want so independent and fiery a girl for his wife? Yet he certainly did not want a woman like his mother.

He still remembered the shock of learning that his mother had betrayed his father and was carrying another man's child. His father had shouted the facts to him as he attempted to protect his mother from his sire's anger yet another time. He recalled his father shouting that his mother was no better than a common whore. That she had a belly full of another man's seed. That he would kill her if he could, and he finally did. Letting his mother miscarry her child. Refusing her pleas to send for the physician, or a midwife. Laughing at her pain, and then going off with his latest mistress to pleasure himself while his wife had died in agony . . .

"Don't marry and bring this misery on another woman," had been his mother's last advice to him.

But was he his father? Cynara's insistence in pursuing him had begun to raise doubts in his own mind. He did not think young Lady Stuart stupid. Why would she chase after him if she did not see something good in him? Or was it just a matter of her great pride that was at stake here? She had evinced an interest in him. He had ignored her, and now she must win his heart to prove a point. But what point?

"Your horse, my lord," the stableman said quietly, breaking into his thoughts.

"My thanks," the earl responded, tossing the man a coin. He mounted his stallion, the very one he had ridden in the park with Cynara. He departed Audley's End, traveling down the same road on his way to his house in Newmarket. Tomorrow he would ride early in the morning; and he would try to sort the jumble of his troubled thoughts. Was he a fool to even consider that he might marry like other men? The more he thought about it, the more confused he became. He kicked his horse into a canter, and let the cool night wind soothe his soul as he rode.

Chapter

18

A delicate mist-like mauve haze hung over the rolling heathland that surrounded Newmarket and vicinity. The air was barely still, and the faint scent of the newly greening field perfumed the early morning. A fox moved stealthily through the grass hunting its breakfast, which even now nibbled upon new clover unaware. Above the land, the sky was a cloudless and clear blue as the sun rose over the horizon in a blaze of reds and golds causing a nearby blackbird to burst into sweet song.

In a small grove of trees crowning a hillock, Lady Cynara Stuart sat atop her black stallion watching and waiting. He rode this way every morning, she had learned from a groom in her father's stables, who had been well paid to uncover this very fact. He would not escape her today. And then she heard the *thrum-thrum* of hooves coming at a canter. She reined in Fluffy, who, hearing the sound, too, began to grow restless.

"Not yet, my beauty," she cautioned him. "Not quite yet." And then as the earl of Summersfield's horse came almost abreast with her, Cynara kicked her own stallion and burst forth from the grove at a gallop dashing ahead of the other animal in challenge.

The earl's mount reared, and Harry Summers swore quite distinctly. Then he chased after the other rider to whom he intended giving a piece of his mind. The black horse ahead of him seemed to eat up the earth beneath his feet as his own dark chestnut struggled to gain even ground with the other animal. Then suddenly he recognized both horse and rider. He laughed aloud and pushed his own beast harder for he had no intention of allowing the little witch to best him again. Slowly, slowly he began to gain, and then he pulled ahead of the black stallion racing across the heath for another few minutes before pulling his exhausted mount to a sharp stop while wheeling it about to face his opponent.

"Madam" he said, laughing as Cynara drew her horse to a standstill before him, "you are, I think, quite mad. How did you know I ride this path and at this particular hour?"

"My groom told me," she answered. "I had him bribe one of the men in your stables, my lord. Certainly you know that servants, especially lower servants, are always willing to be bribed." She grinned mischievously at him.

He had to laugh again. One of the things he liked about Cynara was that she was so damned frank with him. She didn't pretend or dissemble.

"Haven't you ever bribed a servant?" she asked him.

"I have never felt the need to do so," he told her.

"Then your purse is undoubtedly heavier than mine is," she said candidly. "I have not time to sneak about obtaining the bits of information that I need to know. It's easier to bribe a servant to learn those facts," she admitted.

"Ahh, I see now that patience is not a strong suit with you, madam. You reveal yourself to me without realizing it," he told her.

"I would reveal *all* to you, my lord," she murmured.

"Behave yourself, you bold baggage!" he scolded her.

"I thought you liked women who were open about themselves, and their desires," Cynara replied. "'Tis said of you that you consort with whores because they do not pretend to be other than they are. I would have you see that I am nothing other than a woman who wants you."

"You are not a woman, or so you claim," he said through now gritted teeth. There she sat upon her horse, but inches from him, and he was already lusting after her again with a ferocity he couldn't believe within himself.

"Aye, I am not yet a woman, my lord, and whose fault is that?" she demanded of him. She was a witch!

"I will not marry," he half-shouted, causing his horse to jump nervously for his voice was thick with his emotions.

"I did not ask you to marry me," Cynara responded, "although one day I expect you will. But not until you have come to realize that you love me, my dear Wickedness. I shall not marry a man who does not love me, or have the courage to admit he does. We are not, however, speaking of love or marriage right now. We are speaking of *making love*, which is an entirely different proposition altogether, my lord. *Is it not?*" She smiled seductively at him. "Do you not want to make love to me, darling Wickedness? Many men do, and they would kill for the opportunity I am offering to you."

"Are you offering to be my *whore*, madam?" he asked her scathingly.

"I am offering you my virtue, my lord," Cynara said quietly.

"*Why?*" His look was a hard one.

"Because I love you," she answered him simply. "I have never before said those words to any man, even in jest, my lord." Her gaze was steady and never left his.

"You don't know me, foolish girl! How can you love me when you know nothing about me?" Now he was shouting, and his stallion danced nervously as did Cynara's horse.

"I know *all* there is to know about you, my lord," she told him. "Did you think my family would allow me my pursuit of you without learning all they could? But even before they did, and before they told me, I loved you. I saw the sadness and the hopelessness in your eyes, Wickedness, and I knew that look. I wanted to make it go away even as my father sent it finally from my mother's eyes! You will one day realize my sincerity and wed me as you should. I am, after all, the perfect wife for you, for I understand your demons and can tame them. But until that day comes I see no reason we should deny ourselves the pleasures of our bodies. I want none but you! I shall have none but you! Surely by now even a stubborn-headed man like yourself can understand that simple fact!" Her voice had risen in intensity as she spoke, and she glared at him furiously.

"*My God! My God!*" he said, astounded, and then kicking his horse he cantered away from her. To his surprise she did not follow. He realized with shock that perhaps she did indeed know him well, or at least better than he had assumed. What kind of a girl offered herself so boldly to a man? Women, even the best of them, simply could not be trusted. Had not his own mother proved that point to him? And had she not with her dying breath warned him against marriage?

But he wanted Cynara Stuart with every fiber of his being. She tempted him. She taunted him. She had begun to people his dreams so that he dared not sleep for too long lest she come to him, seducing him with her innocence. Yet this was a duke's daughter, and kin to the king himself. Unless he was willing to make her father a respectable offer for Cynara's hand in marriage, he would not have her. And what if he dared to make that offer and was refused? Cynara might say what she would, but she was still nothing more than a female and subject to the will of her guardian, in this case her father, the duke of Lundy. He had to put the wench from his mind!

She watched him ride off, struggling with herself not to go after him, to press her case further. But she knew that her admissions had probably startled him enough. He would need time to come to terms with her love. It would not be easy for him. He distrusted women, and he feared marriage. *I shall have to seduce him,* she thought to herself. *And when he proposes marriage out of guilt, I shall refuse him, and I shall keep refusing him until the day he admits his love for me. On that day he will be ready to wed, and not a moment before. We will be divinely happy.*

It was an audacious plan, Cynara knew, but she could not see that she had any other choice in the matter. Why men could simply not listen to their hearts she did not know. He had a heart, and it was troubling him, she realized else he would have never ridden away from her. Had he been the rogue he fancied himself, he would have lifted her down from her stallion and made love to her right there in the new grass upon the heath. After all, had she not given him permission to do so? But he had not. Instead he had fled her.

Another less astute girl might have considered that the earl of Summersfield did not want her, but he did. Cynara had seen the longing in his green eyes every time he looked at her. She respected the power of his will that he did not give in easily to his desires. It bespoke a man of good common sense, although Harry Summers might have laughed at this analysis of his character. Cynara gently moved Fluffy into a canter as she rode home, considering just what her next move was going to be.

When she arrived back at her father's house, she found her grandmother alone in the dining room. She was surprised for it was unusual for Jasmine to arise this early, and even more unusual for her to break her fast publicly. Cynara knew at once her grandmother wanted to know what had transpired and was not willing to wait for Cynara to come to her.

"I met him along the path, and we rode together," she said to the older woman, as helping herself to eggs and ham, she sat down.

"You learned his route and waited?" Jasmine replied.

"Aye," Cynara admitted, eating heartily.

"*And?*" her grandmother demanded.

"I do not know yet," Cynara answered honestly.

Jasmine nodded. "It is wise of you to consider carefully what you will do next. You are certain?"

Cynara nodded. "I hate every moment I am not with him! I ache that his heart is so bruised, Grandmama. I would heal him if he would but allow me, but he is not yet ready for my tenderness," she said quietly. "I must practice patience," Cynara mocked herself.

"It is not a Stuart trait," Jasmine chuckled. "You remind me of myself at your age, but you also remind me very strongly of your grandfather, Prince Henry Stuart. Hal was not a man to be denied. When he wanted something he took it, and he never regretted his actions."

"Papa is not like that," Cynara said.

"Your grandfather died before his nineteenth birthday, my dear child. Who knows what he would have been like at your father's age.

At nineteen, however, he was still filled with the joys of his youth. Your father is now well into his middle years. You cannot judge them side by side," Jasmine said. Then she smiled. "Yet I suspect your father is more like my father. Charlie considers well in advance the consequences of his actions. My father was very much like that. Prince Henry was certainly not." Jasmine reached out and took Cynara's hand in hers. "You would do well to consider the affects this battle you wage with the earl of Summersfield will have upon you both when it is over and done with, my dear child. His soul may be too damaged for you to reclaim."

"Nay, Grandmama, it is not," Cynara assured Jasmine. "He has already exhibited a conscience to me."

"So," Jasmine replied with a smile, "you are tempting him, are you?" She laughed. "Try not to cause a scandal, Cynara. I do not think your poor papa could countenance it. As for your mama, I believe she used all of her strength up in those years you lived alone on your hilltop. She is more fragile now than she used to be."

"I cannot promise to be good," Cynara responded.

Jasmine laughed. "Whatever happens, child, I am here for you, I assure you," she told her granddaughter. And then she changed the subject. "The king is to hold a special race in two weeks. He will offer a plate flacon worth thirty-two pounds to the winner. Of course, it is the honor involved that is of importance, not the purse."

"The jockeys will not think so, Grandmama. Thirty-two pounds is a small fortune to any of them. Papa will enter a horse, I assume."

"Naturally," Jasmine answered. "And Tom Jenkins will ride it, I'm certain. He's the best jockey in England, and we are fortunate to have him in our employ."

"Hmmm," Cynara said thoughtfully as she mopped her plate with a piece of bread. "Wickedness will surely enter one of his horses, Grandmama. I must learn more. When is the race to be held?"

"On the thirtieth of March," Jasmine replied. "What mischief are you planning now, girl? *Remember!* No scandals!"

"Not at all, Grandmama," Cynara said sweetly. "Now tell me how

Fancy gets on? And is Siren really expecting a child? I cannot imagine her a mama. My uncle in Scotland must be delighted."

"Little Lady Christina thrives and is, I am told, showing signs of cutting a tooth," Jasmine said, "and yes, Diana is with child. It should be born nine months to the day of her marriage to Damien. Your uncle Patrick could surely ask no more of her than that," Jasmine chuckled. "They will not come to Queen's Malvern this summer. Flanna will go to Roxley in mid-August to be with her daughter, but you know Patrick. He will not give up his grouse season even for his first grandchild. He will come later. I shall see them both there after the child is born."

"I do not know if I shall go home this summer," Cynara ventured.

"And why not?" her grandmother demanded.

"I am afraid to leave him," Cynara said softly.

"We will ask him to Queen's Malvern," Jasmine answered.

"He will not come, I suspect, unless, of course, I can make greater progress between now and June," Cynara replied. "He is not the Roxley boys panting after my cousin, Diana."

"Nay," Jasmine sighed in agreement. "He is not. Perhaps, however, your best course would be to leave him, and let him realize just how much he needs you, Cynara."

"I don't know," Cynara said slowly.

"You will not until it is time to return to Queen's Malvern, my child. Your parents will not allow you to remain at court unchaperoned, and your father already chafes to return home. You will be fortunate to get him to return to Greenwich in May and then Whitehall before the king adjourns to Windsor for the summer months."

"I cannot go home from Newmarket next month," Cynara said in desperate tones. "*I cannot!*"

"I will see your father allows you to return to court until June," Jasmine pledged to her granddaughter. "But I can promise no more, child."

"It will have to be enough time," Cynara said almost to herself. Then she smiled at Jasmine. "Will you be attending the races today?"

"I shall not miss a one," Jasmine said returning the smile. "And with luck I shall win a great deal of money."

"You might lose," Cynara said.

"I never lose," Jasmine responded.

"Neither do I," Cynara replied with a chuckle.

The race course at Newmarket was four miles of short meadow grass in length. It was marked at specific intervals by tall white-washed posts that had been driven deep into the ground. It was the custom for the king and his court to wait upon their own mounts on either side of the course at the halfway point for the racers, who once past, would be followed to the finish line by the king and the court.

Charles Stuart, the king, kept four jockeys in his employ and had a large stable at Newmarket. He was known to race occasionally himself and insisted upon winning fairly. A good sport, he was always known to congratulate those who beat him, and he held no grudges. Many in the court could neither afford horses nor wagering, but they came to Newmarket anyway, living in tents and pavilions that had been set up about the town for their accommodation. Cynara knew how fortunate those who had horses were.

She did not see the earl of Summersfield for several days after that morning ride. He seemed to have disappeared, but she knew he was there. He obviously enjoyed playing hide-and-seek with her. But Cynara spent her time learning what the earl would do regarding the king's plate race on the thirtieth of March. It took more coin than she had anticipated this time, for the earl had obviously scolded his servants for accepting bribes. Eventually, however, her groom was able to learn what she wished to know. The earl of Summersfield would be racing his own stallion himself in the king's race. If he won it would be an honor. If he lost, it would have been nothing more than a good ride and would cost him nothing.

The duke of Lundy's jockey, Tom Jenkins, would be riding her father's current champion, Shadow Wind. Cynara knew that she could not bribe Jenkins with any amount of gold. His reputation and his pride in his employer would forbid it. Still, if the earl of Summersfield was to ride in the race, then so would Cynara Stuart.

She didn't think any woman had ridden at Newmarket previously. When she was discovered, it would cause quite a stir. Cynara laughed to herself. She fully intended beating Harry Summers, and she fully intended that he know it.

"What mischief are you planning?" Jasmine asked her granddaughter, sensing that something was afoot.

"No scandal, Grandmama," Cynara laughed, "but perhaps I shall give the court something to chatter about."

The day of the race was upon them. It dawned sunny but windy. The court assembled at the track to enjoy the horses. The plate race would be the third gallop of the day. The crowd milled about chattering, some upon horses, others in fancy carts, and others on foot. Jasmine upon her Arab mare found herself next to a charming little carriage containing the king's mistress, Nellie Gwyn.

"You seem to be missing one of your party," Nellie remarked low, her bright hazel eyes looking about for Cynara. Only Jasmine heard her.

"Would you know what she is about, Mistress Gwyn?" the dowager asked the royal favorite.

Nellie shook her chestnut red curls. "I have hardly seen her since we arrived at Newmarket, madame."

"It is something to do with her passion," murmured the older woman. "She says she will cause the court to chatter." Then Jasmine laughed. "I was every bit as headstrong at her age, but I had not the Stuart's blood coursing through my veins as well."

"And who kept you in check, madame?" Nellie asked, curious.

"My grandmother," Jasmine smiled. "I am trying to be the friend to Cynara that Madame Skye was to me, but as I remember it, I was not quite as reckless. At least not all the time," she amended.

"Oh, look!" Nellie cried. "I can see the first of the riders coming. It is a large field for the king's cup." Then Nellie stared hard. "Lord love a duck!" she gasped, her hand going to her mouth. "Oh! Oh! It cannot be! *It can't!*"

"What is it?" Jasmine demanded of the young woman. "Tell me, Mistress Gwyn! What is it you see?"

"Do you see the first three riders in the lead, madame? They are practically neck and neck with each other," Nellie replied. "One is your son's jockey and horse. The second is the earl of Summersfield. But look to the third rider. The one in black, wearing the black-and-white domino cap. I would stake my life that it is Cyn herself on that big black stallion of hers. Look, madame! Look closely as they pass us," Nellie cried as the thunder of racing hooves drew abreast of the spectators on either side of the track.

Jasmine stared, and then the oath issued forth from her mouth. *"God's bloody blood!"* For Nellie Gwyn was absolutely correct. It was Cynara upon her stallion racing toward the finish for all she was worth. Jasmine saw the duke's jockey lash out with his whip toward the rider of the black stallion, but the girl saw it, too, and blocked the blow with her own crop, which knocked Tom Jenkins's cap from his head. The crown roared its approval. There were several shouts of *Well done!* at the defense put up by the black stallion's rider against Jenkins's unsportsman-like conduct.

Cynara bent low over her horse urging him onward. She had always known that Fluffy was extremely fast. He and her father's entry were brothers, born to different dams but sired by the same father. Shadow Wind had begun to fall behind slightly, but the earl's dark chestnut was neck and neck with her. Cynara leaned forward in her saddle, her legs gripping her mount hard. "Come on, boy! Just a bit longer!" she begged him, and she actually felt him increase his speed just slightly. The chestnut, however, kept pace with him, for the earl of Summersfield was every bit as intent upon winning the race as was she.

Cynara saw the finish posts ahead of her. One or the other of them had to gain a bit more speed, but she could feel Fluffy beginning to flag just slightly. She raised her whip, not to strike her mount, but to gain the attention of her opponent. The earl of Summersfield saw the movement out of the corner of his eye. He turned his head to look. His eyes widened with surprise, and in that moment Cynara spurred her stallion forward by just a head and propelled them over the finish line laughing, even as she pulled off her cap, allowing her sable black hair to cascade forth in the breeze.

A roar of surprise went up from the crowd. Around her the other riders came thundering over the finish. From the look on Harry Summers's face, it was clear he didn't know whether to be angry or amused. He decided upon the latter. What a girl she was, he thought as he began to laugh himself at the huge joke she had played on them all. The king rode up slowly and, seeing what all the fuss was about, raised one very black eyebrow.

"Well, Cousin Cynara, it would seem you have fooled us all, and bested even your papa's jockey, whom I believe will protest your victory," he said with a chuckle.

"I know of no rule that says a woman cannot ride in your race, Your Majesty," Cynara said pertly. "Tom Jenkins was a distant third. If anyone has call to protest, it is the earl of Summersfield."

"And do you protest, Wickedness?" the king asked, curious as to what the earl's reply would be.

"I do not, Your Majesty. It was a fair race, fairly run, and fairly won. Lady Stuart bested us all. The prize should be hers," Harry Summers said graciously.

"Well, Cousin, it would seem you have surprised everyone this day," the king said.

"I have indeed, Your Majesty," Cynara replied grinning mischievously, and the king laughed heartily.

"You are a true Stuart, Cousin," he chuckled. "*A true Stuart.* You must promise me, however, that you will play no more merry pranks such as this one. It was very dangerous. Your poor mama looks near to swooning with your naughty conduct. Your grandmama, however, is more amused than angry. Your papa, however, is another matter, pretty Cyn. I will present you with your prize and then leave you to make your peace with him." And Charles Stuart, the king, handed his cousin the plate flacon while Charles Stuart, the duke of Lundy, glowered nearby at his daughter.

Cynara thanked the king prettily and then turning said to her father, "Here, Papa, is a trophy for your stables as Fluffy is one of our horses. I apologize for besting Shadow Wind, but you must certainly reprimand Tom Jenkins for striking out at another rider."

"*Go home at once!*" the duke of Lundy said in tones such as Cynara had never before heard her father use.

"Yes, Papa," she said, for one look at his face had told her this was neither the time nor the place to argue with him. She turned meekly away and departed the track.

"Be careful, Charlie," his mother warned him. "She has done nothing wrong, only outrageous. The king is not angry so neither must you be."

"She could have been killed! Crippled! Trampled to death!" the duke almost shouted at his mother.

"But she was not," Jasmine replied quietly.

"I think," the duchess of Lundy said in a weak voice for she was still horrified by her daughter's risky conduct, "that we must make a match for Cynara now, Charlie. She has to be married and settled before she ruins herself entirely! I have always thought myself a strong woman, but I can bear no more of her reckless conduct."

"I agree!" the not-so-royal Stuart said.

"*I do not!*" his mother interjected her own opinion. "The worst thing you could do right now is attempt to force Cynara into a marriage she does not want. She has made her wishes in the matter quite plain to all of you." The dowager turned her glance to the earl of Summersfield and said, "Will you allow this happen, my lord, because you have not the courage to admit the truth to yourself?"

Harry Summers looked stricken, and then with a muffled sound of distress, he turned and walked away.

"*What is this?*" the king inquired, curious.

"He is in love with Cynara, but will neither admit it to himself nor marry her. And all because he fears it will turn out like the marriage of his wretched parents," Jasmine said in decidedly irritated tones.

"It is said he killed his sire," the king noted.

"*Your Majesty!*" Jasmine said, now fully exasperated by the entire situation. "Do you think I should encourage my granddaughter in her pursuit of the Earl of Summersfield if that were true? I have fully investigated him, *and his family*, for I have my sources. I do not wish to see any member of my family harmed if I can prevent it. The story is too long and involved for me to tell here, but I assure you that the earl of Summersfield did not slay his father. Although from what I have learned of the man, it is a wonder he lived as long as he did!"

"Your judgment has always been impeccable, madame," the king said. "I hope that eventually you will tell me the entire tale."

"Her judgment is impeccable except where Cynara is concerned," the duke of Lundy said angrily. "My wife is correct in this matter. Cynara *must* be married to a respectable man as soon as I can find a man to take her and given her behavior, I do not know who would want her at all!"

"Ohh," his mother said scathingly, "I am certain you will find someone delighted to take her for her fortune and her position. Someone who will mistreat her and make her utterly miserable, but then Charlie, she will not be your problem. She will be his, whoever he is! I never thought I should live to see the day when you would relinquish your responsibilities to your own child."

The duke of Lundy was stunned by his mother's criticism, but before he might reply, and drive a wedge between them, the king intervened.

"Cousin," he said, "will you trust me to negotiate this matter for you, for are we not family? Look discreetly about, if it pleases you, for a suitable match for Cynara, but make no match for her. I agree with your mama that she must be allowed to pursue her passion for Wickedness to its end, whatever that end may be. If she cannot bring him to the altar, then you must certainly make another arrangement for her. But mayhap she will breach the earl's strong defenses and become his wife. I know you would not have her unhappy, and you, my dear Barbara, certainly understand better than most the unhappiness that comes of true love." The king's dark eyes met those of the beautiful duchess of Lundy, and he patted her soft white hand. Then he turned his look back to his cousin. "Are we agreed, Charlie?"

The duke nodded. "Very well, Cousin, I shall try to keep a rein on my temper, but God only knows it has never been tried as much as by my youngest child."

The king chuckled. "Stuarts, as you know, Cousin, are not known for being easy."

"But they always have great charm," Jasmine said softly, and she gave the king a smile.

'Odsfish! he thought to himself. *She may be an old woman, but for just a moment there I could see what the legend is all about.* He took Jasmine's elegant hand in his and kissed it reverently. "Good day, madame," he said, his eyes meeting hers. Then turning, he walked away.

"I have had more than enough excitement for the day," Jasmine announced "as I am certain you both have. May we go home now?"

The duke of Lundy nodded. Escorting his wife and mother to their carriage, he gave the coachmen orders to return to their house. Both Barbara and his mother hurried upstairs once they had arrived. The duke walked slowly into his library and closed the door behind him. A fire was burning in the hearth, and his daughter was curled in one of the big chairs by the blaze sipping a sherry. She turned and smiled at him.

"I love this room, Papa. I hope that you do not mind sharing it," Cynara said.

The duke poured himself a whiskey and came to join her, sitting opposite his daughter, cradling the crystal tumbler in his cupped hands. "I am sorry for all those years we lost," he began, "and you are intelligent enough to know that I love you, Cynara."

"But?" she said, a little smile touching the corners of her mouth.

"You cannot go on like this," the duke told her. "You will be seventeen in June, Cyn. It is past time you were wed. I have promised the king that I will give you the opportunity you need to capture Harry Summers's heart, but if you have not done so by year's end, Cynara, I will make a match for you, *and you will marry.*"

She said nothing to his great surprise.

"What?" he asked, half teasing. "No cries of protest?"

"It would do no good to argue with you, Papa," Cynara replied. "Your mind is quite made up even as mine is. We are alike in that way. A Stuart trait, I suspect."

"You would defy me then?"

"Let us not quarrel, Papa. It has not yet come to that, has it?" Cynara said logically. "What does Grandmama say?"

"She is your champion as always, Cynara," he responded dryly.

Cynara laughed softly. "She is an amazing woman, Papa. What a life she has lived!"

"Times were different when she was your age," he said. "And she was a princess born. You are not. You are *my* daughter."

"Be patient with me, Papa," Cynara pleaded prettily. "If you are, we shall both get our way. You shall see me wed, and I will have Wickedness for my husband."

Leaning forward slightly he gently touched her sherry glass with his crystal tumbler. "May God hear your prayers, my daughter."

"I love you, Papa," Cynara told him.

Charlie, the not-so-royal Stuart, sighed deeply. "And I love you, Cynara Mary Stuart," he answered her.

"Even when I drive you to the brink of madness?" she teased.

"Even then," he admitted with a grin.

The peace once again restored between father and daughter, it was decided that despite her outrageous behavior, Cynara would be allowed to go to Audley End tonight, but she would go alone. Both the duke, the duchess and the dowager needed time to recover from Cynara's racing adventure. And it was past time, Jasmine told her son, that Cynara was allowed to go on her own.

"She can get into just as much trouble with you in another room as she can if you remain home," Jasmine said wisely. "Let her go and accept the plaudits she will receive for her daring."

"Barbara will fret," Charlie said.

"Barbara has taken a small sedative in her wine and gone to bed," Jasmine chuckled. "She will never know that Cynara is gone."

"And whose idea was the sedative, I wonder?" the duke murmured.

Jasmine laughed again. "Barbara will be fine once Cynara is safely wed. She fears Cynara's passionate nature, which is not only yours but hers as well. Your daughter cannot help but being filled with the juices of youth."

"Do you really think she can bring Harry Summers to the altar of matrimony, Mama?" the duke wondered.

"If anyone can, it is your daughter," the dowager replied.

And concerned by her father's ultimatum, Cynara even now was bathing while Hester chattered about how all the servants were talking about Lady Cynara's daredevil race this day. "More bath oil," Cynara said, and she took the flask from Hester before she could tip it. Pouring some of the exotic oil into her palm, she massaged it into her arms, her shoulders, her breasts. She rubbed the oil slowly around her neck from throat to nape. She had been as discreet as she had known how, but now she must press the earl's back to the wall and gain an admission of his love. Once he had said it, he would surely propose to her. She poured some of the oil onto her wet head, which she had just washed and glossed it through her sable locks. Then she rinsed her hair, but the fragrance of the gardenias remained.

"Which of yer crow's gowns will you have this evening, m'lady," Hester asked. She always referred to Cynara's black dresses as such.

"No black tonight, Hester," Cynara surprised her maidservant. "I want that pale yellow silk gown. The one with the deep scooped neckline and the puffed sleeves with the lace cuffs. It has a looped-up overskirt, and the underskirt is striped with a slightly deeper yellow."

"Jewelry?" Hester asked, recovering.

"Grandmama has a yellow diamond on a red-gold chain and ear-bobs that match. Go to Orane, and fetch them for me," Cynara said.

"Ohh," Hester laughed. "Yer going to really stick their noses in it tonight, aren't you, m'lady? Or are you, perhaps, going fishing?"

"The latter," Cynara replied frankly. "It is past time that Wickedness admits his passion for me. My father has threatened to make a match for me if he has not declared himself by year's end. I believe it will be far less troublesome to bring the earl around than to have to fend off unwanted suitors."

Laughing, Hester hurried off to fetch the required jewelry. When she returned to her mistress's bedchamber, Cynara was already out of her tub, wrapped in a drying sheet, seated by the fire brushing her hair dry. Within the hour, she was dressed and ready to depart. Her gown was flattering, and both her father and grandmother approved of the color. Her hair was affixed in an elegant chignon with a single lovelock falling over her left shoulder. It was far more suitable than the currently fashionable little curls on either side of the head. Cynara kissed her relations good night and entered her coach. Stretching her legs out, she admired the dainty yellow satin slippers with their pearl daisies. She drew the mink-lined yellow silk cape about her shoulders to keep the evening chill away.

The coach moved off in the direction of Audley End several miles away. For the first time in her life, she was being treated like an adult, Cynara thought. No chaperon, discreet, or otherwise, accompanied her tonight. Her grandmother had calmed her father and convinced him that at almost seventeen she was old enough to go to court without him. It would be no different, of course, except that she would not have to look over her shoulder every now and again to see if she was being observed. Cynara grinned pleased. Tonight she would begin her seduction of the earl of Summersfield in earnest. The day after tomorrow was the first of April. She had but nine months left in which to win him.

At Audley End she was immediately surrounded by courtiers, all interested in speaking with her about her ride in the king's race today. Some were admiring of her skill. Some were openly scathing about her unladylike behavior. Others were suddenly seeing Cynara Stuart in a brand-new light and were anxious to pay her court. She accepted with grace the compliments of her admirers and haughtily ignored her detractors. To those whom she recognized as suitors, she was ambivalent. But nowhere in the crowds that evening did she see the earl of Summersfield.

"Drat!" she muttered to herself when she was satisfied that he was not there. She had won a handful of coins at both cards and dice. She had chatted with the queen, who rumor had it, was with child. She danced with several eager young men. Finally she decided that if he would not come to her, then she must go to him. "Have my coach brought around," she told a passing footman. And then she slowly made her way from the Great Hall, making the excuse that she was exhausted after her adventures today.

Her carriage was waiting, and she called up to the coachman as she entered the vehicle, "Drive me to the earl of Summersfield's residence at once." And she jiggled the bag of coins she had won at him.

"Yes, m'lady," was the immediate reply. It wasn't up to him to question the duke's daughter, the coachman thought.

The carriage pulled away from the king's residence and down the graveled road. Inside Cynara thought about what she was going to say to him, coming to his home, uninvited. Outside the night was dark. There was a smell of rain in the air. When they finally reached the earl's dwelling and Cynara alighted, she said to her driver, "You will wait for me, Greenleaf."

"Yes, m'lady," the driver called after her as she entered the earl's house through the front door, opened by a servant. Then he settled back upon his box, pulled up the collar of his cape against the damp night air, and brought out his pipe.

"You may tell his lordship that Lady Cynara Stuart is here," Cynara told the liveried majordomo.

"Yes, m'lady," came the polite answer, and the majordomo turned disappearing through another door in the circular foyer.

Cynara looked about her. It was all surprisingly tasteful for a bachelor and very modern. The floors were black and white marble squares. A large crystal chandelier hung from the ceiling. There was a sweeping staircase to her left. The majordomo reappeared.

"His lordship says he was not expecting you, m'lady," he told her, looking extremely uncomfortable.

"Where is he?" Cynara asked in measured tones. "And bear in mind that I will be your mistress one day. What is your name?"

"Statler, m'lady. You will find his lordship in his dining room. Allow me to escort you."

"Thank you, Statler," Cynara said sweetly, and she followed the servant across the room and through the door he held open for her and then closed behind her.

"You are persistent," the earl said.

"You did not come to congratulate me at Audley, and so I have come here so you may correct that oversight," Cynara said boldly. God! He was so damned handsome tonight. He was not formally dressed but wore brown velvet breeches and no coat. His shirt was opened, and his bare chest with its light covering of dark hair was visible.

"If you remain here, you know what must happen," he told her, and he drank deeply from the cup in his hand.

"Yes," Cynara said softly. "I know what will happen, but it must happen eventually between us, mustn't it?" She walked over to the table where he sprawled in his chair, and taking the cup from his hand drank from it too.

"I will never marry," he said almost despairingly.

"Of course we will marry one day, Harry. I am not your poor mama, and you are certainly not your dreadful papa. We are Cyn and Wickedness, and we were meant for each other. If you must have me in order to believe my love for you, then so be it."

"If you are not a virgin, I will kill you," he growled.

"Why?" she demanded of him.

"Because the thought of any other man touching you or loving you drives me to madness," he admitted, his eyes meeting hers.

Cynara did not flinch from his gaze. "You had better be very good at this lovemaking, my lord," she told him.

"If you are a virgin," he said, "how will you know if I am or not?" His look was smoldering.

"Women, even virgins, my grandmama says, know such things instinctively," Cynara answered him.

Reaching out, he pulled her between his legs and buried his face in her cleavage, inhaling the exotic fragrance that seemed to surround her. "Oh, vixen!" he cried low. "You weaken my resolve."

"Make love to me!" Cynara commanded him. "Make love to me, my darling Wickedness! I am yours, and you are mine. The game between us is finished. By the dawn we will have both won."

He stood and towering over her, he grasped her by her slender shoulders, looking into her beautiful face. "I dare not marry," he said once again, but Cynara put gentle fingers over his lips to silence him.

"Hush, my love," she said. "Think not about tomorrow, or even yesterday. There is only now, Harry. *Only now!*"

Chapter

19

He was kissing her. He held her head between his two big hands, his thumbs lightly brushing over her cheekbones as his lips moved softly over her lips, her face, her trembling eyelids. He lifted her up onto the table, unlacing the bodice of her gown, drawing it off even as he undid the tapes that fastened it to her skirt. He drew the skirt off first and then her fine lawn petticoats, leaving her in just her lace-edged chemise. Silently he ripped the delicate garment away. He removed her pearl-decorated yellow slippers one at a time. She wore black silk stockings, and he stared, fascinated at the startling contrast between the stockings and her snow-white skin.

"You would deflower me on your dining room table," Cynara whispered. Unable to help herself, she reached out, pulling his open shirt off. His smooth broad chest with its subtly pleasing dark fur was broad and tapered into a narrow waist. Her hands could not help but stroke his wide shoulders.

"You are a feast for the eyes, and to be devoured slowly," he said low. His big hand swept away the few porcelain dishes behind her. They crashed to the floor shattering. On the sideboard was a silver basket of new strawberries. Walking across the room, he brought it back to the table and fed her one.

"Where do you get strawberries this early?" she asked him.

"My gardener has a greenhouse," he told her. "Lie back now,

Cynara," and he gently pushed her down upon the linen cloth although her legs were still draped over the edge of the table. One by one he placed the berries upon her bare torso. Then lifting the silver creamer from its niche in the berry basket, he poured it slowly over the fruit.

Cynara's blue eyes were wide with both surprise and excitement. She gasped softly as lowering his dark head he began to devour each of the berries he had set so carefully upon her naked flesh. And when he had eaten all of the little tart-sweet fruits, his tongue began to lick the cream from her body. *"Ohhhhh!"* Cynara cried.

"You are delicious," he told her low, his warm tongue stroking her gardenia-scented flesh in a sensuous manner. "Do not move now, Cyn," he advised, placing the remaining two berries atop her nipples, and drizzling the remaining cream on them. The dark head was lowered again to quickly eat first one berry and finally the last. Then he began to lick her breasts, removing all the cream, seeking in the deep valley between them for any errant drop of sweet liquid that might have gone astray. The tip of his tongue dipped into her navel removing the last drop he could find. "Did you enjoy that?" he asked her.

"Yes!" she answered him without hesitation.

He pulled her up into a seated position again. "Unlace my breeches, Cynara," he commanded her.

"Are your servants usually so discreet?" she asked as her fingers undid the garment.

"From the moment you entered this room, they knew not to come in unless called," he explained. He drew off his breeches.

"You wear no drawers!" she said, and she blushed.

"Neither do you," he countered, and she laughed. He kissed her again, one hand moving to fondle her breasts. He caressed her slowly, feeling her pulses beneath his fingers as they moved across her body. Gently, he pushed her back again onto the table. "Now, my bold little vixen, I am going to teach you to please me in ways you cannot imagine." The fingers of one hand threaded itself through the thick dark brush upon her mons. He felt her quiver. "Are you afraid?" he asked her softly.

"*No!*" she denied.

"Liar!" he replied, and he laughed. "Give me your hands," and when she obeyed he put them upon the dark curls. "Now, vixen, draw your nether lips asunder for me that I may view your treasures. Do not tell me that you have never touched yourself there, for I am certain that you have. All virgins are curious."

Wordlessly Cynara opened herself to his hot gaze. She watched him curious. So far the things he had done to her were such as she had never imagined.

"Impossible," he finally said softly. "You are perfect." He knelt before her open legs, and then leaning forward he began to touch her with just the tip of his tongue.

"*What are you doing?*" Cynara cried out, and she shuddered.

He lifted his dark head, his eyes were slightly glazed. "I am tasting you," he told her. "Did your grandmama not explain these things to you, my bold vixen?"

"It has been explained to me how a man and a woman couple themselves," Cynara said. "And I have been told that lovers touch."

"I am touching you," he responded.

"I did not know tongues were involved!" she answered nervously.

"My tongue will not hurt you, vixen. Let me have my way with you. You knew that I would from the moment you came here tonight," the earl of Summersfield told Cynara. "And did you not come for the express purpose of being made love to, Cyn?"

"Yes," she whispered, "but I did not know . . ."

"No, you would not if you are the virgin you claim to be, but until I take your maidenhead from you I cannot be certain," he murmured. Then his tongue began to touch her again.

Cynara closed her eyes, and allowed the sensations his actions seemed to arouse in her their free rein. The broad flat surface of the fleshy organ swept over her, birthing sensations that both excited and frightened her. The very tip of his tongue began to worry an acutely sensitive bit of her flesh. "*Oh! Oh!*" Cynara half-sobbed as she experienced an amazing wonder.

He laughed. Her sweet pink flesh was pearlescent with her innocent juices. The look of astonishment upon her face told him more than any words could have. He stood and pushed her back so that she was now spread her full length upon the dining table. He climbed up, sliding between her outspread legs, and kneeling back upon his haunches he stroked her silky thighs, marveling at their whiteness above the black silk of her stockings with their pearl-studded garters. "Did you wear these for me?" he asked, fingering one.

Her heart was hammering. Her entire body felt more alive than she had ever felt, and she was yet a virgin. "I dress to suit myself, Wickedness," she told him pertly.

"I like it that you are not shy about your nudity," he told her. "You have an outrageously beautiful body, Cyn."

She blushed at the compliment, but her gaze did not drop. "When are you going to fuck me?" she asked him directly.

"There is more to making love than just that," he told her.

"Like eating strawberries off my naked form," she teased.

"Yes," he said smiling. "A virgin should be more nervous about fucking for the first time. I have but sought to put your fears at ease, vixen. Are you eager for it then?" God knew he was, the earl thought. Why was he being so considerate and tender of her? His rod was as hard as iron with all of this love play. He wanted to drive himself deep inside of her and make her cry out with pleasure.

Cynara reached out with a single hand, and her fingers wrapped about his engorged love lance. She squeezed it, marveling at its thickness and its great length. "I think I am eager," she told him. "I am in love with you, Wickedness. I have made no secret of it. I should not be here now but that I want my body joined with yours. I want us as one." Her blue eyes looked seriously up at him.

The warmth of her hand enclosing him sent his senses reeling. "Release me, vixen," he growled at her. "I can do nothing while you have me in your grip."

"Take me then, dear Wickedness," she instructed him softly, and her little hand fell away from his member only to reach out, wrapping about his neck, drawing him down to her waiting lips.

With a groan he began to kiss her again. What was it about her that so excited and fascinated him? *You love her,* a voice in his head said loudly, but he silently denied it, and forced the words from his consciousness as her dainty little tongue began to tease at him, taunting his senses into a frenzy as she licked at his face, his throat, and his chest. He forced her back by her shoulders, kissing her beautiful round breasts, still tasting the mixture of gardenia and cream on her nipples, which he suckled roughly making her cry out. His teeth grazed her skin, and her teeth sunk into his shoulder. Their breaths were coming in hard, short pants. Their passions were loosed and fast racing out of control.

"Remember what will happen if I find you are not a virgin," he growled in her ear.

"Why do you dally then, my lord Wickedness?" she taunted him. "Are you afraid to learn the truth and see the proof of my love for you?"

He positioned himself for the onset of her deflowering, his manhood pressing into her flesh inch by inch. She gasped at this new intrusion of her person. He groaned unbelieving at the tightness of her hot and wet sheath. It encased him and squeezed him strongly. A madness overcame him momentarily. He needed to fill her fully, or he would perish with his longing. He pushed forward once again and suddenly found himself blocked in his passage. She had been telling him the truth! He was overwhelmed with a feeling of guilt. *She really was a virgin.* He had to stop! He couldn't do this to her. Not when he had no intention of ever marrying.

But sensing his sudden reluctance Cynara bravely thrust her hips up against him bringing about her downfall. She screamed softly with the pain of her lost virginity. Several tears rolled down her pale cheeks. But then the pain began to subside and drain away. She almost laughed at the stunned look upon his handsome face, but then he bent down and licked the tears from her cheeks.

"You are very willful," he said softly, and then he began to move within her, slowly at first with the long deliberate strokes of his manhood. Then more swiftly until she was gasping for breath.

Her head whirled with the knowledge that she was no longer a virgin. Her body was fiercely and most acutely aware of his hard length as it plumbed the depths of her very soul. She clung to him as if she were afraid of falling. Her head was thrown back on the hard table, and he growled almost savagely as his teeth bit gently into her straining throat. The rising pleasure was almost unbearable as he pistoned her relentlessly yet she cried to him, "Don't stop!"

But he could not have stopped even if he wanted to stop. His need for Cynara Stuart was almost painful in its desperation. Again and again and yet again, he drove himself into her. He couldn't get enough of her and began to believe that he was going to go mad. And then she cried out sharply. Her body stiffened, and shuddered. At that moment, his own juices exploded into her newly awakened body with a tremendous force. Cynara fainted beneath him as the earl slumped still half atop her. When his heart had ceased hammering so violently he pulled himself off the girl and slipped off the table. He stared.

She lay pale and fragile in a swoon, her thighs smeared with her own virgin's blood. The white linen cloth beneath her also gave evidence to her lost innocence. His own manhood bore traces of it. He had known it in his heart all along, the earl admitted to himself. For all of her reckless behavior, there was a sweetness about her. And now he had ruined her for a respectable marriage. And he had done it deliberately because he wanted her. But she had obviously wanted him too. He had not forced her. She had come to him. He had warned her when she began her relentless pursuit of him that he would not marry, and that he would have her virtue of her. Well, now the game was played out, and he had won. Yet he was not satisfied. He wanted more of her. He doubted that he would ever get enough of her.

"That was marvelous!" Cynara said, opening her eyes and sitting up. "Oh, Wickedness, is it always like that?"

"I don't know," he replied slowly, and then he admitted to her, "I have never known it to be such before."

"That was because you were making love to the wrong woman," she told him. "Grandmama says it is perfect with the right lover."

"I think your grandmama may be right," he answered softly. Then he said, "You must go home, Cyn. You cannot remain with me now."

She sighed. "I know," she said, "but could we not do it just one more time tonight?"

He shook his head. "You are too newly opened, vixen."

"When then?" she demanded. She pouted at him, but began to draw on her petticoats, pursing her lips at the shredded chemise, which was beyond repair.

"There will come a time," he told her.

"Yes, there will!" she replied. "Lace my bodice up for me, my dear lord." She looked about the room which was a very beautiful setting with its paneled walls, and crimson draperies, and paintings of landscapes with horses. Then her eye spotted the scarlet stain on the tablecloth now drying to a brown. Her eyes widened.

"You were indeed a virgin," he said quietly. He pulled on his shirt, which extended over his buttocks.

"I shall never be able to repair my hair," Cynara said fretfully. "I shall have to tell Hester that she did not fasten my chignon tightly enough, and it came down while I danced."

"You are very resourceful," he noted.

She nodded. "I am," she agreed, picking up her cloak. Did a woman always feel so sore after coupling? She didn't care!

And in the next few weeks at Newmarket, the earl of Summersfield learned just how resourceful Cynara could be and how determined she was that they continue as lovers. What was worse to his mind was that he couldn't resist her now. With each passing day, he needed her more. A day did not go by that they didn't find a place, a way to make love. She was adventurous and inventive to boot. One afternoon she sat next to him at Audley End by the river. Before he realized it she had unlaced his breeches and was fondling his manhood, which responded in shockingly little time. Then she was lifting her skirts, and encasing him within her body as she sat upon his lap, her skirts now artfully draped about them.

"My God, Cynara!" he had gasped. "What if someone comes along?"

"Have you never made love in public before?" she teased him. "I find it rather stimulating."

And so did he. They rocked back and forth while several courtiers strolled in the distance, but in their full view. Their passions were completed together, and afterward they laughed. They rode together one morning, and he took her on a mossy bank, riding her hard until she screamed her pleasure. And afterward when they returned to his stables, he had her again in the dim light of a box stall upon a pile of sweet-smelling hay. One evening they found a deserted hallway at the king's residence, and backing her against one of the room's marble pillars he slid his hands beneath her skirts, and lifting her up plunged himself into her sweetness until they were both well satisfied.

Jasmine saw the subtle change in her granddaughter's face and knew the reason for it. She hoped that Charlie and Barbara would not notice that their daughter bloomed these days. That the earl of Summersfield was most willingly in her company now. The court would be decamping from Newmarket shortly for Greenwich as the month of May was almost upon them. The duke of Lundy had had enough of court and wanted to return home to Queen's Malvern. He wanted his family with him.

Cynara protested. "You said I might remain at court until summer, Papa."

"Your earl seems no closer to marriage," Charlie grumbled. "I want to go home, damn it!"

"Papa, there is no reason I cannot go to court alone," Cynara said. "Girls of fourteen and fifteen are there without chaperons. Have I caused any gossip since the race? And you have been allowing me my freedom for several weeks now. All you and Mama do is go to the races. You are home and in bed by dark each night. I will be seventeen in a few weeks. You have said I have until year's end to bring Wickedness to the altar. How can I make future progress with him if I am at Queen's Malvern?"

"She has a point," Jasmine said quietly.

"I do not know," the duke said.

"I will come home in August for Grandmama's birthday," Cynara said. "I promise! Please let me remain."

"If you are worried, then ask the queen to watch over her," Jasmine said. "Cynara is, after all, a member of the family."

"What an excellent idea," the duchess of Lundy said. "My mind would be at ease if the queen were to watch over Cynara."

"Very well," the duke finally agreed. "The queen shall be your guardian, Cynara, but you must come home in August."

"Ohh, I will," Cynara agreed, relief flooding through her entire being. To be separated from her darling Wickedness now would have been just too awful.

Afterwards her grandmother had taken her aside and said, "You will be careful, my child." It was a warning, and Cynara knew Jasmine knew.

"I am not foolish, Grandmama," she replied, feeling the flush coloring her cheeks.

"No, but you are young. You are in love. And you are basically inexperienced, my child. You have begun a love affair, and whether that is wise, I cannot say. You know your earl far better than I, Cynara. You must marry eventually whether it be Harry Summers or another. For God's sake be discreet! Only the worst sort of man will overlook a scandal, and he will do so for the very reasons you have feared all along. Your wealth, and your family name."

"He loves me, Grandmama!"

"Has he said it?" she queried the young woman.

Cynara shook her head. "But I know he does!" she insisted.

Jasmine sighed. "Aye," she agreed, "I think he probably does, but unless you can get him to admit to it, it is unlikely you can get him to wed you. Damn! Men can be such fools, and there is simply no help for it at all." She put a loving arm about her granddaughter. "Whatever comes of this, Cynara, you will have me to rely on, I promise you. But do try not to cause an open scandal. As he grows older your father becomes more like his grandfather, King James. He wants to make everything all right, and he will go to any length to obtain his goal no matter how anyone else feels. That was what happened to me with Lord Leslie. It was a miracle it all worked out the way it should."

"You have led such an exciting life, Grandmama," Cynara said. "I thought I should like to have many adventures, and then I met my darling Wickedness. Now all I want is to be his wife and the mother of his children. What a dullard I have turned out to be," she laughed.

Jasmine chuckled. "I could have done without a few of my *adventures*," she told Cynara. "There is a great deal to be said for the quiet life, my dear child."

The court left for Greenwich on the twenty-sixth of April, and Lady Cynara Stuart was among the many members of the court traveling with the king. The queen had been consulted and agreed to watch over her husband's young cousin. To that end the duke of Lundy's apartments wherever the court went would be reserved for his daughter.

"I don't know what the hell you can do with your earl in the next few months," Charlie told his daughter, "but I know that I shall be seeking out suitable gentlemen once I get home. These things cannot be done quickly, and you, my fine girl, will be wedded and bedded before your eighteenth birthday, I promise you. I don't know why you couldn't have settled on a respectable fellow like your sister, Sabrina."

"You were just fortunate that Brie fell in love with our cousin, Southwood, Papa. She was as rough as Highland cattle when she came down from Glenkirk after all those years. Grandmama had a time turning her into a fine lady again. That's why she took Diana, and now her little sister. But you will be as lucky with me as you were with Brie, and I will indeed be wed before my eighteenth birthday." She kissed his cheek. "Thank you, Papa, for letting me remain with the court."

"Until August, Cyn, and then you are home again," the duke said sternly to his daughter. "Neither you, nor your grandmother will wheedle me further after that." He returned the kiss. "What is it about you lately, Cyn? You bloom, I vow, but then a girl is at her prime at seventeen, they say. Bag your earl before your bloom fades, or I will be forced to pick a husband for you."

"Yes, Papa," Cynara said meekly. Then turning she kissed her mother, bidding her farewell, and finally her grandmother.

Jasmine hugged the girl, whispering into her ear, "Do your best, my child. Bring me a birthday gift of a betrothed husband for yourself, and I shall be content."

"You are beginning to sound like Rohana and Toramalli," Cynara teased her grandmother. She kissed her cheek, and then was gone.

The court rode from Newmarket on a bright April day. The duke had bidden his cousin farewell and now prepared to leave for Queen's Malvern with his wife and mother. He made arrangements for the horses in his racing stable to be transported home to Queen's Malvern. He paid off his two jockeys and requested their presence in September when the racing began again. The house was packed up, and finally with their servants in tow the duke and his family departed for home.

Arriving at Greenwich after several days of traveling, the court swung into a round of midspring amusements. There were picnics and boating upon the river. There were sporting competitions. Cynara was particularly good with a long bow, having been taught by her aunt Flanna. She enjoyed shooting at the butts set up in the fields near the palace. Tennis she found too rough a sport, but like all the Stuarts she enjoyed the game of golf, which they had brought with them from Scotland. And she rode each day with her lover.

But both she and the earl lived for the nights when the dancing had ceased, and the palace was quiet. It was then that he slipped into her apartments and into her bed. His presence put Cynara's maidservant, Hester, in a quandary. She knew her mistress should not be entertaining a gentleman in this manner, but her loyalty to Cynara was such that she could not go to the king or report her mistress's behavior to the duke. She spoke with Mistress Gwyn's serving woman, Nan.

"She's already been breached, that's obvious," Nan said bluntly. "You can do naught about it but pray she don't get a big belly."

"But how can you be certain?" the naïve Hester asked.

"Why, lass, look at your mistress. Have you ever seen her so blooming beautiful? That inner light comes from good and regular fucking. Look at my own mistress. And now that the poor queen's miscarried of her child, my mistress will work His Majesty to put a babe in her belly, but that's different. Him is the king. Such behavior is forgiven of a king and his mistress. 'Tis not of a duke's unmarried daughter and her lover, no matter 'im's an earl. Why don't they wed? They are perfect for each other, my lady says."

Hester sighed. "He says he'll never marry, but my mistress says he will one day."

Nan shook her head. "Men can be difficult, and that's a truth. Of course he will wed her, but until she puts her foot down he'll take the privileges of a husband, and she'll wear no ring. You tell her that I says it."

And Hester did exactly that, adding, "It ain't right, m'lady! What if someone should find out about these midnight trysts of yours? Your reputation would be ruined. You don't want folk to say he *had* to wed you. That your da made him."

"Nay, I do not," Cynara answered Hester. She had been so wrapped up in their shared passions that she had lost her perspective.

That night they lay naked together in her bed. He was massaging her feet for she had complained they hurt from all the dancing they had done that night in celebration of the king's birthday. His strong fingers kneaded a foot, pressing and easing the ache, kissing each toe as he worked it. Cynara purred with pleasure. When he had finished she turned herself that she might lick at his torso. Her tongue moved in a leisurely fashion, tasting the salt of him, concentrating upon the nipples on his chest. Slowly, slowly, she encircled each one with her tongue.

"Damn, wench, I love it when you tease me," he told her.

She responded by drawing her long sable hair over his skin as her head moved lower and lower. She nibbled at the taut flesh of his belly, the tip of her tongue pushing into his navel briefly.

His breath caught in his throat. She had never before been as daring in her lovemaking. He almost whimpered aloud as she rubbed her face in the dark thatch of curls between his legs. Her fingers delicately lifted his manhood, even now stiffening with his desire for her. Her tongue slowly licked the entire length of him. He groaned low. She took him into her mouth for the very first time.

"*Oh, God! Yes!*" he half-sobbed.

"What do I do?" she whispered softly, her tongue brushing strongly over the tip of his manhood before she absorbed him between her lips once again.

"Whatever you want, Cyn!" And his voice was pleading.

She suckled him, drawing him deeper and deeper until she was close to gagging for his size had increased swiftly. She squeezed him between her lips, her tongue working him until he was whimpering quite distinctly with his need for her. Releasing her hold upon his manhood, Cynara encased him within her love channel, her back to him. Immediately he half-rose, his big hands slipping around to cup and fondle her perfect round breasts. Keeping him between her thighs as she would her stallion, she pistoned him until, with a feral growl, he forced her, his hand on the nape of her neck, facedown in the bed. His hands grasped her hips, and now it was he who dictated their passions.

"So, naughty Cyn, you would attempt to rule me, would you?" He thrust hard and deep into her eager body.

"You cried like a child," she shot back.

"But now it is you who will call out, Cyn." His rhythm grew fiercer and quicker in tempo. "*Won't you? Won't you?*"

"*Make me!*" she taunted him cruelly.

He knew what drove her wild, and he proceeded to execute it. Slowly, slowly, he pushed deep. Slowly, slowly he withdrew until he was almost, but not quite free of her. Then he pushed himself into her body again. *Slowly. Slowly.* And Cynara began to whimper with her need for completion, but he would not give it to her. "Not yet, my angel," he told her. Then he thrust harder and deeper than he had ever before gone.

She was panting hard with her own lust. There were starbursts behind her tightly closed eyes. A wave of sensation began to rise up from deep within her until she felt as if she were drowning in a pool of white-hot desire. "Y-You're killing me!" she sobbed. And at that moment she was overwhelmed by a tidal wave of delicious delights. Cynara screamed as the pleasure washed over her, rendering her prostrate. She swooned, and felt as if she were tumbling into a warm, all-enveloping darkness that left her weak but more than satisfied. She heard him groaning and felt his juices filling her as he collapsed atop her. With a sigh she floated away.

When she finally became aware once again, she found that she was lying in the protective circle of his embrace. His hand was stroking her long hair. She smiled to herself.

"You frighten me when you faint like that," he murmured, realizing that she was conscious once more.

"'Tis only the second time," she reassured him. "It is just so wonderful, Wickedness. Sometimes I cannot help it for you make me soar. Do I not have the same affect upon you?"

"Yes," he admitted, and then he said, "I want you to come home with me to Summersfield Park, Cynara. I am now bored with court life, and I need to be on my own land again."

Cynara stiffened slightly, and she turned so she might see his handsome face. "What is it exactly that you are asking me, Harry?"

"To come to Summersfield," he repeated. And then he realized her confusion, and said, "I have warned you all along, Cynara, that I should not wed."

"Despite the fact that you love me," she answered softly. "And you do love me, Harry, even if you will not admit it. There are some things as I have told you before that are instinctive in a woman's nature. One of them is the ability to recognize when she is loved. Your father did not love your mother, nor did she love him. He raped her because she injured his pride by refusing his advances. Then they were forced into marriage by virtue of that single act and the fact that you were already in your mother's womb. But that is not the situation with us, my poor Wickedness. Have you not yet realized that you are free to love? I have given you everything that I could to prove that to you, and you are in love with me. Yet you will neither admit it to me or to yourself."

He was silent.

"I will not stop loving you, Harry, even if you are a fool. Nor will my father force me into marriage with anyone else."

He released his tender hold upon her and arose from the bed, quickly pulling his clothing back on. "I will ask you again, Cyn," the earl said to her. "Will you come to Summersfield with me?"

"No," Cynara replied quietly. "I will not."

He left her then without so much as a kiss, and when the door had closed with finality behind him, Cynara did something she rarely did. She wept. In the morning she arose to learn that he had already left Greenwich. Angrily she directed Hester to pack their belongings.

"I want to be gone from court today!" she told her maidservant furiously. "I will not remain here another night!" And she began pulling possessions out, and flinging them on the floor.

"M'lady, I do not know if I can pack us up that quickly," Hester pleaded with her mistress. "In a few days, of course . . ."

"Today!" Cynara shouted. "I am going now to take my leave of their majesties, and tell the coachman to be ready." And she slammed from the apartment.

Hester sighed, looking about her. Then with a determined look, she began to haul her mistress's trunks from their storage, and pack. About her Cynara's spaniels yapped excitedly, and the usually good-natured Hester swore at them to be silent.

Cynara hurried through the corridors at Greenwich to Nell Gwyn's apartments. A guardsman outside the royal mistress's rooms jumped to open the doors for Cynara never slowed her stride. "Nellie!" she called as she entered.

"I'm in me bath," came the answer.

Cynara directed her footsteps into a small tiled room where Nellie now reclined in a large brass-bound oak tub, her chestnut curls piled atop her head. "I'm leaving court today!" Cynara said. *"Now!* As quickly as Hester can pack. May I borrow one of your women to help her? I cannot remain another moment! *I will not remain!"*

"What has he done?" Nell asked quietly.

"He has departed for Summersfield Park!" Cynara said.

"Without you?" Nell was astounded. "The damned fool loves you, Cyn. I suppose he ran away to avoid facing his feelings."

"He asked me to go with him," Cynara told Nellie.

"And you refused," Nellie responded. "Of course you had to refuse. Why he could not see that before he even asked . . . Men are such fools!"

"You know he has been in my bed," Cynara said low.

Nellie nodded. "I knew."

"And did the rest of the court know?" Cynara wondered aloud.

Nellie shook her head. "You have both been very discreet. Some may have suspected, but even they are not certain of what has transpired between you and Harry Summers. Your reputation is yet intact, my friend."

"If I had gone with him, it would have exposed me to the world as his whore," Cynara said. "Why would he do that to me? He loves me. *I know that he does!*"

"By publicly making you his whore," Nell answered wisely, "he prevents other men from approaching you with offers of marriage."

"But he refuses to offer himself," Cynara wailed.

"Go home," Nell advised. "You are close to breaking him, Cyn. Fleeing you is his last attempt at facing himself and his emotions."

"I hate him!" Cynara declared.

"They why are you so distraught, Cyn?" And Nellie laughed softly as she arose from her tub and stepped out into the wrapping sheet that her maidservant held. Tucking it about her, she beckoned Cyn into her bedroom. "I will send Nan to help your Hester. Have you yet spoken to His Majesty?"

Cynara shook her head.

"Then go, and do so. You will find him in an excellent mood despite Her Majesty's tragedy. I have seen to that. It is now time, I believe, that I have a child. I will give the king another son," she smiled. "It is past time someone other than the Castlemaine flaunted her bastards about the court."

Cynara sighed. "I will come and see you before I leave," she said. "Ohhh! Wickedness has surely lived up to his name now!" And the sound of Nellie Gwyn's merry laughter followed her as she hurried off to speak with the king. In the royal antechamber there were already many waiting for a word with His Majesty. Cynara pushed through the crowd and looking directly at the guardsman at the door said, "I would speak with my cousin immediately!"

"My lady! My lady!" One of the king's secretaries hurried up to her. "You must wait your turn along with the others."

Cynara turned on the man, her blue eyes blazing. "Do you know who I am, fool?" she demanded. "I am Lady Cynara Stuart, daughter of the duke of Lundy, His Majesty's most beloved cousin. I am not the *others*, and I wish to see my cousin now! Unless he is with Her Majesty then you had best allow me access at once before I box your ears for your presumption!" She glared ferociously at the man, who quailed before the girl. He was new to his appointment at court.

The guardsman did not wait for further instruction, instead opening the doors to His Majesty's privy chamber to allow young Lady Stuart inside. Cynara caught his eye and nodded faintly as she moved past him as the door closed smoothly behind her.

The king looked up and smiled a welcome to her as Cynara swept him a deep curtsy. "Cousin, what a pleasure," he said.

"I have come to bid Your Majesty farewell for now," Cynara said. "I am leaving Greenwich today for home."

"You do not intend coming back to Whitehall and then Windsor, Cousin?" the king asked.

"I promised Papa that I would return home if he would allow me but a bit more time at court. I hope I shall be allowed to return, Your Majesty," Cynara told him.

"You know, Cousin, that you are always welcome. I understand that the earl of Summersfield departed early this morning for his home." The dark eyes scanned her face.

Cynara suddenly and quite unexpectedly burst into tears.

The king arose immediately from his chair, and put comforting arms about her. "There, there, little cousin, for pity's sake, do not weep. The man is not worth your tears that he cannot admit to what everyone else can plainly see. That he loves you." The king pulled a large silk handkerchief from his satin coat, and handed it to

Cynara. "Dry your eyes, Cousin. I could, you know, order him to wed you. You are, after all, a member of my family."

"No! No, Your Majesty," Cynara sniffled, attempting to regain a mastery over her emotions. "I do not want him forced into marriage as his father was forced. He must admit to loving me, and he must ask me properly for my hand. Only when he does will I wed him." She blotted the tears from her beautiful face. "I know he loves me, and he knows it as well, but he will not say it. Why are men such simpletons?"

The king chuckled and gave her shoulders a small squeeze of comfort. "I cannot tell you that, Cousin, being a man. And I will admit to having my moments of foolishness if you promise not to tell on me," he said with a smile.

Cynara giggled, her good humor restored. She flung her arms about the king's neck and kissed his ruddy cheek. "Ohh, I do love you, Your Majesty!" she told him. Then she backed away from him, and curtsied once more. "Have I Your Majesty's permission to retire home to Queen's Malvern?"

He nodded. "After you have made your farewells to Her Majesty, yes, Cousin, you have my permission to leave us. But you must promise me that you will come again after your summertime. I know that your family gathers at Queen's Malvern at that time. Give my cousin Charlie, and his fair Barbara, my felicitations. And do not despair. I suspect that your earl has but gone home to consider how to proceed next."

"That is just what Nellie says!" Cynara told him. "Thank you, Your Majesty."

"Farewell, Cousin," the king said as she backed from his privy chamber.

By mid-afternoon, by some miracle known only to Hester, they were packed and on their way. They could only travel as far as Greenwood House on the edge of London that day given the late hour, but Cynara was satisfied that they had at least departed court. And she was not unhappy that they would spend tonight in a familiar setting. There had, after all, been no time to send to her father's secretary to arrange for the accommodations along the way. They traveled with six of her father's men-at-arms as well as the coachman and his assistant.

"We will leave as soon as the sun is up," Cynara instructed the men, "and we will travel the day long, stopping only briefly at midday. The weather is good, and we should be able to make excellent time. I am anxious to be home again."

The coachman had made the trip between London and Queen's Malvern enough times that he knew just where the best inns were located. Cynara's escort kept them safe from highwaymen, and her status allowed her the best accommodation each night when she stopped. As each day passed Cynara found herself growing more anxious to be home. The midlands, where her father's estate was located, was a land of gently rolling hills, and green, watered valleys. When they had at last reached the hills above their little valley, which was set between the Severn and the Wye Rivers, Cynara stopped her carriage, and mounting her stallion who had traveled tethered behind the coach, she looked down on the ivy-covered mellow pink brick house. She was home at last, and home right now was where she very much needed to be. Kicking Fluffy into a trot, a loping canter, and finally a gallop, she raced down the hill road to where her family was waiting. And behind her the great traveling coach lumbered along, the horses eagerly smelling home.

Chapter

20

The duke of Lundy was very pleased to see his child returned home almost two months before she had promised to return. The duchess was openly relieved. But Jasmine was curious. She knew, however, that her granddaughter would eventually tell her all. She had but to wait.

"So, you have given up on Summers," Charlie said in pleased tones. "I knew that you would eventually come to your senses, Cynara."

"Now, Papa, because I have returned home earlier than you anticipated, do not read anything into it. Remember that I have your word you will give me until the year's end to gain my heart's desire. I have not given up on the earl. Harry wanted to go home to Summersfield Park to inspect his estate. He has been gone for some time. It pleases me that he is so careful of his lands. Are you not impressed, Papa? I'm certain that you have believed Wickedness's only interest in his patrimony was the monies he gains from it." She laughed. "I shall be back at court in time for the hunting season. The king made me promise that I would. Mama, Her Majesty sends you her regards, as does our cousin, the king."

Cynara's sophisticated world-weary attitude intimidated her mother, but Jasmine was not in the least taken aback.

"The duke of Cranston is looking for a wife," Charlie said to his daughter. "The first one died in childbirth along with the child. 'Twould be a good match for you, Cynara. You'd be a duchess, and your son would be the next duke. I've inquired, and he is interested."

"No," Cynara responded. "You had no right, Papa, to do such a thing. You gave me your word I would have until year's end."

"Cranston will not wait forever, Cynara," her father said testily. "This is an excellent opportunity."

"I know to whom you refer. He is old," Cynara said.

"He is but thirty-five," her father snapped. "Young enough to sire children on you. And old enough to be tolerant of your behavior."

Cynara couldn't help but laugh. "Oh, Papa, are you that afraid of what I might do?" Then she grew quite serious. "Make no matches for me, Papa, I beg you. If I cannot have Wickedness, then I want no other. Would it be so dreadful a fate if I remained unwed and stayed home with my parents?"

The duchess burst into tears. "I want you to be happy," she sobbed at her daughter. "You think that the earl of Summersfield is the only man who can make you happy? When I fell in love with your father I was just your age. And then Madame Skye separated us and had me wed to Squire Randall. I thought I should die when I learned of it, but I did not. I was a good wife to my first husband. I even came to love him though not as I have always loved your papa. A woman needs to be settled with a good husband, Cynara."

"I am sorry, Mama, but I am not a mercer's daughter from Hereford, accepting of the lot chosen for me by my betters. I am a duke's child, and I will have the man I love, or I will have no man!"

Jasmine could see that the situation would soon be out of hand, and Cynara's homecoming become a nasty quarrel. "I do not think this is the time for us to discuss such matter," she said quietly in a tone that brooked no nonsense. "Cynara has just arrived home. And, indeed, Charlie, you did promise your daughter until the end of the year before you began attempting to make matches for her. I realize that the duke of Cranston is certainly a possibility, but if he is truly interested in Cynara he will consider her sensibilities and bide his time. If he is not, then he is certainly not the sort of man I would want my granddaughter to marry, Charlie. And when you consider the matter with the seriousness it merits, neither would you."

The duke laughed. "Mama, you should have practiced the law in the city for you reason like a barrister."

"I have been told such on several occasions," Jasmine replied archly, but she did smile at her son.

Cynara's eyes met those of her grandmother's in silent thanks. A dispute had been avoided for now. She was home, and once the exhaustion of her trip had subsided, she must consider her next move carefully. She was certain her grandmother would have some good suggestions. "When are the Glenkirks coming?" she asked brightly.

"Not until Diana's child is born, and they will go to Roxley. We shall not see them at Queen's Malvern this year," her mother quickly answered. "Imagine, Diana became enceinte upon her wedding night. Is that not wonderful? The duke is ecstatic."

"Siren is fortunate," Cynara said candidly. "She married the man she loved. Perhaps I shall go and visit her, and Fancy too, once I have recovered from my travels."

"An excellent idea," Jasmine said. "I shall go with you."

"Where is my cousin, Mair?" Cynara asked. "Have you been having fun with her, Grandmama? She is such a pretty child."

"She is with her tutor learning the history of this land," the duchess told her daughter. "I suspect she will not be quite as amiable as Diana was, but she is a lovely child nonetheless."

"What you mean, Mama, is that Mair, has a mind of her own and chooses to use it. Hopefully by the time she is old enough to go to court that will have subsided, and she will behave exactly as you would wish her to," Cynara noted.

"You speak as if good manners were a bad thing," the duchess said sharply.

"My manners are flawless," Cynara murmured.

"I think that perhaps you should go to your room now, my child," Jasmine remarked. "I will see that a light supper is brought up to you. After your journey, you will want to retire early."

"Yes, Grandmama," Cynara responded meekly, and then curtsying to her family, she removed herself from the family hall and went upstairs.

"She is very tired," Jasmine said to her son and his wife. "Do you not see it?"

"Her pursuit of Summers is fruitless," Charlie grumbled.

"Let her be, my son, and no more talk of the duke of Cranston, I beg you. Cynara will come to her own conclusions if you allow her the freedom to do so. Press your own agenda right now, and she will fight you to the death. She is not home an hour, and you are quarreling with her. Let me speak with her and see what has happened."

"Very well, madame," the duke of Lundy said to his mother. He did not look content, however. He wanted his youngest child settled and happy, yet his daughter seemed to resist all their efforts for her happiness.

For several days Cynara led a quiet existence. She ate. She slept a great deal. She walked through the beautiful gardens that belonged to Queen's Malvern. She realized as much as she enjoyed the court—and certainly of her cousins, Fancy and Diana, Cynara was the one who had enjoyed court the most—she was now aware of how exhausted she was. The court was so exciting and there was so much for her there to do that regular meals and sleep were the least of her worries. Home was for resting, Cynara thought to herself amused, as her humor was finally restored.

She joined her grandmother in her apartments one morning, bidding the ancient twins, Rohana and Toramalli, a pleasant good day. She was frankly amazed that they still both survived for they were in their late eighties and dangerously frail. Still they lived on in comfort, waited upon by women young enough to be their great-granddaughters. But each day they joined their mistress as they always did.

Jasmine was sitting up in her bed. "Ahh," she said seeing Cynara, "you are looking more rested. Court can be such chaos. Come and sit next to me, my child. We have had no time to talk since you arrived home. I want to hear all about your pursuit of your earl."

"*I hate him!*" Cynara said, suddenly annoyed.

"Then why do you resist your father's efforts at matchmaking?" Jasmine asked mischievously, for she knew the answer.

"Because I love him too!" Cynara replied. "Ohh, Grandmama, why are men such dunderheads?"

"What did he do that sent you home almost two months before we were expecting you?" Jasmine inquired.

"He left court! Without a word! I awoke one morning, and he was no longer at Greenwich. How could he?" she wailed.

"You had no idea that he was leaving?" Jasmine gently probed.

"Well," Cynara amended, "he did ask me to go with him to Summersfield Park," Cynara responded. "I refused, of course."

"Of course," Jasmine agreed. "You must not allow your good name to be sullied by unseemly behavior. You have been discreet in your association with the earl, I assume." Her look was searching.

Cynara bit her lower lip, but then she answered. "Yes, Grandmama, I have been extremely discreet. There is naught that can be said about my behavior with the earl."

"Your public behavior, I assume," Jasmine responded, "although I shall not inquire if you have a private behavior with the earl."

Cynara blushed furiously, which told her grandmother precisely what she needed to know. "Grandmama!"

Jasmine just laughed. Thank God she had had the foresight to give Hester the potion for Cynara that would prevent any difficulties. "Would you like to go and visit Diana for a few days, my child?" she said. "I am certain she will be interested in all the news of the court."

"I should like to go," Cynara responded, "but Diana really does not give a fig for the court. Still, I shall tell her about my race at Newmarket. She will be deliciously shocked and make my visit most worthwhile," Cynara chuckled wickedly.

The duke was pleased that his daughter was to go and see her cousin. "Mayhap when she realizes how happy Diana is," he said, "she will seriously seek that same happiness for herself. 'Twas very clever of you, Mama, to suggest such a visit."

Jasmine smiled briefly. Her main concern was removing Cynara from her father's reach so they would not quarrel with each other.

That would drive Cynara away. Both her son and her granddaughter were determined to have their own way. While both sought the same end, their routes were very different and quite diametrically opposed. And Cynara, now rested after a week at home, was becoming restless and beginning to think too much. She even now questioned her judgment in refusing the earl's invitation.

"Who would have known, Grandmama?" she said. "Not anyone at the court, nor my father either as long as I came home in August. I could have told the queen I was coming home and then gone to Summersfield Park."

"You were correct in refusing such an invitation," Jasmine reassured her granddaughter. "It is one thing, my child, to discreetly take a lover. It is another to behave like a common trull. You would have lost the earl's respect had you gone, and had no chance at all of bringing him to the altar. By refusing and returning home you have but increased his appetite for you, and for your passion."

"Grandmama! I did not say—" Cynara began.

"No," Jasmine quickly responded, "you did not, but I am no fool, Cynara. I know what I know. Your papa, however, being a man and your father, has not yet ascertained what you are about. I told you that I trust your judgment with this man, and I do. But if you cannot bring him to see reason by year's end, then I will support your papa in his desires. Do you understand me?"

"I shall tell any man who attempts to court me that I am no virgin," Cynara said defiantly.

Jasmine laughed. "Do you think they will care, my child? It is your wealth, and your connection to the king that will matter to gentlemen like the duke of Cranston. You know that as well as I do. Your little missteps will be kept quiet and overlooked in light of the advantages of marrying you, Cynara. Revealing your rather naughty behavior would embarrass you far more than it would anyone else. It would be said that you are a Stuart, and Stuarts are known to be wild. It would be said that your mama's low birth was to blame. Is that what you want?"

"I love him so very much, Grandmama!" Cynara burst out. "Why can he not see reason?"

"What is meant to happen, my child, will happen. You have done what you could. Now leave it in the hands of fate, Cynara," Jasmine advised her granddaughter. "I expect that the earl of Summersfield is even now regretting your absence."

And he was. Harry Summers had arrived home to find himself immediately lonely and bored. There was nothing for him to do. His tenants were industrious, and his estate manager, a distant cousin from Ireland, competent. His estates were more prosperous than they had ever been. His cattle and his horses grazed sleek and fat in his green meadows. His field and orchards thrived. He closeted himself in his privy chamber and went over the accounts. Absolutely everything was in perfect order. The servant girls and milkmaids, who in the past had provided him with amusement, no longer appealed to him. And the nights were the worst of all.

He missed Cynara. He wanted her here with him, and at first he was angry that she had refused his invitation. But on reflection he knew that she was right. She was seventeen now, and it was long past time that she wed. But the thought of Cynara Stuart marrying anyone but him set him to gnashing his teeth. It was why he had given in to her seduction. To spoil her for anyone else. *She was his!*

He sighed. He could not have it both ways, and he knew it. She had given herself to him because she loved him. Because she wanted to be his wife. And she had indeed been a virgin that first time. She had known no other. And never would if he could but overcome his fear of admitting his own love and of marriage. Cynara had said she was not his mother, and God only knew that was the truth. His mother had been his father's victim from the start. Only once had she dared to defy her husband, and grasp at a bit of happiness for herself. And she had paid for it with her life. No. Cynara was not like his mother in the least. But was he his father?

Had he not done exactly what Devil Summers had done when he had allowed his father to die in pain, alone, and tortured by the sounds of his son's lust in the room next to his? He might have called for the doctor. He might have sat by his sire's bed despite the fact he hated the man. He might have kept his hands from his father's mistress until his parent had died. But he hadn't. Just as when his mother had died, and his father had left her alone, in pain, and with the sounds of passion ringing in her ears. But would a wicked man feel the guilt that wracked him over his actions towards his parent?

Cynara knew his history, yet she did not condemn him. It was obvious that she saw something in him that pleased her. She was the king's cousin, and had access to their whole world. Many, given the least encouragement, would have sought her hand in marriage. Some far more important than he was. *But she chose him.* Why?

Because she loves you, fool, he voice in his head answered. Yet how could she? he questioned himself. *Because she does,* came the reply. His mother had advised him not to wed with her dying breath, but her words were those of an embittered woman, he knew. Did he even dare to consider marrying? Marry Cynara Stuart? He thought a moment. His pedigree was acceptable. He had his own wealth and did not need hers. He could even live with the odd arrangement regarding her personal wealth that all the women in her family made before their marriages. The duke might consider a better match for his youngest child, but he would never forbid Cynara, and Cynara loved Harry Summers. Certainly the duke of Lundy would take that into consideration. Aye. She loved him. *And he loved her.* He did.

Harry Summers rode back to court, now settled at Windsor Castle for the summer. He learned to his disappointment that Lady Cynara Stuart had departed for her own home on the very same day he had left for his. It was said she would return in time for the hunting season.

"You might," the king said to him when he learned that the earl of Summersfield was seeking Cynara, "go to Queen's Malvern."

"You have missed her then," Nellie Gwyn said. She would have her secretary write Cynara on the morrow with this news. The poor lass needed a bit of good news.

"Aye," Harry said, "I do miss her."

"And that is all?" Nellie probed further.

The man known throughout the court as Wickedness flushed.

"'Odsblood!" Nellie swore, her blue eyes dancing wickedly. "Do you mean to make an honest woman of her then?"

"Mistress Nellie," the earl pleaded helplessly.

"*You do!*" Nellie crowed.

"I must return to Summersfield Park," Harry Summers said. "I will come in the autumn when Lady Stuart returns."

"Do not be a laggard, my lord!" Nellie warned him. "Lundy is considering a match for her with the duke of Cranston, but it is you who has her heart."

"Perhaps she would be better off with someone else," he replied.

"You do not believe that for a minute!" Nellie said. "Go to Queen's Malvern, my lord."

But the earl of Summersfield returned home. It was better that he wait, he told himself. Perhaps the separation from a satisfactory mistress had dulled his judgment. He still missed her, he admitted to himself, but what difference would a few months make? Come October he would return to court for the hunting season. He would reacquaint himself with Lady Cynara Stuart, and they would proceed from there. Was she thinking of him too? he wondered.

She was. Cynara and her grandmother traveled to Roxley in the company of Mair Leslie who claimed to want to see her sister, but Jasmine knew Mair's interest was the marquis of Roxley. Diana's gracious home, her happiness in her life, and the child she was expecting had an odd affect on Cynara. She became envious, and Cynara Stuart had never before in all her life been jealous of anyone. She was, as she so often reminded herself, a Stuart, which was more than enough. But now it wasn't. Now she wanted what Diana had, and she wanted it with Harry Summers. She would run away. She would hide herself, but she would not let them marry her off to the duke of Cranston!

Diana, advised by her grandmother as to the lay of the land, wisely refrained from asking Cynara about the earl of Summersfield. The visit, however, was successful, for Mair's open quest of the marquis of Roxley kept them all amused. And when it came time for them to return to Queen's Malvern, Diana asked her grandmother to leave Mair behind.

"I could use her company now, and my parents will want to see her when they arrive."

"Ohh, Grandmama, may I remain!" Mair begged.

"Two months without lessons?" Jasmine pretended to consider the matter seriously while Diana and Cynara smiled behind their hands.

"Ohh, Grandmama, I promise I shall study all the harder when I return to Queen's Malvern in exchange for this time with my sister," Mair vowed.

"And the marquis has nothing to do with it?" Jasmine teased.

"*Grandmama!*" At eleven Mair Leslie was now old enough to at least pretend chagrin at having been found out.

"Well," Jasmine said, "for your sister's sake I shall leave you here at Roxley, but you must return to me in the autumn, Mair."

"Oh, yes, Grandmama!" Mair said, her eyes shining.

Cynara bid her cousins farewell, promising to return when Diana's baby was born.

"If it is a girl you must stand as its godmother," Diana said. "And Fancy too. But if it is a lad, then it is you I choose."

The cousins kissed, and then Cynara joined her grandmother in their carriage for the two days' ride back to Queen's Malvern. But the rocking of the coach seemed to disagree with Cynara, and she left it after a few miles to ride her horse, but even so she felt poorly.

"I hope I am not sickening with some summer's flux," Cynara said to her grandmother that evening at the inn where they were staying. "I would not want Diana to have caught something from me or Mair."

"We will see how you feel in the morning," Jasmine said.

In the morning, however, Cynara felt fine, but she rode the rest of the way home to Queen's Malvern rather than be enclosed in the vehicle with her grandmother.

"'Twas but a passing fancy," Cynara declared.

But two evenings later she left the dining room to puke her guts in a chamber pot. She was pale, and her skin felt clammy. Cynara took to her bed.

It cannot be, Jasmine thought. *It must not be!* She sought out Hester. "You have been giving your mistress her strengthening tonic each morning, have you not, Hester?" she asked the girl.

"Oh, no, madame," Hester said. "My lady did not like the taste of it and bade me throw it out."

"Ohh, foolish girl!" Jasmine cried. "By obeying your mistress rather than me, you have caused our undoing! When was your mistress's last moon flow?"

Hester thought a moment, and then her eyes grew wide with her understanding for she was a country woman. "Ohh, madame! She has had no moon flow since early May! But 'twas not my fault!"

"Yes, it is, for the potion I gave you was made to prevent just such an accident as has now occurred," Jasmine told the serving woman. "But until I am certain of this, you will keep what little knowledge you now possess to yourself, or by God, I will strangle you myself!"

Hester began to cry. "Ohh, my lady, I did not think it important. My mistress needed no strengthening medicine. She could run on her nerve alone. I saw no harm when she said she did not like it. What shall I do? Ohh, I shall never forgive myself."

Jasmine shook her head wearily. "The fault is mine as well, Hester. I should have told you the truth, but I hesitated to shock you with the knowledge of what I brew." She sighed. "Perhaps I am wrong. We will wait a week or so, eh?"

But in the week that followed, with Hester looking more stricken at every turn, and Cynara vomiting at the slightest thing, Jasmine knew that they could not hide from the truth. Her granddaughter was enceinte with the earl of Summersfield's child. Cynara must be confronted, and then the duke and duchess of Lundy must be told. When they had all recovered from the initial shock, Harry Summers would be sent for in order that he might do the right thing. *I am getting too old for this sort of thing,* Jasmine thought irritably.

"Ohh, God!" Cynara cried when forced to face the fact that she was with child. "What am I to do?"

"I will have him thrown in the tower for this . . . *this rape!* He is just like his father!" Charlie, the not-so-royal Stuart, shouted.

"He did not rape me!" Cynara told her outraged parent. "Rather I seduced him, Papa, and he is nothing at all like his father!"

"He is a man of the world," Barbara told her daughter. "You could not possibly have known what you were doing. He coerced you into believing that 'twas you who was the aggressor, Cynara, when the truth was it was he. Ohh, my poor baby!" She attempted to hug her child.

Cynara, however, shrugged her mother's embrace off. "I was a virgin, Mama, not the village idiot. For mercy's sake it is sixteen sixty-nine, not fifteen sixty-nine! Virgins are far more knowledgeable these days. Believe me when I tell you that I seduced him and not the other way around."

"I did not raise you to whore yourself," Barbara said suddenly angry.

"I am *your* daughter, madame. Did you not lay with my father when you were sixteen? I believe he had your virginity of you, or so you told me when I was still a small girl. And you were his mistress even while the duchess Bess was alive. Do not dare to criticize me, Mama! I love Harry Summers no less than you have loved my father," Cynara told her parents defiantly.

"I will send for the earl of Summersfield tomorrow, Cynara," the duke of Lundy said. "He must be made to make this right. So you will have your heart's desire after all, my lass, though I should have wished you to choose another way of gaining it."

"No," Cynara said quietly.

"*No?*" the duke looked surprised. "What do you mean by no?"

"I will not marry him, my lord. I will not begin my marriage in the same manner as his poor mother was forced to begin her marriage. Besides, he has not yet told me he loves me."

"But you know he does," Jasmine noted softly.

"Aye, but he has not said it," Cynara answered. "If you send for him, Papa, I shall never know if he wed me for myself, or because I carry his child. I have fought so hard to marry a man who will love me because I am Cynara. Not for my wealth, or my connections, or because I am going to have his son. Please, I beg of you, do not send for Harry. If he comes for me, and speaks his heart then I will wed him gladly, but I will not allow his family's history to repeat itself for his sake, for mine, and for that of our child."

Barbara Stuart began to weep softly. Her husband looked unsure of himself and very perplexed.

Jasmine, however, nodded. "She is right, you know."

"But the babe will be born a bastard," Charlie said.

"So were you. So was Cynara. It was remedied in time, and this can be too," Jasmine said. "Cynara must have charge of her own destiny now, my dears. And we must support her with all the love that we can. For her sake, and for her child's."

"What are we to do, Mama?" the duke asked helplessly. He could not believe that his beloved Cynara had put herself in this position.

"I think we must ask Cynara what she would like to do," Jasmine responded calmly. She turned to her granddaughter. "Well, child?"

"I do not know, Grandmama," Cynara answered. "I realize it is unlikely we can avoid embarrassment in this matter. Should I remain here at Queen's Malvern, or go somewhere I am not known? I suspect this is a situation in which we must all be in agreement."

Jasmine nodded.

"Mair Leslie cannot return here until after your child is born," Barbara Stuart said firmly. "I would not have her follow your example, Cynara. The marquis of Roxley may not wait for her to grow up, and I do not want her taking matters into her own hands."

"She is eleven, Mama, and her flow is not yet upon her," Cynara said dryly. "Besides, Mair is far more practical than I am."

"I agree with Barbara," Jasmine said. "Mair will remain at Roxley until this business with Cynara is over and done with, my dears."

"Hilltop House!" Cynara said. "I can go to Hilltop House. I was born there. Why can my child not be?"

"It is so isolated," Barbara said nervously.

"It is, but it does not have to be," the duke responded. "You preferred the isolation by virtue of the times and our situation. You wanted no one to know you were there alone. But the house is perfectly comfortable and can be refurbished completely to make a nice little nesting box for Cynara. Hester will be with her, and I will place several men-at-arms about the place to discourage visitors. We can supply the house with everything it needs. We'll know our daughter is there. I think Cynara has come up with a good solution."

"When do you think the child is due?" Jasmine asked.

"Late winter, or very early spring," Cynara replied.

"Your belly should not show until autumn. You will remain here at Queen's Malvern until Diana's child is born so you may stand as its godmother. Afterward you will go to Hilltop House."

"But after the baby is born?" Barbara Stuart asked.

"I will not give up my own flesh," Cynara responded. "I can remain at Hilltop House, Mama."

"Your absence would be noted, Cynara," her grandmother said. "Then there would be a scandal, I fear. We may still marry you off respectably, my child. The child can remain at Hilltop House, raised by its nurse and by our family. You may see it when you are not at court, but should you suddenly disappear for any amount of time, there would be too much gossip, and we could not contain it."

"I don't care," Cynara said. "I cannot bring myself to marry anyone but Harry Summers. And if I do not, then I shall remain here to raise my infant. It does not matter to me what people say."

"There is time for this matter to be resolved," Jasmine said. "For now you are here with us, and your secret will be safe."

Cynara nodded. "I will raise my own child up," she said softly. "I will make up for the fact that he has no father by being the best mother I can be." She turned to her own mother. "You were an excellent example to me, madame, in those days when we could not be certain my father would ever come home." Then Cynara curtsied to her elders and walked slowly from the old family hall where they had all been seated.

"We can put the child out to foster," the duke said. "It would hardly be unusual, and while I am not pleased at all by this turn of events, Cynara is not the first high-born girl to birth a bastard. I am almost relieved she will not have him now."

"She will not have him if he does not admit to his love for her," his mother reminded him. "'Tis an entirely different thing. Cynara is very proud, and she has always sought to be loved for herself, being a wise girl. I am frankly surprised that he has not come after her already, but I guarantee you that come the autumn, and she does not reappear at court, Harry Summers will come to Queen's Malvern looking for her. This will right itself, Charlie."

"It is all my fault," Barbara Stuart, duchess of Lundy said. "I was always so frank with her about our situation, about our family history. How could she truly believe it was wrong to lie with the man she loved without benefit of clergy? Did I not do the same thing and then boast on it? Now the pigeons have come to roost." She turned her beautiful face to her husband. "How can you ever forgive me, Charlie? I know how much you wanted for Cynara."

"What I want, or have wanted for our daughter is of no account, my darling Barbara," the duke said. "Cynara is a Stuart, and we are known to be heedless of the consequences of our actions. The facts are simple. Cynara is with child by her lover. The world as we know it will not crumble because of this. Our lives will go on, and we will survive it. So will our daughter. Now tomorrow I shall write to the duke of Cranston, and tell him to seek elsewhere for a wife. That Cynara's heart is engaged elsewhere, but that she thanks him for his interest." Charlie put an arm about his stricken wife. "Cynara alone is responsible for what has happened, Barbara. Never again let me hear you say that this is your fault, for it is not." The duke of Lundy kissed his wife even as she burst into fulsome tears, which but caused him to laugh. "Damn Cromwell, and his pocky Roundheads," he said, using an oath his youngest sister had once used, "for all those years you and I were separated."

"Ohh, Charlie," Barbara sobbed, "you are so good to me!"

"He is like his father," Jasmine said, and she smiled with her remembrance of the golden boy who had once loved her, and who had given her this wonderful son.

Having come to terms with the truth of the situation, Jasmine and her family now settled down for a quiet summer as the Leslies of Glenkirk would not be with them. They were all relieved by this as none of them relished having to explain to Patrick Leslie, the duke of Glenkirk, who would use the excuse to take his second daughter, Mair, home to the Highlands. As long as Mair remained at her sister's home, and Cynara was gone from Queen's Malvern when she returned, there could be no cause for complaint. And it was possible that the secret could even be kept from the Leslies as well for now.

July and August passed. The harvest was beginning to be gathered in, and in the orchards the trees were weighed down with a sur-

plus of fruit. On the third day of September a messenger arrived
from Roxley to announce that the duchess Diana had given birth to
a healthy son on the first. The christening would be held in Roxley
church on the fifteenth of the month, and the family was expected.
Cynara's belly was just beginning to round slightly but not enough
to reveal her secret. She was now past the stage where anything
could sicken her. In fact she bloomed and had never appeared more
beautiful in her entire life.

They traveled to Roxley where Diana was already up from her
childbed. Fancy and her husband, Kit Trahern, marquis of Isham,
arrived shortly after the party from Queen's Malvern. The three
cousins were almost giddy to be together again. It seemed so long
again since their sojourn at court. Forewarned, however, neither
Diana nor Fancy asked Cynara about the earl of Summersfield.

James Patrick Charles Esmond, heir to Roxley, was baptized the
following day in Roxley church where his parents had been wed just
over nine months ago. The duke's tenants lined the road from the
castle to the church, cheering the infant who would one day be their
master. The infant was held by his godmother, Lady Cynara Stuart,
radiant in a teal blue gown with lace trim. He howled at the appropriate moment, indicating to all that the devil had flown out of him
with his baptism. The guests returned to the castle where a feast
was held.

That evening when all the adults but the three cousins had gone
off to bed, Cynara told Diana and Fancy of her own impending
birth. Diana's hand flew to her mouth, stricken, but Fancy nodded
understandingly.

"You are not telling Wickedness?" she asked quietly.

"Nay," Cynara answered. "I cannot do to him what was done to
his father. If he loves me he will eventually come to admit it, and all
will be well. If he cannot, then he shall never know he has a child."

"You would deny your child its inheritance?" Diana finally spoke.
Her face was troubled.

"If he cannot love me, then how can he love our child?" Cynara
asked. "It is a kindness to my child that he never know a father who
would reject him."

"But what will you tell your child one day when he asks you?" Diana persisted.

"I do not know," Cynara said, "but I will know when the time is right."

"You assume that the earl of Summersfield will not prove worthy," Fancy spoke. "I hardly know him, but of what you have written, Cyn. If what you have said of him is true, then I believe he will tell you of his love and be a good father to his child."

"Who knows your plight?" Diana queried her cousin.

"Grandmama, Hester, my parents," Cynara said, "and now you two."

"My father will use it as an excuse to take Mair back to Glenkirk. You know how he can be," Diana declared. "He is due here in October. Not even a grandson bearing his name would dissuade him from hunting his damned grouse."

Her cousins laughed.

"I am going to Hilltop House," Cynara said. "It has been refurbished for me these past weeks. It will be believed that I have returned to court. Mair will never know, and neither will your father."

"You will foster the child out, of course," Fancy said.

"So it has been suggested, but I shall not do it. The babe will nurse at my breasts and know my face before any other. I will see its first steps and hear its first word. Nothing can dissuade me from my course, but I do not discuss it with the family. Let them believe what they will. In four years I shall be of age, and my fortune will be in my hands. Until then I do not think Papa will allow me to starve even if I do not make a *respectable* marriage," Cynara told them.

"It is a difficult road you have chosen, Cousin," Fancy said, "and I admire you for your courage and determination."

"And we shall be here for you, Cyn, no matter!" Diana declared.

"I know," Cynara answered. Then she laughed. "Who would have believed two years ago when we were preparing to go to court that we would end up with two wed and one about to birth a bastard?"

Fancy nodded. "I know. I should have never believed that I would be a king's mistress, a girl from the Colonies, and then find such great happiness as I have found with Kit."

"And when I first saw Damien and Darius," Diana noted, "I never believed I should be able to choose between them, let alone make the perfect choice for me. And I have even done the right thing by birthing a son nine months from my wedding day." She laughed.

"And proud Cynara Stuart has done the wrong thing," Cyn said softly.

"Nay, Cousin, it is never wrong to love," Fancy told her. "I do not comprehend how you will find happiness, but you will find it one day. I know it! If it could happen to me, then it will surely happen for you, Cyn."

Cynara leaned over and kissed her cousin upon her cheek. "Thank you, Fancy." Then she smiled at them both. "I am so glad that you are my cousins. Even if I have turned out to be the naughty one, I hope that we will always be friends."

"Aye!" Fancy agreed.

"We will," Diana echoed. "And our children will grow up together knowing each other too. That I promise."

"Let us make a pact on it," Cynara said, and she held out her hand.

Her cousins placed their hands atop one another's.

"*Forever!*" Cyn said.

"*Forever!*" Diana replied.

"*Forever, and always!*" Fancy concluded.

Chapter

21

After the autumn racing at Newmarket, the court decamped for the New Forest for the hunting season. This forest, like all the royal preserves, had been restocked after the Restoration. Now, almost ten years later, the woods where only the king and his guests were allowed to hunt, teemed with game of all kinds. But the earl of Summersfield, newly returned to court from his home, could not find the prey he sought. As the hunting season began to draw to a close, he sought out Nellie Gwyn, for he knew that the king's favorite had a correspondence with Cynara. Nellie did not write, nor could she read, but in her position as the king's mistress, she did have a secretary who took her dictation, read to her, and wrote for her.

Nellie did not enjoy the hunt, which was fortunate as the queen did. It was one of the few things that Catherine of Braganza and her husband had in common. So while many in the court spent the day out in the forest chasing deer and boar, Mistress Nellie held her own court in a cottage close by the royal hunting lodge. She eagerly awaited their return to Whitehall and the city she loved. It had become common knowledge that the king's mistress was with child. She would deliver in the spring.

Harry Summers found Nellie alone, a rare thing. He smiled and asked, "Do you want company, Mistress Nell? Or do you prefer your solitude?" He admired the feisty little actress who had caught the king's attentions and held them.

"I'm bored to death, Wickedness," Nell answered him. "Come in and amuse me. I'm finally past puking me guts out."

"I know little of such things," the earl replied, and he came and sat next to Nellie. "You know why I'm here, and I know you must know why she is not back at court. For mercy's sake, Mistress Nell, tell me, I beg of you!"

"Her da don't approve of you," Nell said as she considered just how she could taunt Harry Summers into going after Cynara. They would be well matched. Both proud, and stubborn, and neither willing to admit defeat, but one of them was going to have to if this matter was to be resolved. "The duke of Lundy is determined to match Cyn with this duke of Cranston. Do you know him? I don't think he's ever been to court. An older gentleman, Cyn says, who lost his first wife in childbed and wants another to get an heir on. Sounds a bit cold-blooded to me, but Cyn says her da is anxious to have her wed, and the fellow is no fortune hunter. This duke is well off, and most eager to have Cyn, though she resists her father's wishes for love of you, Wickedness." Nellie peered closely at her companion.

Harry Summers said nothing. *"Does she?"* he attempted nonchalance.

"She can't withstand her family forever," Nellie said. "Jesu, Harry Summers, admit aloud your love for her, and then go after her! This duke of Cranston won't be too pleased to discover someone else has traveled the road he alone hoped to traverse."

"If her family does not approve of me . . ." the earl began, but Nellie waved her hand at him impatiently.

"She loves you, damn it! You know what you have to do, Wickedness! I cannot believe you to be such a dolt and a simpleton! And do not tell me again about your parents' horrific union. They had no love for each other, but you and Cyn do. Did you know His Majesty attempted to intervene? He offered to order your marriage to his cousin, but she would not have it. She could not, she told him, force you to the altar as your father and mother were forced. How much more can you demand of her, Harry Summers? All she wants from

you is an admission of your love for her and a proper proposal. Will you let her be compelled into marriage as your mother was coerced? Desired only for her youth and ability to bear children? Do you want her to end as your mother did? Brokenhearted and alone? If you let this happen, I shall wash my hands of you!" Nellie told him angrily.

The earl of Summersfield stood up. His handsome face was brimming with a mix of emotions. His heart was pounding. *"I love her!"* he said.

"I know," Nell replied calmly.

"I do want to wed her!" he cried, a smile suddenly lighting his features as he admitted what had been in his heart all along.

"I know," Nell responded, and she began to smile.

"I have to go to her!" he cried.

"Best to hurry before her da leads her to the altar, and another man's bed," Nell suggested mischievously.

The earl of Summersfield took Nellie Gwyn's hands in his, and raising them to his lips, he kissed them fervently. "Thank you, Mistress Nellie," he said. "I am always at your service."

"So they all says when they runs off to another woman," Nellie chuckled. "I'll tender His Majesty your farewells. He will be pleased when I tell him your destination, Wickedness. I suspect that you have outgrown your sobriquet, but I shall always think of you that way. Go along now, for I do not know how much time you have to prevent this misalliance. You had best ride hard, my lord." And she watched as dropping her hands he hurried off. *"There!"* Nellie Gwyn said well satisfied. "That should do the trick, and is his lordship in for a surprise," she chortled to herself for Cynara had confided her secret to a final person, her friend, Nellie Gwyn. "Beasley!" Nell cried for her secretary. "Come, for I have a letter to write!"

The earl of Summersfield went to his rooms at a nearby inn, packed a few of his belongings up, telling his valet to settle the accounts with the innkeeper, and then to return home with the rest of his possessions.

"Where will you be, my lord?" his valet inquired.

"I am going to Queen's Malvern, the duke of Lundy's home near

Worcester. Tell the staff that I will be bringing home a bride and to make Summersfield Park beautiful for her. I shall send ahead when we are ready to travel." Then he was out the door with his saddlebags.

It was late November, and the weather was turning foul. Worse, the daylight hours were few and though he rode from daybreak until sunset, the journey took him longer than he had anticipated for there were not that many hours of daylight. He rode alone, a dangerous thing for his stallion was worth stealing. The highwaymen, however, were holed up for the weather was nasty. The roads were muddy with icy rains. The winds from the north cut into him, pushing through his cloak and freezing his face, but he pushed on. He would arrive unannounced, but so much the better. The duke of Lundy would be caught off guard, and Harry Summers would press his case as to why he would make a better husband for Cynara Stuart than this duke of Cranston. He would even fight the man if necessary.

He arrived at Queen's Malvern just after sunset one early December evening. The western sky was edged in dark red at the horizon, but above him the night was black with another impending storm. A stableman came forth to take his mount as he slid from the stallion's back. The horse was led off, and the earl of Summersfield walked through the open door of the beautiful house telling Becket that he wished to see the duke of Lundy.

"The family is in the old hall," the majordomo said. "Please to follow me, my lord," and he led the earl into the lovely paneled room with its twin fireplaces which were burning cheerfully. Colorful tapestries hung upon the walls. "The earl of Summersfield, Your Grace," Becket announced.

Charlie did not look particularly pleased with his guest's arrival. "My lord," was all he said. He did not bother to stand.

Jasmine, however, arose from her chair by the fire, and walked slowly toward the earl. "Welcome to Queen's Malvern, Wickedness," she greeted him, holding out both her hands to him. He had come at last, she thought relieved. "You will, of course, be staying the night. Barbara, do have a chamber made ready for the earl. Have you eaten, my lord?"

"No, madame, thank you," Harry answered the elderly woman, kissing the elegant hands offered him.

"We dine shortly," Jasmine said, taking her hands back, and smiling. "Have you met my granddaughter, Lady Mair Leslie? But you would not have as she hasn't yet gone to court."

He could bear it no longer. "Where is Cynara?" he begged. "For God's sake don't tell me you have forced her into marriage with this duke of Cranston I have been told of, madame!"

"My cousin is at court," Mair piped up.

The duchess of Lundy arose quickly from her own chair. "I think, Mair, that it is time for you to practice your pianoforte. Come, and I will listen to you, my child." She swiftly ushered young Mair from the hall before she might realize that something was wrong.

Harry Summers looked confused, and it was then that the duke of Lundy got up speaking harshly.

"Why should you care where my daughter is, my lord? Why would you possibly care?" Charlie demanded, angrily.

"Because I love her," the earl said without hesitation. "Because, my lord, I have come to ask Cyn to marry me, and there is nothing that you can do that will prevent me from making her my wife."

"There is much I can do to prevent such a marriage from taking place," Charlie said. "Do you forget who I am, my lord? One word from me, and you could spend the rest of your days in the tower. It has not, I understand, been used to house a royal prisoner in some time, but I am sure it could be made ready for such a special guest who could then be quickly forgotten."

"Does it mean nothing to you that Cyn loves me too?" Harry Summers demanded. His look bordered on desperate.

"How could you possibly know if Cynara loves you?" the duke said.

"Because she told me," the earl answered simply. "You are, my lord, I am told, a man who puts a great deal of weight upon love."

Charlie flushed, then he said, "You are not the man I would have chosen for Cynara. Know that from the start, my lord."

"Then you have not forced her into another union?" Harry cried joyfully.

Charles Stuart, the duke of Lundy, snorted irritably. "You love her, but do not know her well enough to know that you can force Cynara to nothing she does not choose to do."

"Indeed, I do know it, my lord, but I also know that she loves her family and would do her best to please them," the earl answered.

"But not marry the duke of Cranston," Charlie said. His tone had softened considerably for as much as he hated to admit it to himself, he could see that the young man before him spoke the truth.

Jasmine leaned over, and murmured softly in her son's ear. "Say nothing, Charlie. He does not know, I am certain."

The duke gave his mother a barely discernible nod.

"She is not wed?" The sound of happiness in Harry Summers's voice was palpable. "Then, please, my lord, may I see her?"

"She is not here," the duke responded.

"But she is not at court either, my lord," he cried.

"No, she is not. I gave her until the end of the year to give up this foolish pursuit of you. She decided she would return to her childhood home to consider her choices. Hilltop House is but a half-day's ride, my lord. If you are still of a mind to marry her on the morrow, then I will give you directions and send the vicar with you. If her heart still leans toward you, Harry Summers, you had best wed her immediately before she decides otherwise. I have never before known my daughter to set her mind on something so hard. If you are still what she would have, then I have no choice but to accept you into the family." He signaled to a hovering servant who hurried up with a tray containing two goblets of wine. The duke took one, and nodded to his guest to accept the other. "You know, of course, that the women in this family control their own wealth? You must sign a legal document to that effect before I will let you go to Cynara."

"Gladly, my lord," the earl agreed and took the other goblet.

"Good luck to you both then," the duke of Lundy said, and he drank down his goblet in two swallows.

Beside him his elderly mother gave a small sigh of relief, and from the corner of her eye she saw her son force back a grin.

The earl ate a good country meal with the duke and his family, and admired the dining salon that had been added to the house. He was grateful when he was shown to a warm chamber for the night. He had been on the road for many days, and a comfortable bed was most welcome. He suspected that given the hospitality at Queen's Malvern that he had, his stallion was faring just as well as he was. He was asleep almost as soon as his head hit the feather pillow.

In the hall below, the duke, his wife, and his mother discussed this latest run of events. Lady Mair was asleep in her chamber. Charlie was curious as to why his mother suspected the earl knew nothing of Cynara's coming child.

"Because he made no mention of it," Jasmine said, "and, too, he was very concerned that you might have pushed your daughter into another marriage. He knows you are an honorable man, Charlie. An honorable man would not force his enceinte daughter into marriage with a man not her child's father. *No.* The earl of Summersfield does not know Cynara is expecting his child. *And we will not tell him.*"

"But why should he not be told?" Barbara Stuart wondered. "Do you think he would be unhappy at such news?"

"There is naught that Cynara could do except marry another that would make Harry Summers unhappy, Barbara. No, this has to do with your proud daughter. If Cynara believes that her earl seeks to wed her only because she carries his child, she will not have him. It is better he go to her unknowing and learn of the babe from her. He does indeed love her. He will not let her escape him now that he had admitted to it himself and to the world," Jasmine concluded wisely.

"Should we warn her he is coming?" the duke queried aloud.

Jasmine laughed wickedly. "Nay, my son, I think not. Their surprise should be a mutual one, I believe." She arose from her chair by the fire. "Now, my dears, I am going to bed. It has been a long day," she told them, and slowly walked from the hall.

The duke took his wife's hand in his, and his arm slipped about her plump shoulders. "Well, my darling," he said, "Mama was correct as she usually is, and it has all worked out quite well. Now if my sons would but settle down and marry, I should have no more worries."

Barbara laughed. "What a simple man you are, Charlie," she teased him.

He grinned back at her and arose, drawing her up with him. "I think it is time we found our bed too, madame. The morning will be here soon enough, and our guest will be champing at the bit to go to our daughter and declare himself. And damned well about time too!"

In the morning, however, Charlie came down to his dining room to break his fast to learn from his majordomo that the earl of Summersfield had departed at first light.

"He would not even remain to eat, Your Grace," Becket said. "He asked for directions first to the church and then to Hilltop House. He said to thank you for your hospitality, and that he would return the vicar with good news as quickly as he could."

Charlie, the not-so-royal Stuart, burst out laughing. "Well, damn me, Becket! He does love her!" Then he sat down at his table saying, "I find I am quite ravenous this morning. Fill my plate, and bring me a pot of tea."

"Yes, Your Grace," Becket responded, a smile upon his face too.

"What's the day like?" the duke asked.

"'Twill be a fair ride, my lord. The storm passed in the night," Becket told his master.

It was cold, but clear. There was yet a bit of a wind that shredded the clouds in the blue sky above him as he rode, the duke's vicar, gathered up from the village nearest Queen's Malvern, at his side. The plump cleric was curious as to this hurried mission he was being brought on. The young man who had arrived at his door just as the sun rose, had introduced himself, and then said he had the duke's permission to take him to Hilltop House where the vicar was to perform a marriage ceremony between the earl and the duke's daughter. The clergyman had gathered up the few materials that he would need for such a duty, and rode off with the stranger.

Cynara was outside cutting the last of the sweet and medicinal herbs in her garden when she heard the *thrum-thrum* of hoofbeats. From his nearby pasture she heard Fluffy whicker at the passing riders. Drawing her cloak about her she walked from the little sheltered garden at the dwelling rear to the front of the house, just as Harry Summers arrived in the company of the Reverend John

Jobson. The earl leaped from his stallion even before it had come to a skittering stop.

"*Cyn!*" he cried joyfully.

"And what, my lord, are you doing *here?* And in the company of the parson too?" she demanded suspiciously, fending him off.

"*I love you!*" he cried.

"*What?*"

"*I love you, Lady Cynara Mary Stuart! I love you!* I have from the first moment our eyes met, but I could not, would not, admit that I was capable of such emotion. Not after the example that I had been set. But I can no longer deny my emotions. *I love you!*"

"Indeed, my lord," Cyn said sharply. "Well, now that you have told me so, you are free to go."

He quickly knelt before her, and grasped at her hand. "Please, my darling Cyn, please do me the honor of becoming my wife," the earl of Summersfield said. His eyes were warm with his love for her. "*Please!*"

"And just why is it that you want to marry me, my lord?" she asked.

"*Because I love you, you impossible creature!*" he shouted. "Do you not understand?"

"And there is no other reason?" she demanded suspiciously.

"What else could there be but the fact I love you?" he replied.

And then Cynara realized that he did not know that she was carrying his child. *He really did not know.* He wanted her for herself, and for no other reason. A wave of happiness threatened to overwhelm her, but she said, "You will have to speak with my father, my lord, and you will have to sign a certain paper."

"'Twas done last night, my darling! I went to Queen's Malvern when you did not return to court. Your papa was not at first very pleased to see me, but I have finally managed to convince him that I love you and want you for my wife. He said if that were the case I had better wed you immediately before you changed your mind. I fetched the vicar at first light, and here we are." He grinned at her pleased.

He didn't know. Her enveloping cloak was concealing her now-visible belly. "Very well, my darling Wickedness," Cynara said, "I shall accept your most charming proposal, and we shall wed here, and now. I have won both the game and the match." Then she laughed. "It will certainly be a wedding night as you never expected."

"Shall we go into the house, my lady?" Reverend Jobson suggested.

"Nay," Cynara surprised the man, saying, "you shall marry the earl and me here beneath the blue sky. God would surely not disapprove. Hester! Fetch Jack and Bobby, to come to me now. My servants shall witness our union, my lord."

"Whatever pleases you, Cyn," he agreed happily.

Hester came with the two men-at-arms, and they all stood together upon the hillside before the house. Above them the December sun shone brightly. The air was clear, and the breeze had gone. The vicar spoke the words of the Anglican wedding ceremony; and when he asked if there was any man present who believed these two persons should not be joined he should speak now, or forever hold his peace; there was only the sound of the sparrows chattering away in the ivy that covered a wall of Hilltop House. When the sacrament had finally been concluded, and they were pronounced man and wife; the vicar insisted on returning to Queen's Malvern before the early nightfall that he might tell the duke. They watched him as he trotted off back down the hill.

"Go with him," Cynara ordered the two male servants. "He should not ride alone."

They nodded, and running to the stables to fetch their horses they sped off after the cleric.

"I'll go, and fix you a nice wedding supper," Hester said smiling. She bustled back into the house.

"You have not yet kissed me, wife," the earl said.

"Let us go to our bedchamber, my lord husband, where I shall welcome you properly," Cynara smiled seductively, taking him by the hand and leading him inside.

"I am happy, madame, to see that your appetite for bed sport has not abated," the earl told her, grinning in anticipation.

Cynara laughed. "Ahh, my dear husband, you have no idea how

great my appetite for bed sport is these days." She brought him up-stairs, and in the hallway outside her bedchamber, she said, "If you will but give me a few moments, my lord. I will call you when I am ready."

He nodded. "Do not keep me waiting, my lady wife."

Cynara laughed again as she entered her room, closing the door behind her. Quickly she laid her cloak aside. Then she divested herself of all her garments, stockings, and shoes. She loosed her sable hair about her shoulders, calling to him in the most dulcet and enticing of tones, "You may come in now, my lord." The candles flickered as he opened the door and stepped eagerly through.

His jaw dropped with his astonishment. She was completely naked. Her breasts were swollen to twice the size they had been when he had seen her last. Her great blue-veined belly protruded before her. He stared, and then suddenly grew angry. "You were not going to tell me that you were carrying my child!" he shouted at her. "It is my child, I presume?"

Cynara picked up her silver hairbrush and threw it at him. "Of course it is your child, you dolt! And no! I had no intention of telling you. Do you think I would have forced you into marriage as your mother and father were forced? I prayed that you would come to me, Harry! That you would admit the love for me that I knew you felt. That you would ask me to be your wife. *And you have!* You came, my darling Wickedness, because you loved me for myself, and not because you needed to give this child we have created a name, or because I am the king's cousin, or a wealthy heiress. *You came only because you loved me even as I love you!*"

"I don't know whether to kill you or kiss you," the earl said.

Cynara placed a protective hand over her belly. "Are you happy?" she asked him. "We shall, I fear, have to postpone our honeymoon, my dear lord. I am no fit bed companion right now as you can see."

"And that, my darling Cyn, is what I have always loved about you," he answered her. "Despite your elegant veneer of sophistication, you are a true innocent. Did your grandmama not tell you that even with a babe in your belly, lovers may mate, and gain pleasure, if it is done carefully? Get into bed, Wife. I am going to show you a

few little diversions, but only because it is our wedding night.
Afterward we shall be most circumspect in our behavior until after
our heir is born."

"You are convinced it is a son I carry," she said, climbing into
their bed.

"Summers usually throw lads first," he told her as he pulled off
his clothing and his boots. "Now, madame, move over," and he
joined her beneath the down coverlet. Rolling her onto her side, he
began to stroke her lovingly. "My God, your titties have become so
full. Our child will be well nourished, my darling." He placed a kiss
upon the nape of her neck, and Cynara shivered deliciously.

"Should I be so lustful now?" she wondered aloud. "It somehow
seems so naughty to have a belly filled with a kicking babe, and a
terrible itch in my private place."

He chuckled in her ear, his breath hot. "I am going to adore being
married to you, my darling Cyn," he said. He reached between her
legs and found her already very wet with her need, which suited his
purposes as he was very aroused by her lush fertility. "Now, my darling," he said, "Trust me to make us both quite happy." And he proceeded to do just that, sliding his length into her slowly and
carefully as she lay upon her side, their legs entwined. She whimpered with pleasure. And such was their need for each other that
they gained their heaven swiftly and together.

Afterward Cynara lay sprawled between her husband's legs while
his big hands caressed her blue-veined white belly. When the baby
kicked, his tiny foot quite visible, they both laughed. "He is very ac-
tive these days," she told the earl. "When will we go to Summersfield Park, darling Wickedness?"

"Not until after the child is born," came the answer, "and you are
both able to travel safely. "We shall see our home by the summer,
my darling wife. I would take no chances with you, or our child."

"I was born in this house," Cynara told him. "Let us remain, and
I will birth our son here. We will have our privacy too. I am not of a
mind to share you with anyone else right now, Harry Summers."

"Nor I you," he agreed. "You are so deliciously ripe, Cyn. When
is our child to be born?"

"At the end of February," she answered him. "Harry, do you know what day it is today? We should know the date that we were wed, my lord."

He thought a moment. "It is December the ninth," he told her.

Cynara smiled. "We have the three of us—Fancy, Diana and me—been wed in December. I think it a good sign."

There was a discreet knock upon the bedchamber door, and Hester's soft voice called to them. "The supper is ready, my lord and my lady." Then they heard her footsteps retreating quickly back down the stairs.

"We must keep Hester with us," Cynara said. "I cannot cook."

"Then by all means we must keep Hester," the earl of Summersfield agreed. He arose from their bed, and began to dress. "Come along, madame," he said to her. "You do not want to shock poor Hester."

"There is little I could do that would shock Hester," Cynara laughed, but she got up from her bed, and began to pull her clothes back on as well.

"But I, madame," he teased, "could most certainly shock Hester. But as we shall need her, I will not," he promised.

"I can see, Wickedness," Cynara murmured, "that being married to you, and expecting a child, has not dulled your sense of fun."

"'Tis not what Nellie Gwyn says," he told her. "She says I shall now have to give up my court sobriquet."

"Ohh no, you shall not!" his bride replied. "We shall always be Cyn and Wickedness, my dear husband. Cyn and Wickedness forever!"

"And ever and ever and ever!" the earl of Summersfield agreed, and together they went down to supper.

Epilogue

QUEEN'S MALVERN

August 9, 1670

Jasmine awoke to a perfect summer's day. She lay quietly in her great bed listening to the birdsong outside her open window as the birds welcomed the new day. It was August ninth and she was eighty years old. God's blood! Where had the time gone? Then she laughed softly to herself. That was a question she had no doubt most people asked themselves at one time or another. Well, she certainly had no regrets. Her years had been filled with living.

The door to her bedchamber opened, and Orane's iron gray head popped into the room. "Madame is awake?" she asked.

"Madame is awake," Jasmine acknowledged.

"I shall fetch your tea, madame," her serving woman said, and she closed the door behind her as she departed.

What a treasure Orane was, Jasmine thought. She had originally come from France with Jasmine's daughter, but she found life in Autumn's house exceedingly dull. Jasmine had offered her a position. The servants who had been with her for her entire lifetime were much too old to care for her now. Rohana and Toramalli had been eleven years old when she had been born. Jasmine's turquoise eyes misted with the memory of the twins who had served her so loyally. They had died within just a few weeks of each other this spring past. But they had attained their ninety-first year in January. They were buried in the family graveyard with Jasmine's beloved servant, Adali. And with the passing of Rohana and Toramalli had gone the last of her early history. There was nothing left of her youth now but several caskets of jewelry that she no longer wore. *God's blood,* she swore silently again. *I grow maudlin. I shall not become one of those old women who becomes sentimental, and mawkish about the past. I am eighty years old today. I have the greatest gift I could possibly receive. I have my children here with me, and many of my grandchildren as well. Today we shall all celebrate that day in India so long ago when I entered this world as Yasaman Kama Begum, the Mughal's daughter.*

Orane returned with a tray that had been set with a red rose in a silver bud vase. Jasmine smelled the rich aroma of the black tea from the pot upon the tray. The servant set the tray upon a nearby table, and plumping the pillows on the bed she aided her mistress into a sitting position. Then bringing the tray she set it on Jasmine's lap. Jasmine smiled, for along with the tea was a small bowl of peeled apricots, and yogurt which she very much enjoyed.

"You spoil me," she told Orane with another smile.

"It is madame's natal day, and a time to be spoiled," came the reply.

"Are they all up?" Jasmine asked.

"Nay, just some of the gentlemen, and your daughter, Lady Fortune, madame. Such a beautiful, but sad lady," Orane noted.

"Aye," Jasmine agreed. "She misses her husband. Such a tragedy! Who would have thought that Kieran Devers should die in such a similar fashion to Autumn's first husband. Poor Fortune misses her Maryland, but I am so glad she has returned home to England. I certainly thought never to see her again in this life, Orane. Autumn was but a baby when she left. It must be close to forty years."

"Eat your breakfast, madame," Orane advised. "The festivities are scheduled to begin at the noon hour."

"And this time tomorrow," Jasmine said, "I shall be exhausted, and even older." She chuckled to herself, and set about eating her meal while slowly sipping the dark tea.

And what a celebration it was to be! All of her living children were in the house. She had never before had them all under one roof at the same time. Her five sons, and three daughters now ranged in age from sixty-two to thirty-nine. Eight children born from two husbands, and a lover. She shook her head. As her three favorite granddaughters were so fond of reminding her, she had lived a very exciting life. Almost as exciting as her own beloved grandmother, Skye O'Malley.

Jasmine finished her breakfast, and Orane took the tray away, leaving her mistress to her thoughts as was Jasmine's custom. The maidservant busied herself seeing to madame's bath.

Well, almost as exciting. Jasmine smiled to herself. She had nothing to regret. She had seen her children happily wed. They had given her forty-seven grandchildren among them. Now most of her own offspring were grandparents, and she a great-grandmother. Excitement, she concluded, was greatly overrated. It was family that counted. Madame Skye had known it, and preached it.

"Your bath is ready, madame," Orane said, coming to help her from her bed. "Which gown have you finally chosen for today?"

"The turquoise blue one that matches my eyes," Jasmine said.

"'Tis a bold color for an old woman," Orane noted tartly.

"What?" Jasmine said, leaving her bed, "Would you have me in black, or dark purple, or worse, dusky rose? Aye, I am an old woman, but I have never been a dull woman, Orane. Too bold a color indeed! I have yet to go crepey about my neck and shoulders!"

"No," Orane admitted, "you haven't, madame. Women many years your junior do not look as good, and well you know it."

Jasmine smiled archly. She might still look respectable, but God's blood! Sometimes she felt every bit of her eight decades, especially in her knees. And when it rained now her fingers ached more often than not. Well, she would tolerate a little pain if she might continue to be considered a beauty. She stared into the mirror on her dressing table. Her eyes still held their color, and her skin was soft. Her face showed but the faintest hint of slackening about her jowls, but nowhere near as bad as some old women. There were tiny lines etched into her skin around her eyes, but she had all her teeth. It

was a great sight better than most women, twenty—nay, thirty—
years younger. She could hardly complain. She bathed, and then she
dressed.

 Her gown was a beautiful watered silk the color of a Persian
turquoise. It had a wide cream lace collar, and the neckline in deference to her years was not as low as fashion might have dictated. The
long sleeves were puffed, and tied with ribbons of a slightly deeper
hue. The lace cuffs of her gown matched that of the collar. Her hair
was dressed as it always had been, in a chignon, low on the nape of
her neck. She wore a turquoise pendant surrounded by diamonds on
a gold chain about her neck, and matching earbobs in her ears.

There was a knock upon the door to the apartment. Orane
opened it permitting the duke of Lundy to step inside.

He bowed to his mother. "Everyone is assembled in the hall awaiting you, Mama. Are you ready to go down?" He offered her his arm.

She nodded, but said, "Such a fuss, Charlie. If I were a hundred
today it might be warranted." She took his arm.

He chuckled. "We have every intention of doing it again when
you are one hundred, Mama," he assured her.

She snorted with laughter as they exited her apartments, and descended the stairs. He led her into her favorite room, the old family
hall. They were all there, smiling, and Jasmine felt tears pricking
the back of her eyes.

Her eldest child, India Lindley Leigh, came forward with her
husband, Deveral, the earl of Oxton, who kissed his mother-in-law's
hand graciously. India kissed her mother's cheek saying as she did,
"Happy birthday, Mama." India's four children followed their parents in tendering their greetings.

Next was Henry Lindley, the marquis of Westleigh, his wife,
Rosamund Wyndham, and their five children. Adam Leslie, Baron
Leslie of Erne Rock and his wife stood with Duncan Leslie, Baron
Leslie of Dinsmore and his wife. These two youngest sons of her
union with James Leslie had inherited her estates in Ireland.
Between them they had produced eleven children. They reminded
her strongly of her late husband.

Her eldest Leslie son, Patrick, the duke of Glenkirk and his wife, Flanna, were here too as were all of their seven children.

Barbara Stuart stood smiling with Cynara and Harry Summers. Cynara held little Lord Henry Summers in her arms, and it was obvious that Harry had a serious rival for his wife's affection. The duke of Lundy's three eldest children from his first marriage were with their father, and stepmother. Sabrina, and her husband, the earl of Southwood, had brought their children up from Devon. Her two brothers, Frederick and William flanked them. They were both yet bachelors.

And her lost child, Fortune Lindley Devers, who had surprised them all by arriving unannounced in England the previous month. Her husband, Kieran, had died suddenly the winter before, and Fortune, who had sworn never to venture across the ocean again, had done just that. Her eldest son, Shane Devers, had inherited the plantation that she and Kieran had carved out of the Maryland wilderness. It had been her home, yet without Kieran she had felt lost, and a stranger. So she had bid her seven children and their families a farewell, returning home to England to be with her mother. Fancy and Kit Trahern had offered her a home with them. Fortune, however, thanked her youngest daughter and son-in-law, but told them she preferred remaining with Jasmine.

"One day," she said, "I will accept your offer, but not now. It has been so long since I have sat with my mother, and talked with her over a cup of her beloved tea. Being with her comforts me."

And finally there was Autumn, her baby, with her husband Gabriel Bainbridge, the duke of Garwood. They had come with their seven-year-old twin sons, their two daughters and their four-month-old infant son. They had brought with them Autumn's two French daughters, Mademoiselle Madeline d'Oleron, daughter of the marquis d'Auriville. She was now seventeen, and a great beauty who was considering a marriage offer from a neighbor whose vineyards matched hers. She greeted her grandmother in her native tongue, bringing down scorn on her head from her younger half-sister, Marguerite de la Bois, the daughter of King Louis XIV.

"Oh do speak English, Maddie, and stop being a snob!" the twelve-year-old said. "Happy birthday, Grandmama!"

"Thank you, my little Daisy," Jasmine responded. She was particularly delighted to see these two girls as she had not been with them in some time.

Finally when each member of her family had greeted her they all chorused, *Happy birthday, Madame Jasmine!*

"Thank you! Thank you all," Jasmine replied as she was seated with great ceremony in a highback tapestried chair at the center of the high board.

The servants began bringing in the meal that was to begin the day's festivities. The guests all seated themselves. Jasmine gazed out over the hall, astounded by her numerous progeny, her descendants. Then she remembered that she was but one of several hundred of Madame Skye's posterity. How amazing, she considered.

The meal was a simple one. Prawns in white wine, and thinly sliced salmon to begin. A side of roasted beef, and several turkeys stuffed with apples, onions, bread and sage. There were artichokes in olive oil, creamed onions, boiled beets and green beans. There was freshly baked bread, and sweet butter. Several varieties of cheese. The wines came from the family vineyards at both Archambault and d'Auriville in France. There was cider, and there was ale. And finally a great tart of plums, fine spun-sugar crowns and exotic animals.

The meal finished, presents were produced and offered to the matriarch of the family. She accepted them all graciously, but when the parade of relations had finally ceased she smiled at them all saying, "Thank you, my dears! Thank you! But the greatest gift I have this day is you. My beloved family. My children, my grandchildren and great-grandchildren. And I am told there will be more great-grandchildren in the coming year. Is that not the greatest of blessings?" She arose from her chair, and lifted her goblet up. "Let us drink a toast, my dears."

And the family rose up as one.

"On this, my eightieth birthday," Jasmine said, "Let us drink a toast to the originator of all our good fortune. *I give you Skye O'Malley!"* And she drank her goblet down.

"Skye O'Malley!" the assembled shouted with one voice as they turned to the portrait hanging over the fireplace in the hall, goblets raised. And afterwards everyone of them agreed that it appeared for a brief moment as if their ancestress smiled down on them all.

The meal concluded, they moved out of doors for games, and for dancing. A messenger arrived from the king bearing his wishes for Jasmine's happy day, along with a silver-and-gem-encrusted flask of scent. Jasmine enjoyed watching her family as they chattered and played upon the lawns. Musicians arrived, and there was even a Leslie piper. The day continued fair, and warm. Finally the sun began to set over the western hills in a glorious show of colors. Still they remained outside watching as the stars came out, and finally the moonrise. It was full that night.

"It was full, I am told, the day I was born," Jasmine noted.

The younger children began to fall asleep in the grass. The nursemaids came to take them inside. The day had ended. Jasmine bid her family good night, leaving them behind in the hall talking with one another as they had done in their youth. She walked slowly up the staircase, and down the hallway to her apartments where Orane awaited, ready to prepare her for bed.

"Madame had a wonderful day," Orane said.

"Madame did," Jasmine agreed.

And when she was comfortable in her bed, and Orane had gone, Jasmine gazed out the open window at the moonlight. It had been a good day. It had been a good life. And there was going to be much more to come. Oh yes! There was more. Perhaps she would live to be one hundred years old, Jasmine thought with a chuckle. Had not Rohana and Toramalli lived into their nineties? Closing her still beautiful turquoise eyes, the dowager duchess of Glenkirk fell asleep at last, dreaming of her youth, and of the many men who had loved her.

ABOUT THE AUTHOR

Bertrice Small is a *New York Times* best-selling author and the recipient of numerous awards. In keeping with her profession, she lives in the oldest English-speaking town in the state of New York, founded in 1640. Her light-filled studio includes the paintings of her favorite cover artist, Elaine Duillo, and a large library. Because she believes in happy endings, Bertrice Small has been married to her husband, George, for almost half a century. They have a son, Thomas, and four grandchildren. Longtime readers will be happy to know that Finnegan, the long-haired bad black kitty, and his housemate, Sylvester, the black-and-white tuxedo cat, remain her dearest companions.